Praise for
Nancy Thayer and *Beachcombers*

"Ms. Thayer captures her beloved Nantucket like no one else, celebrating the island's nature and beauty, using it as a rich backdrop."
—LUANNE RICE

"Heartwarming . . . Will appeal to fans of women's fiction, especially those who read Debbie Macomber and Elin Hilderbrand."
—*Library Journal*

"[Thayer] captures the essence of summer."   —*Charleston Gazette*

"Thayer has the knack of creating likeable characters who grapple with problems that will strike a chord with many readers."
—*The Boston Globe*

"Fun and engrossing."   —*Publishers Weekly*

"Nancy Thayer's gift for reaching the emotional core of her characters [is] captivating."   —*Houston Chronicle*

"If you are looking for a good, late-summer beach read, you can't go wrong with *Beachcombers*. . . . Another winner for Thayer's fans."
—*The Roanoke Times*

"It's a 'beach' book, but it's also a comedy of manners that's fun to read."   —*Huntington News*

"Thayer gives readers a charming summer read, filled with family and love."   —*Booklist*

Beachcombers

NANCY THAYER

Beachcombers

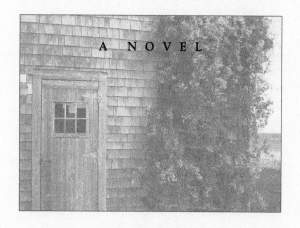

A NOVEL

Ballantine Books Trade Paperbacks
New York

2011 Ballantine Books Trade Paperback Edition

Copyright © 2010 by Nancy Thayer
Random House reading group guide copyright © 2011 by Random House, Inc.
Excerpt from *Heat Wave* © 2011 by Nancy Thayer

Published in the United States by Ballantine Books,
an imprint of The Random House Publishing Group,
a division of Random House, Inc., New York.

BALLANTINE and colophon are registered trademarks of Random House, Inc.
RANDOM HOUSE READER'S CIRCLE & Design is a registered trademark
of Random House, Inc.

Originally published in hardcover in the United States by Ballantine Books,
an imprint of The Random House Publishing Group, a division
of Random House, Inc., in 2010.

This book contains an excerpt from the forthcoming book *Heat Wave*
by Nancy Thayer. This excerpt has been set for this edition only and
may not reflect the final content of the forthcoming edition.

LIBRARY OF CONGRESS CATALOGING-IN-PUBLICATION DATA
Thayer, Nancy.
Beachcombers / Nancy Thayer.
p.   cm.
ISBN 978-0-345-51829-3
eBook ISBN 978-0-345-51830-9
1. Sisters—Fiction.   2. Female friendship—Fiction.
3. Nantucket Island (Mass.)—Fiction.   I. Title.
PS3570.H3475B43 2010
813'.54—dc22   2010010064

Printed in the United States of America

www.randomhousereaderscircle.com

6 8 9 7 5

For
Martha Foshee
The best sister in the world!

Acknowledgments
.....

I would like to thank: Karol Lindquist, lightship basket virtuoso, for the many things she teaches; Libby Oldham, who knows about Nantucket history; Dionis Gauvin, who knows about fashion; Tricia Patterson, who knows about everything; Josh Thayer and Sam Wilde Forbes, who make me proud and make me laugh; Adeline and Ellias Forbes, who make my heart do cartwheels; David Gillum and Neil Forbes, beloved of those I love—I love you, too. Thank you, my friends, for being there, and Charley, for being here.

I also want to thank Meg Ruley, for her guidance, acumen, and friendship. Enormous thanks to those at Ballantine: Junessa Viloria, Kim Hovey, Katie Rudkin, Sarina Evans, Libby McGuire, and Gina Centrello, and especially that goddess of editing, Linda Marrow.

For whatever we lose (like a you or a me)
it's always ourselves we find in the sea

—e. e. cummings, "maggie and milly and molly and may"

BEFORE

Look," their mother said to them.

It was late October, and Danielle had brought her daughters here to Surfside, the beach that faced, unprotected by bulkhead or harbor or jetties, the immense sweep of the Atlantic Ocean.

The water was sulky today, deep blue and aloof, the erratic autumn wind stirring its surface into restless waves. By now the girls knew how the ocean had its moods. On summer days it would be playful, sparkling, seductive, tossing up its lacy foam with sounds like kisses. In November, it would hiss as the tides spat and sank into the sand, dragging cold nets of froth back into its hungry depths, as if the sea itself were hunting. Winter made it warlike, hurling its waves toward the shore in battalions that rose up and thundered down, carrying the shrieking wind on its back. And when the skies were blue and the wind was mild, the ocean would shine, as if deep within, its own blue sun glowed.

Whatever the weather, the surf always brought treasures; their mother had taught them that. It was their mother who started the Beachcombers Club.

The universe is always speaking to us, Danielle told her daughters. Sending us little messages, causing coincidences and serendipities, reminding us to stop, to look around, to believe in something else, something *more*. And those of us who are lucky enough to live surrounded by the ocean have more opportunities than many to see, to know. You have to be willing to step away from what we consider normal life. You have to have imagination. You have to be aware that we're all part of a wonderful, mysterious game.

They came to the beach at least once a week, no matter the season or weather. They stalked the edge of the beach, the mother and her three daughters, heads bent forward as they scanned the sand, stopping when someone discovered a prize, and usually they tossed their finds back into the watching waters, but occasionally they slipped the rock or shell or glass into their bags to take back to their house on Fair Street.

At home, they'd gather around the kitchen table and wait until their mother had set out cups of hot chocolate frothy with marshmallows or lemonade tinkling in icy glasses. Their mother would sit at the head of the table—she was the ultimate judge—and the girls would present their discoveries: a mussel shell with the glossy indigo iridescence of a starling's head. A broken whelk, its interior twisted into a perfect spiral staircase, as smooth as bone. A flat square of blue glass like a pane of summer sky fallen to earth. Sometimes a human object: the handle of a translucent china teacup, a bracelet or hair clip or key chain, a bottle.

They'd hand their treasures around, then vote to see which one was the best, and the winning find was proudly placed between the cookbooks—on the lowest shelf so little Lily could see—until a new find was brought in. The unchosen ones were usually returned to the beach the next week, but a surprising number of them remained in the house. The windowsills of each girl's bedroom were littered with ocean trophies.

Abbie, who was the oldest and wisest, might go into a tidying fit and decide to clean her room and toss it all out, and then she would spot a rock, thinking, this is only a funny old rock, there are zillions of them on the beach. But when she picked up the rock, she would suddenly remember why she kept it, because of the way it fit into her hand like a secret promise or the weight of safety, and she kept another rock, the white one, because it was marked with a crooked blue-gray vein like a scribbled message she was sure to interpret someday, if only she had patience.

Emma liked slipper shells. Turned upside down, they became cradles for her many babies. Twisted bits of driftwood became sofas, chairs, bureaus, and beds for the dollhouse her mother had helped her create out of several packing boxes.

Little Lily liked the pretty things best. The fluting of a snow-white angel's wing or the twist of deep coral from a channeled whelk pleased her, but best of all was the discovery of sea glass, and her favorite of colors was a deep cobalt blue. Sometimes her mother glued colored yarn to a shell to make a bracelet or necklace.

Now Emma called out triumphantly to the others. She'd found

a bottle, complete, unbroken, an old-fashioned, long-necked thing of pale, clear turquoise. Lily and Abbie clustered around to scrutinize the object, checking first of all, of course, for a letter rolled up and tucked inside. But the bottle was empty. They inspected it for writing, because sometimes on this beach they found items inscribed in Portuguese or French. No writing on this one. They held it up, trying to guess what it once contained.

Only Abbie was aware that while they concentrated on the bottle, their mother, standing near them, gazed out at the sea, her longing so extreme it hurt Abbie to see it.

"Mom," Abbie said, calling her back to them.

Their mother immediately focused her attention on Abbie. "I'm here."

She dropped to her knees. She put her arm around Lily's waist and held her close as she said, "Girls. Look." She wet the tip of her finger, pressed it into the sand, and held her finger up for them to see. She blew gently and most of the grains fell back down. "See this grain of sand? This one, here. Now look at the ocean. Think of the size of the ocean compared to the size of this grain of sand. This is what we are in the universe. Think of it. How enormous the universe is. How tiny we are."

Emma shivered. She didn't like it when her mother talked like this.

"Think of the creatures swimming in the ocean depths," their mother continued. She was beautiful, with long auburn hair she allowed the wind to toss into tangles. "Whales and mermaids and monsters and long squirming eels and fish striped with gold and silver. We haven't even discovered all that hides in the deepest parts of the ocean." She looked out at the water. "So many mysteries," she told them. "Never think that there is only here."

"Mommy, I'm cold!" Lily, bored and hungry and chilled, pulled away from her mother.

Their mother kissed the top of Lily's head. She stood up. "Okay, kids, let's race for the car. The winner gets the front seat."

"Yay!" Lily yelled and took off running down the beach.

Abbie and Emma followed, pacing themselves, letting little Lily win, because it meant so much to her.

Abbie turned to look back at their mother. She was standing very still, facing the ocean, yearning for its depths.

NOW

1

· · · · ·

Abbie, Lily, and Emma, Sort of

SUBJECT: HELP!
FROM: Lily
DATE: June 5, 2009
TO: Abbie

Oh, Crabapple, I hate it when I can't reach you by phone. Where are you? Why isn't your cell phone on? Would you please please email me right away? We're all in a mess here and we need you to come home.

SUBJECT: But don't panic.
FROM: Lily
DATE: June 5, 2009
TO: Abbie

Disregard that last email. Well, don't disregard it completely, but no one is dead or anything. It's just that Dad's in financial trouble, plus a sexy woman's after him, and Emma lost her job AND Duncan broke off their engagement. Emma came home from Boston and just lies on her bed, crying all day long. She's so thin, I'm kind of scared for her. I'm trying to keep up with the house and everything, but my crazy busy season's started with the magazine. And I guess you'd bet-

ter not call me, because you're six hours ahead or behind or whatever and I probably can't talk when you can plus I know you hate
the expense of a transatlantic call. Just please, please, come home.

SUBJECT: Help
FROM: Abbie
DATE: June 5, 2009
TO: Lily

I'll email Emma today. But honey, isn't it about time Dad had a girl-
friend? Mom's been gone for fifteen years. He's probably lonely. And
maybe you're overestimating Dad's money problems. I mean, everyone's having trouble this year. Has he told you he's worried about
money?

FROM: Abbie
DATE: June 5, 2009
TO: Emma

Hi, Emma, what's going on? Lily tells me you're back home. God,
you *must* be desperate. ☺ Email me, let me know you're okay, okay?

SUBJECT: The Playhouse
FROM: Lily
DATE: June 5, 2009
TO: Abbie

Dad hasn't *said* he's worried, but he acts worried, and he's rented the
Playhouse (to that woman, wait till you see her!), plus he said he
might put the boat up for sale. And I know a lot of the people who'd
hired him to renovate their houses have canceled. I can see with my
own eyes how little work there is for him this summer. I think if you
were here, he'd talk about it. I know he thinks I'm still a baby.

SUBJECT: Please
FROM: Abbie
DATE: June 7, 2009
TO: Emma

Just send me one little email, okay? You don't even have to say anything. Just hit reply!

SUBJECT: I'm coming home.
FROM: Abbie
DATE: June 8, 2009
TO: Lily

I've got a reservation on British Air. I'll be home tomorrow. Probably around three, if my connections go smoothly.

2

. . . . .

Marina

So here she was, on Nantucket. In a small rented cottage in the middle of an enchanted island. At least she hoped it was enchanted. She was waking to another day without family or love or plans for the future.

Still, she felt just a bit better.

Lying curled in her bed, she forced herself to name just five things for which she was grateful. It was an exercise Christie had advised her to perform first thing in the morning and last thing at night. If nothing else, Christie had told her, it will give you a little bit of structure, one tidy line to start the morning and end the day to make you feel enclosed and on task.

All right then.

Marina was grateful that she'd slept through the night without needing a sleeping pill. She'd been afraid she was becoming addicted to them. Over the past few months, the divorce had plunged her into a state of grief and despair that at night turned into a raging anger and a kind of burning terror—what was her life *about*? Did she mean *nothing*? But here on the island, for the past three weeks, she'd discovered that something in the sea air worked like a charm to make her fall into a deep, relaxing sleep. Christie had been right to tell her to come here to heal.

Two—well, she was grateful she'd found the cottage. It resembled a dollhouse, with wild roses rambling all over the roof and clematis and wisteria blossoming on the trellis on the outside walls. The windows were mullioned like a fairy-tale cottage. The door was bright blue. Inside, one large room served for living, dining, and kitchen areas. A ladder led up to the loft with the bed. Windows on three sides provided views of the birds nesting in an apple tree on her right, a pine tree on her left, and a hawthorn tree straight ahead.

Inside, the décor was—well, there was no décor, actually. The few furnishings had a cast-off and shabby air, but were basically sound and comfortable. No curtains hung from the windows. No paintings graced the walls. No rugs brightened the floors, but she could understand that. It was so easy to track sand into the house, and the floors were wood and felt cool and smooth to the soles of her feet.

She was grateful to be in the heart of the town. That was the third thing, and it had been on her list every morning and every night. The cottage was off an idyllic lane in the illustrious historic district. She could walk to the grocery store, the pharmacy, the post office, the library. Tucked away at the far end of a long garden, it had once been the Playhouse for the family that had grown up in the huge old house at the front. The owner and one of his daughters lived in the house. Their presence made Marina feel not so alone. She liked seeing the lights come on in different rooms of the house. The daughter, Lily, was pretty, but not very friendly. Well, she was only twenty-two. Marina must seem ancient to her.

Jim Fox, on the other hand, was really nice. He'd brought her fresh fish several times already, and often in the evenings when he came home from work, he jumped out of his red pickup truck and sauntered down the lawn to chat with her. Did she need anything? If she did, she had only to ask, he'd be glad to help. Had she enjoyed the bluefish? Would she like some more when he went out fishing again? He was so attentive that Marina sometimes wondered if he were hitting on her. She doubted it. She was sure she wasn't giving off any sexual vibes, since her sexuality was hiding under its shell like a wounded turtle. Although she could still recognize that Jim was an awfully attractive man, tall, muscular, and comfortable enough in his powerful body to be easygoing and kind.

Fourth, she was grateful for Christie's enduring, sustaining friendship and especially for her wisdom this summer.

Odd, how things turned out.

Long ago, when she started seventh grade, Marina had teamed up with two very different best friends. Christie was her *good* friend, pretty, cheerful, popular, and smart. Dara was her *exciting* friend, always ready to try something new and outrageous, more sexy than good-looking. They remained best friends when they all started at the same gigantic university in Columbia, Missouri, but by their sophomore summer, things changed. Christie and Marina decided to go off to Nantucket to work as waitresses. They'd heard that the pay was good, the island was gorgeous, and they could party like crazy on their time off. Dara couldn't believe they were going to be waitstaff—she considered such a job way too far beneath her. She didn't need the money the way Christie and Marina did, and she went off with other college friends to backpack in Europe.

Marina and Christie had so much fun, they returned to the island for the next two summers. During the academic year, they still spent time with each other, but Dara ran with a new, fast crowd, and the trio was never the same after that. After graduation, they went their separate ways. Dara wanted money. Marina wanted to turn her love of color and design into a career. Christie just wanted her high school sweetheart, Bob.

Christie married Bob right after college—Marina was her maid of honor. A few years later, when Marina married Gerry Warren, Christie was Marina's matron of honor, lumbering down the aisle, eight months pregnant. After that, Marina had seen little of Christie. Their lives were so different, and they were so busy. Christie and Bob lived in happy chaos with their hundreds of children—really, only an eventual five—on a lake outside Kansas City.

Marina and Gerry met in college. He was handsome, with thick, straight blond hair and sapphire eyes. He was smart, too, and witty. At first she thought he was just a bit too smug and shallow, but he wanted Marina, he *pursued* Marina, and his varied and creative attempts to charm her were irresistible. Perhaps she didn't love Gerry, but she was helplessly seduced by his desire.

Their ambitions were similar, too, and that drew them together as a natural pair. He was a dynamite salesman; she was artistic and creative. Marina and Gerry started a graphic design/ad agency in the Kansas City area. They invested their own time and some start-up money borrowed from their parents, and they worked day and night.

For a few years, work was the very air they breathed. They established themselves, grew a name, became successful, and paid back their parents. They bought a condo and the posh cars they displayed as ads for their success—a Jag for Gerry, a Saab convertible for Marina. But somehow, as the months and years went by, they never found time to relax. They were like a clock, their lives the two hands ticking around the face of the day and night, with never a second to stop.

As their agency grew in size and reputation, their office became a kind of battleground that they had to storm daily. Marina and Gerry worked out five days a week, keeping their bodies lean and sleek. Marina wore tight black suits and four-inch heels and kept her blond hair cut short, chic, and easy to care for. She did less creative work and spent more of her time dealing with clients, executives, lawyers, techies, and accountants. At night she and Gerry often worked late, or took clients out to dinner. She felt glamorous, accomplished, successful. She was having fun, making money, and looking fabulous.

In the meantime, sexpot Dara got married, twice. Marina was Dara's maid of honor the first time. The second time, Dara flew off with her wealthy lover to Pago Pago for their wedding and extended honeymoon. Dara's second husband owned a megabucks Kansas City real estate company. When he signed on with Warren Design & Advertising, his business and his contacts sent Marina and Gerry's company skyrocketing into the economic stratosphere.

Marina was grateful to Dara for this. Their friendship took on a new energy. Marina and Dara attended the same parties, went on shopping sprees together, and gossiped over lunch at posh restaurants. Dara was obsessed with her appearance—she got breast implants when she was thirty, and a face-lift at thirty-two—but Marina understood. After all, she was in the ad business. She appreciated the importance of presentation.

Over the years, Dara lost interest in their domesticated friend, but every few months Marina made time to visit Christie. In the midst of her pack of children, dogs, and cats, Christie was a calm, contented center, moving slowly, in no rush to finish any project and be somewhere else. She was right where she wanted to be. Marina admired the pace, the depth, the comfort of Christie's life.

Marina felt like she was always straining, rushing, pushing, to get somewhere else.

And as the years passed and Marina grew older, she discovered that she was beginning to envy Christie, too.

One sultry July afternoon, she confessed a deep and powerful secret to Christie. She told Christie before she told Dara. She told Christie even before she told Gerry. The words felt so odd in her mouth.

"Christie, I want a baby. Actually, I've gotten kind of obsessed with it. I don't want five kids like you have, I couldn't do that. But I do want a child of my own."

"Well, honey," Christie replied, laughing, "that's one thing you can get without wearing those killer tight suits."

Christie gave her the courage to confide in Gerry. He seemed amused, but he liked the idea. So in the middle of the hurricane that was their life, Marina and Gerry tried to make a baby.

But the baby wouldn't come.

They were both shocked. Their history together was one of achievement and success, not failure.

They tried everything. Tests. Charts. Positions. Herbal and hormonal supplements. Nothing worked. They saw several doctors, who all pronounced Marina and Gerry healthy and perfectly capable of reproduction. Yet still nothing happened.

She confided in Dara, and Dara said, "Oh, honey, consider it a blessing. A baby would ruin your figure."

Marina couldn't understand it. She tried to be relaxed about it all, but when she saw another woman with a baby, she burned with envy. She dreamed of babies at night and longed for one every waking hour. As each month passed in failure and sorrow, she began to hate herself.

One afternoon she sat in her slick chrome-and-glass office, staring at her computer screen, thinking over and over again in a relentless circle of pain: Why couldn't she get pregnant, what was wrong with her? She felt something wet on her hand. It wouldn't be tears. She didn't allow herself to cry in the office. She glanced down to discover that she had been stabbing the palm of her hand with the tip of her silver letter opener. She gasped and tossed the letter opener onto the desk. She pressed tissues against her hand, grabbed up her purse, and raced from her office. She didn't even stop to tell her assistant where she was going. She didn't even know where she was going—she just needed to be away from the pain.

Once in her car, she understood exactly where she wanted to be, and she drove out to Christie's house. It was January and a new snow had blanketed the roadsides and rooftops with the pure sparkling white of confectioners' sugar. The sun was out in a high blue sky and the air was sharp and tangy.

Christie had a fire going in the rec room. Her children were all in school. She was knitting a sweater and listening to music—in the middle of the day! Marina couldn't imagine living such a life.

Christie told Marina to kick off her shoes and curl up on the sofa. She brought her hot chocolate and cookies, as if Marina were one of her children. She listened to Marina, and she cried with her—how grateful Marina was for that, to have her friend genuinely share her loss.

"I'm so angry, Christie," Marina cried. "I'm so *hurt*. Why me? What's wrong with me? I know Gerry thinks I'm at fault, even though the doctors say we're both physically fine. But it's turning our marriage inside out. And I'm getting obsessed and bitter and angry; I'm turning into a person I don't like being. I don't know what to do!"

Christie was quiet, knitting a row as she thought. "You could stop trying," she suggested. "You could stop hoping. You could give up. You could adopt."

"Gerry doesn't want to adopt."

"Then let it go." Christie reached over and put her hand on Marina's. "Just let it go. You have so much, Marina. You have work you enjoy, you have a husband you love. You're gorgeous, you're free. You should love your life."

"I want a family. I want your life," Marina insisted. "I want your children."

Christie burst out laughing. "Are you kidding me? I tell you what, you stay here for the weekend with my bunch. Bob and I will go off on a little jaunt together and leave you in charge." She saw the alarm on Marina's face and laughed even harder.

Marina laughed, too. She felt better already, and as she drove back home in the winter twilight, she decided she would tell Gerry that if she wasn't pregnant by her fortieth birthday, she was going to stop trying. They would have to move on. And she told him, and he accepted her decision.

Perhaps Marina had secretly hoped that her ultimatum to herself—to Fate or Destiny or whoever gave women babies—would make her body sit up, take notice, and get to work. Get pregnant.

Then her fortieth birthday arrived.

And everything changed.

Now Marina reminded herself: *No wallowing! Move on!* She sat up in bed, planted her feet on the cool wood floor, and surveyed her funny little loft bedroom.

Focus, she told herself.

What was number five? Okay, the fifth thing she was grateful for was to be on this island. The flamboyant, generous beauty both hurt and healed her. Some days the intensity of the wild blue sea, the dense clouds of pink climbing roses, flew straight to her heart like an arrow, spearing her with emotions, so that she had to crouch to the ground, pressing her knees into her chest to keep from crying. But some days the beauty soothed her, even cheered her.

She believed that someday, someday *soon*, she would walk on the beach, and she would smile.

3

. . . . .

Abbie

Abbie!"

The instant Abbie stepped out of Jason's truck onto the drive-way, her youngest sister opened the front door and flew out of the house. Lily had been waiting, watching out the window, and this tugged at Abbie's heart. Lily was twenty-two now, a grown woman, but she would always be Abbie's little sister. And Lily *was* little, four inches shorter than Abbie, and petite.

"Abbie, I'm so glad you're here!" Lily was almost jumping up and down.

"Me, too, kid." Abbie wrapped her sister in a big hug.

Lily was the beauty of the family, with her red hair and green cat eyes. She was sexy, too, and not unaware of her charms. Abbie felt Lily's attention shift to Jason, the island man who had been on her plane and offered her a ride home from the airport.

Jason was lifting Abbie's luggage from his truck. He was two years older than Lily and six years younger than Abbie. He'd just gotten out of the army, and he was grown up and bulked up. He'd been a hunk to start with, with his dark hair, black eyes, and the ex-otic looks he'd inherited from his Cape Verdean ancestors.

Abbie reached for her duffel bag and roller suitcase. "Jason, thanks for the ride."

"No problem." Jason nodded at Lily. "Hi, Lily."

"Hi, Jason. Thanks for bringing Abbie home." Lily batted her long lashes at Jason. "Would you like to come in for some iced tea or something?"

"Another time, maybe. Abbie tells me she hasn't been home for a while. You guys have some catching up to do." With a smile, Jason climbed up into his truck and drove away.

Lily grabbed her sister's arm, pulling her toward the house. "I can't believe you're really here! I went out to Bartlett's and got a bunch of their arugula . . ."

The front hall was cool and dim; the back of the house got the sun. As she dropped her bags down by the stairs, Abbie saw the dust powdering the baseboards, the frame of the mirror, and the etched glass globes of the overhead light.

"Look!" Lily nodded toward the hall table, where a vase of wild-flowers stood next to the brass bowl where the family tossed their mail and keys. "Just for you!"

"How nice, Lily! Thanks." Abbie hugged her sister again, but she couldn't keep her gaze from sweeping over Lily's shoulder. She'd been gone for just eighteen months. How could the house have become so cluttered in that short space of time?

"Where's Emma?"

"She's in her room. She might be asleep. She sleeps a lot." Lily studied Abbie's face. "We haven't gotten around to washing the windows for a while. I never think about it, until, well, I never think about it."

And then it was as if the entire house came crashing down all around Abbie, the weight of the windows and the sofa and the chairs and the dust all balancing right on her shoulders, weighing her down so much she could scarcely breathe. And she hadn't even made it into the kitchen yet.

Since she was fifteen, Abbie had been in charge of the house, taking care of Lily and Emma, cooking and cleaning. She hadn't been able to go to college, not with the death of her mother and the family responsibilities that had brought her. Sometimes she'd thought she would never be able to have her own family, her own life. She loved her family, but she'd longed to see just a bit of the world.

When she turned twenty-eight, two years ago, she accepted an au pair job with a summer family and traveled with them to London.

She was being paid for work, yet she'd never had so much time to herself. The children she took care of were ten and twelve, good-natured and easy. With them she went to museums, concerts, plays, and to watch the changing of the guard in front of Buckingham Palace. At night, she helped herself to a book from Mr. Vanderdyne's library. She read Dickens, Hardy, and T. S. Eliot. She watched DVDs of Noël Coward plays and Truffaut movies. She sat with her charges during their French lessons and began to learn French herself—the Vanderdynes were going to France this summer.

Then Lily's worried emails arrived. Abbie had to come home.

It had felt good, at first, to feel needed. Yet how good a job had she done of raising Lily if Lily was still dependent on Abbie?

Sensing the drop in Abbie's mood, Lily was babbling, "We've been too busy working to pay attention to stuff like dusting. Even before the stock market crashed last fall, Nantucket was kind of falling apart. People have stopped building new homes. Several of Dad's clients backed out of deals. He always has some work, but you know he puts his crew first, and he's kept paying their salaries and health insurance. I've helped out financially as much as I can. I pay for some of the groceries and stuff like that."

Okay, *this* was a change, and a good one. When Abbie had left eighteen months ago, Lily hadn't had any idea about the amount of money it took to run a house. With both her big sisters gone, it sounded like Lily had learned a lot.

Lily went on, "I want to talk to you about money. You're always so good with stuff like that."

"Okay, sure. We can ask Emma, too, since she's the money expert."

"I don't think Emma's feeling too *expert* about anything," Lily said.

Abbie's attention was caught by the photograph on the mantel. Their Aunt Stella had taken it at her daughter's wedding ten years ago. The three sisters were dressed in matching bridesmaid's gowns, lavender tulle fantasias.

Abbie's curly brown hair was feathered close to her scalp, accentuating the elegant shape of her head, and the length of her neck. She'd inherited her father's tall, lanky, wide-shouldered swimmer's body and stood with an ironic tilt behind the froth of dress. Abbie had worn her hair short all her life. It was easy to keep—she often trimmed it herself—and it made swimming easy. She was twenty then, but clearly she was an adult. She held herself with authority. Her smile was genuine but perhaps just a little sardonic.

Emma was a few inches shorter than Abbie—it was always remarked upon, how the three sisters were like stair steps. Like Abbie, she had big hazel eyes. Unlike her older sister, she was round, as their mother had been. Not fat, not even plump, just *round*. Her bosom bulged at the strapless neckline. Her waist was small, her hips wide. Her brown hair was as curly as Abbie's but Emma had freckles sprinkled over her nose and cheeks and her face was less angular than Abbie's. She was the "cute" one, and it drove her crazy. She set and rolled and ironed and blew her hair dry, and for photos she jutted her chin out, trying to look sophisticated. She always just looked cranky.

Lily had been only twelve that year. She'd sleeked her wild red curls into a formal chignon and lined her gorgeous green eyes with kohl. She was the shortest of the sisters as well as the youngest, and the most dainty. For the photo she'd turned a bit sideways, curling her shoulder up to her cheek in a kittenish come-hither gesture. She looked like a child playing dress-up.

"Why is this thing on the mantel?" Abbie wondered aloud. "We all look so young."

"Dad likes it there," Lily said. "It's the last formal photo taken of the three of us together."

Abbie did a slow turn around the room. "It's like entering a time machine." She quickly held her hand up. "Not criticizing! Just saying." She took a moment to study her baby sister. "Wow, you have really turned into a bombshell, haven't you?"

Lily blushed. "Do you think so?"

"How could I not? You've got some Rita Hayworth stuff going on for you now."

Pleased, Lily hurried to return the compliment. "And you look like—Audrey Hepburn."

"Ha. I think I'm more Sigourney Weaver in *Alien*."

Lily nodded enthusiastically. "I can totally get that!"

"What's Emma looking like these days?" Abbie idly ran her fingers over the piano keys—it was just slightly out of tune.

Lily tugged on Abbie's arm. "Let's go up and see her."

4

. . . . .

Emma

Emma lay on her bed like the letter S with a cat nestled into the crook of her knees and her ancient Paddington bear squashed up against her chest. Much of the stuffed animal's fur had worn away, and his left ear was held on with a safety pin, but she only loved him all the more for that. Paddington had seen her through many crises. His fur probably still held all the salt from the tears she cried the year her mother died.

Downstairs, the screen door slammed. Voices floated up, Lily's rapid girlish soprano, Abbie's lower, slower phrases. It had been two years since she'd seen Abbie.

Emma had been so happy for Abbie when she went to London. No one knew better than Emma how Abbie had sacrificed her own life to keep the family going after their mother died. Perhaps Emma hadn't been really aware of it when she was a teenager, caught up in her own grief and desires. Certainly when she got a scholarship to U. Mass./Amherst, she'd accepted in a flash, and gone away for four years, assuming that Abbie would stay home to take care of Lily and run the house. It was what Abbie did. Had she taken Abbie for granted? Yes, she had. They all had. Even, especially, their father.

Jim Fox was a contractor, a reliable, friendly, even-tempered man who never let his clients down. He was not ambitious, or if he was, his ambition was simply to enjoy each day. He loved the island and the community. He loved taking the time to talk, over a sandwich lunch at the drugstore where he could jaw with his buddies, or leaning against his truck shooting the breeze with a friend—another contractor, a realtor, the police chief, a fisherman.

He was a good father, patient and decisive and loving. He taught his daughters to sail, to clean a bluefish, to use a Phillips screwdriver. He took them to the summer fairs and he built them the Playhouse at the back of their yard.

But he'd been hit hard by their mother's death. He'd gone quiet, paralyzed by grief, and without Abbie taking over the way she had, who knows what would have happened to their family. Their father had continued working, and working hard, so the family never suffered financially. But the light had gone out of his eyes, and even his smiles were sad.

Emma had been thirteen when their mother died. As she grew older, Emma wanted to do something to help her family, but she didn't have the homemaking talents or the natural bossy authority Abbie had, so for a few years she felt lost. During high school, she gradually learned that she was smart, and by the time she started college, she had formed a plan. Perhaps she couldn't run the house the way Abbie could but she could help in other ways. She determined to save herself, and her family.

In college, she majored in economics. It didn't come easily to her, but she studied hard. She didn't party much and she didn't fall in love. She worked part time at a copy center and saved her money instead of spending it on lipstick and clothes. After graduation, she went to Boston and landed a plum job in a high-powered investment firm. She started on the lowest rung, but she worked industriously and diligently, and gradually she made a name for herself as a broker. She scrimped her pennies and saved them until they grew into dollars, then invested her own money in high-risk–high-payoff stocks.

Emma earmarked one account for Nantucket. For her father. When it reached a nice fat sum, she was going to come home and present him with a check. So he would be safe, and could continue to work in his peculiar leisurely way, or not work at all.

By her third year, she was living the good life. She started dating Duncan Fairly, another broker in her firm, an ambitious, energetic type A who liked her style. They quickly became a couple. She va-

cationed with him in the Caribbean. They bought each other designer clothing, and reveled in their image. They were the glam
couple of the firm. He asked her to move into his Back Bay apartment.

She invited him to Nantucket. At first, she worried that their
eccentric old house and her father's way of life were a little too
downscale for Duncan, but Duncan never criticized. He knew Nantucket was a great place to make contacts. He liked sailing, playing
tennis, eating out at the posh restaurants. And it was on Nantucket
that Duncan proposed to her, in August, while they were walking
on the beach at sunset. It had been perfect, almost as if Fate were
following a schedule Emma had drawn up.

By then, fourteen years had passed since Emma's mother's death.
Her father was less paralyzed, happier in his life, more *there*, but
Emma had another idea for brightening his life. She would give him
grandchildren. He would *love* having grandchildren. He would be
such a great grandfather, patient and instructive, showing them the
berries on the moors, the shells on the beach, the fish sparkling like
magic firecrackers in the harbor waters.

Emma wanted to wait until it was all ready, the bank account
bulging, her pregnancy begun, and then she would spread the future
before her father like a magic carpet. She would present her father
with a nice fat check and instructions to fix up the house, because
she wanted to bring her children to the island as often as possible.

In October, the stock market was hit by a death blow.

The money Emma had invested vanished like smoke in the
wind. Her savings were gone. The money in the aggressively-
invested, high-risk account for her father disappeared in a blink of
the eye.

The firm fired her. She tried to remind herself that dozens of
brokers had been fired along with her, but the comfort that brought
was ice-cold.

She tried not to be desperate. For a few months she hung on,
frantically searching for a new job, networking at parties—the few
parties that anyone gave. It was difficult in the new economy to be
optimistic, but she was young. She was in love. Duncan had not
been laid off, after all. He made enough money. He could support
her and a baby or two. Of course they couldn't have the lavish wed-

ding they'd been planning, but she really didn't mind. Their new life together was what counted.

In May, Duncan broke off his engagement to Emma. He had, he told Emma, fallen in love with Alicia Maxwell, another broker at the firm. Another broker who hadn't been fired. The daughter of such old family money that this financial blow was a gnat's bite to her.

Emma was stunned with loss.

Duncan didn't give her time to grieve. He tore through his apartment like an exterminator, snatched up her possessions, tossed them into boxes, and shipped them back to Nantucket. She had no address of her own, no place to go, but back to the house where she'd lived as a child.

Now cardboard boxes grew up from the floor of her old childhood bedroom like stalagmites in a dark cave. She didn't have the heart to unpack them. She didn't have the heart for anything.

She was defeated, and beneath the loss ran a vein of fear. She didn't want to be paralyzed like her father had been. But how could she climb out of this pit of sorrow?

She heard her sisters' voices as they came up the stairs. It would be so good to see Abbie. It was comforting that she was here. Emma and Abbie had always been close. They were only two years apart, while Lily was the baby. The adorable, darling, baby-doll child, perhaps a little bit spoiled, a bit of a princess now.

But Emma had to give Lily credit. Since she'd graduated from college, she'd been home taking care of things. She bought and cooked decent food; she kept the house pretty clean. This year when Emma came home for Christmas dinner, she found a tree elaborately decorated by Lily, as well as a real Christmas dinner.

Now that Abbie was back, Emma wondered cynically just how quickly Lily would weasel out of any household responsibilities. She gave herself a mental head slap. After all, just how many responsibilities was *Emma* willing to take on? She couldn't even find the energy to get out of bed.

Her bedroom door flew open.

"Emma, look who's here!"

Emma rolled on her side and sat up in bed, dislodging Cinnamon from his warm nest. The cat yawned, arched his back, and fixed the newcomers with a disdainful glare.

Abbie sat on the side of the bed and gave Emma such a warm, affectionate hug that Emma had to hold her breath to keep from bursting into tears. Oh, Emma thought, she'd forgotten how wide and strong her older sister's shoulders were, as if she'd been built to comfort and care for them all.

But this time, not even Abbie could help.

5

Lily

Lily was surprised at how the old childish jealousy surfaced as she watched Abbie hug Emma. Good grief, she was twenty-two, she was an adult; when would she stop feeling so third wheel whenever she saw her sisters together?

It was only natural that they'd be close. They had only two years between them, not the eight-year ravine that existed between Abbie and Lily, or the six years between Lily and Emma.

Her two older sisters looked alike, too, both of them with their father's curly brown hair and huge hazel eyes. Lily got her coloring from her mother, which was a good thing; Lily liked being a redhead. But still, she was set apart.

Now Emma collapsed in Abbie's arms and was sobbing and blubbering out in choking gasps. "Duncan . . . money . . . want to die." She wailed so terribly that Cinnamon leapt up, startled, and raced from the room.

Abbie kept her arms around Emma. Over and over she said, "I know, honey. I know."

Lily stood by the end of the bed. Wanting to be closer, to be included, she leaned down to put her hand on Emma's leg. "Want some iced tea, Emma? Maybe a beer?"

"Oh, sure," Emma wailed. "Iced tea would change everything."

"I'm only trying to help." Lily moved away from the bed and sat down in the old wicker rocking chair in the corner of the room.

After awhile Emma's sobs subsided. She leaned back against the headboard. Abbie handed her a tissue and Emma noisily blew her nose. Her voice was clogged with tears when she said, "I don't know what to do. I don't know how to go on."

"First," Abbie said, and the authority she'd had when they were growing up rang steadily in her voice, "you're going to get up, take a shower, wash your hair, and put on some clothes."

Emma sagged. "I don't want to."

"I don't care," Abbie retorted calmly. "While you're in the shower, Lily and I are going to change your sheets."

"Hey, let her change her own—" Lily began to protest, but Abbie shot her a look.

"Then we're going for a walk around town, and we'll stop someplace for a drink."

"I don't have the money for a drink," Emma objected sulkily.

"My treat." Abbie gave her sister an affectionate pat on her thigh. "Get moving." She stood up and nodded at Lily. "You get the sheets. I'll strip the bed."

Lily stood up, too, and snapped a brisk salute at her sister. It was really mind-boggling, she thought as she wandered out into the hall and down to the linen closet at the end, how Abbie could just waltz in like this after eighteen months away and take over. Plus, suddenly everything was all about Emma. Abbie hadn't even asked Lily how she was!

Back in Emma's bedroom, Lily dropped the sheets on the bureau, found the bottom sheet, and sailed it out over Emma's double bed. Abbie grabbed the other side and together they lifted the corners and slipped the sheet over the mattress.

"Well done," Lily told Abbie, and trying to create a sense of conspiracy between them, she nodded toward the bathroom, where the shower ran full force.

"Poor kid," Abbie said. "She worked so hard."

"*I* work hard, too!" Lily protested.

"Oh, right." Abbie hefted the mattress to tuck the sheet under. Of course she did it quickly and perfectly, as if she'd been trained by the order of excellent innkeepers or something. "You're writing a weekly social column for *Nantucket Talk*. Tell me about it."

"Oh, it's such a cool job." Lily vigorously stuffed a pillow into the case. "It *is* hard work, though. I have to drive all over the island;

I have to go right up to people I don't know to ask if I can interview them; I have to take notes and remember a million things at once because I can't use a tape recorder; I have to try to remember everyone's face and name and be really nice."

Abbie laughed. "That sounds like fun, Lily, and perfect for you. Is it a year-round job?"

"Absolutely! Something's always happening on the island now. Armchair theater, concerts, community events like the spelling bee."

Abbie tilted her head. "Are you really so busy off-season?"

Suddenly Lily felt under attack. "I run the house, too. I buy groceries, I make Dad healthy dinners, I vacuum . . ."

"I know, I'm just wondering . . . The curtains need to be washed, and stuff like that."

Emma walked into the room, wrapped in a towel, her brown hair curling around her face, smelling wet and strawberry-scented from the shampoo.

Abbie ran her hand over her forehead. "You know, I'm whipped. I mean, I started the day in London, and it's nine o'clock in the evening for my brain. Jet lag must be catching up with me."

"Take a nap," Emma said. "I don't feel like going out, anyway."

"Actually, I think I will take a nap." Abbie stretched and yawned. "Emma, would you wake me in a couple of hours? I want to get back on U.S. time."

"Sure." Emma dropped her towel on the floor and slipped into her bed. She reached for the clock on her bedside table and set the alarm, then slid down between the covers, turning her back on her sisters.

"See you in awhile," Abbie said over her shoulder as she left the room. "Man, it's really hitting me. I'll unpack later."

Lily stood for a moment, then she left the room, too, mumbling, "You could have said thank you for changing the sheets."

Emma must not have heard her, for she only said, "Pull the door shut, would you, Lily?"

Suddenly Lily found herself alone in the hall. The doors to both sisters' rooms were shut, as blank and forbidding as they'd been when they were teenagers gossiping about exotic secrets while silly little baby Lily, too young to be included, hung around in the hall, waiting to be invited in, hoping to overhear even one intimate word.

Well, she wouldn't be like that! She had a life! She had work!

But she'd turned in her column this morning, and tonight, Tuesday night, nothing was happening on the island. It was still too early for the big parties, galas, fund-raisers, even for the art openings.

Well, then, she had friends! Clattering down the stairs, she yanked out her cell phone and punched in Carrie's number. Carrie was always at home with her baby and eager for adult company.

"Hey, Carrie, I thought I'd come over for a while."

"Hallelujah! I haven't had a real conversation all day. And Tommy's going to be out fishing until dark."

"Need anything? Wine, pizza?"

"If I have to eat another pizza, I'll go mad. So will Tommy. I never seem to have the time or energy to shop for real food, let alone cook it."

"Tell you what, I'll stop at the grocery store and pick up some pasta and mussels and clams and fresh parsley. You have olive oil and garlic, right?"

"I do. You're going to cook dinner for me?"

"I can't do anything fancy, but I can do a mean pasta with seafood."

"I utterly love you. I will give you my firstborn child. Really."

Lily laughed. "See you soon."

6

. . . . .

Abbie

After their naps, Emma and Abbie sat on the back deck, sipping red wine, enjoying the soft evening air. Emma wore khaki shorts and a loose cotton shirt and her brown curls frizzed because she hadn't blown her hair dry.

Abbie had napped and showered and pulled on an old sundress she found in her closet. Her head buzzed with jet lag and her stomach grumbled.

"Where's Lily?" Abbie wondered. She hooked a wicker stool with her toes and dragged it over to rest her feet on. "Has she organized anything for dinner?"

"I have no idea," Emma replied listlessly.

Emma weighed less than Abbie had ever seen her, and she had dark circles under her eyes. She'd always been organized, energetic, determined. It was just wrong, having her seem so defeated. Abbie considered her next words carefully, then said, "Lily's worried about you, and I can see why."

Emma twitched in her chair. "I'm fine."

"Yeah, I can tell."

"I'm not going to pull a Mom, if that's what you're worried about."

"You'd better not!" Abbie glared at her sister. "Suck it up, Emma. It will get better."

"Will it? I don't know. I don't even care."

"But you will. You'll get over it. Lots of people—"

"How do you know?" Emma shifted in her chair so she could zing a glance at Abbie. "When have you *ever* made yourself vulnerable to a man? When have you ever lost your heart?"

"Get back, Jack!" Abbie said. "For your information, I've been involved a few times."

"Really."

"Really."

At the same moment, Abbie and Emma turned away from each other and took a huge swallow of wine. Aware of their parallel actions, they both laughed.

"So why did you never tell me about any of them?" Emma asked.

"I don't know. I'll admit I never was really serious about anyone." She studied Emma. "How long are you planning to stay here?"

"Planning?" Emma snorted. "I honestly don't know. I can't think about it. Hell, I can scarcely move. Plus, it's not like investment firms are searching for young brokers. I'm worthless, you know?"

"Don't say that!" Abbie snapped. "You're not worthless."

"I am, though. It's the truth. Might as well face it."

"Oh, Emma—" A movement at the end of the garden caught Abbie's eye. "Is that The Dreaded Seductress?"

For a moment they were silent, like hunters spotting prey. The woman came out of the Playhouse with a clear plastic bag in her hand, walked around the garage to the other side where the trash barrels were kept, and returned empty-handed. She was short, slender, and blond, but they were too far away to tell whether or not she was pretty. She wore khaki shorts and a black tee shirt.

"She looks pretty normal to me," Abbie observed quietly. "Have you met her?"

"I haven't," Emma said. "I don't especially want to."

"You don't especially want to do anything," Abbie reminded her.

"That's true."

The woman didn't seem to notice them. She walked around the Playhouse, studying it, stopping here and there, nodding to herself.

"What's she doing?" Abbie whispered.

"Well, *I* don't know, do I?" Emma frowned. "Maybe she's going to paint the trim? It certainly needs it."

"But why would *she* paint the trim? She's only renting. How long is she renting for?"

"The summer, I think. I admit, I haven't exactly paid attention to anything Lily or Dad said recently."

"Dad must be worried about money if he rented the Playhouse."

"I think he is." Emma began to cry. "I was going to take care of Dad. I had a special savings account earmarked for him. And it all just—*went*."

"Oh, honey." Abbie reached over and took her sister's hand. "No one ever expected you to do anything like that."

"But I *want* to!"

"I know. But come on. Dad's not that old. He's what, fifty-two? And you have to admit, he looks ten years younger."

"And I wanted to give him grandchildren."

"You will. 'Course you will. You're not even thirty yet. You'll meet someone new."

"I don't think so, Abbie. I'm so tired. I could go back to bed right now."

"Maybe you should see the doctor. Maybe try an antidepressant?"

"Yes, because meds work so well for our family." Emma stood up. "I can't do this anymore. I'm going back to bed."

"I'll call you for dinner."

Perhaps she shouldn't have mentioned antidepressants to Emma, Abbie thought as she sat alone in the garden. It was a tough subject for them all. But Abbie couldn't help but worry about Emma and she knew Lily was right to call her home. Emma had always been the determined one, the ambitious one, the optimist. Seeing her like this was just wrong. Abbie didn't think *she* had the depression gene, if there was such a thing, but Emma was close to the mark when she accused Abbie of not letting herself get vulnerable. Abbie didn't want to put herself out there emotionally, because she wasn't sure she could take a fall. And as for her youngest sister, Lily seemed to be naturally lighthearted, fun-loving, superficial. Plus dramatic Lily probably shed any unpleasant pressures by turning even the slightest problem into a soap opera.

How odd it was that of the three sisters, optimistic Emma was the one who had struggled with a tendency for depression. All her life, Abbie had been aware of this. Weeks and months had passed

when they were children when Emma would get quiet and melan-
choly. But she'd always bounced out of it. And when she got to college, she seemed to have burned away any despondency with the
strong bright light of hope.

Now this. Now Emma's world had crashed down around her. But
Abbie was sure Emma would recover. And it was the beginning of
summer on the island, a languorous time of year when each day was
blessed with natural riches—sunshine, blue sky, sparkling water, soft
breezes. It was a good time for starting over.

As she sat musing, Abbie idly observed the woman at the far
end of the garden. She had walked around the Playhouse, tilted her
head up to scan the sky, and studied the fence that ran along the
back. She went into the Playhouse by the blue front door and returned carrying an old red wooden chair. An apple tree arched pos-
sessively over the Playhouse—also, Abbie noticed, covered with
ivy. The woman set the chair in the shade of the tree, stood with her
hands on her hips for a moment, nodded to herself, and went back
into the house. She returned carrying a small table.

You've got our tea table! Abbie thought indignantly. Then she
laughed at herself. It had been over a decade since any of them had
even thought of the old table.

The woman set the table next to the chair. She sat down on the
edge of the chair. Abbie was hidden in the shade, or at least the
woman didn't seem to see Abbie. She rose several times to adjust
the position of the chair and table.

I'd face the fence. It's covered with honeysuckle and clematis, Abbie
thought.

As if the woman had heard Abbie's thoughts, she stood and an-
gled the chair and table so she was facing the fence. She walked
back into her house and returned carrying a glass—it looked like a
wineglass—and a book. When she finally settled, her back was to
Abbie, which for some obscure reason offended Abbie.

Now she began to understand why Lily had been so bent out of
shape. Their lives had not been without sorrow, but certain periods
of it had been heavenly. Abbie couldn't remember a time when the
Playhouse didn't exist. Her father had begun building it when his
first child was born. He'd built small chairs and a little table, and
their mother had made curtains for the windows. Over the years
their parents had furnished the place with miniature tea sets and

bunk beds for their dolls and stuffed animals. They even had a little bookshelf and a hutch for the dishes. An old mattress was dragged up the stairs to the Playhouse loft and flopped on the floor, to be covered by a variety of tattered blankets.

As the years passed, Abbie and Emma had dragged in cast-off furniture that fit adult bodies to mingle with the smaller furniture Lily still used. When Abbie became a teenager, she used the Playhouse as a refuge and inner sanctum. She would lie on the old love seat covered with cabbage rose chintz and read to her heart's content while the rain thundered down all around her.

When Abbie was fifteen, she took Andy Mitchell up to that mattress in the loft. They were in the middle of some pretty serious cuddling when they heard the door slam and Abbie's father came thundering up the stairs. He chased Andy out and gave Abbie holy hell and the next day he dragged the mattress into his truck and took it out to the dump.

Perhaps that was why their father had started on a long, complicated, DIY project, adding the bathroom and a real kitchen to the back of the Playhouse. He told them he was turning it into a guesthouse, for when they brought friends home from college, but really, Abbie thought now, he was probably just trying to keep her and Emma out of it while they were teenagers. It took him five years to do it all, to build the frame, add the shingles, have someone install electricity and run water and plumbing from the same lines that fed his shop at the back of the garage. It was too bad for Lily, really, because she was still little and would have loved the fantasy world at the back of their yard. Lily was twelve when the Playhouse was ready again. She used it, Abbie had always thought, for escape, in the same way Abbie had, except it was Abbie that Lily was escaping. It was Abbie who had taken their mother's place, running the house, cooking and cleaning and acting as disciplinarian and protector. It was Abbie who freaked out when she caught twelve-year-old Lily and her friends smoking in the Playhouse, and it was Abbie who chased Lily's first boyfriend away from the sagging sofa when Abbie caught them with their clothes off.

Now as Abbie sat reminiscing, a truck pulled into their driveway and parked next to the house. Her father got out. Eager to greet him, Abbie half rose, but he didn't notice her. To her surprise, he headed toward the Playhouse. He was carrying a cooler. When he got to the bottom of the garden, he called out—Abbie could hear his voice but not the words—and the woman turned in her chair, then stood. As Abbie watched, her father set the cooler down, reached into it, and handed the woman something. The two talked easily; Abbie could tell by the music of their voices that they were friendly.

She took the opportunity to study her father. She hadn't seen him for nearly two years but he appeared pretty much like he always had, tall and broad-shouldered, with the muscular posture of a contractor.

Her father said a few more words to the woman, picked up the cooler, and came toward the house.

When he was only a couple of yards away, Abbie stood up. "Hey, Dad!"

To her surprise, her father's face turned bright red. Was he *blushing*?

"Well, my gosh, Abbie, I didn't even see you there! Sweetheart, you look grand!" Jim Fox strode toward his daughter, dropped the cooler on the terrace, and embraced her in a grizzly bear hug. "Lily told me you were coming, but I didn't realize it was so soon. How are you?"

"I'm great! How are you? Man, you don't look a day older! What's your secret?"

Her father blushed again. And his hazel eyes sparkled.

"So you've rented the Playhouse."

His face continued to flame as he turned toward the bottom of the garden. "Well, yes, in this economy I've got to say I can use the money."

"Who's the renter? Is she nice?"

Jim Fox cleared his throat. "Her name's Marina Warren. She's from the Midwest, and yes, she's very nice. I just gave her some bluefish, actually. Iggy Holdgate hauled in a large catch and gave me some." He opened the cooler. "A big guy."

"Super! I'll cook it for dinner!"

"You'll cook? Honey, you just got here."

"Oh, I'm fine, I had a good nap. I love bluefish."

As they talked, they went into the mudroom and on into the

kitchen. Her father put the fish in the refrigerator, then said, "I'm going to take a shower."

"Fine. I'll get started in the kitchen."

"Where are your sisters?"

Abbie squatted down to dig through the crisper and found a bag of fresh lettuce and two bunches of asparagus.

She told her father, "Lily's taken off—I don't know where—and Emma's upstairs in her room."

Worry flashed across her father's face.

"We had a great talk." Abbie handed him a cold beer. "I'll have one, too, while I cook." With forced enthusiasm, she said, "I'm so glad to be back!"

"Are you really?" her father asked. "I know it's not London."

"It's summer on Nantucket!" she told her father. "Nothing could be better!"

She moved around the kitchen. Everything was familiar, everything was right where it had always been: the knives in the wooden block, with the bread knife space still empty—they never had figured out where that knife went. New heat-proof rubber spatulas hung out with old wooden spoons and slotted spoons in the blue speckled container, while the less popular utensils mingled messily in the top drawer to the left of the sink, along with so many crumbs Abbie suspected the drawer hadn't been cleaned since she was last here.

The red enamel colander and the salad spinner were on top of the refrigerator, and just inside the pantry door hung their mother's apron. It said Kiss the Cook and their mother had given it to herself for Christmas, laughing as she showed it off. That had been the Christmas Abbie was fifteen. Whenever Abbie came in from a school event or the beach at dinnertime, her mother would be wearing that apron as she prepared dinner. She'd tap her apron and arch her eyebrow.

"Oh, Mom, you are such a dork," Abbie would say, and she'd huff over, rolling her eyes, to peck a kiss on her mother's cheek before stomping out of the room.

Now Abbie touched the apron, allowing the memory to flood back. She wished she had been nicer about kissing her mother.

And there by the far wall, on the low shelf with the cookbooks, was a large white oyster shell she'd found at the beach at Pocomo, the last time the sisters had gone beachcombing. Abbie picked it up and held it in her hand. She'd wanted, after their mother's death, to keep up the tradition of the Beachcombers Club, but the first time she'd forced her younger sisters to go to the beach to search for prizes, they had all ended up sobbing in helpless wrenching grief. She marshaled them out to beachcomb the next year, but their hearts weren't in it; the beach held no magic—it just wasn't the same with their mother gone. They never tried it again.

Anyway, as the girls grew older, they lost the time and interest for beachcombing. Months passed, and then years, and the gripping sorrow eased into an ache, and then into something more like the memory of an ache. Their father had changed after his wife died. He'd retreated deep inside himself, and he seldom talked about their mother or shared his own grief with his daughters. But on Danielle's birthday, he always took the girls out to dinner, and he always proposed a toast. Abbie could remember lifting her juice glass, saying, "Here's to Mom. Happy Birthday, wherever you are." It was her father who coined the phrase. The girls knew it was exactly what their mother would have liked them to say. It was what she had believed.

Perhaps once a year, every year, Abbie pestered her busy sisters into giving up an hour from their social lives to go down to the beach together, and two years ago, just before she left for her au pair job, she marshaled them into a trip. They were all in their twenties then; Emma was just home for a week, Lily had finished her junior year of college. They were in their adult lives, but Abbie could be forceful when she got really bossy, so they all went. No one found anything terribly unusual. Abbie won the prize with the oyster shell, a big one with a creamy interior around a spot of deep abalone blue. When she was a girl, she'd used these shells as carriages for her small troll dolls. That summer she'd put it on the trophy shelf and forgot it almost immediately.

And here it was, a little dustier than before. So much time had passed, so many things had changed, yet here, Abbie thought, was this ordinary shell, sitting on the shelf like an ivory platter full of memories.

She touched the shell with her fingertip, then went to the sink to wash the lettuce.

7

. . . . .

Marina

As she put the bluefish in the refrigerator, Marina discovered she was smiling. Jim Fox was really attractive, and the electricity that sparked between them had her blood buzzing.

He was up at his house now, talking with his daughters. She'd been very aware of their presence when she was setting up her little outdoor nest. Their laughter made her smile, even though an awareness of loss plunged through her whenever she overheard any two women laughing together.

She sank onto the couch and put her head in her hands.

Six months ago, Marina had started her period on her fortieth birthday. The moment she woke she wanted to break into a howl of sorrow, but she choked it back as she rose from bed and rushed into the shower. Recently Gerry had been cool, abrupt, even irritated when she talked about her infertility. Their marriage was in one of those distant phases all marriages went through, probably because of problems at the office. Today she and Gerry both had crowded schedules. She needed to ignore her private life and concentrate on her accounts.

Sometimes she and Gerry drove to work in the same car, but he had a meeting elsewhere in the city today, so they drove separately.

She was glad, really. She needed to talk to a friend. Christie was busy with a new baby, so she put on her headset and punched in Dara's number.

Dara sounded groggy. "Marina. What's up?"

"Dara, my period started today."

"Oh, hell. Oh, Marina, fucking damn. I'm sorry. How are you?"

"Not so great. And work is a rat's nest, which actually is not a bad thing. It will keep me from brooding."

"Good for you, Marina. Positive attitude. Move forward. How are you celebrating your birthday?"

"Oh, forget my birthday." Marina sped up and passed an ancient Toyota dawdling in front of her. Dara's chipper attitude irritated Marina. She needed someone to help her mourn, to help her mark this occasion. Dara remained silent on the other end of the line. "Gerry hasn't planned a surprise party for me, has he?"

Dara laughed. "And I would tell you if he had?"

"Because I'm not in the mood for a party. I think I'd just like to get hammered. I'd like to sit down with you and drink tequila and wail."

"No Gerry?"

"No. We haven't been very close lately. Anyway, he's sick of me blubbering around."

"Well, honey, if that's what you really want to do, let's do it. Shall we meet at Hoolihan's?"

"Great. No, wait. I'd better ask Gerry if we have plans. I mean, it is my great-big fat fortieth. I'm sure he has something planned. I'm here. Talk to you later."

"Marina? Listen, honey—I just want to tell you . . . I think you're going to be just fine. I think you're a tremendously strong person."

"Thanks, Dar'. I love you, too." Marina clicked off.

Later, she would remember her final words to Dara, and they would crash a world of humiliation down on her heart. How had she ever been so blind?

How had she ever been a friend anyone could so easily betray?

There *was* a surprise fortieth birthday party, thrown at Dara's house. It was a mob scene, with champagne and every other kind of liquor flowing like Niagara Falls, and music pumped up by a DJ and people dancing and getting properly smashed and yelling out all sorts of inappropriate things. In the midst of such revelry, Marina hardly saw Gerry or Dara. She got good and hammered, and she thought her husband had, too, so when Dara insisted they sleep at her place because they were too wasted to go home, Marina accepted gratefully.

Saturday morning she awoke in Dara's guest room with a dry mouth and a bad headache. She expected to see Gerry snoring in bed next to her, but she was alone. She pulled on a robe of Dara's over her naked body and shuffled down the hall to the kitchen, toward the smell of coffee.

Gerry and Dara weren't kissing or embracing or even touching. They were sitting on opposite sides of the kitchen table, quietly talking.

Yet something about the way they were leaning toward each other slapped Marina wide awake.

She said, "What's going on?"

Their heads snapped toward her in identical rhythm.

"Marina. You're awake." Dara stood up, poured a cup of coffee, and put it on the table.

Marina sat down. She took a sip of coffee—it was strong and rich. Dara was a good cook.

She looked at Gerry, whose mouth was pulled tight the way it always got during an argument, especially when he was in the wrong.

Slowly, Marina said, "I'm not going to like this, am I?"

"I don't know," Gerry countered. "You might like it a lot, if you stop to think about it. I want a divorce, Marina."

She stared at him. They'd been married for ten years. They must have made love a million times. She knew everything about him, how stupid he looked when he was flapping around the office in a tantrum because of something at work, how tender he could be when they were alone together. He was handsome, and he worked hard at it, exercising at a gym, spending lots of time buying clothes and moussing his hair, he was even considering having a face-lift because he needed to keep his image young and fresh. She knew how his older brother's success as a physician overshadowed Gerry, how his parents scarcely *saw* their younger son because of the blinding light of their older son's brilliance. She'd held Gerry in her arms as he wept bitterly after they spent Christmas with his parents. Her love for him had been the motivation, really, for the fury with which she attacked her own part in their business. She had wanted to protect him.

True, they weren't getting along very well recently. Their time and conversations together revolved around work. He was probably sick of her relentless failures to get pregnant, and for her own part, Marina had to admit she hadn't felt close to him for a long time. Still. To bring up divorce like this, in front of Dara—what was he thinking?

"Gee," she said snidely, "nice of you to wait till I had my birthday party to tell me."

From the other side of the table, Dara spoke up. "Marina. There's something else."

Marina turned toward her friend. Christie and Dara had been the first to know when she'd gotten her period, the first to know when she'd lost her virginity, the first to know when she'd fallen in love with Gerry. Marina had been Dara's go-to person during her two marriages and grisly divorces. Dara was a beauty, apple-cheeked and bosomy, sensual and seductive.

Oh.

Gerry had found comfort with Dara. Which was why Gerry was talking in front of Dara.

"You and Gerry," Marina said flatly.

Dara nodded. "Yes." She raised her chin defiantly. "And Marina, I'm not going to apologize. You're not in love with Gerry anymore. I know that."

"Really. Did I ever say that?" Marina demanded.

Dara blushed. "Marina. There's something else."

"Good God," Marina cursed. "What more could there possibly be?"

Dara's eyes flew to meet Gerry's. Her face became radiant. Her smile was absolutely Mona Lisa.

It felt like a knife slicing through her entire torso. The pain made her breathless. "You're pregnant."

"With my child," Gerry added, unable to keep the pride from his voice.

It was almost dazzling, how quickly Marina's life changed after that. Of course, Gerry and Dara, in their eager selfish joy, had already plotted the path. With Dara's money, Gerry bought out Marina's half of the business. Gerry had already spoken to an agent who had a buyer lined up for Marina and Gerry's condo. With no children or financial issues, the legalities of the divorce were dealt with in a flash.

Suddenly, within a matter of weeks, Marina lost her husband, her work, her home, and one of her very best friends. Most of her current friends were Gerry and Dara's friends, too. They strained to be supportive to Marina without insulting Gerry or Dara, and that just made it difficult for everyone. Marina had to let them go.

Her parents had retired to sunny Arizona. Over the phone, they offered her love and understanding, but they were just a little bit *I-told-you-so*. They'd never liked Gerry. She saw a couple of therapists, but their advice was what she expected: You have to go through this loss, you can't go around it. The Japanese sign for "crisis" also means "opportunity." Their words were not much help in the middle of the night. Cartons of ice cream and old black-and-white movies worked better.

Christie saved her life.

"You've got to get out of town," Christie advised her. "Here, you're just mired in misery like an old horse stuck in mud."

Marina had snorted out a laugh in the midst of her tears. "Thanks for the glamorous image. And where would I go?"

"Where do you *want* to go?" Christie countered.

Marina blew her nose and shook her head. "I don't know."

Christie bellowed at her sons, "I told you boys, not in the house!" She turned back to Marina. "Why not Nantucket? Summer's coming up. We had so much fun those summers, remember?"

Marina leaned back in her chair and thought about that. During college, she and Christie had gone east to work as waitresses in a huge swanky hotel. They didn't make much money, but they had free lodging, free nights, and a few free afternoon hours. They swam, partied, worked a bit, and returned to Kansas City as brown as nuts and grinning at themselves.

Marina protested, "Oh, Christie, we were *young* back then. I'm old and worn out and pathetic."

"You certainly will be if you don't move your ass," Christie insisted. "If you stay here indulging in self-pity. Think of it, Marina, the blue ocean, the salty air, the *freshness* of it all."

"I won't know anyone," Marina said.

"Well, isn't that the point?" Christie replied.

Now Marina found herself smiling. It was good, just to think of Christie and her practical optimism.

And Christie was right. Being here, away from *there*, was a kind of therapy. While out of sight was not completely out of mind, the reality of Gerry and Dara was not such an oppressive reality.

But she ached with loneliness. Leisure did not come easily to her. She'd worked hard to learn her trade, and she and Gerry had labored diligently and ceaselessly to build their business. She was accustomed to the sound of phones ringing, people chatting, footsteps hurrying past her office; she was used to the pressure of presentations and the dozens of little victories of accounts won and money made. She'd been such an excellent multitasker, scanning reports while she ran on her treadmill, dictating memos while she drove to a meeting, flirting with new business contacts during the intermission at a symphony.

Now, on this bright, airy island, she felt like a piece of flotsam lost at sea, without a compass or any way to communicate to others. The ocean expanded all around her. She was alone, as insignificant as a little cork bobbing on the surface.

But she wouldn't give up.

She grabbed up the newspaper and a pen, and began to circle anything that caught her eye. Noonday concerts at the Unitarian church. A comedy presented in the evening by the Theatre Workshop. She hadn't realized how many museums there were. The Nantucket Whaling Museum was right in town. So was the Maria Mitchell Science Library and Observatory. And the Coffin School. And someone was offering painting classes. Hm. She'd have to consider that. Gerry had always been the visual guy; but it might be fun to learn to do watercolors. She'd get a library card, too, and stock up on all the juicy novels she'd never had time to read.

And maybe she'd get to know Jim and his daughters better. Anything could happen, right?

8

· · · · ·

Lily

Driving home from Carrie's, Lily felt wistful. Carrie and her baby existed in their own sensual world of love and touch and cooing voices. Carrie had gotten slightly plump and she moved as if her limbs were heavy and when she held her baby in her arms, Lily could walk through the living room on her hands and Carrie wouldn't glance her way. Lily didn't want a baby, but she would like to live, for a while, in such a lazy world of love.

What she'd *really* like to have was another car, she thought, as she steered the rusty Old Clunker through the narrow streets. She wouldn't even ask for a *new* car. Just a newer one. Her father had bought the Toyota sedan when Abbie was seventeen for her to use on the island. As the years passed, all the sisters had used it, referring to it with fond aggravation as the Old Clunker. She hadn't minded its humble state when she was a kid, but now that she worked for the magazine, she hated showing up at posh events in such a tired tin can.

Her father's truck was in the drive, so she parked in front of the house. He would probably leave before she did tomorrow morning. As she walked up her drive, she heard laughter. She walked around to the back of the house and went in the back door.

Her father and two sisters were seated at the kitchen table.

"Hi, honey," her father greeted her. "Want some ice cream? We saved some for you."

"Oh, but I made a pie, especially for Abbie's homecoming!"

Abbie raised a skeptical eyebrow.

Emma said, "We didn't see any pie."

"It's on the windowsill in the pantry." A little panic washed through Lily. Had her sisters assumed Lily had just blown off responsibility for tonight's dinner? Well, in a way, she kind of had.

She went into the pantry and found the pie. Somehow a box of cereal had been shoved against it, so you wouldn't notice it unless you knew it was there. She carried it out and set it on the table. "Ta-da!"

"Wow, Lily!" Abbie said. "What a masterpiece!"

Lily flushed with pleasure. "Let me cut you a big piece."

"Tomorrow," Abbie said. "I just finished all that ice cream."

"I'll wait, too," said Emma. "I'm stuffed. Dad brought home fresh bluefish and Abbie cooked it perfectly."

Well, Abbie would, wouldn't she, Lily thought. She felt both jealous and guilty. *She* should have prepared dinner for Abbie's first night home. She'd intended to. She just got waylaid at Carrie's.

"I'll have some pie," her father said.

As Lily cut a piece for her father and settled in at the table, Abbie told her, "We were just talking about all the changes in town since I've been gone. So many restaurants have closed, and so many stores downtown!"

"The economy is rough everywhere," Emma said.

"I guess that's good," Lily offered, trying to be upbeat. "In a misery loves company kind of way."

"Dad," Abbie asked, "how are you doing?"

Their father took the time to finish his pie before answering. He nodded at Lily. "That was delicious, honey." He leaned back in his chair and seemed to be physically summoning up his strength. "I'll be honest with you, Abbie. Times are tough. I had three different clients back out of their contracts to have new houses built and one actually shut down on the renovations I was doing and didn't pay me. I think I'm going to have to take him to court to get any money out of him, and I don't know that hiring a lawyer wouldn't end up costing me more."

"So what jobs do you have going on?" Abbie asked.

Their father shrugged and shook his head. "Just small ones. A couple of renovations. Nothing substantial. That's why I rented the

Playhouse. I always knew in the back of my mind it would come in handy someday."

Abbie asked, "How long is the rental?"

"Marina's got it for six months." When he said the woman's name, their father blushed.

The three sisters exchanged glances.

Their father cleared his throat. "While we're on the subject, I probably ought to tell you . . . I'm going to sell the boat."

"Dad!" Their voices came out in one surprised chorus.

"You can't sell the boat!" Abbie continued.

"Honey, I know how attached you are. We all are. I don't want to sell it. But if I can . . . it might keep me going for a little while longer . . . and things might change . . ." Clearly he was having trouble speaking about this. "If I sell the boat, that might buy me a little time until a new job comes in, and then I won't have to sell the house."

"Sell the house!" the girls cried.

"I know, I know, I hate it, too, but it might come to that. Now, it might reassure you to know that I do have some savings in an IRA. Not a lot, but with social security, I should be able to live pretty comfortably for the rest of my life. The thing is, I can't take out the money until after I turn fifty-nine and a half or I'd have to pay some fees and penalties. So I've got a few more years to go before I can touch those IRAs. I think I can make it, if I watch my pennies, but . . ." He held his hands out in a what-can-I-do gesture.

"Oh, Dad, this is terrible," Abbie said.

"Well, I'm not putting it on the market right away. I just want you to know it's got to be an option in my life." He shrugged. "And come on, it's way too big for me. If Lily weren't home, I'd rattle around here like a marble in a bathtub."

Lily watched her sisters for some kind of wisdom. But Abbie and Emma just sat there stupefied.

"You know," their father said, "it might not be such a terrible thing for me to sell the house. I mean, I don't think any one of you wants to live the rest of her life on the island, and if I sold the place, I'd make a nice fat sum of money and I'd have something to give each of you." He studied his daughters' faces. "Abbie? You look like I've just hit you over the head with a board."

Lily could tell her sister's smile was forced. "Sorry, Dad," Abbie said. "I think jet lag is clogging my mind. I can't seem to think right."

"Well, don't worry about it," her father told her. "I don't want you girls to worry about anything. I mean, if any of you were to get married, have some children to come here for summer and holidays, then I can see this big old house might be worth struggling to keep. But as it is . . ."

Emma made a choking noise and burst into tears. Shoving her chair back, she rose. "Sorry." She ran from the kitchen and up the stairs to her room.

"She's really taken it hard, Duncan breaking off with her," Abbie observed quietly.

"Duncan was an asshole," their father said, surprising Lily. He seldom swore.

Lily smiled. "You're right. She's better off without him."

He pushed back his chair and stood. "Well, I think I'll catch some of the ball game before I go to bed. Let you two catch up on some girl talk."

"Night, Dad," Abbie said.

He pecked a kiss on their heads. To Abbie, he said, "It's great to have you home. And thanks for cooking dinner." He left the room.

"I was at Carrie's," Lily blurted out. "She's got a baby now, a little girl only seven months old, and Carrie's exhausted. I went over to help—"

Abbie interrupted Lily by leaning back in her chair and yawning enormously. "Oh, man, it's hitting me now." She stood up. "I've got to go to bed or I'll fall over on the floor. Good night."

"Um . . . good night," Lily replied. She stood alone in the silent kitchen, with all the dirty dishes for a meal she hadn't eaten.

9
· · · · ·

Emma

Rain streaked down the windows like teardrops. Perfect for Emma's mood. She checked the clock: 6 a.m. She groaned and rolled on her side, trying to fall back asleep. Instead, her thoughts flashed a slide show in her mind, a private DVD of images of Duncan and Alicia, happy, together. Perhaps she dozed.

Someone tapped gently on the door. "Emma? Honey?" It was her father.

She didn't answer. She didn't want to see him.

The door opened. Her father came in and sat down at the end of her bed. He smelled of Old Spice and his own particular scent of soap and wood dust.

"How're you doing?" he asked softly.

She muttered, "I'm fine, Dad. Don't worry."

"It's raining," he told her. "It's down in the lower sixties, if you can believe it. Be sure to wear a sweater when you go out. It's supposed to be cool and rainy all day."

If she could remember how to smile, she would have smiled. That was so Dad, presenting the daily weather—the *hourly* weather—in detail. He always had been a devotee of the Weather Channel. She supposed it was his way of taking care of his daughters now that they were grown.

"Thanks, Dad. I'll wear a sweater." *If I get out of bed, which I won't.*

"Well, then, I'm off." Her father leaned over to kiss her forehead. "See you tonight."

"Right."

Her father closed her bedroom door behind him. Emma remained pinned to her bed by the needles and knives of her misery.

Where was Duncan at this very moment? He had never lingered in bed. When their alarm went off at six a.m., Duncan would be awake instantly, and he'd roll on top of her, whispering, "Hey, baby, let me give you one," which now that she thought about it was ironic, because their morning sex was always over so fast it didn't give her anything at all. She knew, for Duncan, it was a kind of start-up point, a way of checking his first item of the day off his list. He'd jump up from bed, rush into the bathroom, and shower. She'd shower while he shaved, they both dressed, and he drove them to work while she put her makeup on in the car. As they rushed into the building, they'd grab a double java jolt coffee from Starbucks.

She thought that with Alicia, Duncan probably could slow down enough to enjoy making love. With Alicia, who was already rich, and safely rich, Duncan didn't have to move so fast because he didn't have so far to go to get to what he wanted. Would Alicia sleep at Duncan's apartment, or would he sleep at hers? What would her apartment be like? Emma had Googled the address. It was on Commonwealth Avenue, in the pricey, elegant part of the city, not far from the building where they worked. So probably Duncan would sleep at Alicia's, rather than at his place, which was in a nice but not posh apartment in Watertown. This would give them even more time to lounge around in bed.

Alicia's hair was a sleek brown pageboy. It never frizzed—she'd been born with sophisticated hair. While Emma's stupid hair would coil into curls at the slightest whisper of humidity. She had to blow her hair dry, then iron it to get it to lie down and look groomed; she could never hope for sophisticated, not with freckles. It was one of the things that drove Duncan mad about her; he hated how long she took to dry her hair. He was always afraid they'd be late for work, which they never could have been because they always got into the building an hour before everyone else, so they had time to scan the news streamers and Asian stock reports.

Now, with Alicia with the perfect hair, Duncan would have even more reason to relax. And at night, they wouldn't have to

argue about what to have for dinner or who would fix it. With Alicia's money, they could just go out every night, to whatever restaurant they wanted. Everyone would admire them when they walked
in—just like they'd admired Duncan and Emma. Duncan was so
handsome, so tall, with sleek brown hair and a patrician profile. His
clothes were expensive, and he wore them well, his body shaped by
the hour's exercise he did every day instead of eating lunch.

What a glam couple they'd be, both thin and reeking of power
and sexual conquest . . . while she lay here on her childhood bed, on
stupid sheets with idiotic *violets* on them! While her hair curled like
a Scottish sheep's and her bank account gaped emptily and no hope
waited anywhere. Duncan and Alicia could zip over to Paris for the
weekend. Emma couldn't get out of bed.

"You should keep your engagement ring," Duncan had told her
the day he broke off with her. "It might help you get back—"

"I don't want your charity!" she'd screamed. "This ring is a sign
of your love! This ring is a sign of our hopes for the future!" She'd
thrown the ring at him. The two carat, square-cut diamond ring.

Idiot.

She couldn't stand it that he pitied her. But of course he did.
She was a loser. She'd lost her job. She'd lost her savings. She'd lost
all hope for the future.

10

......

Marina

All morning long, rain fell in shining, stinging needles. Marina whistled to herself as she buzzed around cleaning her little nest. She emailed Christie, played a few games of computer solitaire, then made a fresh cup of coffee and curled up with a book she'd bought at the airport, reminding herself what a luxury it was to lie around reading on a rainy day. But the book didn't hold her attention.

Her mind sidetracked back to its endless loop of self-pity and memories, replaying the moment in the kitchen with Gerry and Dara. Dara's contrite, triumphant announcement that she was pregnant with Gerry's baby.

Replaying the moment she walked into their ad agency to clean out her office, down the corridor past the receptionist and the desks of copywriters and all of them beaming at her with such *charitable* smiles.

Replaying the pain, and the hopelessness, and the crushing sense of defeat.

"Okay, that's enough!" She tossed her book on the coffee table and began to pace around the little cottage. She wiped down the already clean kitchen counter, adjusted the candlesticks on the little wooden table, and now she craved something to *do*. It was not her style to sit alone in a room with a book and the rain clicking away on the roof like someone nervously tapping her fingers.

She would go out for lunch, and to the library for a new book.

She pulled on white jeans and a pink shirt and slid her feet into espadrilles. She took her time putting on just a touch of makeup and selecting earrings, because why shouldn't she take her time? She had all the time in the world. Time was all she had.

She belted on her khaki trench coat and stepped out into the rain. *Umbrella,* she thought. She'd packed so few things when she flew out here. Her first stop would be at Nantucket Pharmacy to buy an umbrella. The wind batted at her, whipping rain in her face. She walked down the drive, taking care to avoid the deepest puddles.

Just as she reached the street, a red pickup truck turned into the drive with Jim Fox at the wheel.

He slid his window down. "Where are you off to?"

"Oh, just into town. I have to buy an umbrella."

He laughed at that. "If you stayed home, you wouldn't need an umbrella."

"If I stayed home, I'd go stir crazy." Quickly, she continued, "Not that it isn't a nice little cottage."

"Little being the crucial word. Listen, let me take you out to lunch."

"Oh," she said, surprised, and her vision did a kind of wriggle, so that the man in the pickup truck suddenly came in clearer. He was handsome, and he was definitely hitting on her. She was astonished to feel something deep inside her raise its little hopeful head, like a flower sensing rain. "Well. Okay!" She opened the passenger door and stepped up inside.

"I'm going out to the Downy Flake," he told her as they headed along the street.

"When I used to come to the island, the Downy Flake was in town," she said.

"Right. They moved more than fifteen years ago. Good thing, actually. In the summer, all the restaurants right in town get plenty of foot traffic from tourists, but the places out of town still have room for us locals." He glanced over at her. "So you used to come here?"

"For three summers, with my friend Christie. To work—and play." She idly reminisced as Jim drove along the narrow lanes. When other cars inched out of side streets, he braked and waved them ahead.

"No one would do that in the city," she told him.

"What, let someone go ahead? Not everybody does that here. People from the city bring their hurry with them." As he spoke, a black Jag shot away from the curb, making Jim, who wasn't going fast to start with, slam on the brakes. "Like that fellow." He laughed. "Bringing a Jag to the island! He might as well have a bumper sticker saying, I need a flashy vehicle to compensate for my little"— he shot Marina a cautious glance—"um, balls."

Marina laughed. "My ex-husband drove a Jag."

"Really. Good thing he's your ex, then."

Surprised at his response and the complete absence of anything like pity in his voice, Marina said, "You know, I think you're right."

"So how's your summer going?" he asked.

"Oh, I'm just getting settled, really. I've been to the library, and I want to visit all the museums, all of the island. It's so different, perceiving it as an adult. I realize there are huge chunks of the island I've never seen, not to mention all the historical spots that I couldn't appreciate when I was younger." She glanced over at him. "How is *your* summer so far? I don't think I know what you do."

Jim blushed when she turned to him, and her own pulse quickened in return. What was going on? She thought he was probably ten years older than she was, and really not her type. Gerry was six-two, lean as a whippet, with sleek blond hair. Jim was tall and burly, with unruly brown hair. Plus, she'd gone off men in general. She didn't think she'd ever be able to stand being in bed with a man again in all her life.

Jim was talking. "I build houses. Summer's always busy for me, but this year things are slowing down, with the economy and all. I'm trying to take advantage of it, trying to enjoy the summer."

She laughed. "Isn't it funny, how we have to work to make ourselves have fun!"

"We're fortunate if we can carve out some fun for ourselves," Jim told her. "I mean, people are struggling now. My crew all have families to support. My three daughters are grown, so I don't have as much to worry about financially."

He'd left an opening as big as a conversational Grand Canyon. Marina cleared her throat. "I wasn't fortunate enough to have children. And I just got divorced. So I've only got myself to worry about." She didn't want to seem maudlin, so she continued, "I just sold my half of an ad agency, so I'm comfortable for a while. I want to sort out my next step. But first of all, I want to just *be,* and this is just about the most spectacular place on the earth to be in."

"I envy you, having the opportunity to see parts of the island for the first time. Have you ever been to the moors?"

"Never. I just noticed them on a map I was studying."

"You like maps? I've got some great Nantucket maps. Maps of the shoals and shipwrecks. Geological maps . . ."

Actually, Marina thought, she didn't know whether she liked maps or not. She'd never considered them. But Jim's enthusiasm was contagious and she was a bit sorry when their arrival at the restaurant interrupted his train of thought.

As they entered the Downy Flake, all the waitstaff and most of the customers nodded or waved a greeting to Jim. They were given a table and were quickly brought their lunch: cheeseburgers and salty fries. Their attempts at conversation were sketchy because so many people stopped by to chat. Jim introduced her to everyone. "This is Marina Warren. She's from Kansas City. She's renting our cottage for the summer and she wants to learn all about the island." By the time she'd finished her lunch, Marina had been invited to two churches with coffee hours after the service, and one woman suggested she help them sort books for the local library book sale.

She wasn't surprised at Jim's popularity. He had a confidence about him, and a kind of contentment in his voice, a deep resonance that seemed to spring from a profound comfort with himself. And he *was* handsome, with his tanned skin and curly brown hair and large hazel eyes. He had told her when he first showed her the cottage that he was widowed. She wondered whether he had a girl-friend, and what she would think of him taking Marina out for lunch. Probably, given Jim's gregariousness, it was not unusual at all.

As they got back into the truck, the rain diminished and sud-denly the clouds parted and the sun shone down.

"Do you still want to go into town and get an umbrella?" Jim asked her.

"Absolutely," Marina told him. "I remember how much it rains on this island."

She settled back in the seat, rolled down the window, and took a deep breath of the clean rinsed air. "I hope you don't mind my asking this, but could I have your permission to paint the walls of the cottage?"

"Well, of course, but you shouldn't have to do that. I know those walls need some brightening. I can do it or have my crew come over while you're out."

"Oh, I wouldn't mind at all. In fact, I'd enjoy the painting. I like painting walls, seeing the new color rise, and I like the actual work. It's kind of like a Zen activity."

He laughed. "If you really want to, then please do. But let me reimburse you for the cost of the paint."

"It's a deal," she told him.

"Have you ever been out on the west part of the island?"

She shook her head. "I don't think so. Mostly we went to Cisco or Dionis, to the beach."

Jim pulled into a parking spot on Main Street. "Here you are. I've got to go back to work."

"Well, thanks so much for lunch!" She turned to face him, and something *zinged* between them. Startled, she blurted out, "The food was delicious and I loved meeting all your friends and maybe I will volunteer in the library. I hadn't really thought of volunteering, but maybe I will—" She shut her eyes tight, took a deep breath, and opened them. "I'm babbling."

"And you do it very well," Jim told her with a grin. "I'm going over to Tuckernuck someday soon. Want to go? We could have a little picnic."

"Oh. Do you have a boat?"

"I do. A little runabout out in the Madaket Harbor. Nothing elegant. Smells like fish, probably."

"I'd love to go out with you," Marina told him.

"Then we'll do it," he promised. "Soon."

She stepped down from the truck and waved good-bye and set off walking down the sidewalk, and all the while she just couldn't stop smiling.

11

·····

Abbie

See what I mean?" Lily and Abbie were peering out the window.

Abbie let the curtain fall. "She doesn't have a car. Dad probably agreed to drive her somewhere."

"It's lunchtime. I think they're going on a date."

"So what if they are, Lily? Dad's allowed to date." Abbie padded barefoot down the hall to the kitchen. She'd slept late, and she was starving. Opening the refrigerator, she scanned the contents. "No bacon? No eggs?"

"Dad has to watch his cholesterol," Lily informed her. "And I need to watch my weight. We're a bran and granola family now."

"Ugh." Abbie opened the cupboard and took down a bowl and a mug. "Where's Emma? Did she go out?"

"Did she go *out*? Are you kidding? You saw her yesterday. She's been *flattened*. She hasn't gone out since she got here." Lily eyed her sister assessingly. "I was right to get you back here, wasn't I?"

"Oh, I don't know, Lily!" Abbie sounded irritable. She bumped the silverware drawer shut with her hip. "Don't you guys drink coffee?"

"Dad does. He keeps it in the freezer door. Don't ask me why. Listen, I have to bike over to the magazine for a staff meeting. I'll see you later, okay?"

"Wait a minute, Lily." Abbie leveled a serious look at her sister.

"Don't think I'm going to *fix* Emma right away or even at all. She's going through a really tough time, that's for sure. But she's an adult. I can't kiss her owie and make everything okay."

"But you can keep an eye on her, right?"

"I can't spy on her twenty-four hours a day."

Tears welled in Lily's eyes. "I don't want Emma to be so sad."

Abbie put the bowl down and crossed the room. She took her baby sister in her arms. "I don't want her to be so sad, either, honey. But sometimes life is just plain hard."

"But Emma will be okay, won't she?"

"Of course she will." Abbie kissed her sister's forehead and gave her a little shake. "Get to work. I'll make some coffee and take a cup up to Emma."

Abbie tapped on Emma's bedroom door. No one answered, so she pushed it open and went in.

When they were girls, their mother had decorated each room with painstaking detail. Abbie's was yellow, Emma's lavender, and Lily's peppermint pink. One wall of Emma's room was lined with shelves populated by dolls of all shapes and sizes. Abbie and Lily had both altered their rooms as they grew older, Abbie slapping up posters of other countries, Lily thumbtacking pictures of rock stars and actors. But Emma had never packed her dolls away.

Emma was in bed, and Abbie knew she was awake, because Emma slept like a starfish, all limbs spread out, and now she was on her side, facing the wall, her covers pulled up to her ears.

"I know you're awake. Here's some coffee." She put Emma's mug on the bedside table and sat down with her own at the end of the bed, leaning against the bedpost.

Emma didn't move.

Abbie said, "We saw Dad pick up that woman and drive off with her." She sipped her coffee. "I don't know why Lily's so freaked out. Well, she's obviously younger than Dad, and she's not from the island, but still. Why shouldn't Dad have a girlfriend?"

Without turning to face Abbie, Emma muttered, "Lily's afraid she'll take Dad away from us."

"Well, that's silly. We're all grown up. We should be starting our own families. Plus, you and I haven't even been living on the island."

"But Lily has. Lily came right back the minute she graduated from college."

"She says she wants to meet the right people and get a job in New York."

"Yeah, she says that, but can you see Lily in New York? She—" Emma's mumbled words disappeared beneath the covers.

Abbie nudged Emma's bum with her foot. "Turn over. Sit up. I can't even hear you."

Emma didn't move. Abbie dug her foot into Emma's back.

"Stop it!" Emma yelled.

Abbie didn't stop.

"God, you're irritating!" Emma turned over and sat up.

"Now drink your coffee," Abbie ordered.

"I don't want it."

"Drink it anyway."

"No, Abbie, I mean it. I can't drink coffee. Anything with caffeine makes me kind of freaky. Like I want to run down the hall and jump out the window."

"Oh, Emma."

Emma shrugged. "So I'm better without coffee. This way I just want to lie here and die."

"I hate when you talk like that."

"Then don't talk to me. Go away."

Abbie studied her sister, trying to evaluate her health. Emma was thinner than she'd ever been, and everything about her was dull: skin, eyes, hair. "You look like Iceland in January."

Emma snorted. "That's way too optimistic an image."

"Really."

"I feel like a piece of shark shit on the bottom of the ocean. I've been chewed up and shat out. I've got nothing left."

"Oh, Emma, that's terrible." Abbie leaned forward to stroke her sister's arm. "Honey, it will get better. Remember how it was after Mom died? And it got better."

"Not for Mom."

"Oh, I don't know. Maybe for Mom."

"It was better for Mom to be away from her three daughters, to be dead in the ground?"

"We've talked about this, Emma. We don't know what's on the other side. Mom might be happy where she is, and watching us."

"Oh, bullshit."

Abbie didn't want to talk about their mother anymore. She could go into as deep a dark place as her sisters if she allowed herself. At least she'd prodded Emma from apathy to anger. She changed the subject. "I've got to get a job. After what Dad said last night, I want to contribute some money."

"How long are you staying?" Emma asked.

"I'm not sure. I might as well stay the summer. It's the time to make money on the island." Abbie rose, set her mug on the table, and ranged around Emma's room. Emma's suitcases were still on the floor, unpacked clothing spilling out. Idly, she picked up a camisole and wrapped one of the dolls in it. "I'm not particularly qualified for anything. I don't want to wait tables or tend bar, I did plenty of that when I was younger." She put the doll back, picked up a shirt flung over a chair, and hung it in the closet. "What do you think you'll do?"

Emma had scooted back down in bed. "I think I'll go to sleep."

"No, silly, I mean, what kind of *work* do you want to do?"

"Don't want to work. Don't want to move." Emma turned on her side, facing the wall. "Go away."

"Eventually, Emma, you're going to have to eat," Abbie reminded her sister. She grabbed her sister's feet. "I know what. I'll take you out to lunch." It was difficult with the sheet and blanket over Emma's feet, but Abbie managed to tickle them.

All at once Emma jerked away and shot up in bed like a whale breaching. "Stop it! Just fucking *stop it!* How can you not get it that I want to be left alone? *You* can float along on the surface of the world but I can't be like you. I've done my best, I tried my hardest, and I've *failed!* It's over for me, Abbie. Everything I've ever wanted is gone and there's no hope in hell of ever getting it back!"

"Emma, you are only twenty-eight years old," Abbie said softly.

But Emma was in a rage. "Yes, and my life is *over!* I have worked as hard as I could, I've struggled, I've tried to be smart, I've done everything the best I could, and it's all turned to shit! And if this is what fate or destiny or God or whatever wants to do with me, then what the hell can I do about that? Some people are lucky, some people aren't. I'm unlucky. How more clear can that be to me?"

Emma was so upset she was crying and spitting as her words flew into the air. "Emma, Emma," Abbie cooed, "calm down, honey."

Emma buried her face in her hands. "I hurt, Abbie. All I do is hurt. I can't stop hurting. I hurt with every breath I take. I don't want to breathe. I don't want to live."

Abbie tried to wrap her arms around her sister, but Emma pulled away. "Emma—"

"I'm not going to kill myself. I wouldn't do that to you and Dad and Lily. But I have to tell you, Abbie, I don't see any reason for me to live. Or any way."

"I think you should see a doctor, Emma."

"No."

"Well, Emma—" Abbie didn't know what to say. "You don't want Dad to see you like this."

Emma sniffed and gulped and wiped her face. "I know. Just leave me alone for a while, Abbie."

"Will you come down for dinner tonight?"

"Yeah, okay."

"Promise me. Promise you'll come down for dinner."

"All right," Emma conceded. "I promise."

Abbie shivered as she left Emma's room. She felt unsettled, anxious, as if she'd left the stove on and couldn't get back to the house. She needed to *do* something. She stomped down the stairs and grabbed up the car keys and headed off to the grocery store. They could always use groceries.

At Stop&Shop, she filled her cart, then joined the long line snaking from the cashiers. In front of her, two summer women were moaning about how they couldn't find help. One needed someone who knew computers for a data entry job, and the other needed a companion for her cranky old mother-in-law who was developing macular degeneration.

As Abbie listened, an idea bloomed in her head. The more she thought about it, the better she liked the idea, and by the time she was through the checkout counter and loading the car with groceries, she was talking out loud to herself.

At home, she quickly stashed anything that needed refrigeration, and let the rest wait while she grabbed up a pad of paper and pen. Then she thundered up the stairs and into Emma's room.

"I've got the best idea!"

Emma moaned and pulled her pillow over her head.

Undaunted, Abbie sat on the side of Emma's bed. "I was at the grocery store, and I heard two women talking about how they need summer help, and I thought, we could do that stuff, and we can get fab references from tons of people on the island. We can do anything, but we don't want to lock ourselves into a nine-to-five grind, at least I don't, so listen to this!" She cleared her throat, then read:

" 'Do you need an educated, responsible young woman for a temporary job? A babysitter in two hours for seven children ages two months to sixteen years? Someone classy to take Grandmother to church or theater? An instant secretary who can fax, email, type or text? Nantucket Mermaids has it all. Excellent references. Discretion guaranteed.' What do you think?"

Emma didn't say a word.

"Great! I knew you'd love it! Mermaids—mer*maids*, get it? Okay, I'm off to the newspaper now to get the ad in for this week's issue. See you!"

Abbie rushed out of the room without shutting the door behind her. At least that would make Emma get out of bed, even if only to shut the door.

12
· · · · ·

Marina

Thursday morning, Marina walked into town. The woman Marina had met at the Downy Flake had told her the book sorting would be done on the ground floor of the library, which Marina realized meant the basement. She felt oddly shy as she walked down the stairs from the main floor, and she was kind of pleased by that. At least she wasn't feeling pathetic.

The door to the room at the end of the corridor was open. Marina could see towers of boxes of books, and long tables holding more books, and people lifting books from boxes and carrying them here and there. It all had the peaceful, appealing industry of an anthill.

She stepped inside and scanned the room for the woman she'd met at the Downy Flake. She didn't see her, but a slender woman in her early fifties noticed Marina and smiled.

"Hello. Have you come to help us?"

"Yes. Hi. I'm Marina Warren. I'm renting here for six months, and a friend of Jim Fox told me you all might need some help."

"Oh, *you're* the woman renting Jim's cottage! Welcome. I'm Sheila Lester. And we're *so* glad you're here. Half our volunteers haven't shown up, but who can blame them on a heavenly day like this. I'm sure they're all out swimming or fishing or working in their gardens." She chuckled.

Sheila Lester wore her salt-and-pepper hair short and spiky. Above her coral tee shirt she wore a black cord with one deep turquoise bead that accentuated the clear turquoise of her eyes. Marina liked her at once.

"Well, I can come as often as you'd like," Marina said.

"That's swell. Now, let me show you the ropes. Although, as I'm sure you can tell, it doesn't take a rocket scientist. Basically, you grab a box and sort the books, putting them on whichever table they belong."

On large white sheets of cardboard, written in enormous red letters, were the categories: Fiction, Nonfiction, Cookbooks, Gardening, Mysteries, Children, and Nantucket.

"Take that corner," Sheila suggested, pointing to a tower of brown boxes.

Marina set to work. The closest table was already piled with books, so she shoved them aside to make room for a few piles of her own. Soon she was moving around the room, placing the books in their categories. The other volunteers were all older than Marina, but they were pleasant and funny, and it felt good, to be part of this productive, literate group. Before she knew it, it was noon.

"Lunchtime, everyone," Sheila announced. "Thank you all for coming. See you tomorrow morning."

Marina lingered by the "Nantucket" table. "I wonder, could I buy a few of these now?"

"If you want, just borrow them," Sheila told her. "Bring them back when you return—you are coming back, aren't you?"

"Absolutely," Marina told her. She gathered five books up in her arms. As she walked out of the library, she took a moment to stand on the wide front steps and consider the day. On either side of her, in the shade of the overhang, people sat talking into their cell phones. In the Atheneum garden, people lolled on benches, reading books, eating ice-cream cones, and watching their children swing from the sturdy crabapple trees. At the corner of the street, three women in bright sundresses stood chatting.

Crossing the street from the post office came a woman with hair in a French braid, like Dara wore hers. She was pushing a stroller with a fat baby in it.

Marina clutched her books to her chest, but the arrow of envy had already struck her heart. She knew she could recover from the divorce, and even from the loss of her best friend, but it would take her a long time to resign herself to childlessness.

A light touch on her shoulder broke her away from her thoughts. She turned to see Sheila Lester there.

"Want to have lunch?" the other woman asked.

"Oh. Sure!"

"I've only got an hour," Sheila said. "Let's go over to the Fog."

At the restaurant, they settled into a booth, leaned toward each other over the table, and began to chat. Marina gave Sheila a very condensed account of her past, but rather than get mired in the mud of Dara, Gerry, and the divorce, she turned the conversation back to Sheila. Over salads with walnuts and cranberries, Sheila told her about her own work.

"I make lightship baskets. Do you know about lightships?"

"Not a thing," Marina admitted. "Tell me."

"Lightships were floating lighthouses in the nineteenth century, stationed at certain places around the island to warn passing ships of dangerous shoals so they didn't get lost in the fog and run aground. Crews stayed out in the lightships for six months at a time. Needless to say they didn't have television, so they did craft work. Some made sailor's valentines, intricate little combinations of shells put together to form a pretty picture. Some made lightship baskets, which involved lots of patient weaving of canes." She held up her own basket, which she carried as a purse.

"It must take patience to make one," Marina said.

"It does," Sheila agreed. "You might want to give it a try. I teach classes and give individual lessons, too."

"I'll think about it," Marina told her. "Patience isn't really my strong suit."

After lunch, they went their separate ways. Marina gave herself a gold star for making a friend and not whining and moaning about her pathetic past year. There was a kind of tranquillity about the other woman that Marina felt terribly appealing. It was rather like the calm that Jim Fox radiated. Both people paid attention to her when they talked. They weren't looking over her shoulder for something better.

Back in her cottage, Marina spread the books out on the coffee table, loving the way the covers brightened the room. The one on découpage had such a gorgeous cover of blue hydrangea that she propped it on the table like a painting.

She checked her calendar. Determined not to spend her life hiding away weeping, she had gone through the arts and entertainment section of the newspaper and scheduled events in throughout the week. She would absolutely go to them, every single one. And now that Sheila had reminded her of all the museums on the island, she would add those to the mix.

And of course, she reminded herself, there was the island itself. She hadn't been swimming yet. She studied her calendar. It read: Book sale. Swimming. Theater.

The closest beach was Jetties, which would be a long walk from her cottage. She decided to rent a bike. She changed into her bathing suit, slipped a tee shirt over it and slid her feet into flip-flops, and filled a bag with a bottle of water, a towel, a paperback novel, and sunblock. As she sauntered down the sidewalk back toward town and the bike shops, she realized she was relaxed in a way she hadn't been for years. She kept thinking of that turquoise bead Sheila wore. She wanted one just like that.

She rented a bike at Young's Bicycle Shop, hopped on, and headed toward the beach. She hadn't been on a bike in years, but after a few wobbly moments, she found herself pedaling with ease, and feeling surprisingly graceful and pleased with herself.

At the Jetties, she locked her bike in the parking lot and carried her beach bag along as she clomped down the boardwalk to the sand. The afternoon was brilliant, the sun dazzling on the water, the beach crowded with swimmers and sun lovers. She spread out her towel, anchored it with her beach bag, and strolled toward the water.

During her college days she and Christie had swam here, and Marina remembered now how the beach at the Jetties was broad and shallow. She waded far out and swam, stiffly at first, and then surrendering to the slow-rocking waves. She'd forgotten how impossible it was to think while swimming—the ocean engaged all her senses. She floated for a long time, kicking her feet, loving the warm sun on her face.

Wading back up to the beach, she felt luxuriously tired and relaxed. She gathered up her things and biked back to the cottage. She showered and dressed, pleased to see that she'd gotten a little tan, a nice little glow. This was a good day! She'd done some volunteer work, made a friend, learned about the island, and had a refreshing swim.

She tucked her paperback into her purse, and set off walking into town. She would find a bench in the library garden and read until six or so, when she'd have a drink and dinner on the patio at the Boarding House, and then she'd stroll around town until the play began.

She was happy, she realized. She was here, and alive, and happy. And that was a lot to be grateful for.

13

· · · · ·

Lily

Thursday night, Lily sat in the back row of the theater, scribbling as fast as she could, listing the names of all the people she'd just seen at the gallery opening on Old South Wharf. She'd clicked quite a few photos with her digital camera, and she thought most of them would be usable. The problem was, some of the people she knew from seeing them at other parties or openings, and they assumed Lily knew their names, so she hadn't double-checked for fear of insulting them. Now she jotted down reminders of who they might be and where in the past six weeks she might have seen them.

People were filing into the little makeshift auditorium here in the basement of the Methodist church. The seats were banked, and she always sat in the corner in the back, where she could see everyone. She disliked being solo at any event, although she did enjoy the looks people shot her as she sat engrossed with her tablet and pen. Maybe they imagined she was from a city newspaper.

Something caught her eye. She saw *that woman*, the renter, walk in. She was slender, delicate, and terribly chic in a long-sleeved black tee, pencil-legged black pants, and high black heels. Her straight blond hair was held with a simple clip at the back of her neck. That was a great look, sophisticated without fuss, easily elegant. Surely the woman was too stylish, too severe, for her father. He was a margarita at a clambake. This woman looked like a martini at the opera.

And what am I? Lily wondered, sneering down at her flowered peach sundress with its ruffled skirt. I'm a hopeless Shirley Temple, she decided, a too-sweet drink garnished with sucky little pieces of fruit. She'd worn this dress in high school, for heaven's sake. But she knew it would be hot in the theater, and her wardrobe was so limited, she had to recycle everything. Plus, she'd be bored in simple clothes. Deep in her heart she longed to wear flashy, fabulous, look-at-me clothing and jewelry. Perhaps, with both her sisters back, Lily could keep a little more of her paycheck for clothing and give a bit less of it to her father for food and utilities. She'd never really sat down with her father to talk about it. She'd always just offered money, and he'd taken it. But of course, if she didn't live at home, she'd have to pay rent and buy her own groceries; she knew that. She didn't really know whether she was helping her father or costing him money. He paid the insurance on the Old Clunker . . .

The houselights dimmed. The stage lights came up. Lily turned her attention to the play.

Friday morning, Lily took a glass of iced tea and headed up the steep stairs at the back of the house to the attic.

"Hey, kid!" Abbie stuck her head up into the attic heat. "What are you doing up here?"

"Oh, I'm kind of messing around with some old clothes," Lily told her. "I need more things to wear to all my events, and I think there are some of Mom's clothes up here."

Abbie came up the stairs and stood in the middle of the attic with her hands on her hips. "Good God. There's tons of *everything* up here. What a mess." Her eye fell on a batik cotton bedspread in swirls of turquoise and blue. "Oh, my gosh. Mom threw that over the old chaise in their bedroom to hide all the rips and stains from poor old Rover. This can definitely go to Take It or Leave It."

"Don't be so hasty," Lily advised absentmindedly. She was pawing through hanging wardrobes.

"Well, do you want it? I can't see it ever fitting in with your décor."

"I don't want it," Lily answered. "I'm changing my style. No more yellow butterflies and daisy sundresses. I want something black."

"That sounds very Goth. I thought that was a teenage phase."

"Not Goth, silly. Sophisticated." Narrowing her eyes at her sister, she snapped, "Stop smirking! *I* can be sophisticated!"

"Of course you can," Abbie replied without a touch of condescension in her voice.

Lily unzipped a quilted wardrobe and reached in. "Ugh. Grandmom's old fur coat. Why are we saving it?"

"Because," Abbie replied, her words muffled as she bent over a box, "this family is psychotically anal. We can't seem to throw away anything. For example! Our old Scrabble game."

"Great. Bring it downstairs. We can play it some rainy night."

"No, we *can't*, because don't you remember? Some of the letters are missing. We just stuck it up here because what, we thought it would magically reproduce the letters? God, we're a strange family."

"No, Abbie, we thought we'd use those letters for some kind of game, scavenger hunts or spy games or something."

"Well, it's going to the dump!" Abbie added it to the pile of discards.

Lily knelt down next to a chest full of stuffed animals. "I suppose some of these should go, too. I mean, we can save some for our children—I want to save my dolls for my children—but some of these are just mangy and gross." She held up an elongated rabbit with a ripped ear and a missing eye. "I don't even remember this guy, do you?"

Abbie glanced over. "Nope. Dump it."

It was really nice, having Abbie's company up here in the gloomy attic. Lily loved her father, but she'd been lonely for the companionship her sisters provided. She wouldn't admit it aloud, but she'd been especially lonely for Abbie. Of course it was because when Lily was seven and their mother died, it had been Abbie who stepped into the maternal role. Lily understood that. She'd talked to counselors and therapists, she'd read books. But she wasn't *dependent* on Abbie. Abbie had been gone for almost two years, after all. And Lily was making her own way in life. It was just that with Abbie around, Lily felt . . . well, less lonely.

"Abbie?" Emma's voice came from the bottom of the stairs. "Abbie, we've had a couple of phone calls."

"Come up here!" Abbie yelled, her head down inside a trunk.

Emma slowly ascended the steps. She sat down at the top with her feet on the last step. "What are you guys doing in the attic? It's a steam bath."

Abbie said, "Cleaning it out. Check out the mess." She waved her arms. "It's ridiculous."

"Why are you cleaning out the attic now?" Emma asked.

Abbie shrugged. "I don't know, actually. I came up here because the door was open and Lily was up here."

"And I came up here to search for some clothes," Lily said. "I'm sick of my wardrobe. I need more sophisticated clothing. And you know I can't afford anything from the island stores, especially not in the summer."

To Lily's surprise, Emma nodded. "I might have some things you could use. We'd have to hem them, you're such a little hummingbird."

Pleasure rushed through Lily like a river. "Oh, Emma, that would be cool."

"What are the phone calls?" Abbie asked, dumping a pile of old bed linen on the floor.

"One woman phoned about a nanny slash housekeeper. Sounded snippy and hurried. The other call was from Sandra Bracebridge. Her mother-in-law is Millicent Bracebridge, remember her? An old lady, used to be involved in all the local organizations. Well, she's in her late eighties now, and her eyesight's going and Sandra wants someone to read to the old bat."

"Did she actually call her mother-in-law an old bat?" Abbie asked.

"Well, no, but don't you remember? Millicent Bracebridge was always pretty mean."

"What are you two even talking about?" Lily asked, looking from one sister to the other.

"Oh, didn't we tell you?" Abbie sat down on a pile of discarded clothing. "Emma and I are starting a new business. Nantucket Mermaids. We'll do any kind of odd job someone wants us to do. The ad just came out in yesterday's papers."

"Oh." Lily bit her lip. Here they were again, her two sisters, partners, a pair. She sucked up her courage and asked, "Why didn't you tell me about it?"

"Lily, honey," Abbie said, "because you already have a job, and from what you said, it keeps you busy."

Lily felt a bit better. "You're right, it does. I mean, that's why I'm up here. I need more clothes to wear to all the events I've got to go to." Still, she thought, it would have been nice if they had at least included her in the conversation. She would always be the baby of the family, but couldn't they see she wasn't a *baby* anymore?

"I hope you find something," Abbie said. "I'll help you take all this other stuff to the Take It or Leave It later. Right now I've got to cool off."

"I'll be down in awhile," Lily told her.

As her two older sisters went down the attic steps, Emma and Abbie talked about how to schedule interviews and who could give them references and how to divide up the jobs. They went down the hall together, their voices twining like vines. Lily stood alone, holding an old slip in her hands.

14

. . . . .

Abbie

From the outside, the house resembled any other, with gray shingles, white trim, and a picket fence. As she walked up the slate path, Abbie decided the blue hydrangea, climbing pale pink roses, and pots of multicolor petunias were so perfectly placed, groomed, and tended that the yard must be professionally landscaped.

The blue front door stood open. Abbie hesitated, then knocked. As she waited, she studied the décor. The house had been renovated and decorated to a glossy perfection in Nantucket style, everything blue and white and simple. Simply expensive. In the front hall alone, she saw two Claire Murray hand-hooked rugs, an antique table holding the white pitcher of blue hydrangea, and a Pamela Pindell oil painting above the hall table. Sailor's valentines lined the stairway wall and several lightship baskets were set decoratively by the doors leading to the living room and to the back of the house.

The good news, Abbie reminded herself, was that these people could afford to pay her well.

She called, "Hello?"

She heard voices raised in argument coming from the back of the house. She waited until a moment of silence fell, then called again.

"Hello?"

"Oh, for Christ's sake, Howell, go see who's at the door. Harry, this is your last chance. Mommy is leaving!"

From the back of the house came one of the most handsome men Abbie had ever set eyes on. Tall, broad-shouldered, with sandy hair that fell over his forehead, and startling blue eyes, he was somewhere in his thirties. That he appeared embarrassed and hesitant made him even more attractive.

"Oh, hello, sorry, we're in the middle of . . . of course you can tell that, can't you?" He had a pencil stuck over his ear. He wore shorts and a blue-and-white-striped shirt with the buttons done up wrong.

"I'm Abbie Fox." She smiled at him, keeping her posture straight and her head high. She wanted to appear confidant, capable. "I'm here about the nanny/housekeeper job."

"Well, thank God! Come in, come in." He hesitated, seeming baffled. "Um, come meet Harry."

Abbie followed the man down the hall and into the kitchen. It was large, gleaming with its state-of-the-art stainless steel refrigerator, stove, and ovens. The slate countertops held every conceivable new appliance.

In the middle of the kitchen stood a woman wearing a navy-and-white pin-striped suit and navy high heels. Her dark hair was blunt-cut at chin level and moved all in a piece, like black satin.

"All right, Harry. The sitter's here. Mommy's leaving. I won't be back for four nights. If you don't let me kiss you now, you won't get a Mommy kiss for a long, long time."

Abbie followed the woman's gaze. Under the table sat a little boy with shaggy white-blond hair. He wore a swimming suit and cowboy boots and he was holding a large plastic horse. He didn't respond to his mother but glared furiously at the floor.

"Fine." The woman turned and performed a rapid-fire up-and-down inspection of Abbie. "You're Abbie? I checked the references you emailed. You'll do. I've made lists for you and Howell can tell you the routine."

Outside, a horn honked.

"There's my taxi," the woman said. She picked up a handsome black leather briefcase and stalked out of the room.

Howell followed her.

Abbie was alone in the kitchen. She sat down on the floor,

crossed her legs Indian-style, and faced the little boy. "I'm Abbie. You must be Harry."

He didn't reply. But Abbie could see how tightly he clutched his horse, how white his knuckles were, how fiercely he clenched his jaws, just like an older man would do to keep from crying.

"You know what? You're only four years old. You're allowed to cry when your mother leaves to go off to work."

Harry didn't blink.

Howell returned to the kitchen and sat on the floor next to Abbie. "Well, old boy, it's just you and me now," he said to his son. "Oh, and now we've got Abbie. Abbie, do you ride horses?"

"No, but I've got a friend who does. She's got a stable off Hummock Pond Road. She has three horses." Howell nodded encouragingly at her, so she continued. "One is buckskin with a white mane and tail. And one is an Appaloosa." She could see the tension ease from the child's body as she talked. "Do you know what an Appaloosa is?"

Harry's response was to set his jaw more firmly closed. His father prompted her, "No. What is an Appaloosa?"

"It's an Indian horse with a spotted coat. Some of them are dark with huge white spots here and there and some are spotted like a leopard."

"Maybe you could drive Harry out to see them someday," Howell suggested.

"Um, yeah, sure. I could do that. That would be fun." She peeked at Harry. Still no response.

"I tell you what, Harry," Howell said. "I think we all need a little cheering up now that Mommy's gone back to the city, so let's walk down and get an ice-cream cone." Hurriedly he explained to Abbie, "It's too early in the day for an ice-cream cone, and we have to be careful not to give him too much sugar, at least I do, but sometimes rules have to be bent just a little, right?"

"Right," Abbie agreed.

"Which reminds me, Sydney left some on the table for you."

"Some what?"

"Oh, rules. A list of rules. I think you'll find them very, um, comprehensive." He turned his attention back to his son. "Ice cream? Strawberry or vanilla? Maybe pistachio."

Harry didn't budge.

"You know what? I'd love to see Harry's room."

"You would? Well, but Harry—"

"I'll bet Harry will stay right here. He'll be fine."

Howell opened his mouth, as if to argue, then closed it. "Sure. Come on, I'll show you."

Abbie rose and followed the man out of the kitchen, down the hall, and up the stairs. The first door on the left led to an enchanting child's room decorated in a blue-and-white nautical theme. Along one wall shelves ranged, covered with toys and games, mostly involving pirates, boats, and whales.

"Tell me about Harry," Abbie said.

Howell looked worried. "He's a great little boy. Smart and loving. But sensitive and stubborn. Leaving him alone will not make him come out from under the table."

Abbie ran her hands over the toys, picking up a stuffed octopus, a wooden lighthouse. "He's upset that his mother's going back to the city?"

"Right. He's always been an obstinate child, but recently he's become, well, I suppose you could call him defiant. I mean, he's always liked routine, and recently, I admit, his routine has changed a lot. He had the same nanny for about a year now, but this spring she got married and moved away. And my wife was just made partner at her law firm, and she's got piles more work, and in addition, she's taken on a high-profile divorce case. She is stressed and rushed to the max, and we thought that spending the summer here would be good for Harry."

"Do you stay here all the time?" Abbie asked.

"Oh, sure, I do, of course! Well, I'm fortunate that my company allows me to work at home, although I can't be available every moment, you see. I'm on the staff of environmental health and safety for Franklin Pharmaceuticals. I've got a major research report to put together and my deadline is September first, so this is a do-or-die summer for me. But I can work at home, so I can be with Harry every morning and every night. I mean, I want to be, if you can take over in the afternoons."

"Will you need some housekeeping?"

"I don't think so. We've got a team of cleaners who come in

twice a week. What we need, I guess, is someone to buy groceries, take stuff to the cleaners, do laundry, that kind of thing. Again, I think Sydney covered it pretty comprehensibly in her list."

"Good." Abbie wanted to reach across to button up Howell's shirt properly. Instead, she grabbed a plastic horse off the shelf. "Why don't you go on to work, and I'll sit in the kitchen and read Mrs. Parker's list and keep an eye on Harry. I'll see if I can't cajole him out from under the table and down to the beach."

"Oh, good, well, but, here's the thing, you won't drag him out, will you?"

"Of course not!"

"I mean, Sydney sometimes gets impatient—Christ, I don't mean she ever hurts the boy! But I mean, if we *have* to be somewhere . . . but she's his mother."

"I won't drag him out, I promise," she reassured him. "I'll sit there all day, if I have to."

"Good. That's good." Howell walked out into the hall. "That room down there I've taken for my office. I work in there. But if you need anything, anything at all, just knock on the door, okay? I won't mind if you interrupt."

"Got it," Abbie said. She smiled at him. "Okay, I'm off to the kitchen floor."

"And I'm off to work." But Howell didn't move. Instead, he stood staring at Abbie, as if he had something else to say to her.

It was a moment, Abbie thought, like others she'd known, when she and a man looked at each other and were caught in the exhilarating grip of mutual attraction.

Wow.

Wait. Was she nuts? He was married. She'd just met his wife.

Flushing, Abbie ripped herself away and hurried down the stairs to the kitchen. "See you later!"

Harry had changed positions. He now lay on his stomach beneath the kitchen table. He was rocking his horse back and forth in a galloping movement. When Abbie sat down, he froze.

Abbie lay down on her stomach, parallel to the boy. She placed her horse parallel to Harry's horse, just a few inches away. Harry whipped his head around so that he faced the other way.

Abbie rocked her horse back and forth on the floor and made

clicking, horse-walking noises with her mouth. "Okay, Licorice. It's time for lunch. Here's some hay."

"Thunder. His name is Thunder."

Abbie smiled to herself. "Okay, Thunder," she said, "come over here and I'll give you a nice pile of fresh hay."

For the next hour, she sat and lay on the floor, clopping the plastic horse around, talking to him, speaking for the horse in a series of whinnies and neighs. Harry didn't speak to Abbie, but gradually he began to walk his own horse over the floor, winding in and out through the table legs. Abbie developed a cramp in her neck and turned over, lying flat on her back. She drew her knees up and made Thunder slowly, with much huffing and puffing, ascend the mountain her legs made.

"This mountain is so high!" she huffed in the best baritone she could muster—she thought Thunder should have a masculine voice. "But I know I can reach the top. I just have to keep trying." She could sense that Harry had turned on his back and was watching her. Slowly she walked the horse up her leg and brought him to rest on top of her knee. "Wheeeee!" she whinnied. "I made it!" She brought the horse into a triumphant pose, rearing to stand on just two back legs. "Wheeee! I'm Thunder, the king of horses!"

Howell walked into the kitchen. He smiled down at Abbie, who felt ridiculous, lying there on her back.

"I just want to get a soda from the refrigerator." Howell squatted down to his son's level. "How're you doing?"

Harry turned on his side with his back to his father.

"It's a hot sunny day, Harry. Wouldn't you like to go down to the beach with Abbie?"

"We could bring the horses," Abbie said. "We could make an awesome corral for the horses out of sand. A barn, too."

Harry shook his head.

"Maybe tomorrow," Abbie said easily. "Anyway, it's going to take Thunder a long time to get down this mountain."

"Thunder looks kind of lonely up there," Howell said.

"I know," Abbie agreed. "It sure would be nice if Thunder had a friend to do things with."

Howell said, "Harry, what do you think? Would Storm like to climb the mountain with Thunder?"

Harry didn't respond.

"Well," Howell said. "I guess I'll get my drink and get back to work."

Abbie waited until Howell left to begin the dramatic progression of Thunder down the leg mountain. "Thunder is exhausted, he's going to take a nap. And I'm going to get a drink. I'm thirsty." She stood up, brushed off her shorts, and opened the refrigerator. It was fairly empty, although there were plenty of juices and soft drinks.

"Would you like some juice, Harry?"

No answer.

She grabbed a soda for herself and poured a cranberry drink for Harry.

"Here you are!" she said, leaning over to put the drink near him.

He didn't respond.

She leaned against the counter as she drank, staring out at the sunny day. She wondered if she could somehow persuade Harry as far as the backyard.

"I've got to pee," she said. "I'll be right back."

She found a half bathroom off the kitchen and was in and out in minutes. When she sat down on the floor again, she saw that Harry's juice glass was empty. Harry was on his side, eyes closed, sound asleep.

15

· · · · ·

Emma

Good," Sandra Bracebridge said, "you're on time."

They were standing on the brick sidewalk outside the Bracebridge mansion, a towering white Greek Revival with a broad front porch and columns. The Bracebridge property was protected from the riffraff by a wrought iron fence with spiked railings.

Emma forced herself to smile. She'd read somewhere that human beings responded in like fashion to stimuli like smiling, yawning, crying, so she was performing a kind of experiment.

But nope, Sandra Bracebridge did not move her lips. It was possible the woman wasn't human. During the brief interview Emma had endured earlier in the day with Sandra Bracebridge, the other woman had remained composed to the point of paralysis. And from everything she'd heard, Millicent Bracebridge, in her eighties and struggling with various infirmities, was going to be even less friendly.

Millicent Bracebridge, her daughter-in-law had told Emma, had fallen this winter and broken her hip, and had never really walked after the operation. At eighty-eight, she had seen her husband and most of her friends into their graves, and pain from arthritis and other minor ailments made her cranky. Now the macular degeneration that had plagued her for years was worsening her eyesight. And she tended to live in the past, which worried Sandra. Sandra's husband, Millicent's son, had died a few years ago, and Sandra was responsible for Millicent. She did not want her mother-in-law getting gaga. Millicent would not tolerate any kind of formal assisted living and, driven by her pride, she had given her lawyer durable rights of attorney, along with written instructions that if she had to be institutionalized, it would be in a nursing home on the Cape or near Boston, not on Nantucket. She had told Sandra that she did not want people who had known her when she was in her majestic prime to see her in her infirmity.

The Bracebridges were one of Nantucket's founding families. Millicent Bracebridge's collection of Nantucket arts and crafts was rumored to be extensive and significant. Emma couldn't believe she was about to work for one of the island's old legends, a wealthy, prominent woman from an important Nantucket family. Of the various jobs Emma had accepted, this one seemed the most interesting.

Now Emma followed Sandra Bracebridge up the wide steps, across the porch, and in through the wide front door. The black-and-white tiled foyer floor was covered with priceless antique Oriental rugs, and a crystal chandelier sparkled from the ceiling. In a polished cherry case a grandfather clock ticked away, its face artistically decorated with the sun, moon, and planets. An oil painting of a whaling ship took up most of one wall.

"Wow," Emma breathed. "What a magnificent room."

Sandra ignored her and swept on into the living room. "Millicent? We're here."

Emma followed her employer into a large room crowded with antiques. Oil paintings in elaborate gilt frames spanned the walls. Elaborate boxes of ivory scrimshaw were set along the mantel. In the window seat, seven lightship baskets of varying sizes were displayed, the darkened cane a testimony to their age. Small tables held Tiffany lamps and cloisonné vases. Obviously no children were allowed to enter this room, where one careless movement could provoke a disaster.

"Millicent? This is Emma Fox. She's come to read to you."

Millicent Bracebridge sat in a wheelchair with a tartan blanket tucked around her legs. Her white hair was styled like a 1940s movie star, finger-waved in strict ridges. She wore a light wool suit with a diamond brooch at the collar, and heavy hose and lace-up, high-heeled shoes.

"Well, let me get a look at you," Millicent said, gesturing impatiently.

Emma stepped close to the wheelchair. Sandra had told her to dress conservatively; her mother-in-law did not approve of the current style of showing off so much skin. Today she wore a white shirt, khaki trousers, and sandals. It was hot outside, but in this room with its high ceilings and heavy draperies drawn against the sun, the heat was moderate, although the air was heavy with humidity.

"Hello, Mrs. Bracebridge," Emma said.

"Lean down so I can see you. I've got macular degeneration. If you come close, I can get bits of you, though."

Emma obediently leaned down. As she did, she caught the scent of the older woman, a mix of talcum powder and a light floral fragrance.

Millicent Bracebridge turned her head slightly, seeming to aim her black eyes away from Emma's face. "You're a very pretty girl. Pick up that book over there and read a few sentences for me."

"*Moby-Dick!*" Emma exclaimed. "I loved this book." Opening it to the first page, she began to read.

After a few sentences, Sandra Bracebridge interrupted. "All right, Millicent? Does she read to your satisfaction?"

"She's fine." She waved her hand. "Go on along. Don't worry."

"The bathroom is just down the hall," Sandra Bracebridge told Emma. "And the kitchen's at the back of the house if you need a drink of water, or there might be iced tea in the refrigerator."

"Sandra, the girl is not an imbecile." Millicent's voice was sharp.

"All right, then." Sandra leaned over to kiss the older woman's forehead. "Three hours, right?" she asked Emma.

"Right," Emma affirmed.

Sandra left the room, and a moment later, the front door closed. Emma picked up *Moby-Dick* and settled on the corner of the sofa. "Can you hear me from here, Mrs. Bracebridge?" she asked.

"Very well, thank you. But before you get settled, I'd like you to get another book. Do you see the glass-fronted secretary in the corner? On the top shelf, far left, you'll find Agatha Christie's *Murder in the Links*."

Emma obeyed. She opened the door, found the book, and returned to the sofa. "Got it."

"Good. Now, this is important. When you are through reading, every day, you must remember to replace the book exactly where you found it."

"Oh. All right. I'll do that."

"It's Sandra, you see. She worries about me. She's afraid I'm getting senile. Getting lost in the past. And here's a little secret. I do get lost in the past. As often as possible. I love it there. But Sandra knows I've read Agatha Christie's entire oeuvre several times over. I don't want to cause her any alarm, and she will become alarmed if you tell her you're reading Agatha Christie to me. So this is our secret, all right?"

Emma grinned. "Absolutely. I'm very good at keeping secrets. I—"

Millicent cut her short. "All I care about is that you keep *my* secret. Now please read."

Emma read.

After thirty minutes, Emma excused herself to fetch iced tea for herself and Millicent. The tea provided a necessary pick-me-up; the warm dim room with all its heavy rugs, sofas draped with afghans, and antiques piled on top of antiques began to seem claustrophobic to Emma. No sounds came in from the street, no children laughing, no birds singing. Only the ticking of the clock in the hall provided any counterpoint to Emma's voice. As she read, she found herself giving a distinctive voice to each character, using a French accent for the Belgian detective, a pompous British one for Hastings, and high fluttering voices for the women. She was rewarded by seeing Millicent smile whenever Poirot spoke. Emma read along, stopping only to refresh her throat with some tea, and soon the clock struck four.

"It's time for me to go, Mrs. Bracebridge," she said.

"Very well, mark the place where you stopped. There's a bookmark over on the secretary. You'll have to remember where you left off on the page. I don't like my books marked with pencil or pen."

"Is there anything I can get you before I leave?" Emma asked after she'd put the book back on its shelf.

"I'll be fine." Mrs. Bracebridge felt around on the table next to her until her hand closed on the remote control. "I'll listen to television until the girl comes to bring me my dinner and help me to bed."

"Well, then, I'll see you tomorrow. Same time, same station," Emma said.

Mrs. Bracebridge was pleased by that. "Yes. Same time, same station."

Stepping out into the sunlight made Emma squint. The fresh air revived her, brought her back to the present. She stood for a moment, enjoying the sight of a family biking down the street, the children ringing their bells and laughing, a man with curly black hair walking his black standard poodle, the window boxes of houses along the street radiant with color. The blue sky, illuminated by the golden sun, spread like a luminous canopy over the trees and rooftops. Summer. How hard it must be to lose all this, Emma thought.

Sandra Bracebridge had told Emma that if she spotted any signs of senility, Emma was to inform her immediately. Emma smiled. As far as she was concerned, Mrs. Bracebridge's desire to enjoy more of her beloved Agatha Christie was only a sign of good mental health.

It was time for her to drive out to Surfside to pick up four children, drive them out to Annye's health food store to choose whatever they wanted for dinner, and deliver them to their house in Sconset. The Bennett father was still in London on business and the Bennett mother had her hands full with social engagements, so she'd hired Emma as a chauffeur and maid of all jobs for two hours in the late afternoon. The four kids were noisy and quarrelsome, but after the tomblike quiet of the Bracebridge house, Emma welcomed the clamor. At the house, the children shoved and pushed one another, yelling, as they fought their way out of the car.

"Grab your towels, kids!" Emma reminded them. "And your beach bags!"

She'd forgotten she was as invisible to them as a gnat. She crawled into the backseat of the SUV and gathered up the sodden sandy beach towels. She carried them and one of the beach bags to the back of the house. She made two more trips to take in the beach paraphernalia and food. Once everything was out of the car, she went to the back of the garden to shake the sand out of the towels before lugging them past the outdoor shower and into the laundry room. She stuffed the towels into the washing machine and started the wash cycle, then went into the kitchen and began to empty and clean out the beach bags and coolers. As she worked, she heard Mrs. Bennett trying to rein in the children, who were in the family room with the television volume on high.

Emma had just finished with the coolers when Jody Partridge came in the back door to begin her shift as babysitter for the evening. Jody was an island woman in her late thirties, married, with two children of her own.

"How are the maniacs?" she asked Emma.

Emma dried her hands on a dish towel. "Maniacal. Have fun." She hurried out of the house.

She had a free hour before she went to her next job, babysitting for a couple staying at a local B&B. As she drove back into town, she tried to remember what food was left in the house. She wasn't hungry, really. She'd forgotten what it felt like to be hungry. But she couldn't remember when she'd last eaten and she was shaky from low blood sugar.

What were Duncan and Alicia doing now? Perhaps they were strolling around the Public Garden, holding hands and enjoying the soft summer air before meeting friends for dinner at the Taj. The friends would be wealthy, like Alicia, and perhaps as they lingered over dessert, they'd discuss vacations . . . oh, no. *No.* Duncan and Alicia wouldn't come to Nantucket on vacation, would they? Duncan's family had a summer home in Maine. Surely they'd go there. On the other hand, Duncan had loved Nantucket. He had a lot of friends here, and a lot of contacts. What if Emma were working, pushing a baby stroller around town or running into a store to pick up something for one of her clients, her hair frizzed with humidity, and she ran into Duncan and Alicia ambling down the street in all their sleek perfection?

It was a nightmare thought. It took her breath away. And now that she'd imagined it, she couldn't get the scene out of her head. It played itself over and over, filling her with dread.

16
· · · · ·

Lily

Tonight the Hennersons were holding a fund-raiser for the next senatorial candidate. It was going to be a crush of the wealthiest people summering on the island. It was just the kind of event where she could meet someone. The One. So she wanted to *shine*.

But her look just wasn't coming together. Lily was on the verge of tears as she stood in the middle of her bedroom, surrounded by every dress and skirt and top she owned. She'd tried them on in every possible variation, but nothing *worked*. She wanted to look sophisticated. She wanted to look *fabulous*. She wanted to be able to just go out and buy herself a new dress.

Emma had the sort of clothes Lily coveted. City clothes. Sleek silks and crepes, expensively subtle. And Emma had said she'd loan Lily some of her things.

Lily went into Emma's room. Emma's bed was unmade but she'd finally unpacked her bags. Lily rooted around in Emma's closet and came out with a filmy silk shirt in pale olive that would be dynamite with Lily's red hair. She took it into her room and tried it on. Wow! It was perfect. She slipped into a pair of cream silk capris, clipped on a dangle of earrings, and slid her feet into high-heeled sandals. All right. In fact, very nice. She smiled at herself in the mirror. If she were a man, she'd be attracted!

She heard voices in the kitchen. Good. Her sisters were home.

She hurried down the stairs. Wait till they saw her! Wait till they heard she was going to see inside the fabulous Hennersons' house!

Abbie and Emma were in the kitchen. Emma was pawing through a cupboard while Abbie squatted down as she searched through the vegetable crisper.

"Where's Dad?" Abbie was asking.

Emma replied, "Out fishing. Said he'd get dinner at Henry's."

"The peanut butter's all gone," Abbie said. "And there is only one slice of bread, and it's the heel."

Lily positioned herself in the doorway, hip stuck forward, model-style. "Ta-da!"

Abbie's face when she saw Lily was not full of admiration but of irritation. "Lily, weren't you the last person to have breakfast this morning?"

"Well, I guess, so what?"

"So you used the last of the bread for toast, right?"

"Well, why not? Honestly—"

"So didn't you notice there was no bread left? Didn't it occur to you that you should have gone to buy bread? Not to mention fruit, cereal, milk, yogurt?"

Impatiently, Lily shot back, "Why should *I* buy the stuff? You guys are here now. You eat here, too."

Emma joined the argument, crossing her arms and glaring at Lily. "Just because we're here doesn't mean you get to be a baby again."

Lily sniffed. "Well, that's mean!"

Abbie said reasonably, "Come on, Lily, Emma and I work. We were out of the house and working while you were still in bed."

"I work, too! I have to leave for work right now, actually!" She hated how her sisters treated her, as if they were adults and she was a hopelessly silly little girl.

"Wait a minute," Abbie said. "Are you taking the Old Clunker?"

"Of course," Lily said. "The party's up on Cliff Road. I can hardly walk there in high heels!"

"*Lily.*" Now Abbie was tense. "I was counting on using it. I'm babysitting for a family out in Monomoy."

"You can bike there," Lily protested.

"Monomoy's farther than Cliff Road," Abbie argued.

"Not much farther and besides, you can't expect me to *bike* to a fund-raiser in my good clothes!"

"But you can expect me to bike to Monomoy after I've worked all day."

Lily crossed her arms defensively. "Well, I didn't know that, did I?"

Emma's voice was calm and serious when she weighed in. "Lily, you know we have jobs. We told you about them. Abbie and I both got up at six and worked all day. You slept until God knows when and had the whole day free, right?"

Lily insisted, "My work schedule is different from yours."

"You had the whole day free," Emma repeated. "Did it occur to you to buy groceries?" She waved her arms around. "It certainly didn't occur to you to clean up the kitchen. What did you do today, Lily? Wait, don't tell me, I know what you did! You went to the beach, didn't you?"

"You don't understand. I need to keep tanned for my job. I don't want to look pale like—" She'd gotten herself into a corner and didn't know how to get out.

"Like the rest of us?" Abbie suggested. "The rest of us, who are too busy working all day to lie on the beach and soak up the sun?"

"Okay, I'm *sorry*!" Lily snapped. "Perhaps I should have bought groceries. I'll buy them tomorrow. But I've got to go now, this fund-raiser is a big deal. I'm lucky I got a press invitation. Oh, stop being so mean to me. If I cry, I'll ruin my mascara!"

"Oh, go on." Abbie gave in. "I'll go do some shopping after I finish babysitting. Stop&Shop's open all night now."

"Wait," Emma said, moving toward Lily. "Is that *my* top?"

As Emma walked toward her, Lily suddenly felt like Cinderella in the Disney movie with the two wicked stepsisters looming over her, ripping her clothes to rags. "I was *going* to ask you," she babbled. "I don't have anything nice to wear, and this is a very big deal, and I knew you wouldn't be using it tonight, oh, please don't make me take it off, I don't have anything sophisticated—"

"Stop acting like someone out of Dickens," Emma ordered. "Go ahead and wear it. You just should have asked first. And actually, you can keep it. It fits you better than it ever fit me."

"Oh, Emma, thank you! Does it really look good on me?"

But Emma turned away from Lily. "Listen, Abbie, I've got a babysitting job tonight right in town, just a short walk from here. I'll stop by Grand Union on the way home and grab some milk and bread for tomorrow morning."

"Oh, great, Emma, thanks." Abbie looked at her watch. "We can make a grocery list tomorrow morning so we can stock up for the week or at least a few days."

"I've got to go," Lily said softly.

Abbie didn't respond to Lily. She was on her tiptoes, searching through the highest shelf in the cupboard. "Don't we have any soup or *anything* in this house? I'm starving."

Lily hurried down the hall, grabbed the keys to the Toyota, and went outside. She felt terrible, guilty because she *could* have bought groceries today and it was too bad Abbie was hungry, and also furious because not everything was her fault. After all, Abbie had traveled abroad, she was übercompetent, she wasn't actually *starving*, she was just trying to make Lily feel bad, and also hurt, because there they were again, her two older sisters ganging up, the perfect pair, turning their backs on their dumb little sister.

She blasted the radio as she drove over to Cliff Road, hoping the summer rock would help her change out of her sullen mood. It was a gorgeous hot evening, and even if she was only going for work, still she was going to one of the most elite parties on the island. She found the house on a street already lined with convertibles, Hummers, and sports cars. She had to drive three blocks before she could find a place to park. As she hurried toward the house, she put a little swing into her walk, just in case anyone was watching.

A handsome guy in a tux was at the door, checking invitations. As Lily joined the throng of people streaming into the house and out onto the long deck with its ocean view, she caught a glimpse of herself in a mirror. The way her long red hair fell past her shoulders was cool. She looked *good*.

But not as good as the other women there. She strolled along, tossing off easy smiles and checking for a chance to start up a conversation, privately intimidated by the other guests. All the women were tanned and shimmery, with sleek hair pulled back into casual low ponytails or chignons, and diamonds, emeralds, and sapphires clustered around their necks in fabulous arrangements. Their clothes made her burn with envy. Some women wore real true gowns whose skirts swept the floor, with halter tops or asymmetrical bodices or beaded bustiers. Others wore tunics so short that their slender legs seemed endless. Few wore pants, and why should they, this was summer, time to show off one's long sleek legs.

Stop it! Lily ordered herself. She had work to do.

First, perhaps, a little drink to soothe her nerves. She made her way to the bar at the end of the deck.

"Hey, Lily," the bartender said.

Lily gawked. "Jason! What are you doing here?"

"What does it look like? I'm working." He was scooping ice into a glass as he talked.

"I thought you were a contractor." She couldn't believe how sexy he was in black jeans and a white button-down shirt with the sleeves rolled up. His forearms were so muscular, his shoulders so broad. His brown hair was cut brush-style and he was, not surprisingly, very tanned.

"Contractor by day, bartender by night. I'm a man of many talents. What can I get you?"

Lily surveyed the table. "Oh, good, you have Prosecco. I'll have that, please."

"So you're here for your column?"

He knew about her column? Lily blushed. "Right." She took a sip of sparkling wine. "Here's my courage," she told him, holding up the glass. "I have to approach complete strangers and ask if I can take their photos and names. Sometimes it's fun, but sometimes people are offended."

"I can't imagine anyone being anything but nice to you, Lily," Jason said.

"You'd be surprised," she told him.

"Actually, I don't think I would. Remember, I work for people like this."

As if to prove his point, an older man in a blue blazer slammed his glass down on the table. "Again," he ordered Jason, then turned away, scanning the crowd.

Jason cleared his throat. "Would that be Scotch, sir?"

"Right." The man answered without looking at Jason.

Jason got a clean glass, scooped in some ice, added the Scotch, and held it out to the man, who snatched it and walked off without a word of thanks.

"Point made?" Jason said, smiling at Lily.

Lily nodded. "Still, it's a job." She fluttered her fingers and forced herself out into the crowd.

She knew the hostess wanted her photo taken; she'd discussed it briefly with her a few days before. Mrs. Hennerson was a familiar face in the society pages and it didn't take Lily long to find her in the crowd. The older woman grabbed the senatorial candidate and they posed willingly while Lily clicked off several shots. After that, buoyed by the wine, Lily plucked up her courage and wandered through the group, introducing herself to strangers, chatting with them, taking their pictures, and carefully writing down their names.

"Hey, Princess, do me a favor."

Lily was just squeezing between two groups of people when she heard the low, raspy voice. She looked toward the end of the deck. An older woman sat there in a swirl of crimson and diamonds. She was probably around seventy, but obviously had had face-lifts and Botox and heaven knew what else, so that her face seemed strangely ageless and also oddly alien, as if she were from another planet and just masquerading as a human.

"Were you talking to me?" Lily asked.

"I was." The woman held out her glass. "I'm dry. Get me another."

Slightly insulted, Lily hesitated. "I'm not—"

"I know you're not a waitress. But I need another drink and I don't have the energy to fight through the mob. Get me a drink and I'll let you take a photograph of me. Your editor will like having my picture, believe me. And I'll tell you who's who in this crowd."

"All right." Lily reached out to take her glass. "What are you drinking?"

"Gin martini. Tell the bartender I don't want him even thinking the word vermouth. Two ice cubes, no more. Fill it to the top." She'd barely finished with her instructions before a couple of older men came up to her. "Darlings!" she bellowed at them. "Give me a cigarette before I perish!"

Lily made her way back to the bar, told Jason how to fix the drink, then asked, "Do you know who that woman in red is?"

"God, yes. That's Eartha Yardley. Countless husbands and end-less money."

"That's Eartha Yardley? She looks so old!"

"She *is* so old. She's got to be in her late seventies. The latest rumor is that she's got a younger lover—a much younger lover."

"Well, well." Lily held out her own glass. "Better fill mine, too."

"Sure," Jason said. "But Lily, a word to the wise. Be very careful what you say around her. She's got a reputation for being a ruthless gossip."

"Thanks, Jason. I'll remember that." She took her new glass of Prosecco. "See you later."

"Hey, Lily."

She turned back toward him.

"Want to go out sometime? Maybe this weekend?"

She nearly dropped both drinks. "Oh, Jason, I'd love to!"

"I'll call you." Jason turned his attention to a pair of women wanting wine.

Lily squeezed her way back to Eartha Yardley. The summer had just gotten much more interesting.

17

· · · · ·

Marina

Marina stood in the morning sun with a coffee cup in one hand and a paintbrush in the other, surveying her work. She was painting the walls of the cottage a dreamy, pale Caribbean blue. She enjoyed the rhythm of painting, the way everything changed so quickly, with a few sweeps of her brush.

She set her coffee cup down and knelt on the newspapers she'd spread to protect the floor from spatters. As she cut carefully in a low corner, she let her thoughts drift.

It was early July. She'd been here for a month, and she thought she was doing a pretty good job of going forward with her life. She wasn't sitting around moping, she was making herself get out into the world, she was doing things! She was attending lots of lectures and plays and concerts. She was helping at the library. She was even making a friend in Sheila Lester.

She'd decided to go to Sheila's studio to learn how to make a lightship basket. It would be a good discipline for her. It wasn't the sort of work she was used to, it wasn't high energy, high stakes. It would require steadiness and patience and that would make it a challenge for her. It would help her to learn how to move slowly through the world.

And she'd bought a little bike. She rode out to the beach on the Atlantic side of the island and took a swim almost every evening.

Then she would walk along the beach, idly checking out the shells and pebbles and gazing out at the vast, indifferent ocean, and she'd throw this question out at Fate:

What good am I on this earth? Why am I here?

She didn't have children, so that wasn't her purpose in life. Her husband left her so she wasn't here to love and support her life's mate. She'd sold her share of her business. So what worth did she have?

She didn't expect something to rise up out of the ocean holding a sign that told her the answer. But she hoped to come up with some kind of answer before she left this island and returned home.

Her life did seem more like a work in progress now, not something ruined or stunted.

She really did need to slow down. She'd been sloppy at first, spattering paint on the windowsills and floor as she slapped the brush against the wall. She had to grab herself by the scruff of her own neck and metaphorically shake herself, reminding herself there was no need to hurry. Being in a rush was a habit she could get rid of—needed to get rid of.

As she smoothed the creamy blue paint up the wall, she understood, suddenly, that all her life she'd been trying to get *there*. She'd been hurrying toward *there*, that mythical place where life would be full and happy, and now *there* was gone. She'd wanted only the normal things, she decided: home, husband, children, work, and plenty of money.

Well, she had plenty of money. And if that was not sufficient to make a life, it was still something to be proud of. She hadn't been given a nest egg to start with; she'd earned everything she had. She hadn't won an Oscar or flown to the moon, but she had, with Gerry, started an advertising agency and built it into a flourishing business. She'd worn some fabulous clothes and she'd taken some exotic vacations. She'd been written up in newspapers and magazines and professional journals. She'd lived in a gorgeous penthouse with a fabulous view.

So had she been *there* all along?

No. Because she had wanted children. If she had had a family, she would have been *there*. If she'd had a family, the business could have disappeared and she still would have been *there*.

She had been a good person, she was fairly sure of that. No torturing animals, stealing from old ladies, polluting the water. So why had Fate denied her her dearest wish? Had she done something wrong and was being punished for it? She couldn't imagine what.

A knock sounded on the cottage door, startling her. She put the brush down, carefully balancing it on the gallon can of paint, got up, and went to the door.

Jim Fox was there. "Hope I'm not interrupting anything."

The brightness of the sun made her blink. "No, not at all. I'm just painting. Want to see?" She stepped back for him to enter.

He came in, a big man in a small cottage. "Good job. Nice color. But hey, today's a great day. I thought you might like to take that boat ride with me."

"I'd love it!" She looked down at her shorts and paint-stained tee. "Should I change?"

"You might want to put on a bathing suit."

"Good idea. And what can I bring?"

"We can pick stuff up on the way."

"All right, then. I'll just clean up my paintbrush and change."

"I'll meet you out at the truck."

Marina felt slightly breathless as she rinsed the brush in the kitchen sink. Jim was older than she was—she couldn't figure out just how much older—but today in his swim trunks and tee shirt, she could tell quite clearly that he was in great physical shape. He had big forearms and huge, muscular, hairy thighs. Just thinking about his thighs made her want to giggle like a teenager.

She pulled on her most conservative, least flirtatious bathing suit, a blue Speedo, yanked her tee and shorts on over it, slid her feet into her flip-flops, and found her beach bag, which she kept ready to go with sunblock, bottled water, beach towel, and paperback. She raced out of the cottage like a schoolgirl released for summer vacation.

As they drove along Madaket Road, Jim pointed out the bike path, and Sanford Farm with its great walking paths, and Long Pond where boys gathered to catch crabs. Jim's boat, a thirty-foot Boston whaler, rocked sedately in the Madaket Harbor. Jim handed her down, stored the beach bags and cooler of food, settled himself behind the wheel, and started the engine. Marina pulled off her tee, slathered herself with sunblock, and leaned back on her arms, letting the sun beat down on her as they slowly chugged out of the harbor and into the wilder waters.

The breeze was slight, and the sea glistened like a great shattered slab of polished sapphire. In the distance white sails cut through the skyline and the distinctive silhouette of a fishing boat loomed on the horizon. The whaler's engine rumbled like a purring cat and today even the ocean seemed content.

A long narrow beach stretched out from the eastern shore of Tuckernuck Island. Already a couple of boats were beached in the shallows. Jim anchored his boat a few yards from shore and they slipped into the waist-high water, carrying bags on their shoulders. The lazy waves were silkily cool against her hot skin. After they'd established their little nest in the sand, they hurried back to the water. Jim swam far out; he was a strong swimmer with a powerful stroke. So that's where he got those muscles, Marina thought. She was less sure of herself, so she swam near shore and spent a lot of time just floating on her back, eyes closed, the sunlight flickering against her eyelids.

After awhile, they came up onto the beach and settled on the blanket to eat lunch. Music from someone's radio drifted in the air, and another boat slowly motored past. The bread was fresh, thick, and hearty, and the bottled water tasted like a fine wine.

"My bones have turned to gelatin," Marina told Jim.

"Take a nap," Jim told her.

"I don't think I have any choice," she murmured. She turned on her stomach, crossed her arms, laid her head down, and was asleep at once.

When she woke, the sun was higher in the sky. Only a few feet away, Jim lay sleeping, his scalloper's cap pulled over his face. She took a moment to study him, liking his strong workman's body. Then, embarrassed by her staring, she rose and headed off down the beach, letting her gaze drift along the water's edge. She stopped to pick up a striped scallop shell, and a white sand dollar, and a shard of cobalt glass. The sand whispered against the soles of her feet, and the ocean seemed to breathe. She picked up an iridescent mussel shell, both sides still connected, and an ivory slipper shell. Perhaps she might make a sailor's valentine, she thought. She needed a container, though, she realized, as she turned around and made her way back along the shore. Her hands were already full.

Jim was awake. "You found some treasures." He held out an empty Tupperware box.

"Thanks." She sighed. "It's so peaceful here."

"Today it is," Jim replied. "One more swim, then we'd better go back."

During the slow, easy journey across the channel to the harbor, Marina stared out at the water as if mesmerized, and when they loaded their gear into Jim's truck, she said, "I feel like I've just had a lobotomy."

Jim laughed. "The sign of a perfect day."

He tuned the radio to a soft-rock station as he drove back into town.

"I have no idea what time it is," Marina said.

"Does it matter?" he asked.

"You know, I guess it doesn't."

When they pulled into the driveway, Marina said, "Jim, this was a wonderful day. I'm so grateful."

"I enjoyed it, too," he said.

"Listen, I'd love to repay you somehow—let me fix you dinner."

"Well," he said, hesitating, and it seemed the color rose in his cheeks, or perhaps it was only a glow from the day's sun. "Well, okay. Don't go to any trouble."

"How about Friday night?" she asked.

"That's fine."

"Thanks again," she said.

Jim hauled the cooler out of the back of his truck and carried it toward the house. Marina handled her beach bag gently. Back in her little cottage, she took her array of shells out and spread them across the table. Each shell was curled or striped with its own distinctive hallmark. She sat down in a chair and began arranging the shells in patterns, making roses, and circles, and garlands, and after awhile she realized that her mind was so full of beauty she had no room for words.

18

.....

Abbie

The Jetties Beach was only a few blocks from the Parkers' house but the Parkers allowed Abbie to drive their SUV to take Harry to the beach, which was a good thing, because Harry was such a dawdler they'd never get there by walking. Abbie had never seen such a slow-moving little child.

On Friday afternoon, Abbie knelt in the sand helping Harry build a complicated sand castle. According to Sydney's meticulous instructions, Abbie had slathered him with sunblock so he wouldn't burn. She'd fastened a floppy sun hat on his head. She'd adjusted the beach umbrella over his thin little body and covered him with a beach towel while he took a little nap after his snack, and she'd walked up and down the beach with him, and tried to lure him more than ankle-deep into the water, but so much water and all the shouting, shoving children leaping in the shallows made him nervous.

Occasionally another child would attempt to play with Harry, but at any overture, Harry would hurriedly retreat to his towel and curl up in a ball like a bug. Aware of the judgmental looks other women exchanged, Abbie wanted to post a sign: *I'm the nanny, not the mother!* Then she chided herself for not wanting to claim the little boy. She knew he was doing the best he could. She didn't think there was anything seriously wrong with him, but he was peculiar.

She wanted to talk with his father about him, but so far the chance hadn't arisen.

Right now, her job, assigned by Harry, was to dip one of the buckets in the ocean and carry up water to moisten the sand just right for building. The perfect building sand nearby, already moist for packing, was too near the threatening surge of tide for Harry. He had constructed an elaborate and lengthy castle complete with a moat and drawbridge. He was a patient little guy. If a wall gave way, he would study it from all angles before beginning the reconstruction.

Abbie had a brainstorm. "You know what, Harry? I'll build a little corral for the horses!" Hurriedly, she corrected herself. "I know, knights didn't call them 'corrals.' I don't know what they called them."

"Pens, maybe," Harry offered. "Yes, that would be a good place for the horses to stay. Maybe we could build a little barn over there so they are out of the hot sun."

"I'll start on the pen," Abbie said.

"After I finish this wall, I'll start on the barn," Harry told her, and he smiled.

As she worked, Abbie told herself she really had to get Harry out to see Shelley's horses. Anything with horses seemed to make him happy, and while he was a pleasant child, he didn't seem like a happy one.

But there were times when he was enthusiastic. At the end of the day, when Abbie brought Harry back to his house, she would first rinse him off in the outdoor shower, being sure all grains of sand were sprayed out of his hair. Wrapped in a clean towel, Harry would run down the hall to see if his father's study door was open. Howell would rise from his desk, cross the room, and pick Harry up, holding him so high his head touched the ceiling.

"Hey, buddy, am I glad to see you!" Howell would say. He'd squeeze Harry until the little boy giggled.

That was when Abbie saw Harry smiling the most, when he was with his father.

Abbie smiled when she saw Howell, too. He just had a way about him, a gentle, friendly aura.

So why was his son such a little knot of neuroses?

Harry finished his wall and moved over next to Abbie to start construction of the barn. They worked for a while in companion-able silence. She could see the shadows lengthening. People were folding up their beach chairs and heading home.

"Harry," Abbie said, "we could get some beach grass from the dunes and stick it around the barn to make a little pasture for the horses."

Harry's face lit up in a smile of real amazement. "What a good idea, Nanny Abbie! I'll go get some!" Off he ran, up the beach to the dunes.

Abbie was surprised to find tears in her eyes. *I've done it*, she thought! *I've made him smile!* She knew he missed his Nanny Donna, and he worried about his mother being gone all week, and if she could forge a bond with this little boy that would provide reas-surance and connection—

From out of nowhere, a bright orange Frisbee came spinning through the air. It skimmed the top of Abbie's head and sliced straight through the sand castle. The castle crumbled as the Frisbee crashed into the sand next to it.

Harry, running down from the dunes with grass in his hands, slammed to a halt, wide-eyed. "Oh, no!" Harry screamed. "You wrecked my sand castle!"

Abbie jumped to her feet and rushed to the child, who stood screaming at the top of his lungs while tears flowed down his cheeks.

"Harry," Abbie said, "honey, it's all right."

She tried to get her arms around the little boy, but he was in a rage, jumping up and down and wailing. All up and down the beach people turned to gawk at him, the source of all this unpleasant noise.

"Harry, calm down." Abbie tried to speak in a calming voice.

A teenage boy with spots on his face ambled up. "Hey, dude, I didn't mean to wreck your sand castle. Sorry, man."

"I HATE YOU!" Harry screamed at the boy. "I HATE YOU I HATE YOU I HATE YOU!"

"*Harry.*" Abbie made her voice stern. "Stop that now."

To her amazement, he obeyed. But she almost wished he hadn't, because it was obvious that he was swallowing his rage, internalizing it. He trembled all over, and his mouth quivered and his bony chest heaved.

She put her arms around him. "Harry, it's almost time to go

home, anyway. We'll build a new one, tomorrow, and it will be better."

"Sorry," the teenager said again, looking miserable.

"It's all right," Abbie told him.

The boy hurried away, sand spraying up from his heels as he ran. Abbie kept her arms around Harry and glared at the other sunbathers who were still studying Harry with a mix of sympathy and glee. After Harry's sobs had subsided, Abbie took his hand and gently drew him down to the beach towel. She settled him so that he would not be facing his ruined structure.

"Here, honeybun, drink some juice. You'll feel better."

He obeyed but now he had retreated into his good little robot boy self with a blank expression, and Abbie was worried. She didn't know if this sort of thing was normal. She'd babysat lots of children and never had this sort of experience. She didn't want to leave the beach now, when it would resound with negative images. She had to direct his thoughts elsewhere.

"Harry, let's go for a walk along the beach and see if we can see anything out in the water. Maybe a mermaid, maybe a whale, maybe a pirate ship."

Obediently, Harry stood up and reached for her hand. It broke her heart, that one little action, the way he reached for her hand. She held it firmly, and together they walked slowly along the beach, looking out into the ocean. She stayed just out of reach of the tide line, knowing how Harry feared the rushing waves.

19

·····

Emma

Millicent Bracebridge seemed half-asleep in her chair, and Emma didn't blame her. The room was stifling hot and the light was dim. But Millicent didn't want the drapes drawn or the windows opened. Outside noises disturbed her, she said. Emma continued to read, imbuing the dialogue with the inflections and accents that made Mrs. Bracebridge smile. Hastings was about to kiss an acrobatic actress named Bella, and Emma was surprised. She hadn't remembered Hastings having any kind of romantic thoughts.

A loud noise coming from the front of the house startled her and made Mrs. Bracebridge wake up.

"Grams!"

A man entered the room, and for the first time since Emma had met her, Millicent Bracebridge's face broke into a luminous smile.

"Spencer." She held out her arms.

Spencer hugged his grandmother and kissed her cheeks, then knelt before her and studied her. "You look *ravishing!*" he told her.

And suddenly the older woman glowed.

"Emma, I'd like you to meet my grandson, Spencer Bracebridge."

Spencer rose and approached Emma, holding out his hand.

He was terribly good-looking, with black hair and ebony eyes. He wore khakis, a white button-down shirt, and a turquoise tie with sailboats on it. Emma was suddenly aware of her frizzy hair and face bare of makeup.

"Nice to meet you, Emma. Mom's told me about you." He glanced at the book in Emma's hands. "Agatha Christie? Mom said you were reading *Moby-Dick*."

"Let your mother keep her illusions, Spencer." Millicent Bracebridge's voice was soft and full of humor. "She judges me rather harshly. I want her to think I'm still intellectually top drawer."

Spencer laughed. "She is hard to please, isn't she! Don't worry. This will be our little secret."

"Thank you, dear."

"But what are you doing," Spencer asked, "cooped up in this gloom on a day like today?"

"I prefer peace and quiet," Millicent Bracebridge began.

Her grandson interrupted. "I've got about thirty minutes free and I want to spend them with you, but not inside." He grabbed the handles of his grandmother's wheelchair. "Come on," he said to Emma. "We're going out to the garden."

"Oh, dear," his grandmother fussed. "It's such a *project*, getting me out there and back."

Emma followed as Spencer steered the wheelchair down the hall, through the dining room, and out the door onto a large wooden deck. The sunlight was dazzling after the dim interior.

"Listen," Spencer said. "Can you hear the birds? I'll bet that's that crabby old cardinal who used to chase all the other birds away from the feeder."

Millicent Bracebridge laughed. "I'd forgotten him."

Emma asked, "Would you like me to make some iced tea?"

"I'd love some!" Spencer said. "And if you've got any cookies, or cake, or anything, cheese and crackers. This is my lunch break. I work at the NHA and they're pretty easy, but this is such a busy season. And Emma, do me a favor. Would you open the drapes and windows and air out the living room?"

His grandmother protested, "I don't like—"

Spencer spoke over her words. "My dear old vampire bat, we will close everything up before I wheel you back in."

Emma stared, shocked at the way he spoke to her. But his grandmother was beaming.

The kitchen of the house was old, with an ancient porcelain

sink built into a metal cupboard and a Frigidaire so old it had to be manually defrosted. As Emma waited for the water to boil for the tea, she searched the cupboards and found digestive biscuits and ginger snaps and Carr's wafers. She put them on a plate with a hunk of cheddar. She poured the water over some Earl Grey, filled a pitcher with ice, and put three tall glasses on a tray along with the sugar bowl and three spoons.

She carried it all out to the patio. Mrs. Bracebridge was laughing.

As Emma served the tea, she couldn't help smiling. Spencer was recounting a disastrous adventure he and his friends had had on the island when they were children.

"Oh, I'd forgotten all about that!" Mrs. Bracebridge chuckled. Her laughter made her cheeks flush rosily. "Your poor mother. How did she survive having you for a child!"

Spencer consumed every cracker and piece of cheese Emma had put out, and when it was all gone, he turned to Emma. "That was great, Emma. Thanks. I was about to starve."

"You always could eat more than anyone I ever knew," his grandmother observed affectionately.

Spencer looked at his watch, made a face, and said he had to leave. Emma hurried in to close the windows and drapes. Spencer wheeled Mrs. Bracebridge back into her spot in the living room, kissed her on each cheek, and smiled at Emma.

"Are you here often?"

"Every day from one till four," she told him.

"Great! I'll try to take my lunch hours then." And he whisked off out the door.

Smiling as they settled back in the living room, Mrs. Bracebridge said, "He always was like that. He was a happy, energetic little boy, and he's a happy, energetic man. He's working on his Ph.D. in history, you know. Specializing in Nantucket history. Wants to live here eventually. Would you like to see him as a baby? He was the cutest baby!"

"I'd love to see him as a baby," Emma said.

"My photo albums are in the bottom shelf of the bookcase, over there behind the sofa."

Emma fetched the albums and brought them to Mrs. Bracebridge. She pulled a chair up next to the wheelchair and helped the older woman hold the albums close enough for her to see with the peripheral vision her macular degeneration allowed her.

Millicent Bracebridge beamed. "Oh, there I am at my engagement party! Look at my dress, wasn't it lovely!"

"And your husband was so handsome," Emma said.

"He was, wasn't he?"

The afternoon flew past. When it was time for Emma to leave, she put away the albums and did a once-over of the room. A glass of water was on the table next to Mrs. Bracebridge, and at five someone would arrive for the evening. She had a hunch that after the excitement of seeing her grandson, Millicent Bracebridge would nap, and she was right. When she said good-bye to the older woman, she saw that Mrs. Bracebridge had already nodded off, her chin resting on her chest.

As she walked down Main Street and through the narrow, charming lanes to her father's house, her thoughts lingered on the sight of the grandmother and grandson. What love existed between the two of them, what joy they had in each other. She remembered her maternal grandparents, who lived outside Boston, and who had been just as loving, devoted, and admiring, until they both passed away when Emma was in her teens. Her father's mother had died years ago, also, and her father's father lived in Florida now with a new wife and had little interest in his three granddaughters. At Christmas, he had sent them each a check for twenty dollars, and the three girls each sent a thank-you note, but when each one turned twenty-one, the checks stopped.

So not everyone had a warm, affectionate relationship with a grandparent. She knew that. She would love to be a grandparent someday. She would love to be as loving as Millicent Bracebridge was to Spencer.

But to be a grandparent, she had to be a parent, and who knew if that would ever happen for her?

At the moment, she didn't have a real job, she didn't have a place of her own, she didn't have a fiancé or even a boyfriend. Alicia Maxwell had stolen her man. Alicia Maxwell had stolen her life.

20

·····

Lily

Lily had been out past midnight at the benefit dance for the science museum, and when she got home, she'd still been wired, so she'd sat on her bed and typed her notes into her laptop while they were still fresh in her mind. She probably hadn't gotten to sleep until almost three a.m., and when her cell phone woke her at ten o'clock, her first instinct was to let it go to the message box. Then she opened one eye, dragged the phone to her from the bedside table, and saw that the call was from Eartha Yardley.

Instantly, Lily sat up, wide awake.

Eartha wanted Lily to come out to her house to discuss a job with her. How soon could she come? Eartha asked. Right away, Lily told her, clicked off the phone, and raced for the shower. She dressed hurriedly, grabbed the keys for the car, and raced outside.

Eartha Yardley's house sprawled between high sand dunes at Dionis. On either side of the steps to the front door, large stone dogs sat holding in their mouths stone baskets filled with fresh flowers. It was eleven o'clock in the morning when Lily knocked on the door.

From deep in the house, a little dog began to yap. As Lily waited, the dog's barking came closer, and then she saw the animal—a Shih Tzu, Lily thought—leaping up at the window, yapping and growling and throwing itself into a kind of gymnastic frenzy. But no person came to the door.

Lily knocked again. The dog's bark rose an octave. Lily peered in the window, but the light was wrong; she couldn't see whether or not anyone was coming.

Her cell phone rang. Lily reached into her bag and opened it.

"Lily, don't stand there like Lot's wife, come in. The door's not locked. Don't be afraid of Godzy, he won't bite." Eartha clicked off the phone before Lily could reply.

She pushed the door open and stepped inside. The little dog danced backward, as if Lily were a seven-headed monster. She knelt down. "Hello, Godzy."

But the animal was not to be won over so easily. It continued to bark so passionately it bounced.

The enormous room was *so* not Nantucket-style. Instead of blue, white, and simple, it was multicolored and crowded with antiques, paintings, art glass, tapestries, rugs, and deep, comfortable furniture more suited to a winter in the city than summer on the island.

The little dog raced down a hall and through a door. Lily followed. The bedroom had one wall that was entirely glass, and facing it was a queen-sized bed with a quilted headboard glittering with glass and colored beads. Lily had never seen anything like it.

In the middle of the bed, among crimson silk sheets, lay Eartha Yardley. Her blond hair, backcombed and sprayed into a stiff helmet, was dented on one side.

"God, I hate morning," she croaked. "Not thrilled by afternoon, either. Get me some water, not tap, that mineral stuff from the refrigerator."

"Sure. I'll be right back." Lily hurried from the room, through the living room, and out to the kitchen. All the appliances were state-of-the-art stainless steel, shining and new. She found a glass, poured the water, and returned to Eartha's bedroom.

"Thanks, dear." Eartha was sitting up in bed now, with Godzy in her lap. She sipped the water, shuddering. "Don't stand there gawking at me. I know exactly what an old horror I am in the morning. Walk around the room. Acquaint yourself with my closet. Sit down at my vanity over there and check out my jewelry. Not just the stuff that's out, open the drawers."

Lily obeyed, feeling like Alice in Wonderland Goes to Heaven.

The room was a tumult of discarded clothing, shoes, handbags, and underwear. The floor of the walk-in closet was a sea of silk and satin. She sat down at the handsome vanity, made of light wood and inlaid ivory, a kind of 1930s look. Jewelry was strewn and jumbled across the top as carelessly as shells tossed on the beach by the tide.

"You have so many beautiful things," Lily said.

"Yeah, well, don't get any bright ideas about taking something. I may act like an old fool but I know exactly what I have." Eartha struggled out of bed and went into her bathroom.

Lily opened the drawers on either side of the kneehole. The drawers were all lined with lots of slots and nests with velvet pockets holding rings, earrings, bracelets, necklaces, brooches. One drawer for pearls. One for sapphires. One for rubies. One for emeralds. Two for diamonds. She started sorting the heap of jewelry on top, matching pieces, and replacing them in their little nests.

Eartha came out of the bathroom. She wore a wildly printed caftan and she'd squashed her hair back into place. "Don't do that, honey." She came across the room, walking with the careful steps of someone with a hangover. She leaned one hand on the vanity. "Here." She pointed to a leather book on the floor. "We need to record everything." She crept around to a white silk chaise and collapsed on it. "I keep a record of what I wear to which events. Don't like to duplicate anything, you see, and I attend too many functions to just remember it all, presupposing I have any memory left in the first place."

Lily opened the book. It was a standard diary, one page for each day of the year. She read the last entry:

Luncheon. Kay's. Red silk. Gold chain. Gold bracelets.

Cocktails. Henry's. Paisley swirl skirt. White tunic. Turquoise and silver.

"So my last girl quit," Eartha announced as she lifted a cigarette from a silver case and stuck it in her mouth. "She'd been with me for a while, but she got engaged this winter, when I was down in my Key Biscayne place, and she just missed her fiancé too much and took off. Stupid girl. I pay well, and this is hardly coal mining."

As Eartha talked, her little dog timidly approached Lily. Lily held out her hand for Godzy to sniff. Godzy sniffed and jumped back as if singed, but gathered his courage and came back. After a few more moments, Lily was able to pick the little dog up and hold him in her lap.

"Godzy likes you," Eartha said. "That's a good sign. And you're pretty. I can't bear anyone unattractive. So what do you say? Six mornings a week, just two or three hours, helping me keep things organized."

"I'd love to do it." Lily couldn't believe she was going to be paid. This would be like playing in a fairy tale. "And it fits in very nicely with the little business my sisters and I have started. We call it Nantucket Mermaids, and we do all sorts of odd jobs."

"Cute," Eartha said dryly. "Just tell me who to make the checks to."

As she drove back to her house, Lily yawned until her jaw cracked. Tonight she had to attend a huge fund-raiser, and she needed to wash her hair and set it on rollers, so it would fall in a long relaxed wave like Angelina Jolie often wore hers. Eartha would be at the fund-raiser. Lily knew what Eartha was wearing but still hadn't figured out what she'd wear herself.

The house was empty and hot with late afternoon sun. She dug a protein bar out of her bag and absentmindedly chewed away at it as she went up the stairs, checked her answering machine, and double-checked her calendar. Good. Plenty of time for a little nap.

Cinnamon lay on Lily's bed, stretched out full length, stoned by sunshine. The sight made Lily so drowsy she couldn't keep her eyes open. She slipped off her clothes and collapsed on the bed. As she curled up and closed her eyes, she conjured up all those mind-blowing pieces of jewelry. Although Eartha talked incessantly, she hadn't disclosed much about herself, and Lily had promised she would use nothing Eartha told her in her arts and entertainment column. But a girl could dream, and Lily let her thoughts drift. Eartha had no children of her own. She'd had several husbands, but was unattached now and it seemed her closest companion was Godzy. As Lily relaxed and drifted toward sleep, she allowed herself a little fantasy. What if Eartha came to really care for Lily? It was not impossible. What if Eartha kind of adopted Lily? What if she said, in her careless way, "Oh, Lily, I have so much jewelry. Whenever I see you at various parties, you're never wearing anything real. Why don't you choose a couple of nice pieces of mine to keep for yourself? I don't need them, and you have such a pretty, smooth neck. They'd look ravishing on you, don't you think?"

Lily fell asleep with a smile on her face.

She was wakened from a deep sleep by a loud thud as the door to her room was slammed open so hard it hit the wall. Emma stormed into the room, her face like thunder. Abbie was right behind, her mouth tense.

"Lily, it is not going to start all over again." Emma was practically snarling.

Lily sat up. "What? What's going on?"

Emma echoed, in a little girl's voice, *"What's going on?"*

"Emma, calm down," Abbie said softly.

"I'll tell you what's going on." Emma's voice was shaking. "Abbie and I have been working all day long and we've got jobs tonight, but *she* cleaned the kitchen before she left this morning and *I* cleaned the bathrooms and washed and dried and folded all the towels and we left the Old Clunker for you. All we asked *you* was to stop by the grocery store, and you couldn't even be bothered to do that?"

"I don't know what you're talking about," Lily protested.

"I'm talking about the list I left on the kitchen table!" Emma retorted. "With your name printed at the top in bright red letters. Don't tell me you didn't see it."

"But I *didn't* see it," Lily insisted.

"Oh, come on, Lily, how could you miss it?" Even Abbie seemed cranky.

Lily thought. "I guess I didn't go into the kitchen today. I just got dressed and drove out to Eartha's, and grabbed some coffee on the way."

Emma threw her hands up. "Of course you did. Of course you just took care of yourself and didn't bother to think of any of the rest of us who might have plans, or need the car, or that we're out of toilet paper—"

Abbie added, "You can't just live here like it's your hotel and we're your maids. You're not a baby any longer, even if you want to be."

Lily stared at her older sister in dismay. Abbie had always been so loving to Lily, so protective, so kind. Lily had been Abbie's little darling. She couldn't believe what Abbie was saying.

"It's not my fault," Lily argued sullenly. "I just didn't go into the kitchen."

"Lily." Abbie's tone was more reasonable now. She took Emma's hand and pulled her over to sit on Lily's bed next to her. "I think you all just assumed that when I returned, I'd take care of the house like I always did."

"I didn't think that," Lily retorted. Her thoughts were whirling. Of course she'd assumed that. That was what Abbie did. Abbie took care of the house and Abbie took care of Lily. Lily wanted the old Abbie back.

"But I'm working now," Abbie continued.

"And I am, too." Emma was calmer now. "We both have morning jobs and afternoon jobs and usually evening jobs, too. It's not fair to expect Abbie and me to do all the house stuff, too."

Lily stared at the wall and didn't respond.

Abbie said, "I have a suggestion. Let's get together, the three of us, and work out a schedule of duties. I'm sure Lily wants to pull her own weight, do her share. Right, Lily?"

Lily nodded, but inside a fierce little devil was throwing a tantrum. No, she didn't really want to do any of the housework. Who would?

Emma said, "That means you're going to have to schedule your chores into your days. You're going to have to set your alarm clock and get up before noon and not spend so much time lying on the beach or visiting your friends."

Lily hated it, how Emma was making her sound so irresponsible! Then she remembered her news. "Oh! I wanted to tell you! Eartha Yardley has asked me to help her organize and take care of her clothes. She wants me to work every morning. So I won't be sleeping until noon anymore!" She looked triumphantly at Emma.

"Eartha Yardley. Wow. How did you meet her?" Abbie asked.

"At a cocktail party. She asked me to get her a drink, and I did, and we talked. She phoned me this morning, and I went over to see her. She said I'm *pretty.*" Pleasure bubbled through Lily as she remembered the compliment.

"Okay, so you have two jobs now," Emma said. "So do we—"

Lily interrupted Emma, rushing to tell the rest. "I told her that my sisters and I have a company called Nantucket Mermaids. I thought it would be a real coup if her name was added to the list of clients."

"That's true, Lily," Abbie agreed. "It would upscale our image and impress prospective employers. Thanks for thinking of us."

"So I'm a Nantucket Mermaid now?" Lily asked.

"Oh, for heaven's sake, Lily," Emma said grumpily. "It's just a name."

But Abbie pretended she had a sword in her hand and touched Lily on both shoulders as if she were being knighted. "I hereby dub you a Nantucket Mermaid."

"But you still have to help with the household chores," Emma said.

21
· · · · ·

Marina

Wednesday morning, Marina helped Sheila Lester and two strong male volunteers carry the boxes of discarded books out to Sheila's truck. Some books were in such bad shape, stained with food or water or worse, that they couldn't be read. Others were out-of-date reference books, and some were old paperback novels and antiquated scientific tomes that had been put out for sale at only pennies and never chosen.

"It's kind of sad," Marina said as she climbed up into the cab of Sheila's truck. "Throwing books away."

"I know what you mean," Sheila agreed, yanking down on the gearshift and steering away from the curb. "But the old has to make way for the new. Besides, a lot of the books are still available, just in a different format." She looked over at Marina. "So, have you been out to the Madaket Mall before?"

"The Madaket Mall? No."

Sheila laughed. "That's what we call the recycling shed. That's where we'll drop off the books. That's where everyone finds treasures. I'm not kidding you. Just follow me. I dive right in. Everyone does. You'll see."

Sheila was right, Marina discovered. At the end of the landfill parking lot was a large wooden shed. Inside the shed were tables piled with discarded but perfectly good items: clothing, books, housewares, toys. Various people pawed through the garments or studied the pots and pans, and some of the people appeared poor and some of the people appeared privileged.

"Aha!" Sheila held up a man's short-sleeved polo shirt. "L.L. Bean. Spotless, not a tear. Perfect for my husband." She dove back into the pile.

A swirl of blue and turquoise caught Marina's eye. She pulled it out from under the mountain of clothing and held it up. It was a batik bedspread. If she folded it just right, it would make a dynamite sarong. She draped it over her arm and set off to search the rest of the shed.

At the back of the building, next to some battered pots and chipped fine china, was an old portable record player. She smiled and reached out to stroke it, as if it were a friendly old beast. Her mother had one like this when she was a child. Did it still work? She'd brought her iPod, but this was kind of tantalizing. On the floor sat a cardboard box of records. She knelt. Patti Page: "Old Cape Cod," "Tennessee Waltz." Rosemary Clooney: "Sway." Jo Stafford: "You Belong to Me." The Mills Brothers: "Up a Lazy River." Lilting melodies drifted through Marina's mind.

"Take it home." Sheila stood next to her, her arms filled with clothing. "If it doesn't work, we can bring it back."

"You know, I think I will," Marina said.

Loaded with loot, they drove back to town.

"How's your summer going?" Sheila asked.

Marina considered her answer. "It's odd. Sometimes it seems to go fast, and sometimes it seems to be absolutely stopped still. When I have something planned, if I'm at a play or a lecture, time speeds along. But if I have a few empty hours, and especially when I come home to an empty cottage at night, then an hour lasts forever. I suppose part of it is that I always used to have someone to talk to about the little things. Insignificant things, like I stubbed my toe on the sidewalk and tripped and felt like everyone was laughing at me. Or I saw a cute dress I'd like to buy. Back home, I always had Gerry, my husband, my ex-husband, to talk to, or one of my friends. Here, I have no one. I'm not complaining. I love being here, and I chose to be here. I guess sometimes I'm just lonely."

"Sometimes you can be lonely right in the middle of a marriage," Sheila told her.

"Yes. I guess that's true. But since I've been here, I've come to realize that my nature is gregarious. I like people. I like working with people. Gerry and I had a really first-class office and a staff of twelve and dozens of clients, and maybe, for sure in the last few years, I let myself get too busy, too pressured. But I liked it all, and I miss it."

"What made you decide to spend so much time here alone?"

Marina took a deep breath. "My husband and my best friend fell in love. They're going to have a baby in September. I sold him my part of the business and my half of our condo. And I came here. To get away, I guess. To get away from all the people who know about them, to get away from my anger. To start over."

"A lot of people come here for just that reason," Sheila said.

"That's good to know."

At the Foxes' house, Sheila pulled into the driveway and parked near the garage. Jumping out, she helped Marina carry her plunder inside.

"Wow," Sheila said, noticing the walls. "What a luscious blue!"

"Can you stay for some tea?" Marina asked.

"Sure."

"I chose the color and painted the walls myself." She took a pitcher of tea out of the refrigerator as she talked, filled two glasses with ice and tea, and garnished them with mint from a little pot in her window. She set a plate of shortbread on the coffee table and sat down on the sofa, facing Sheila. "It's probably an odd thing to do, to paint a place I'll be in for only a few months, but you know, I found it very satisfying."

"I can imagine that. Making my lightship baskets does the same for me."

"How long have you lived on the island?" Marina asked.

Sheila took a piece of shortbread. "All my life, really. I was born here. Went to school here. Went off to college, met my husband. He's a pharmacist, so he could work pretty much anywhere. We moved around for a while but when I got pregnant, we decided to move here for good."

"How many children do you have?"

"Two. Kirsten's twenty-two and Roger's twenty-six. They both live in California now, but I wouldn't be surprised if they moved back here eventually. I hope they do. I love having them around." She paused. "Do you have children?"

"No. I tried. I couldn't get pregnant."

"That's so sad. I'm sorry."

"Thanks. And it is sad. I've spent a lot of time being sad, and angry at fate, and resentful. Now my husband of fifteen years is having a baby with my best friend and I'm driving myself nuts with jealousy. I've got to stop wasting time on regrets and self-pity. I want to move on. I want to enjoy life."

"Well, Nantucket's the right place to come if you want to enjoy life."

"I think you're right. So far, I'm having a great time. And"—she couldn't help smiling—"I'm having Jim Fox here for dinner Friday night."

"Well, well." Sheila's face brightened. "First the Downy Flake and now an intimate dinner here."

"He took me to Tuckernuck a couple of days ago. We spent the afternoon together. He seems like a nice man."

"He is. He did a swell job of raising his three daughters after his wife died."

"How did she die?" Marina asked.

"I think I'll let Jim tell you about that." Sheila stood up. "Let's see if this record player works."

Marina set the little machine on the kitchen counter and plugged the cord into the socket. A small light came on and the turntable began to revolve. Sliding a round black vinyl record out of its jacket, she laid it carefully on the turntable and set the needle gently into the groove.

A honeyed male voice began to sing "Blue Moon." The silken tones swirled up into the air, slow, mellow, golden.

"Gosh, this record isn't even scratched," Sheila said. "You're going to have fun with this." She set her glass in the sink. "I've got to get home. Thanks for the tea."

"Thanks for the ride out to the mall."

"We'll do it again sometime. Have fun Friday. And be good, Marina. Everyone loves Jim Fox."

Friday evening, the air was soft and warm. Marina stepped out of the shower and dressed in a pale blue tee shirt and the blue and turquoise batik swoop of cotton she'd found Wednesday at the recycling shed. She'd washed it, cut and hemmed it, and it fell smoothly around her hips. She creamed her skin, which was nicely tanned and glowing from a day in the sun, flicked on a coat of mascara and a pale gloss of lipstick. She pulled her blond hair back in a low pony-tail and slipped some silver bangles over her wrist.

She didn't use perfume. The cottage smelled tantalizingly of the beef bourguignonne simmering on the back burner. She'd decided Jim might like beef for a change—she knew he had the opportunity to eat plenty of fish. A crisp salad waited to be dressed, and she'd made a chocolate cake this morning as she listened to all her new old records. When had she last made a cake? She couldn't remember an occasion. She'd always taken Gerry out to some posh restaurant for his birthday.

She padded barefoot around the small cottage, not really double-checking everything as much as simply enjoying it. She'd bought new wineglasses and some nice red wines for this evening. She'd taken her computer, newspapers, letters, and other paraphernalia off the little table and set it with the plain white plates and inexpensive utensils that had come with the cottage, then she'd turned off the electric lights and put lighted candles all around. The gentle glow made everything appear antique and lustrous.

It surprised her, how her heart leapt when she heard his knock at the door.

He came in, presenting her with a bottle of red wine. They talked easily as she poured them each a glass and settled on the sofa. She'd put out a plate of cheese and crackers and relaxed as he re-galed her with a humorous account of his day's latest crisis: helping an octogenarian get her cat from its terrified perch in the top of a tree.

"My gosh," she said, "your life is a Norman Rockwell painting."

Jim laughed. He wore khakis and a green rugby shirt. "Some-times it seems like that, I know. One of the good things about living on an isolated island." He took a sip of wine. "Tell me about Kansas City."

"Well, I don't know any octogenarians," she told him. "Actu-ally, now that I think about it, I didn't know any of our neighbors in the condo. We—my ex-husband, Gerry, and I—really used the place as a kind of crash pad, we were so busy working. And I never spent any time near cats or trees, although there's an excellent park in Kansas City, Swope Park. It's got a first-class zoo, and lots of great places to walk or hike. And the Starlight Theater is there. And the Nelson Museum of Art, which has a sensational collection."

They kept to safe, light topics as they ate. Jim had two helpings of her beef bourguignonne, which pleased Marina. He seemed completely at ease. She was relaxed, too, but that was because of the wine. She still couldn't figure out what kind of relationship they were headed for.

When she brought out the cake, he lit up.

"Chocolate cake. I don't know when I've had a homemade cake."

She set it before him. "Do your daughters cook?"

"They're all busy working." He ate the cake as if he were starving, as if he hadn't just had a full meal.

"I've only met one. Lily."

"The youngest." He licked his fork. "God, that was good."

"Would you like another piece?"

He grinned. "Maybe in awhile. Leaning back in his chair, he said, "My two oldest daughters were living off-island—that's what we say when anyone from here lives anywhere else in the entire world—but they've come home for the summer."

"I guess it's the season to make money, with the summer tourists."

"Right. And Emma, that's my middle daughter, well, she's had a tough time recently. She lost her job in Boston, and the man she was engaged to broke off with her to be with another woman."

Marina groaned. "She has my sympathy." But she didn't want to talk about Gerry and that whole sad mess right now, not on this soft, sensual evening, with this handsome and pleasant man sitting so near. "And what about your oldest?"

"Abbie. I'm not sure just why she came home. She's been gone for almost two years. I wasn't sure she'd ever come back for any length of time."

"Would you like some decaf?" Marina asked.

"That sounds good."

She was glad to have something to do as she moved around the kitchen. She could sense how their conversation had deepened. Quite a few of the men she knew somehow kept their work and family life separate, but she could tell that whatever Jim was about, his daughters were an integral part.

She set the cup in front of him. "Tell me about Abbie."

He stirred a bit of sugar into his decaf, slowly, thinking. "She was fifteen when my wife died. She was always a responsible girl, and she really took charge. She pretty much raised Emma and Lily."

"What was she like before your wife died?" Marina asked.

"I think that's the first time anyone's asked me that. You know, I have to think about it." He smiled at a memory. "She was always bossy, even as a child. When she was about twelve, she told us she was going to be an anthropologist. She wanted to travel all over the world and study strange cultures." A shadow crossed over his face. "Abbie didn't get the chance to go to college. Her mother died, and she stayed to help with her sisters. I don't know what I would have done without her." He squinted down into his cup as if seeing the past there. "Perhaps I gave her too much responsibility."

Marina prompted, "And your middle girl? Emma?"

"Emma's our smart one. Not that all my girls aren't smart. But Emma made straight A's in school. Won a scholarship to college. Graduated magna cum laude. Worked for an investment broker until just recently. She's always been the organized one, kept her bedroom neat, had a bunch of dolls, changed their clothes every day." He shook his head. "I'm a little worried about her. She's having a tough time, losing her job and her fiancé, although I never cared for Duncan. I think in the long run it will be a good thing that he's broken off with her."

"And Lily? She's a lovely girl."

"Thank you. She is. I suppose I spoiled Lily. I suppose we all did. She was only seven when her mother died. So we all treated Lily like a fragile china doll. She's kind of used to getting her own way. But to give her credit, she's done a great job over the past year, keeping the house tidy and making us some decent meals." He looked at Marina. "You don't have any children?"

"No." It was always hard to say this. "I couldn't have any."

Jim reached over and touched her cheek. "You would have had beautiful children."

He kept his hand on her cheek, and it seemed the most natural thing in the world, to turn her head so that her mouth touched his hand. She heard his breath change and her own pulse sped up. When he dropped his hand, she was disappointed, but he pushed back his chair and rose and moved next to her.

"Come here," he said softly, putting his hand on her shoulder.

She stood up. They looked at each other and then Jim wrapped his arms around her and brought her close to him. She nestled her head on his shoulder and leaned into him. He kissed the side of her neck and ran his hands down her back. She turned her head, longing for his mouth on hers. But he continued to kiss her neck, her cheek, her collarbone. She put her hands on his shoulders, loving the strong, meaty, male heft of his muscles. She inched as close to him as she could, and felt his erection straining between them.

"Let's go up to the loft," she whispered.

He held her away from him. "You're sure?"

"I'm sure." She kept her hand on him as she bent down to blow out the candles on the table. "I've got candles upstairs—"

A knock sounded at the door.

The door flew open and Lily burst into the cottage. She wore a tight black dress and high black heels and a black velvet headband in her long red hair.

"Hi, guys!"

Marina dropped Jim's hand.

"For God's sake, Lily," Jim said huskily, "you don't just barge into someone's home."

Lily rolled her eyes. "Sor-ry! I just got home from a fund-raiser and saw your note that you were down here, Dad, and I couldn't wait to tell you, I met Joe Kennedy tonight!"

"Would you like some cake?" Marina asked. She hoped the young woman couldn't tell how she was trembling with frustration.

"No, thanks," Lily said impatiently. "I—oh!" Lily stepped back, as if she'd just received a thousand-volt shock. "You're wearing Mom's bedspread!"

"What?" Confused, Marina looked from Lily to Jim and back.

"That's Mom's bedspread. I know it is. I'd know that material anywhere. Don't you recognize it, Dad?"

"Honey," Jim said. "She's wearing a skirt."

"No, Dad! Look! It's a bedspread. Mom always had it on the chaise in her bedroom. Marina's just tied it on like a skirt." Lily reached out and grabbed the knot at Marina's waist. "You shouldn't be wearing this!"

Marina stepped back. "I found it at the recycling bin at the dump. Sheila Lester told me we could take anything we wanted."

Lily's lips thinned in frustration. She glared at her father. "What are you doing here anyway, Dad?"

"Like I said in the note. I'm having dinner. And I was having a nice time."

Lily pouted. "I want to tell you about Joe Kennedy." She shot her father a sullen glance. "I guess I'll just wait till you come home."

"Or you can tell us both now," Jim suggested. "I'm sure Marina would like to hear."

Lily shook her head. "I'm tired. I'm going home to bed." She glared at her father. "Are you coming?"

"In awhile," he said mildly.

Lily spun around and stormed out the door into the night.

"Well, there goes a good advertisement for birth control," Jim joked weakly.

Marina managed to fake a smile.

Jim put his hands on Marina's shoulders. "I'm sorry about that. Can we try all this again, another time?"

"Sure," Marina said. She allowed him to pull her against him, but now they were both stiff and ill at ease.

He kissed her forehead. "Well, thanks for the meal. It was exceptional. And the company was, too."

"You're welcome."

"Listen, Marina. Let's do something tomorrow night, okay? We'll go somewhere—dinner, or a concert, something, okay?"

"I'd like that," she told him.

She hid her disappointment and smiled at him as he went out the door.

22

·····

Abbie

Monday afternoon, Abbie tapped on the front door of the Parker house, then turned the knob and let herself in. Usually Harry and his father were in the kitchen, finishing lunch when she arrived, but today Harry came racing down the hall, jumping up and down with excitement. His striped tee shirt was on backward and inside out, with the tag showing under his neck.

"Daddy sprained his ankle! He fell on his bike and we had to go to the hospital and *everything*!"

Abbie followed the little boy into the living room where Howell Parker lay on the sofa in shorts and a tee shirt, his ankle elevated on a pillow, his computer on his lap. Piles of bound research reports and statistical reprints ranged around the floor.

"My goodness," Abbie said.

"I'm such a jerk." Howell smiled ruefully. "I took Harry out biking last night. Rented one of those cool tandem bikes. We were zipping along—"

"We were going really *fast*!" Harry interjected.

"Hit a bump and stuck out my foot to stop, and hit a brick and *ouch*! In one second, a sprained ankle."

"Does it hurt?" Abbie asked.

"I've got pain pills. Of course they interfere with my work, so I'm trying to stay off them."

"I'm *helping* Daddy!" Harry told Abbie.

"He is," Howell confirmed. "He brings me water, and apples, and sometimes books off my desk."

"And your red pencil!"

"And my red pencil."

"How are you managing meals?" she asked.

"I'm not completely helpless. I can hop around. We did pretty well for breakfast and lunch. And there's always takeout."

"How long will you be in a cast?"

"Four weeks."

"Can your wife come home?"

Howell shrugged. "Maybe next weekend. Maybe not."

From what Abbie remembered of the kitchen, food was not exactly abundant. "I'll just check your supplies."

She went into the kitchen and quickly scanned the cupboards and refrigerator.

Back in the living room, she said, "Why don't I take Harry with me to the grocery store? We can get lots of fresh fruits and veggies and some frozen dinners and some healthy snacks. Oh, and you're almost out of milk."

"That's a great idea, Abbie. You're a lifesaver."

His smile was so warm, Abbie felt herself blush. Any woman who looked at him probably blushed, she thought. He was so handsome. And sitting there like that, with his long legs bare . . . she could just see the line of pale skin at the hem of his shorts. *Oh, man!* Abbie thought, *get yourself in control, girl!*

She knelt down to face Harry. "Let's see. Teeth brushed? Is this the way you want to wear your shirt?" She gently touched the tag on the neck.

To her surprise, Harry's face crumbled. "I put it on backward! I did it wrong!" His arms flew frantically as he yanked his tee shirt over his head.

"That's all right," she quickly assured the little boy.

"Hey, sport." Howell strained to reach his son. "Don't worry about it. It's summer, it's the island, we can dress any way we want."

Howell gathered his son to him, nudging his laptop over onto the sofa to make room for Harry.

Abbie sensed it was a good time to leave the boy with his father. "I'll make a grocery list."

By the time she returned, list in her hand, Harry's shirt was on the right way and he was smiling.

"If you go into the right-hand drawer in my desk," Howell told her, "you'll find my checkbook. Bring it to me, and I'll sign a check for the groceries."

"I'll get it, Daddy!" Harry yelled. He raced from the room.

Abbie smiled at Howell. "He's a good little boy."

"Perhaps too good," Howell softly responded. "I worry about him."

"He worries about you."

"I know. You're good for him, Abbie. You lighten him up. It's only been five days, and already I can see a change." He quickly added, "Not that I intend for you to be responsible for his mental welfare, I don't mean that. I'm just saying I'm happy you're his nanny."

"So am I." Standing there, so close to Howell, Abbie felt a warm glow in her belly. Their connection was more than friendly. She knew that she was more voluptuous, more shapely, than his size-zero wife. When she was a teenager, her weight and lanky form had bothered her, but over the years she'd gained confidence. Her body worked well for her, and perhaps it wasn't the current rage but she didn't care about that. She knew he was very much aware of her full breasts and rounded hips. His gaze was almost a caress.

"*Abbie*." Howell spoke her name as if he were tasting it. "Is that short for Abigail?"

"Right." Wanting to make herself more interesting to him, she added, "I don't feel like an Abigail, though, and certainly not a *Gail*. Still, I have options."

"Interesting. Whereas, with Howell, that's pretty much it." He grinned. "Of course, you can guess what they called me when I was a boy."

"Oh, *Owl!*" Abbie said. "You must have been such a darling little boy."

"And you are a pretty darling big girl," Howell told her.

She flushed, but did not turn away. As he sat gazing at her, a blush rose up his neck to his cheeks.

"Here it is, Daddy!" Harry ran back into the room, brandishing the checkbook.

"I have an idea," Abbie said as Howell bent to write out the check. "It's going to turn cloudy this afternoon. After I take Harry to the beach later on, why don't I come back and make some casseroles? I can make a mac and cheese for Harry and a lasagna for you, and they can last several nights."

"I'd like that," Howell told her.

Rain drizzled down the windowpanes and spattered against the house when the wind tossed it, and the sky had turned inky dark. Abbie turned on the lights in the Parkers' kitchen and she moved around with ease and confidence as she cooked. She loved the smell of sautéed onions and the rich swirl of tomato sauce. She hummed as she worked.

Harry lay on the floor, underneath the table, with his horses and some of the kitchen utensils. She'd suggested he make a pen with spoons and forks. Harry had been appalled at first—his mother didn't allow him to play with kitchenware. They'd get dirty. Abbie assured him everything could go into the dishwasher when the day was over.

Five o'clock came much sooner than she'd expected.

She returned to the living room. Howell was poring over a printout of numbers.

"Is it five o'clock already?" he asked.

"It is." She didn't want to leave. She wanted to be turned to stone, to stand there forever, staring at the man.

No. Not stone. Not just staring.

"Abbie," Howell said. "Don't go. Stay. Have a drink with me. Have dinner with us."

Behind her, Harry yelled, "Yay! Stay, Abbie, *stay!*"

"Well . . ." She had another babysitting job tonight, in town, at eight o'clock. She could bike there in fifteen minutes. "And I could help Harry get ready for bed."

"I'd love it if you'd stay," Howell told her.

"All right," she decided. She knew she was blushing. "I'll just . . . check something in the kitchen."

Because Harry was shadowing her, she took down the salad bowl and washed the lettuces and dried them in the spinner, but when he ran out of the room, she held her hands under running water, then splashed cold water on her face.

What do you think you're doing? she asked herself.

Just having dinner with an employer, she responded tartly.

Cooler, she returned to the living room. Harry was allowed to watch thirty minutes of a DVD before dinner because Sydney believed it calmed him down. He sat before the TV, completely engrossed. Abbie poured Howell a glass of red wine. When she brought it to him, Howell put his papers down and struggled up out of his slouch.

"Abbie, don't you want a glass of wine, too? And move that chair closer so we can talk without disturbing Harry."

She brought the chair near him and poured herself a glass of wine. For a moment they sat together, listening to the rain beat against the windows, watching Harry stare at the DVD.

Howell asked, "So, Abbie, were you born on the island?"

"I was. I'm a real true native. As we say, homegrown."

"Lucky you. And you've always taken care of children?"

"Yes, well . . . My mother died when I was fifteen. My younger sister Emma was thirteen but my baby sister, Lily, was only seven. So I pretty much raised her."

"Oh, gosh, I'm sorry about your mother, Abbie. That's tough . . ."

Abbie nodded and changed the subject. "I love being with Harry. He's a really special little boy."

Howell glanced over at his son. "He is. I often wish I had more time to spend with him."

"But you're here for him most of the time. And you're doing really important work."

"You know, I believe I am. Especially after nine-eleven. This paper I'm working on outlines new guidelines and suggestions for minimizing the volume and toxicity of hazardous wastes in the workplace. For example, we can install more efficient chemical-fume hoods in our laboratories, and more efficient lighting." Howell grew animated as he spoke. Cleary he was passionate about his subject. "Wait. Am I boring you?"

"Not at all," Abbie answered truthfully. He could have been reciting the dictionary and she would have found him fascinating.

Obviously he was eager to talk about his work. He went on until Harry's DVD ended, and then he hobbled into the kitchen and chatted with his son as Abbie put dinner on the kitchen table. As they sat eating, he continued telling her about the proper disposal of hazardous materials and protecting the natural ecosystem. Abbie listened intently, trying to make sense of it all. If it mattered to him, she wanted to understand. She put out fresh fruit for dessert, but Harry was already yawning.

"I think it's time for his bath and bed," she said.

"Right. Right. God, I've done it again, blathered away and bored my child to sleep." Howell reached over to tousle his son's white curls. "Hey, guy, why don't you let Abbie give you your bath. I'll come up and read you a book when you're in bed."

Harry said obediently, "Okay, Daddy."

Abbie loved this time of the day. Loved the soothing tumble of the water into the bathtub and the restful scents of baby shampoo and soap. Loved wrapping Harry in a big, warm, soft towel, holding him on her lap as she rubbed his hair dry. Loved helping him into his pajamas—covered with running horses—and hearing his bare feet pad against the floor as he went into his bedroom. Harry knelt in front of his bookshelf to choose a book.

Abbie called down the stairs. "Harry's ready for his book."

She waited at the top of the stairs as Howell came hobbling up, one hand on the banister, the other holding on to his crutch. It seemed entirely natural for him, when he got to the top of the stairs, to put his arm around her shoulders for support. They went into Harry's room, Abbie aware of the living warmth of Howell all up and down, next to her side. He was taller than she was, and she was tall.

Harry was on the far side of the room, intently scanning books, his back to them. When they got to Harry's bed, Howell kept his arm around Abbie's shoulders. He looked down at her face. He didn't speak. He was close enough to kiss. The physical attraction between them was undeniable. She allowed the connection to last for a few moments, then pulled away.

She knelt next to the little boy. "Harry? Have you found your book yet?"

"This one." Harry held up a book with horses on the cover.

Howell said, "Abbie, stay for a while."

"I can't." She met his glance. "Really, I can't. I have another babysitting job."

"Then tomorrow night?"

"I don't know," she said. *What was he asking her, really?* She hugged the little boy and kissed his sweet-smelling head. "Good night, Harry! I'll see you tomorrow!"

Harry hugged her tight. "Good night, Abbie."

She fled down the stairs and out of the house.

Emma

Emma's days had developed a routine.

She spent her mornings taking dictation from a fragile woman who wanted to write her memoirs but was too afflicted with arthritis to type on a keyboard or hold a pen. Francine had been an administrative assistant for the chief financial officer of an international insurance company, and her memories were rife with tales of office politics, confrontations, and executive backstabbings that she recounted in a rambling, emotional rush of words. Emma couldn't imagine that this memoir would ever be published, but she could tell that the struggle to remember and to relate brought meaning to Francine's days.

After Francine, Emma had a free hour for an early lunch. She returned home, swooped hurriedly around the kitchen, putting together a meal in the Crock-Pot or concocting potato salad or rice salad or macaroni and cheese, something to be eaten with fresh fish if their father had some, or cold cuts. She and her sisters had made a list of the necessary chores to keep their house running smoothly. Because Abbie often worked late out at the Parkers', Emma took on the duty of organizing the family dinners. Abbie went to the grocery store twice a week, at six in the morning, before it got crowded, for in the summers it was always so crowded it was difficult to find a place to park. That left the general housework to Lily, who had agreed she'd vacuum, dust, clean the bathrooms, and mop the kitchen floor once a week, whenever she had some free time. Their plan seemed to be working, so far.

At one, Emma went to read to Millicent Bracebridge. She'd gotten into the habit of doubling the batch of homemade treats she made for her family and taking some with her to the Bracebridge house. Chocolate chip cookies. Lemon squares. Blueberry scones. She pretended they were for Millicent, and the old woman did enjoy them, but really they were for Spencer, who often stopped by for lunch.

Today a steady Noah's Ark rain drummed down. Emma stepped into the Bracebridge front hall, set her umbrella in the stand, and hung her raincoat on the antique coatrack.

"Hello!" she called, hurrying into the living room.

"Who is it?" The older woman raised her head off her chest. Her voice was rusty.

"It's me, Mrs. Bracebridge. Emma Fox. Here to read to you. And I've brought some oatmeal cookies." She wrapped her arms around herself, shivering. "It's cold in here today. Why don't I make a fire?"

"That would be very nice."

"Well, then, let me check to be sure the flue's open . . ." Emma had gotten into the habit of enumerating her actions as she performed them, for Millicent's sake. *She* would want any relative stranger moving around her home while she was unable to see what exactly they were doing, to do the same for her. "All right, now. There's plenty of kindling in the box, but I think I'll need some old newspaper . . ."

"There's a pile in the pantry for recycling," Millicent told her.

"Great. I'll go get it. And I'll put water on for tea."

As she walked down the long hall to the kitchen, Emma felt as if she were in an eccentric sort of museum on a Sunday evening. Outside the pouring rain droned down the windows, keeping all the rooms in a dim gray gloom. Portraits of long-deceased Bracebridge ancestors glowered down at Emma as she went, clearly disapproving of everything they saw. The dish towels hanging in the kitchen were old and thin and embroidered long ago by Millicent or her mother. The old Blue Willow dishes rested on an antique cupboard just as they had for decades, and even the teakettle Emma filled with water seemed ancient.

Returning to the living room, she screwed the papers up into long rolls and stuffed them under the grate, arranged the kindling in a pyramid, and lit a match. The fire flared up and caught, and Emma dropped some split logs on top.

"My, that's just what the doctor ordered," Millicent said. "Wheel me closer, would you, please?"

Emma obeyed. "You must be cold in that light dress. Let me get you a sweater or a shawl."

"I think that would be a good idea. Thank you."

Finally it was all organized, shawl, tea, fire, and cookies on a plate. Emma fetched the Agatha Christie from the bookcase.

"Spencer probably won't come today," Millicent said sadly. "Not in this rain."

"That's all right," Emma told her. "We're at a really good spot in the book, and what could be more perfect weather than this for reading Agatha Christie!"

She curled up on the sofa, opened the book to the marked page, and began to read.

"Hello!"

The front door slammed and Spencer arrived, shaking water off his raincoat and stamping his feet.

"What a day!" He dropped his coat over the back of a chair and crossed the room to kiss his grandmother. Today he wore gray slacks, a white shirt, a blue blazer. "Hello, Grams. You've got a fire. Clever girl. Hello, Emma."

"Emma has brought you oatmeal cookies today," Millicent said.

Emma blushed. "They're for you, Mrs. Bracebridge."

The older woman snorted.

"Well, if they're not for you, then I'll just eat them all," Spencer said. Reaching over, he lifted the cookies off the thin china plate his grandmother was holding. "Yum. Good."

Mrs. Bracebridge touched the plate with her fingers. "Did you take *my* cookies?"

"No, I took *my* cookies." He threw himself into a chair. "Since Emma made them all for me."

"Impudent!" Mrs. Bracebridge scolded, but she smiled in spite of herself. Almost anything Spencer did pleased her.

"Is there enough tea for me, Emma?"

Emma poured him a cup. By now, she knew how he liked it,

without milk or sugar. When she leaned forward to hand it to him, their fingers touched, and Spencer smiled at her. She felt herself blush again.

"Listen, Grams, I have a proposition for you. The NHA is organizing a show about sailor's valentines and other shellwork. You've got so many good pieces here. Would you consider loaning them to the museum for their exhibition?"

"I don't know." Mrs. Bracebridge shifted uncomfortably in her chair. "Some of them are very valuable, you know. Very old."

"That's why we want to exhibit them. It is the NHA, Grams."

"Would they be in cases?"

"Behind glass? Probably. I'll have to check with the curator of the exhibit." He sipped his tea and continued, "Really, Grams, you ought to think about giving some of this stuff to the historical association. Especially since you can't even see it."

"I think your mother expects me to bequeath it to her. She'll want to sell it."

"Is that what Gramps would want you to do? You know how much he loved Nantucket. And come on, Mom's got plenty of money."

Mrs. Bracebridge cleared her throat. "Perhaps we should discuss family matters later."

"Sure," Spencer agreed easily. "But think about loaning us the shell work, okay?"

"Dear child, I almost always do whatever you ask, don't I?"

"You do, I know. I just wish your treasures were available for the public to see."

"You have always been entirely too enchanted by the island," Mrs. Bracebridge told him with a sniff.

"I suppose that's true." He reached over and patted her hand. "But so have you. Tell me I'm not right." When his grandmother smiled, he said, "And by the way. I'm giving a lecture at the Whaling Museum next Tuesday. Why don't you have Emma bring you?"

"Oh," Emma said, blushing. "Won't your mother want to take Mrs. Bracebridge?"

Both Spencer and his grandmother laughed as if she'd said something witty.

"The only things my mother likes about this island are the tennis and the cocktail parties," Spencer explained.

"Yes, my daughter-in-law is not a history buff," Mrs. Bracebridge said. "Funny that you're so connected to it, Spencer."

"I'm rebelling," he joked. He stood up. "I've got to get back. Emma, thanks for the cookies, they were yummy." Leaning over, he kissed his grandmother's cheek. "So, ladies, it's a date for next Tuesday, right?"

Flustered, Emma stuttered, "Well, well, I–I don't know. I'm not sure."

"Please come. There's going to be a little reception afterward."

Suddenly Mrs. Bracebridge began to tremble. "I hate being observed in my wheelchair!"

"Too bad. I want you to attend my talk."

"I won't be able to *see* you."

"You'll be able to hear me. And I want you to hear all the applause. Don't even think you're getting out of this, Grams." Grabbing up his raincoat, Spencer pulled it on and hurried out the door.

"What an impertinent young man he can be sometimes!" Mrs. Bracebridge sniffed.

"He really loves you," Emma assured her. "He wants to show off for you."

"He wants to show off for *you*," her employer said.

Truthfully, Emma objected, "Oh, I hardly think—"

"This is not the first lecture my grandson has ever given. But it's the first he's ever insisted I attend, with my companion. You're a smart young woman. Connect the dots."

Emma rose to put another log on the fire. She told herself that was what caused her burning cheeks.

Sitting back on the sofa, she picked up the book. "Shall I continue reading?"

"Of course. But first, did the wretched child really eat all the cookies, or did he leave me some?"

Emma put three cookies on her employer's plate. Then she settled in to read.

24
· · · · ·

Lily

Could life get more complicated? She liked being busy, but this was ridiculous.

She'd spent all day finishing up her articles for this week's issue of the magazine. She'd told Eartha that on Saturdays she couldn't work because that was the day she had to get everything in, but even so, she'd barely made the deadline. Then she'd biked home, and that was another complication, the fact that the Old Clunker that had been basically hers for the past few years had to be shared with Abbie and Emma. Her sisters had complained about the way she cleaned the house, so she'd traded jobs with Abbie. She'd thought she'd like this better—she'd hated scrubbing the bathroom and the toilets.

But going to the grocery store was, truthfully, like parachuting straight into hell. The parking lot was full, *of course,* and she'd had to drive around waiting for a place to open up and then inside the store you couldn't move for the sea of shopping carts. And how much fun was it, lugging groceries for four adults out to the car and then into the house?

She'd been in such a hurry, putting the groceries away, that she'd broken open the bag of pasta and it scattered all over the floor. No one was around to help her, and she'd cried as she'd swept it all up, then cried in the shower because she didn't have anything new to wear to the evening's events. Then she'd realized she'd have puffy eyes if she didn't stop crying, so she stopped.

Her first event was an opening at a gallery on Main Street. That went pretty well. The artist was local, so Lily knew a lot of the people and snapped a lot of brilliant photos. But the second stop, a cocktail party fund-raiser for a local museum, brought her down. Everyone there was wealthy, and friends with everyone else, and they flicked their eyes at Lily with her camera as dismissively as if she were a homeless kid holding out a tin cup. The men, and many of them were young, in their thirties, looked at Lily without *seeing* her. Obviously she was so clearly not part of the group that counted that they didn't even notice that she was pretty.

She found the bathroom, locked the door, and scribbled down the names to the photos she'd taken. She scrutinized herself in the mirror. She looked good. Not wealthy, but *good*.

And she had a date with Jason—she couldn't forget that! He wasn't at all the man for her long-range plans, but he was a really good guy, and so sexy. For tonight, he'd be just fine.

She left the party without saying good-bye—no one would notice she was gone—and hurriedly walked along the streets and lanes to the Quaker cemetery on Madaket Road. Jason was waiting for her there, leaning against the fence.

"It's a perfect night for stargazing," he told her. "Come on."

She followed him, slipping between the rails and onto the soft green grass. The cemetery was a large open plot of rolling land without trees or headstones—the Quakers had not believed in grave markers.

"Wait a minute," she told Jason. "I need to take off my shoes." She put her hand on his arm to balance herself. It was a natural, easy thing to do. She was surprised at how her senses bloomed when her skin touched his. Jason hadn't paid any attention to her when they were in high school. He was two years older and always had a girlfriend. Lily couldn't wait to tell Carrie she'd had a date with Jason.

It was just far enough out of town that the night sky could be viewed without interference from shop- and streetlights. They walked into the middle of the grassy open space. Jason brought a blanket out of his backpack and spread it on the ground, and they lay down, looking up at the sky.

They saw a million stars.

"Wow," Lily breathed.

"Sort of puts things in perspective, doesn't it?" Jason said.

"We used to come out here when we were kids," Lily told him. "I haven't been here for years."

"We saw skies like this in Iraq," Jason told her. "Even more sky, and many more stars."

Lily asked carefully, "How was Iraq?"

He was quiet for a moment, then answered, "It was okay. I guess you could say I was lucky. But I don't want to go back."

"What *do* you want, Jason?"

"Well, that's the good thing about having been in Iraq. Over there, I used to dream that being back here would be heaven on earth, and now it kind of seems like it is. My construction business is doing really well even with the slowdown in the economy. I'm piling up some savings, and I've got a crew working for me, good guys that I can trust, and now and then I have free time to sail or fish. It's a pretty good life."

Lily sighed. "Maybe I need to get sent to Iraq. I just become so resentful in the summer. All the wealthy people who trample all over the island. They make me feel so poor. And it's as if they're taking something away from me."

"I can sympathize. But it's an unreal world here in the summer, Lily. You know that. It's not balanced. We're not seeing the millions of people who are just like us, struggling to get along. That's how most people are, really. And being normal, well, there are a lot of nice things about that. Plus, being normal on this island can be great."

"Hey, look. A shooting star." Lily pointed and they watched as the bright spot of light flared across the sky, down to the horizon, and vanished. The night was warm, the air was fragrant with salt and roses, and Lily's senses were on fire.

Jason was attracted to her. She knew that. She was attracted to him. But he needed to know who she really was, what she really wanted. "I've never wanted to be normal," Lily confessed.

He reached over and took her hand. "You've never had the chance to be. Not with looks like yours."

She smiled. "Like you ever noticed me in high school."

"Sure I did." He turned on his side and rose up on one elbow, facing Lily. "Anyway, I'm noticing you now."

He leaned down and kissed her. Lily reached up and put her arms around him, loving the width of his shoulders. She pulled him closer. They kissed for a long time, and Jason moved closer, so that he was almost lying on Lily.

Suddenly he groaned and sat up. "We're in the wrong place right now."

Lily agreed breathlessly. "You're right. Where can we go?"

"Your house?"

"My father might be there, or my sisters."

"I'm living with my parents." He laughed. "We might as well be teenagers."

"Where's your truck?" Lily asked.

"Just over there." He stood up. "Come on."

Quickly they grabbed up the blanket. Jason stuffed it into his backpack. He held her hand as they hurried across the cemetery to the side street. When they got to his truck, Jason tossed the back-pack into the rear, took Lily by her shoulders, and maneuvered her so she was leaning against the truck and he was leaning against her as he kissed her. She put her hands on his back, pressing him into her.

"Get in the truck," Jason said, his voice husky.

She climbed in on the driver's side and sat close to him as he drove away from town, toward the center of the island and the bumpy dirt roads of the moors. No streetlights rose here to disturb the natural darkness. Sometimes island kids had parties out here, but as they spun deep into the wilderness, they saw no other cars. He parked the truck in the shelter of a grove of evergreen trees. She had kept her hand on his thigh as he drove, and now he turned toward her with an intensity that made her heart race.

He kissed her, pulling at her clothing. They managed to con-tinue kissing while she removed her skirt and top. She felt like some kind of goddess or spirit in only her bare skin and multistoned neck-lace, and as soon as Jason had pulled his trousers down, she lifted herself over him, one knee on each side. Now they could take their time. She put her hands in his hair and kissed him furiously. He ran his hands all over her body, on her breasts, her hips, between her legs. She moaned with desire, and he entered her.

She had never felt less normal in all her life.

. . .

It was after midnight when Jason dropped her off at her house. All the lights were out but the doors weren't locked, they never were. She carried her shoes in one hand as she ascended the stairs. The house was quiet. And that was fine. She didn't want to tell anyone where she'd been. She was confused; she was wildly euphoric and terrified and angry at herself. What was she doing with Jason? He was a *contractor*. He'd never make real money. He'd never leave the island. She couldn't be in love with him! She *wouldn't* be!

But as she fell, fully clothed, onto her bed, it was Jason she thought of, his mouth, his body, his breath, and it was Jason she dreamed of when she fell asleep.

Sunday morning Lily allowed herself to sleep late. The rush of getting her column in to the magazine was over for the week. She'd start again this evening, of course, collecting more photos and stuff, but for this one morning, she could be lazy. Eartha didn't want her coming in on Sundays, either.

So she lay in bed for a long time, remembering the night before, remembering Jason. She would see him again tonight. And she didn't have any jobs during the day. Bliss. She would be as lazy as a cat in the sun.

Pulling on her shorts and a tee shirt, she padded downstairs and into the kitchen. Her sisters were sitting there, drinking coffee. They both smiled when they saw her, and they damn well should. She had done her damned duty. The kitchen was completely stocked and they wouldn't run out of toilet paper for the rest of the summer.

"Where's Dad?" she asked.

"Fishing," Emma told her.

Lily poured herself a cup of coffee and sat down at the table. "Sunday morning. Heaven."

Abbie had a lined yellow tablet and a pen on the table next to her. "I've taken seven more phone calls for Nantucket Mermaids."

Emma said, "Seven! Wow."

Abbie studied the list. "Mostly they're people here for a week or so who need a sitter for an evening or two."

"I'll take as many as I can get," Emma told her. "I need the money and my evenings certainly are empty."

"I might be able to do an afternoon," Lily offered tentatively. She really didn't want another job, but she loved being part of the company.

"No afternoons so far," Abbie said, consulting the list. She laughed. "Did I tell you about the family I babysat for Thursday night? The mother was freaked out because there was some sand on the bathroom floor and the cleaning ladies weren't scheduled until the next morning. While I was in the kitchen, helping her children finish their dinners, she was *raving* on and on about the sand, she couldn't stand it in the house, she'd stepped out of the shower and her bare foot had touched *the sand*! And her husband came in and told me he'd pay me *fifty* dollars extra if I could sweep it up and be sure the bathroom floor was clean."

Emma snickered. "I had a woman last week who told me that after the kids were asleep, I had to arrange the items in the refrigerator in neat rows. She couldn't abide a messy house, she said."

As her sisters laughed, Lily searched her memories for something to share. With a shriek of joy, she remembered. "Oh! I was at a cocktail party benefit at the Lemerceirs last week, and Donna Sefton, she was catering, told me to sneak in and check out the master bathroom and I did. There was a refrigerator in the bathroom! A little one, hidden behind a cupboard door. It was full of champagne and gallons of milk. Mrs. Lemerceir takes a bath every night in milk, says it's good for her skin, and while she's bathing, she drinks champagne."

"What does her skin look like?" Abbie asked.

Lily thought about it. "Actually, she's got good skin. Very pale, though." Her sisters yelped with laughter—she hadn't meant to be funny, only factual. Lily glowed and giggled, pleased with herself.

"No one gets brown anymore," Emma said. "Everyone's too worried about skin cancer."

"Some people do," Lily argued. "Sailors. Tennis fiends. A nice bit of tan gives your skin a good glow."

Emma looked at Lily. "You got in pretty late last night, didn't you?"

Lily smiled. "Yep."

"Well, come on!" Abbie urged. "What happened? Did you meet another star?"

Lily laughed. "I saw a falling star. At the Quaker graveyard. With Jason."

Emma sat up straight. "Get out! You were with Jason?"

Lily shifted nervously. "I hope you don't care, Abbie."

Abbie shrugged. "Why would I care?"

"Because he brought you home from the airport. I thought maybe—"

"Honey," Abbie said, "Jason is way too young for me. I like older men."

"Oh, really?" Emma turned her attention toward her older sister. "Since when?"

Abbie blushed and fiddled with her cup. "Oh, it's nothing. It's stupid. I just—it's not even worth talking about."

"It absolutely is worth talking about. Look at you! You're as red as a tomato!"

Why did they always do this, Lily thought. Why did her two sisters always find each other so interesting that Lily could be having sex with Brad Pitt on the kitchen table and they wouldn't even notice?

"It's just—this Howell Parker? Whose son I'm taking care of in the afternoons? He's—he's just amazing, really. So fascinating, and nice, and so loving with his little boy."

"I can't even believe what I'm hearing," Emma said. "Abbie, you have more sense than to get mixed up with a married man!"

"I know, Emma. But his wife is a bitch—"

"His wife. *His wife!*"

"And she's never there, she's always in New York working, and he's hurt his ankle."

"Are you kidding me?" Emma crossed her arms over her chest, leaned back in her chair, and glared at Abbie. "Abbie, don't do this. He is married. He is off-limits. He loves another woman. He loves the mother of that cute little boy. What are you even thinking?"

Abbie frowned and sighed. "I know. You're right."

"Is he trying to get you into bed?" Emma demanded.

"Oh, no, nothing like that. He's very proper. But Emma, there's this connection *between* us . . ."

Lily heard footsteps coming up the back porch, and then some-one knocked on the door.

"Come in," she called. Would it be Jason? Who else could it be on a Sunday morning?

Marina Warren opened the door and stepped into the kitchen. "Good morning. How nice to see all you girls together!"

25

·····

Marina

This wasn't the bravest thing she'd ever done, Marina thought as she smiled at the three startled women, but it might turn out to be one of the stupidest. In her past life, in her work for the ad agency, she'd walked into a room full of strangers dozens of times and turned them all into friends, or at least into clients. She'd faced disgruntled businessmen and skeptical retailers and calmly, assuredly, worked with them to ease their doubts.

But she'd had something to offer them—an ad, a selection of graphic designs, a catchy slogan about their own product. Here she had only herself.

They knew who she was, still she introduced herself. "I'm Marina Warren. I'm renting your cottage for the summer."

Now it was their turn to say something. She paused. For a moment—silence.

And then the tallest daughter, the one with the feathery cap of brown curls, stood up and came toward Marina, her hand outstretched. "Hi, Marina. I'm Abbie. It's nice to meet you."

"I'm Emma." A slender woman with curly hair, adorable freckles, and big hazel eyes turned in her chair and offered her hand. "Won't you join us for coffee?"

"I'd love to." Marina chose the chair farthest from Lily, who sat scowling at the far end of the table. "Hi, Lily." She said to the others, "I met Lily the other night."

"Oh?" Abbie set a mug in front of Marina and moved the cream and sugar bowl her way. "We hadn't heard. But we have such crazy schedules in the summer we often don't see each other for days, at least not to talk."

"Yes, your father told me about your company. Nantucket Mermaids. Clever. What sorts of jobs are you doing?"

Another pause. Abbie and Emma exchanged glances that telegraphed clearly their surprise at this announcement that their father had been talking about them to this stranger.

Then Emma spoke. "I'm taking dictation in the morning and chauffeuring around a bunch of kids in the late afternoon. The job I like the best is reading to Millicent Bracebridge. She's an elderly lady with a house crammed with valuable Nantucket antiques, but she's got macular degeneration. Sometimes I read to her. Sometimes I listen to her talk about the past. It's a pleasant job."

"And I'm doing some data entry for a couple who are trying to combine business with vacation. And taking care of a little boy in the afternoons." Suddenly, Abbie glowed. "He's the most darling little boy. His mother, a divorce lawyer, is usually back in New York. His father's working on some kind of scientific report. Harry's a shy little kid."

"And you work for the magazine, don't you, Lily?" Marina faced Lily with a friendly smile.

"Yes, but I didn't get the job through Nantucket Mermaids," Lily clarified. "I've had that job for a year now. It's not temporary. It's year-round."

Abbie asked Marina, "Do you work?"

"Oh, boy, I used to. For the past ten years I ran an ad agency slash graphic design business with my husband. Now he's my ex-husband and I've sold my share of the agency to him." From the periphery of her vision, she saw Emma's eyes flicker with interest. "That's why I'm here. I worked here for three summers back during my college days and loved it. Now I'm giving myself space to decide what to do, how to get my life back on course, or rather, channeled in a new course. I'm trying to be positive. To think creatively. This seems like a good place for that."

Emma leaned toward her. "I lost my job recently. I worked for an investment firm in Boston. I lost my job and all my savings."

"That is really tough," Marina commiserated.

Emma nodded. "And my fiancé dumped me."

"Well," Marina countered with a sardonic smile, "my husband left me for my best friend."

Emma's face brightened. "Get out."

"It's true." Marina laughed and held up her hand. "High five."

Emma slapped Marina's hand. "Glad to know you."

Lily objected, "But that's not funny! How can you two be so silly about it?"

Emma grimaced. "I've been miserable about it. I *am* miserable about it. So it's a novel experience to laugh about it. Do you mind?"

Lily bit her lip, confused. She didn't like this woman being here in their home.

Marina pushed back her chair. "Anyway, I just came up here to invite you all to dinner some night."

All three daughters gawked at her, confusion on two faces, resistance on Lily's.

"Your father's told me how hard you're all working, and I thought you might enjoy coming home to a nice, big home-cooked meal."

"That would be great," Abbie said. "What night?"

"What night is good for all three of you?" Marina asked. "I'm pretty open."

Abbie rose and walked over to a small desk in a kitchen nook. She took a calendar down from the wall and carried it back. "So far, I've got babysitting jobs on Wednesday and Friday. And Emma, you have jobs then, too. So Thursday might be good. Lily, do you have anything on Thursday?"

"I don't know," Lily muttered. "I'll have to check my calendar."

Abbie said, "Check it now."

"It's upstairs in my purse."

"We can wait," Emma told her.

Lily glared at Marina. "Is Dad going to be there?"

"I hope so."

Abbie looked from Marina to Lily and back to Marina. "Ah. Are you dating our father?"

Marina smiled. "We're friends."

"Check your calendar, Lily," Emma said.

Lily flounced out of the kitchen.

Marina waited for a few beats in case the sisters had anything helpful to say, like: *Our baby sister is a bit of a spoiled brat.* But they didn't take the opportunity to talk about her now that she was out of the room, and Marina liked them for that.

"Any suggestions on what I should serve?" Marina turned the conversation toward food. "I know you're very clever with Crock-Pot meals." Once again Abbie and Emma exchanged glances at this revelation that their father had shared so many details about his daughters. "Are any of you vegetarian? I've bought a little grill. I thought you might like steaks."

"God, I'd love a steak," Abbie said.

"Me, too," Emma agreed. "Steak has sort of been out of my budget."

"Then steak it shall be," Marina said, pleased to know she could offer Jim's daughters something good to anticipate.

Lily still hadn't returned. Marina tapped her watch. "I'm sorry, but I've got to go. I'm having a private lesson with Sheila Lester, making a lightship basket."

"That's very cool!" Emma said. "Sheila's the best."

Marina went to the door. "Thanks for the coffee. I'll see you Thursday night."

"And we'll come down and tell you whether Lily can come," Abbie said.

"Oh, your father can tell me," Marina told them casually, looking over her shoulder with a smile.

Marina biked over to Sheila Lester's house, her thoughts churning as she replayed the meeting with the three daughters. She'd liked Abbie right away, and thought Abbie had liked her. Well, Abbie seemed the most adult of the three, and she was the oldest. Emma had seemed distant until the moment Marina announced that her husband had left her for her best friend and then they had bonded a bit. Emma was more reserved than Abbie, but perhaps she would become a real friend. They had so much in common. Emma had also been unlucky in love. Well, what woman—what human?—hadn't?

• • •

The studio where Sheila Lester made her lightship baskets was set at the back of her property, a large, airy, one-roomed space full of light and fragrant with the spicy aroma of wood and cane. Shelves along the walls held molds and bases of all different sizes and shapes, and slabs and slices of wood were piled on the floor. Marina was surprised to see all the machinery in the shop. Sheila took her around, introducing her to the machines, explaining their function.

"Drill, to drill the pilot hole in the base. Router. To route the base. Sander. Lathe. Everything needs to be done to the most minute detail. And done right the first time around. You have to pay attention. *Focus*. Be mindful."

"Sounds very Zen," Marina said.

"It is very Zen," Sheila told her. "Compare the various baskets. Some are round. Some are oval. Some are small, some large. Take your time to decide what kind of basket you want to make. Then you can select your wood for the base."

As Marina studied the completed lightship baskets, Sheila returned to the one she was working on, fastened to its weaving stand. With careful, slow, even motions, she wove a thin strip of cane in and out of the vertical staves, pressing down gently with a little packing tool to be sure the cane was firmly in place.

Marina stood next to Sheila, mesmerized by the other woman's unhurried, methodical movements.

"It looks like slow, deliberate work," Marina observed.

"Right," Sheila agreed. "It requires total attention."

"I think I can actually feel my pulse slowing."

Sheila laughed. "You know they say they teach basket weaving in mental institutions? There's got to be a reason for that!"

Marina turned back to the baskets and considered. She didn't want to make one that was too big—she might grow frustrated or overwhelmed by such a task. She decided to make a small basket with a round base.

"Good," Sheila told her. "Now choose the wood you'd like to have for the base." She directed Marina toward a pile of wooden slices, some with grains in intricate swirls, others with rings.

"I'd like this one," Marina decided. "It's almost paisley."

Sheila instructed her as she placed a round template on paper and drew an outline with a pencil. Sheila placed the wood on the table saw base and carefully cut the wood out. She patiently held it against the lathe to sand and smooth the edge, then moved it to the router table to carve out a small channel in the base.

"Now," she told Marina, "you can varnish it."

Sheila returned to her weaving stand. Marina sat on a stool at the other end of the long table with a brush and a can of varnish and her round piece of wood. As she spread the varnish on, the wood's grain shone out.

"Oh, wow, Sheila." Marina held up the round base. "It's got such an intricate pattern."

"Yes. Each piece of wood has its own spirit. We call what you're doing 'bringing out the life of the wood.' "

Marina smiled to herself. Each piece of wood had its own spirit? How irrational.

And yet, as she worked, her round piece of wood seemed to glow as if it were lit from within. As if, somehow, it held a message that was hers alone, because she had chosen it.

26

. . . . .

Abbie

When Abbie arrived at the Parker house Monday, she pulled the door open without knocking so that poor Howell wouldn't have to struggle up to let her in.

"Hello!" She headed straight into the kitchen.

And slammed to a halt, nearly tripping on her own feet.

Sydney Parker was seated at the kitchen table. Beneath her black bike shorts and a white tee, her body was as flat and angular as her black blunt-cut hair. Abbie imagined Sydney slicing through the air of a courtroom like a razor-sharp blade. "Hello."

Harry was in a chair next to his mother. On a plate in front of him lay three stalks of asparagus. He didn't look up when Abbie entered the room but continued to stare down at the food.

"My plane doesn't leave for a couple of hours," Sydney informed Abbie. "I've made a grocery list. You can do some errands for me while I help Harry eat his *healthy* lunch."

"Of course." Abbie slid into the chair next to Harry. "Hey, buddy. How's it going?"

"I don't like asparagus," Harry muttered unhappily.

"Oh, I *love* asparagus," Abbie cooed encouragingly.

"It tastes like strings!" Harry protested, a quaver in his voice.

"Stop that, Harry!" Sydney's voice was icy. "It does not taste like strings. I steamed it perfectly *al dente*. You've got tortellini waiting for you. Just eat the asparagus." She scowled at Abbie. "The list is on the refrigerator. Howell's in his study. You can get a check from him. When you return, Harry will be able to go to the beach with you because by then he will have eaten his asparagus."

"Righto." Abbie patted the little boy's back. "You can do it, sport."

She found Howell at his desk, sitting in an awkward sideways position with his ankle up on a chair. He wore reading glasses as he scanned a report and strained to type information onto his computer. His blond hair stood out in all directions, as if he'd been running his hands through it.

"Sorry to interrupt," Abbie said. "I need a check for the grocery store."

"Oh, hi, Abbie. I didn't realize it was noon already. Um—" He opened his desk drawer, shuffled through the contents until he found the checkbook, signed a check and tore it out. "So Sydney's with Harry?" he asked absentmindedly.

"She's trying to convince him to eat asparagus."

Howell grinned. "There's a contest of wills I wouldn't want to bet on."

"Well, I'm betting on Harry," Abbie said. "I know how stubborn he can be."

"You ain't seen nothin' yet," Howell told her.

He held the check out. Abbie stepped closer as she reached for the check, and for a moment their eyes met. For a long moment she was suspended in a bubble of sensation. *He wants me,* Abbie thought. *And I want him.*

His child is in the other room! Her conscience squealed. *His wife is in the other room!*

Her voice was shaking when she said, "I need the car keys, too."

His fingers touched hers when he handed her the keys. For a long moment, they didn't move.

Howell said, "I'll see you when you get back."

She drove into town, bought the groceries, picked up the dry cleaning, and stopped at the pharmacy, moving in a dream. *I haven't done anything wrong,* she reminded herself. *I'm only enjoying knowing the man—and the little boy.*

Back at the house, she grabbed up two grocery bags from the SUV and carried them in. She entered the kitchen to find Harry and his mother still seated at the table. Three asparagus stalks still lay on the plate.

"You took longer than I thought." Sydney rose. "I've got to get dressed and get back to the city. You can unload the groceries while Harry eats his asparagus." She raised her voice. *"Because he's not getting down or eating any other food until he's eaten it."*

"I've got the dry cleaning and another bag of groceries to bring in," Abbie said.

"Fine."

By the time Abbie had brought in everything, Sydney had left the kitchen. Abbie heard the shower running upstairs.

As Abbie unpacked the groceries, she kept up a rambling conversation with Harry. A one-sided conversation, it turned out.

"Goodness, Harry. It's such a hot, sunny day. We could go to the beach, or to the school playground. You liked the slide, remember? Oh, look, watermelon! Eat those asparagus and you can have some watermelon for dessert, okay?"

In a very small voice, Harry said, "I have to peepee."

"Oh, honey. Well, come on." Abbie took his hand as he jumped down from the chair. She led him to the half bath off the kitchen and stood in the open doorway while he urinated. Then she pulled the step stool in front of the sink so he could stand on it to wash his hands.

"I *told* you he couldn't get down until he ate his asparagus!"

In her taut black suit and high black heels, Sydney loomed like an action figure, an electronic Dark Queen. Her briefcase was in her hand. Her lipstick was a glossy crimson and her eyes blazed with anger.

"He had to pee," Abbie told her mildly.

"Oh, you are *useless!*" Sydney yelled at Abbie. "How can I rely on you if you're going to let him manipulate you like that! *Of course* he said he had to pee."

"But, but he—" Abbie stuttered.

"You should have let him pee in his pants. That would teach him a lesson. When I tell him to eat something, he damn well better eat it." She took a step closer to Abbie, right into her personal space. "I am his mother. I know what he needs, and I know all his tricks. If I tell you to do something, do it. You are *my employee*, not fucking Mary Poppins, got it?"

"Mommy!" Alarm flashed across Harry's face. He tugged on his mother's skirt. "Don't be mad at Nanny Abbie. I'll eat my asparagus."

The little boy ran to the chair and scrambled up on it. He crammed the asparagus into his mouth and chewed, gagging as he fought to swallow it. His face went blotchy and tears welled in his eyes.

Abbie stood staring, horrified.

Sydney watched warily. When he'd swallowed the last asparagus, her face changed. Suddenly she was all smiles. She went to her son, knelt next to the chair, and hugged him tightly.

"What a good boy you are. What a good boy. Mommy's so proud of you." She kissed his cheeks and forehead. "Mommy has to go to work now, and Nanny Abbie will give you your tortellini, and since you've been such a good boy and eaten your asparagus, you can have watermelon and some grapes for dessert!" She hugged him again, and whispered into his ear, "I love you, love bug. Love you love you love you."

Sydney stood up, smoothing her black skirt over her hips. She shot a baleful glare at Abbie. "He needs his tortellini." She left the room, and Abbie heard her go into Howell's study and not long after that, a taxi honked outside and the front door slammed.

"Do you want your tortellini heated or cold?" Abbie thought she could allow the boy this much control over his food. He liked it cold, so she served it in a bowl, and sat with him while he ate, entertaining him with tales of the phone company cherry picker that she'd seen on his street.

While she talked, she searched her mind for memories of Lily at four. Their mother had been alive then, but she'd always been much more mellow than Sydney. Well, almost any mother would be. Abbie knew that after their mother died, she'd allowed Lily to get away with all sorts of things. Lily probably didn't eat a vegetable for a year after their mother's death. She probably lived on ice cream and chicken fingers. But Lily had turned out okay. Hadn't she? Or had Abbie spoiled her younger sister? Sometimes it seemed that way.

Thumping noises interrupted her thoughts. Howell appeared in the doorway, leaning on his crutch.

"Hi, guys." He rubbed the bridge of his nose. "Harry, check me out, have my eyes crossed?" He crossed his eyes.

"Daddy!" Harry giggled. "You look silly."

"I've been reading for so long it's made my eyes crossed." He uncrossed his eyes and rubbed them. "Seriously. I've got to get out of that room. What are you two doing this afternoon?"

Abbie smiled. "I thought I might take Harry to a secret place."

"And what about dinner tonight?" Howell asked.

"Oh, I'll make chicken with—"

"I meant, will you join us for dinner?"

Abbie hesitated.

"Please?" Howell asked.

"Yes, Abbie, eat with us tonight!" Harry cried.

Abbie took a deep breath. "Well, all right, then," she said, trying to sound casual, as if this were only another insignificant invitation.

Howell sat in the backseat of the SUV with his son while Abbie drove them to the moors and then more slowly over the rutted dirt road until they arrived at the grassy turnoff to the pond. While Howell negotiated his way out of the vehicle, Abbie lifted Harry down. All around, hills rolled in green abundance, wild and free beneath the blue sky.

"Cool!" Harry cried as he ran down the path toward the pond.

"We call this the doughnut pond," Abbie told him. "Because of that little island, right in the middle, like the center of a doughnut." She spread a blanket on the ground and set up the folding canvas chair for Howell. "Come here, Harry. Do you know what this is? A deer path. Want to walk it? It goes all the way around the pond."

Harry's eyes were wide. "Will you come with me?"

"You bet." She took the little boy's hand. The sandy path was tangled with all kinds of wildflowers and vegetation. Abbie bent to touch one delicate stem. "See this, Harry? It's called blue-eyed grass."

"Grass doesn't have eyes, silly!" Harry giggled.

Farther on, she stopped and pointed. "Look, Harry. Deer tracks. See the prints?"

He squatted down, scrutinized the tracks, and touched them. "They have funny feet."

"They have hooves. Cloven hooves. That means like this." She forked her fingers. "The deer come down here to drink water."

"Where are they now?" Harry scanned the horizon.

"Oh, they're hiding. They're afraid of people."

"I wouldn't hurt them," Harry promised earnestly.

"I know. But deer are very shy."

They walked on. At a tangle of wild roses, she stopped to let Harry inhale the fragrance. She pointed out the osprey stand built in the middle of the pond and promised she'd find a book with a picture of ospreys in it. She knelt down to show him a clump of berry bushes with minuscule tight green buds.

"We'll come back in a month and pick blueberries," she assured him. "You'll be able to pick berries right over the bush and pop them in your mouth!"

"*Pop* them in my mouth!" Harry echoed.

When they reached the far side of the pond, they waved at Howell, who waved at them. As they headed back, Harry said, "When Daddy can walk again, we can show him the deer tracks."

"We'll do that!" Abbie agreed, smiling when she said "we."

Back at their picnic spot, Abbie poured Harry, Howell, and herself paper cups of pink lemonade from the thermos. She took off Harry's sandals and put more sunblock on him. He squirmed as she rubbed it in, then grabbed up his bucket and shovel and hurried down to the water's edge. For a moment he hesitated, concerned— there was no sandy beach, only mud.

"Go ahead, get dirty," Abbie told him. "Mud washes off just as easily as sand."

He stepped into the mud, smiling with happiness as it squelched between his toes.

"This is a great place," Howell told Abbie.

"It is." She stretched out on the blanket and let the sun beat down on her. She wore shorts and a button-front, short-sleeved camp shirt. She knew the coral color was becoming to her complexion. She heard Harry talking to himself as he filled his bucket with mud. She kept her eyes closed, sensing that Howell was looking at her body. She hoped he was.

The afternoon drifted by. The heat of the day made her indolent. They took a walk together, stopping to investigate bugs and leaves. The three of them were so comfortable together. So natural.

Finally they returned to the house. Emma hadn't scheduled any work for her that evening, so she had no reason to hurry. As she showered Harry and dressed him in clean clothes, Howell went into his study to work.

Harry lay beneath the kitchen table playing with his horses while Abbie lazily moved around preparing dinner. She knew the things Harry loved to eat, and made plenty of it: rice, and carrots cooked and smothered with butter, and chicken breasts with mushrooms and cream. Harry would pick the mushrooms out, but that was okay. She sliced fresh Bartlett's Farm tomatoes to serve instead of a salad. Harry had eaten his green food for the day, she decided, with a little thrill of rebellion.

While the chicken baked, she went out onto the patio with Harry. They were building a fairy house like the one in front of The Toy Boat on Straight Wharf. Abbie was carefully putting together the house out of sticks. Harry was making a path to the house with tiny moon shells.

Howell came hobbling outside. "What an evening. Harry, I like your fairy house. Abbie, I poured us both a glass of wine, but I haven't figured out how to get it out here without spilling."

She smiled. "Sit down. I'll get the wine."

By the time she returned, a glass in each hand, Howell had lowered himself onto a wicker chair. She took a chair nearer Harry than Howell. She hoped he didn't notice how her hands were trembling. Her throat was dry. She kept licking her lips.

"It's hard to get used to so much peace and quiet," Howell said. "I'm such a city boy."

"What city?" she asked.

He'd grown up in Cambridge, where he lived with his parents and his sister in an apartment. He'd gone to college in Berkeley. He worked in New York and New Haven.

"It was Sydney's idea to buy a house here," he said.

It stung, hearing his wife's name in Howell's mouth. She bit her lip.

"So many acquaintances have places here. It's a good place for her to network."

"Plus, it's paradise for kids," Abbie said.

"Absolutely," Howell agreed. "Of course Sydney figured that into the equation."

"I can hear the timer. Excuse me." Abbie fled into the kitchen. What the hell was she thinking, drinking wine with that man as if they were some kind of couple! She was glad he mentioned Sydney. They should keep Sydney right there in the room with them.

She drank the rest of her wine as she worked in the kitchen, preparing the meal. She called them in, and supervised Harry as he washed his hands. She served the food. She put Harry and his father side by side and sat across the table from Harry.

Howell asked Abbie what it was like to grow up on the island, so during dinner she entertained father and son with tales from her childhood. How the seals gathered on the jetties during the winter, and congregated at Great Point like great snorting, grunting, shiny rubber rocks. The time the whale washed up in Sconset. How the electricity used to go out before the underwater cable to the mainland was installed, and everyone read by candlelight, shivering beneath blankets.

Harry listened, wide-eyed, so Abbie continued to regale him as she led him upstairs for his bath and before-bed ritual. She dressed him in clean cotton pajamas, tucked him into bed, and sat next to him, still talking. He fell asleep almost immediately. Abbie sat for a while gazing down at his dear little face and her heart almost burst with longing.

Downstairs, she discovered that Howell had managed to hobble around the kitchen. All the dishes were loaded into the dishwasher, which churned steadily away, and the kitchen counters were clean.

She stood in the kitchen doorway. "He's sound asleep."

"You work magic with him, Abbie." Howell held up the bottle of wine. "Help me finish this."

"Oh, well . . ."

"Just one glass each."

Maybe he's just lonely for adult conversation, Abbie thought. "All right."

Since his accident, Howell's customary place was on the sofa, with his leg stretched out and elevated on a pillow. Abbie took a chair opposite with the coffee table safely between them. She took a sip of wine with a trembling hand. It was still light outside, but in the house the rooms were dim and shadowy. No lamps were lit.

Her skin glowed from the day's sun. Every cell of her body seemed alive and awake. Alert. *Ready*. She could not look away from Howell. His handsome face, his strong body, his steady gaze . . .

"*Abbie*," Howell said softly. "My God. What are we going to do?"

She didn't try to act coy. "Howell, you're married."

"Let me tell you about my marriage," he said.

"I don't think—"

"I'm not going to disparage Sydney. You've met her. She's an amazing woman."

Of course, Abbie knew that, but still the word pierced her with jealousy.

"She's brilliant," Howell continued. "She's ambitious. She works tirelessly. She might have a future in politics. It's what she wants. I admire Sydney tremendously, even though, as you might have gathered, she can be abrasive."

Abbie's heart was leaping about in her chest. He *admired* her! Now each word he spoke seemed to build a bridge between Abbie and Howell.

"She's your wife," she said, trying to cut through this connection with the knife of Sydney's image.

"By accident. We met just a few days before we graduated from grad school. We each had landed the jobs we wanted in New York. We were giddy and we were stupid. We went out a few times, we slept together a few times, and then we got too busy to even think of dating. I hadn't even seen Sydney for a *month* when she came to tell me she was pregnant."

"Howell—"

"She'd thought she'd missed her period because she was working so hard at her new job at the law firm. She was three months' pregnant. God knows she didn't want a baby." He made a scoffing noise. "She wasn't thrilled about marrying me, either. She didn't love me. I didn't love her. She considered giving the baby up for adoption." Pain flashed over his face. "Imagine giving up Harry." He shook his head. "So we married. We are fairly good friends. We've worked out a manageable life. But I don't love her, Abbie. And I've never felt about Sydney the way I feel about you."

It was everything she wanted to hear. Softly, she said, "I know. I feel that way about you."

"Then come over here."

"Howell—" She hesitated.

"Abbie."

As if she were riding a tide tumbling toward the shore, Abbie allowed herself to be pulled by the irresistible magnetism of their mutual desire. Howell made room for her on the sofa, and she perched on the edge next to him, and he put his arms around her and gently drew her to him and kissed her mouth. Pleasure shot through her. His hands found her breasts, pushed up her shirt and struggled with her bra and touched her skin. She kept her mouth on his as she unbuttoned her shirt, unsnapped her bra, and tossed them to the floor. While she stood to tug off her shorts and panties, Howell shifted on the sofa so that she could straddle him. He fought to tug his shorts off.

"Damn!" he whispered when his clothing caught on his ankle cast. "The hell with it. Come here, Abbie."

She settled herself over him, leaning down to kiss him, and he ran his hands over her body, everywhere. She raised herself and he pressed himself inside her.

Here, her body told her. *Here. This is right. This is perfect. This is everything.*

This is home.

27

·····

Emma

Emma, you are a wonder," Spencer whispered.

She grinned. "I'm pretty pleased with myself, I have to say."

They were standing at the back of the small auditorium in the Whaling Museum. Spencer had just given a lecture about Nantucket shipwrecks and lightships, and Emma had accomplished the brilliant coup of persuading Mrs. Bracebridge to attend.

Really, it hadn't been so difficult. Toots Carlyle was young and strong and his vehicle was equipped for wheelchairs. He easily lifted Mrs. Bracebridge out of her wheelchair and into the van, then lifted her wheelchair into the back of the van and out again at the Whaling Museum. He helped the older woman descend from his van on its little electric lift, and he carefully attended her as she sank back into her wheelchair.

Emma took over then, pushing her charge in front of her through the electric doors and around the visitor's stand to the meeting room at the back. The docents at the door did not ask Mrs. Bracebridge if she was a member. It was obvious from her regal bearing that she belonged anywhere she chose to be.

Emma heard the murmuring as she wheeled Mrs. Bracebridge into the room. After the lecture, half the audience swarmed toward Millicent Bracebridge. People leaned close to Millicent, announcing their names, patting her hand, exclaiming how very happy they were to see her.

Emma stepped back, preparing to wait patiently, but to her surprise three women in their fifties approached her.

"Emma Fox? Is that really you?"

They had been friends of her mother and were still friends of her
father. She'd played with their children, had overnights in their
homes, and now she caught up on all the news. When they asked
why she was on the island, and why she was with Millicent Bracebridge, she bit the bullet and explained that she'd lost her job at a
Boston investment firm. They commiserated, telling her about their
children, all Emma's age, many of whom had also lost their jobs or
their savings in the past year.

Across the room, Spencer was also surrounded by people. After
awhile, the lecture room emptied. Spencer came to his grandmother
and bent down close to her.

"Grams. Thank you for coming. I'm honored."

Millicent Bracebridge's face bloomed with pleasure. "Oh, don't
be silly."

"I'll phone Toots," Emma said, and slipped away, allowing her
employer some private time with her grandson.

When she'd finished her call, she dropped her cell phone into
her bag and returned to the lecture room. Spencer wheeled his
grandmother out of the building and stayed with her until the van
arrived, then kissed her wrinkled cheek.

"Love you, Grams," he said.

To Emma's surprise, he leaned forward and kissed her cheek,
too. "Thanks for bringing her. I really appreciate it. See you tomorrow?"

"Yes. See you tomorrow."

Back at the Bracebridge home, a black SUV sat in the driveway.
As the driver helped Mrs. Bracebridge out of the van and into her
wheelchair, the front door flew open and Sandra Bracebridge exploded out of the house, her face dark with fury.

She stomped down the walk and planted herself right in Emma's
face. "What do you think you're doing!"

Emma began to explain. "I took Mrs. Bracebridge to hear her
grandson—"

"Did I not make it clear that my mother-in-law is in a fragile
state?"

"Sandra." Millicent Bracebridge's voice was strained. "Could we please go into the house for this conversation?"

Sandra stormed ahead. Emma pushed the wheelchair up the ramp and into the house. She parked Millicent Bracebridge in her favorite spot in the living room.

"Would you like a glass of water?" Emma asked the older woman.

"Oh, you're not weaseling out of this!" Sandra snapped. "I want an explanation and an apology."

Sandra's mother-in-law lifted an imperious hand. "Sandra, leave the girl alone. She was only obeying orders. I wanted to go hear Spencer speak."

"You know you don't have the stamina for this sort of excursion."

"Obviously, I'm capable of an occasional outing." Millicent's voice came out in a labored whisper.

"Listen to you, you don't even have the energy to speak!" Sandra scolded.

"I'll get some water." Emma left the room.

When she returned, Sandra was pacing in tight little circles around Millicent's wheelchair.

"—'course they act delighted to see you! You own the greatest collection of Nantucketiana in the world! They want something from you."

"Here's your water, Mrs. Bracebridge." Emma knelt next to the wheelchair and carefully guided the glass into Millicent's hands, waiting until she was certain the older woman had a fast hold on the glass before taking her own hands away.

Millicent Bracebridge sipped the water. "Thank you," she said, turning in Emma's direction. "I'm tired now. I'd like to rest."

"I just hope you haven't made yourself sick, Millicent," Sandra huffed.

"Would you like me to stay?" Emma asked.

"Please. I'll probably only nap for a while and I'd like you to read to me later."

Millicent held the glass out. Emma took it and set it on the table. Millicent closed her eyes.

"Very well, then, I'm going." Sandra glowered at Emma. "I'm

not through discussing this with you! As far as I'm concerned, you've seriously overstepped your duties."

Emma said nothing. Sandra sniffed mightily and strode away.

Millicent awoke after a thirty-minute snooze. Emma made her a cup of tea and read to her from Agatha Christie. They didn't discuss Sandra's anger or whether or not Emma's job was in jeopardy, but they did discuss, in great detail, the brilliance of Spencer's speech, his remarkable stage presence, and how pleased he had been to see his grandmother in the audience.

"It's time for me to go, Mrs. Bracebridge," Emma said reluctantly.

"Please call me Millicent," the older woman said. "And thank you again, Emma, for providing me with such a pleasant day."

"I enjoyed it, too," Emma told her truthfully.

Emma walked home feeling quite pleased with herself. When she turned onto her street, she stopped for just a moment. Really, it was such a pretty street. The houses weren't as imposing as the Bracebridges', but they each had a special charm—a window box spilling with petunias, a mermaid door knocker, a trellis smothered with pale pink climbing roses. A pigtailed girl zipped past Emma on her bike. In one yard some mothers sat talking while their little children ran screaming through the water sprinkler. Emma smiled, remembering being young in the summer.

Her mother had been so very beautiful, and she'd laughed so often. She'd invented great games for her daughters to play. She'd decorated each room so prettily, and she loved doing her daughters' hair in fabulous braids. And when they'd been little girls, her mother had been so loving, always hugging, kissing, holding them— Emma still remembered the scent of her mother's perfume as she rocked Emma in her arms. Emma had wanted a lot of babies to love just the way her mother loved her.

And perhaps, someday, she would have them. Today, for no reason at all, she felt hopeful. Boston and Duncan and all that seemed insignificant and far away. She thought of how pleased Spencer had been when she arrived with his grandmother for his talk. She thought of how he smiled at her, and suddenly, beneath the expansive island sunshine, the day was just too glorious for regrets.

28

. . . . .

Lily

Lily was just settling the white wicker bed tray over Eartha's lap when Godzy began his frantic yipping.

"That will be UPS," Eartha said, waving her hand toward the front of the house. "Go get the packages, that's a dear."

"Stop, it, Godzy," Lily told the little dog, who wound himself around her ankles as she walked to the door.

"Want me to carry these in for you?" the UPS man asked. "They're heavy."

"Um . . . let me ask Mrs. Yardley."

Before she could reach the bedroom, Eartha Yardley yelled, "Tell him to come on in. It won't be the first time I've had a strange man in my bedroom." She laughed heartily.

Godzy bounced and yapped and ran in frenzied circles around the deliveryman's ankles as he made his way into the bedroom.

"Good morning, Mrs. Yardley," he said. "Where would you like these?"

"Hi, Liam. Over there on the chaise, don'tcha think?"

He set them down. "I've got another batch." He went out and returned with five more boxes.

When the chaise was piled high and Godzy curled next to his mistress, longing for a piece of bacon, Eartha said to Lily, "Open them up for me, darling. I love being entertained while I eat."

Lily found the scissors in the sewing basket and began carefully undoing the boxes. She lifted out dresses and caftans and shawls in vivid jewel tones, in silk and linen and cotton. "So many exquisite things," she breathed.

"Hold up that turquoise one," Eartha ordered. "Yeah, that's gorgeous, all right. And it looks like I'll be able to squeeze into it. I'll try those things on after I eat." She sighed. "Trying on clothes is such hard work."

Lily took padded hangers out of the closet and hung up the clothes as she took them from the box. She couldn't imagine why Eartha needed so many more things. Her closets were already crammed full.

"I know what you're thinking," Eartha said through a mouth of bacon. "You're thinking why does such an old bat even bother trying?"

"Oh, no!" Lily protested. "I wasn't thinking that at all. I think it's fun to look fabulous at any age." She smiled at her employer. "And you always look fabulous."

"You should have seen me when I was young. I was a knockout."

"I know. You look like a movie star in that oil portrait in your living room."

"God. Those were the days. People were more fun then. Now everyone is so *earnest*. It's enough to make me gag." Eartha cut off a piece of bacon and held it out for Godzy, who snapped it up. "All right," she said, "I've just got to bite the bullet. Come take this tray off my legs."

Lily carried the tray into the kitchen and slowly cleaned it off, giving Eartha plenty of time to struggle out of her nightgown and into her bra, panties, and slip.

When she returned to the bedroom, Eartha was scrutinizing the hem of an apricot silk dress. "Help me into this," she told Lily.

Lily slid it over the older woman's head and gently tugged it down.

Eartha examined her reflection in the mirror. "Drat. Too small. The color's gorgeous, but it makes my skin turn sallow."

"Let's send it back," Lily suggested. "Exchange it for a larger size."

Eartha flashed a look at Lily, standing behind her. "Check out the color with your hair. Wow. Hey. You take it. With that color, it's absolutely calling your name."

Lily's breath caught in her throat. She held the dress against her. The material was so sensual, so exquisite. "I couldn't," she said carefully. "And it's a little too large."

Eartha laughed. "A *little* too large? Honey, you should run for office. Hey, we'll just have my dressmaker alter it for you. She's coming over later today. Check my calendar. And get my topaz necklace and earrings. I'll bet they'd be dynamite on you with that apricot dress."

Lily tried not to hurry as she went to Eartha's desk and turned her engagement book to the right page. "Seamstress at three."

"Now what about this?" Eartha held a dress up against her. It was cut loose and full in a swirl of yellows and pinks. "I think this will fit. Come help me."

Lily burned to open the jewelry drawers of the vanity, but she hurried to help Eartha undress and dress again. Now Eartha was into the full swing of decision making, yanking clothes on and off with Lily's help. Godzy got bored and fell asleep on the bed. Lily fluttered around Eartha, eagerly helping, secretly praying, *Don't forget the jewelry!*

"God, I'm exhausted!" Eartha let the last dress fall into a silken puddle on the floor. "Honey, get me some Diet Coke. I've got to rest. Jesus, this fashion business is tiring." She crawled back into bed wearing nothing but her underwear.

Lily went into the kitchen and returned with two tall glasses filled with ice and Diet Coke. Pulling a chair next to the bed, she opened Eartha's engagement calendar. The two women went over it carefully, planning what Eartha would wear to each event, and which shoes, and which jewelry. Occasionally Eartha asked Lily to hold some of the jewelry up to a garment to see if it made the colors "pop." At eleven, Eartha headed into her bathroom for a shower while Lily stripped her bed and put on fresh sheets and pillowcases and smoothed the light coverlet over the bed. She went around the room, tidying the clothing. She carried the cardboard boxes out to the recyclable pile in the garage. When she returned, Eartha was ready for Lily to help her dress for lunch. Lily zipped up the beige linen dress and dug around in the closet for the shoes Eartha wanted. Eartha sat at her vanity, applying makeup.

"I think that's it for the morning," Lily said. "I've called your cab. It will be here right at noon."

"Be back at three," Eartha told her. "We'll get that dress cut down for you. You're going to the library fund-raiser, aren't you? Good. We'll be sure she's got the dress ready for you to wear for that. And here." Opening a drawer, Eartha lifted out a pair of intricate topaz and gold teardrop earrings and a matching necklace. "Take these. You can keep them. They're meant for your hair and coloring."

Tears welled in Lily's eyes. She blinked them back. "I can't keep them," she protested, but her voice cracked as she spoke.

"Why not? I never wear them. I've seen what you wear to the parties. You need some serious jewelry, honey. You may think you look adorable and innocent in your little costume stuff, but the topaz will make you stand out." She patted Lily's hand. "And I like my friends to be outstanding."

"I . . . I could just borrow them . . ."

"Oh, cut it out. Surely you can tell I have more money than sense. Take the damn things. And stop that quivering-lip shit. You're beginning to annoy me."

Lily grinned at Eartha's words. "Well, if you're sure. Thank you so much. They are beautiful."

"*You* are beautiful, honey. And young. Enjoy it while you can."

Mary Jo Cushing was holding a luncheon event to welcome a biographer who would lecture tonight about his new book on American presidents, but as Lily biked over to the Cushing house, she didn't review the questions she would ask Austin Abernathy for her article about him. Instead, she gloated over the topaz jewelry and the apricot dress.

At the Cushings' house on Cliff Road, Lily entered through the kitchen, stopping to chat for a minute with the caterers, who were friends of hers. The buffet luncheon was on the long green swoop of lawn overlooking the glistening blue waters of Nantucket Sound. Lily zipped around taking photos and writing down names. After the luncheon, Lily led Austin Abernathy to a quiet spot in the solarium to interview him. He was just as she'd feared—long-winded, pompous, and stodgy. She kept stealing glances at her watch. It had taken her fifteen minutes to bike from Eartha's to the Cushings'. She had to leave no later than two-forty-five; she didn't want to be late for the dressmaker, and it would be rude to keep Eartha waiting after her generosity.

"Now Herbert Hoover," Austin Abernathy droned, "was misunderstood by most of the more eminent historians—"

Lily's watch pointed to two-forty-six.

"I'm so sorry, Mr. Abernathy." Lily closed her notebook and stood up. "I've got an appointment at three. It was an honor to meet you. Thank you so much for giving me this interview."

She thanked her hostess and raced out to her bike. She pedaled as fast as she could, but anxiety strung her nerves tight. Emma had to have the car in the late afternoon because she had to drive the Bennett children around, and Lily understood that, but still it seemed unfair. The sun had grown hot and muggy, the warmest day they'd had yet this July, and she felt sweat break out all over as she forced herself to hurry. She didn't want to be late, but she didn't want to show up at Eartha's covered with sweat and smelling like old socks. Frustration clogged her throat. She sniffed back tears. Great. Swell. She was going to show up at Eartha Yardley's with swollen red eyes, a dripping nose, and sweat-smelling clothes!

She arrived at Eartha's only ten minutes late. The seamstress was just carrying a pile of altered clothing into the house. Godzy was circling her, yipping and prancing and wagging his tail.

"Let me help you," Lily offered, dumping her bike on the ground. Mona Coffin had been a friend of her mother's, and Lily was always glad to see her.

Inside, Lily hid her impatience as Eartha tried on the new dresses that needed altering. Lily took garments off hangers and put them back on, entered the information in Eartha's black notebook, and brought everyone glasses of iced tea. She slid the garments Mona would take back with her into their garment bags and double-checked to see that she'd listed all the details of the alterations. She packed up the rejects for the next UPS visit. She chatted and laughed as the two older women gossiped about movie stars and TV celebrities.

And then finally, Eartha said, "Okay, Mona, now I've got a challenge for you. Can you cut this dress down from whale size to goldfish?"

Mona laughed. "Let's see."

Lily dropped her clothes and slid into the apricot dress. The fabric was as magical as she'd remembered.

"Oh, honey," Mona said. "This is stunning on you." She ran her hands down the side seams, pulling the material, evaluating. "Yes. Yes, I think I can take it in here, and here, like this . . ."

"And you'll need to shorten it," Eartha added. "With legs like hers, it should be as short as possible. Cheese on a cracker, you could get two dresses out of that."

How pleasurable it was to have the two older women circling her, heads cocked, studying her, complimenting her, smoothing the fabric over her back and hips, touching Lily and the dress so gently. It felt like a great tenderness. Lily's heart swelled with gratitude.

"How soon can you have it finished?" Eartha asked Mona.

"It depends where it is on your list of priorities," Mona told her. She waved toward the pile of clothing she had to take with her to alter.

"Get my calendar, Lily. I think the library fund-raiser is next Friday night."

Lily ran her finger down the list of Eartha's scheduled activities. "It is."

"Let's have it by Friday morning, then," Eartha said. "It's going to be a big glam occasion. This dress will be perfect for it." She sat down on her bed. "God, I'm beat. I've got to rest before I go out for the evening."

Lily said good-bye to Eartha and Godzy, then helped Mona carry the clothing out to the car. She jumped on her bike and pedaled away from the house, but when she came to the entrance to Sanford Farm, she locked up her bike and ran into a grove of evergreen trees. No one could see her here. She crumbled to the ground and gave way to a massive storm of weeping.

She missed her mother!

She could remember her mother holding her, caressing her, whispering endearments, and she could remember Abbie holding her, too. Abbie had taken Lily shopping for clothes, Abbie had taken care that Lily had the prettiest outfits, and Abbie had altered Lily's clothes to make them perfect. Abbie had brushed Lily's hair and braided it or tied it in ribbons. Abbie had let Lily experiment with her makeup—oh, there had been lots of times when Abbie and Emma, sometimes, too, had dressed Lily like a live china doll. They had been so proud of pretty little Lily, with her red hair and gem-green eyes. They'd held her hands when they walked into town, when they attended church, when they'd gone to school events. Why, when she was small, Lily hadn't had enough hands, not with Abbie, Emma, and her father all wanting to accompany her!

And now she was so alone! Now Abbie and Emma were like strangers, only caring about themselves, not bothering to spare a single thought for Lily!

Oh, grow up, Lily, she told herself. She pulled a tissue from her pocket and blew her nose and wiped her tears. *You're an adult now,* she reminded herself. How could she forget the best thing about being grown-up—Jason. Love, and sex, with Jason. She took her iPod from her backpack, and as she did, she felt the little padded jewelry bag. Now she had real jewelry, too, another pleasure of being grown-up.

She left the grove of trees, climbed on her bike, stuck her ear-piece into her ear, and biked home with ABBA jazzing up her mood.

Not until she was locking her bike in the garage did she remember.

Emma had arranged to use their father's truck to pick up the children so that Lily could use the car this afternoon to buy groceries. And in her excitement at Eartha's stunning generosity, Lily had forgotten all about buying groceries.

29
·····

Marina

Jim had phoned Marina to tell her he was running late. Could she meet him at Even Keel at eight instead of seven? She'd said of course, and he said he'd change the reservation, and now she was strolling into town on a warm summer evening, and everything around her seemed soft and new and lovely. *She* felt soft and new and lovely, and it wasn't just the pale blue summer dress that drifted around her as she moved, it wasn't just the warm glow her skin carried from the summer sun. It was partly, she thought, that she was falling a little in love with this island, with its golden beaches and shimmering skies and gardens vibrant with flowers. It was also, partly, she admitted to herself, the presence of Jim Fox in her life.

She turned off Orange Street onto Main Street. The stores were still open, spilling light onto the brick sidewalks where people sauntered along, laughing and chatting, their clothes as brightly multi-hued as the flower boxes beneath the shopwindows.

Jim was waiting for her in front of Even Keel. He looked wonderful in khakis and a red cotton button-down shirt, and he was talking with another man. Of course he was; Jim couldn't move a step in this town without running into a friend.

She saw Jim's face light up as she approached. He introduced her to his friend, then escorted her into the restaurant. To her delight, they were seated in the garden patio at the back.

"How was your day?" she asked.

He told her about the house he was renovating, how a guy on his crew had injured his thumb with a band saw and had to go to the hospital to be stitched up. He asked about her day and she told him about working on her lightship basket at Sheila Lester's and attending the noonday concert at the Unitarian church. Jim ordered a bottle of red wine, and they sipped it as they waited for their entrées to arrive. Above them, the night sky changed colors, paling from blue to a radiant dove gray. All around them the other diners were talking and laughing, but they seemed insubstantial to Marina, background for the center of the universe, this table, this moment, this man.

She had not been this happy for a long time.

The waiter set their plates before them. Salmon for her, prime rib for Jim.

"Oh," Marina said. "That reminds me. I've invited your daughters to dinner tomorrow night. I told them I'd grill steak."

Shocked, Jim said, "What?"

"I stopped by your house and asked your daughters to come to dinner. They chose tomorrow night."

Jim put down his knife and fork. "I wish you'd asked me about this first."

Now she was the one who was shocked. "Is there a problem?"

His face was troubled. "It's just that it seems, well, *premature*."

The word was like a slap in the face. Marina sat back in her chair, gathering her thoughts. "It's only dinner, Jim. It's not a serious commitment. It's not even a suggestion that there ever will be a serious commitment. It's just being neighborly. I'm living in their old Playhouse. I see them every day and they see me. It's not like I'm *invisible*." She thought she was going to cry.

Jim shook his head. "I know. It's just that the situation is delicate. I suppose I've tried to protect the girls."

"Do you mean in all these years they've never been invited to dinner by a woman you were dating?" Her voice was shriller than she'd meant it to be. Several other diners glanced her way.

Jim muttered, "I don't think you should sound so judgmental. You don't know the background."

"I'd *like* to know the background," she said quietly.

"I don't want to talk about it here," Jim told her. "Not out in public." He picked up his utensils and set about eating as if he were performing a necessary task.

"Oh, Jim." Marina leaned close to him and dropped her voice to a whisper. "I'm sorry. I had no idea this would upset you so much. I'm not trying to rush things with you. I'm not trying to make it seem as though you and I are *together*. I only thought it would be fun. And I suppose I thought it would be nice for your daughters to meet the woman their father is dating."

"I understand," Jim told her. "I'm sorry, too. It's just—things are complicated." He raised his eyes to Marina's. For a moment, he seemed on the verge of a confession. Then he said, "Let's talk about something else."

But no other topic of conversation held their interest for long. Jim was clearly involved with his private thoughts and Marina just felt miserable.

After dinner, they strolled around town, listening to the street musicians, pretending to have a pleasant time. They walked out on the wharves, looking at the yachts anchored there. Clearly Jim didn't want to talk about his daughters or his life, and Marina acted lighthearted, but she just really wanted to hide away in her bedroom and weep.

Finally it was time to go home. The streets were emptying of cars and people. The sky was dark, a quarter moon riding high overhead. As they wended their way down the narrow lanes to Jim's house, even the birds in the trees were quiet. In some houses lights burned, spilling illumination and shadows on the streets and occasionally a door would open and people would come out, laughing, happy on this hot summer night.

When they got to Jim's driveway, Marina said, "Jim. Come in for coffee, please?" She knew he understood what she was offering.

He sighed. "Not tonight, Marina. I've got to get up early tomorrow." He walked her halfway down the drive before saying, "Good night, then." And he turned and headed for his house, leaving Marina to walk to her little cottage alone.

• • •

As she organized the food for Thursday evening, Marina obsessed over Jim's reaction. She ran their conversation over and over again in her mind, searching for any hints that would help her understand his response. She longed to ask Sheila Lester about him, but remembered how, when she'd asked Sheila about Jim's wife's death, Sheila had shut her off, telling her to talk to Jim about that subject. Part of the time she scolded herself for so eagerly, hopefully, stupidly inviting the girls to dinner. Part of the time she was angry at Jim for his bizarre behavior. It was only dinner! And if Lily hadn't come in that night, she knew she and Jim would have gone to bed together. And enjoyed it. He was attracted to her, Marina knew it, and she felt there was some value in their desire, some significance. Some hope.

Still, she planned to behave with complete propriety when they all came to dinner. She would not touch Jim, she would not sneak an intimate glance his way, she would behave like someone's maiden aunt. The girls would like her. She would like them. It would be a fun evening, not laden with whatever heavy memories Jim seemed to keep safeguarded and treasured.

Jim phoned in the afternoon to tell her he wasn't going to be able to make it to dinner. The interior of a client's house was behind schedule, and he was going to continue working with his crew so it would be ready when the family arrived in August.

Marina was stunned. "I'm sorry you won't be coming," she said, forcing her tone to be cheerful. "I know the girls will miss you. I'll miss you, too."

"They're used to this," Jim told her. "They know what summer's like for me. But thanks for the invitation."

His formality was an insult. She cursed as she put down the phone.

Well, she thought, so much for any chance of a relationship developing between them.

She prepared the dinner with all the care she'd have taken if Jim were coming. She made a potato salad with small red potatoes with their skins still on and capers and bits of dill. She made a green salad spiked with thin slices of pear and crumbles of blue cheese. She concocted meringues with raspberry sauce and whipped cream. She bought fresh Portuguese bread and several bottles of wine. She spread a blue tablecloth on the little table—a tablecloth she'd bought brand new at Marine Home Center, nothing secondhand.

She tucked daisies into a little white pitcher and set it in the middle of the table. She placed candles all around the cottage—to let the girls know she liked candlelight all the time, not just when entertaining a man.

She thought about wearing her shorts and tee shirt for dinner, but decided she didn't want the girls to think she hadn't dressed up because Jim wasn't coming. So she pulled on a yellow sundress and a wild beaded necklace. She coated her eyelashes heavily with mascara and brushed her lips with pink color. When she scrutinized her face in the mirror, she saw how sad she looked, really. How sad her eyes were—just like they'd been a month ago, before she came to the island.

Damn, this was just unacceptable! So what if Jim Fox had lost interest in her. No, so what if she had acted *prematurely*, inviting his daughters for dinner, assuming he would enjoy this, assuming he was comfortable with his daughters knowing he liked her. So what if her rash action had driven Jim away, had cost her the undying love of the last good man on earth. She was not going to allow herself to snivel and whine. Men weren't everything! She was still on a gorgeous island, she'd made friends, she'd feathered a dreamy little nest, and she would enjoy herself!

She put a Glen Miller record on her used record player. ". . . is that the Chattanooga choo-choo?" filled the room. She sang to it as she finished the dinner preparations, and she felt her spirits lift.

When the girls arrived, Marina could tell at once they'd been arguing. Abbie and Emma both greeted Marina pleasantly, but Lily clearly was not amused about being there.

"Oh, wow," Abbie said. "You've done wonders, Marina!"

As the three women walked around studying the cottage, Marina studied them. The family resemblance was striking in the shape of their faces, but their individuality was distinct.

Abbie wore a faded Something Natural tee shirt with a short denim skirt and sandals. Her only jewelry was a wide silver cuff bracelet. She carried herself with a natural authority, no doubt because she was the eldest.

Emma wore baggy cotton trousers, a coral-colored linen shirt tied at the waist, and turquoise and coral earrings. The sprinkling of freckles over her nose gave her an innocent appearance, but the depths of her dark eyes held sorrow, a sorrow Marina could understand.

Lily was the beauty of the family and she played it to the hilt. Her emerald tank top brought out the green of her eyes and accentuated her slender waist. Her skirt was a swirl of green, and everything about Lily sparkled. Her dangling earrings glittered with colored stones, bangle bracelets clattered on her arms, a gold chain glinted from around her ankle, and she even wore a toe ring with her sequined sandals.

Marina poured them all glasses of sparkling Prosecco mixed with peach nectar.

"Bellinis," she told them. "It's a girl drink, but since your father can't come, I thought we could indulge."

Lily brightened. "Dad's not coming?"

"No. He phoned to say he's working late."

Lily couldn't hide a smile. "Oh, too bad."

"I can't believe how you've changed this place," Abbie said.

"The walls are such a dreamy blue," Emma added. "And the pictures. They're so interesting."

"Compliments of the Madaket Mall," Marina told them.

Lily asked, "How did you get out to the dump?"

"Sheila Lester took me," Marina began.

Lily interrupted. "How do *you* know Sheila?"

Marina waited a beat or two before responding, indicating—she hoped—that she found Lily's tone a little rude. Something childish within her wanted to say snarkily, *Through your father.* She bit back her annoyance. "I met Sheila when I volunteered to help with the library book sale. She's giving me private lessons in making a lightship basket."

"Sheila's the best," Emma said. "She knows everything about the island."

Abbie asked, "Would you mind if I climbed the ladder and peeked at the loft? It's just that I haven't seen it in years."

"Go ahead," Marina told her.

Abbie went up the ladder. Emma followed. Lily followed her sisters. Marina relaxed, sipping her drink, listening to the girls as they walked around the loft. Because the loft had no closets, Marina had bought plastic crates in a variety of colors and used them as she had in college like an open chest of drawers, her pastel tees and shorts folded neatly and stacked inside. She'd hung her skirts and dresses on hangers on the hooks nailed into the walls, and all the patterns swirled like abstract art.

"Oh, wow, this wasn't here the last time I came up," Lily said, and Marina knew she'd found the mirror.

Emma said, "Such careful workmanship. It must have cost a fortune."

Abbie stuck her head over the edge of the loft. "Where did you get that seashell mirror?"

Marina smiled. "I made it."

"You *made* it?"

"It's not difficult. You just have to be patient. I gathered the shells whenever I walked on the beach, and soaked them in soapy water and dried them in the sun and arranged them the way I wanted them, then super-glued them on the frame."

"Well, I'm impressed." Emma carefully backed down the loft ladder. "I love what you've done up there."

"It's very summery, isn't it?"

"Doesn't it get awfully hot at night?" Emma asked.

"That's why I bought that fan." As she chatted with Emma, Marina strained to hear Abbie and Lily, still up in the loft. Abbie hissed at Lily, "Stop that, Lily. That's private." She suspected that Lily was opening the drawer of the bedside table, and she didn't know if that was a good thing or bad—she'd bought a box of condoms at the pharmacy recently, just in case. If Lily saw them, tough luck. Marina had the right to have sex with whomever she wanted.

"Come on, Lily." Abbie's voice was louder. "We've seen everything there is to see."

Abbie came down the steps, and Lily sulkily followed. They chatted about the island arts and crafts while Marina served dinner, and because the little table was too small for four, they sat on the sofa and chairs, holding their plates on their laps as they ate. Marina asked the girls about their day and refilled their Bellinis. Gradually, as twilight fell, the girls relaxed their guard. Emma seemed the most responsive to Marina's conversation, but Lily answered in abrupt monosyllables. Marina focused her attention on Abbie.

"So you've been traveling for a while, I hear. Where did you go?"

Abbie lit up. "I lived with a family in London."

"Oh, I love London. It's such a great city for walking."

"Exactly! Sometimes on my time off, I'd just wander around the city, ogling the shopwindows, Buckingham Palace, Westminster Abbey, Trafalgar Square—"

Lily broke in. "Well, *I* love being on the island. It's good enough to last a lifetime, for most people."

"Oh, come on, Lily," Emma scoffed. "You're always talking about wanting to live in New York."

"Could I ever just say something without you correcting me?" Lily snapped.

Emma began, "I wasn't—"

Lily glared at Marina. "How long are you renting our Playhouse for?"

Marina blinked, startled by Lily's abrupt change of subject.

"I mean," Lily continued, almost snarling, "since you love cities so much, you're probably bored here."

Marina couldn't stop herself. "Oh, Nantucket's got lots of other . . . *pleasures*." Her tone was gloating, and she was immediately ashamed of herself. Rattled, she rose. "Let me get dessert. Would any of you like coffee?"

Conversation was easy as they ate their meringues, centering on how Marina had baked them, and which island cookbooks were the best. Lily excused herself the moment she'd finished her dessert, explaining that she had work to do for her magazine article. Abbie took her leave shortly after, but to Marina's surprise, Emma remained.

Emma perched on the sofa, holding her dessert plate. She'd hardly eaten all evening. Marina leaned against the kitchen counter and waited.

"How do you do it?" Emma asked quietly. "How do you recover so quickly?"

Marina answered honestly. "I haven't recovered, Emma. I still cry myself to sleep some nights. It helps that I've left the place where Gerry and Dara live, where all our friends live, where every day I have to pass the stores where we shopped together, the restaurants where we ate. And where we worked . . . I think I miss my work as much as my husband. Ex-husband."

"But you seem to enjoy life," Emma said, and as she spoke, her false cheer disappeared and her eyes were full of pain. "I can't believe I'll ever enjoy life again."

Marina took a deep breath. "It's still early for you," she said. "And I'm older than you." She glanced out at the night, so soft and full of stars. "You know what? Let's go for a swim."

Emma shrugged. "My bathing suit—"

"Use one of mine." She climbed the loft stairs, dug out her Speedo and tossed it down to Emma. She pulled on her bikini and tugged a tee shirt on over it.

It was only a few blocks from the Fox house to the Jetties beach, and as they ambled along, Marina found herself telling Emma about finding out about Gerry's affair with Dara, about Dara telling Marina she was pregnant with Gerry's child.

"That's so terrible," Emma said. "How does anybody get over something like that?"

"I guess you just do everything you can," Marina told her. "I saw a therapist, but I have to say she wasn't much help. My friends were all divided between Gerry and me, so they were uncomfortable if I let loose with my anger and misery. A change of scene helps. Being *here* helps."

They had reached the beach. It was after ten, fully dark. All the families were gone, but here and there couples strolled along the water's edge, holding hands and laughing as the gentle tide rinsed over their feet. From the distance, the Sankaty lighthouse winked at them.

Marina waded into the water. The night air was hot, the shallow waves cool.

"It does seem magical here," she told Emma, who had waded in next to her. "Perhaps that's because I'm here as a tourist, and my ex-husband and all that horrible stuff is far away."

"Perhaps." Emma was slowly moving deeper into the water, letting the waves lap at her fingertips, her wrists, her elbows. "As much as I love the island, being here makes me consider myself a failure. Because I failed at work and I failed at love and I have to come home."

Marina gasped a bit as the water lapped against her rib cage. They were far from the shore now. Beneath her feet, the sand was cool and firm.

"Maybe there's another way to think about it," she suggested. "Perhaps you were meant to come home. Perhaps this is where you should be."

"I want to be married," Emma confessed, more to herself than to Marina. "I want to have children. And I want to have enough money to help my father. Perhaps I want too much."

The waters of Nantucket Sound billowed against Marina, lifting her and dropping her with each gentle wave. Far above, the night sky glittered with stars, and in the distance, lights gleamed from boats and laughter drifted from the boats moored in the harbor. All around her the water, so blue in the day, shimmered indigo, only slightly darker than the air around them, and full of glitter.

"Tonight," Marina told Emma, "we have all this." She held her arms out. The last Steamship ferry was approaching, slowly gliding toward the pier, like an enormous swan.

The beach here was wide and gentle. Marina knew she could swim for a long way without coming to any danger. Next to her, Emma flipped on her back and lazily stroked along, her feet making little splashes as she kicked. She felt brave and slightly adventurous, swimming at night, and safe because Emma was next to her. For a while, Marina was a creature of the sea, she could swim forever and never drown. All her sorrows were as far away as the moon, her limbs were strong and willing, and her heart swelled and sang with the pleasure of this unfamiliar act.

She glanced over at Emma. Emma's eyes shone as she turned onto her stomach and did a lazy crawl beside Marina.

"It's like swimming in honey," Marina said. "But we're awfully far out. Let's turn around and go back before we get too tired."

"I don't think I'll ever tire out here," Emma told her, but she ducked under the water and reversed direction.

They swam side by side back to the beach, and the lifting and falling waves carried them gently toward shore.

30

· · · · ·

Abbie

When Abbie arrived at the Parker house, she found Harry in the living room, on his father's lap, while Howell read to him.

"Abbie!" Howell's eyes held a warm smile especially for her. "I'm going mad with this cast thing. Can't drive anywhere. I've got to get out. Will you drive me and Harry somewhere?"

She laughed at his desperation. "Of course. Where would you like to go?"

Howell said softly, "Anywhere you'll take me."

She felt herself blushing. "I was going to take Harry out to r-i-d-e today. You could come watch. Or we could hit one of the beaches."

"I'd love to watch Harry ride," Howell said.

Harry began to dance up and down with excitement. "Horses! Horses!"

"Let's get your sneakers and socks, buddy," Abbie told the little boy. "You can't ride barefoot."

Abbie had already checked with her friend Shelley to be sure it was a good day for a visit. She helped Harry into his booster car seat. Howell leaned on her as she helped him negotiate his ankle into the backseat next to Harry. Her spirits were flying. As she drove out to Hummock Pond Road, she sang silly songs that made Harry giggle, and in the rearview mirror, she saw Howell's eyes resting affectionately on her face.

They arrived at Shelley's farm, parking behind the house in a wide dusty yard opening to a barn and a corral. Shelley came out of the barn to greet them, wearing faded blue jeans and an even more faded tee shirt. She led a white horse spotted with black and brown toward them.

"Hi, guys! Harry, meet Slappy."

Harry was frightened now that he was faced with a real-life, head-tossing horse. He clutched his father's hand and huddled next to him.

"It's okay, buddy," Howell said, bending down to reassure his son. "You can do it."

"He's big, but he's an easy rider," Shelley promised. She fished a bit of carrot out of her pocket and gave it to Harry. "Hold this flat on your hand. Slappy loves treats."

Abbie knelt behind Harry, wrapping her arms around him and enclosing his hand in hers as he held out the carrot. The horse craned his humongous head, pulled back his lips, and snatched up the carrot with his humorous long teeth. He snorted in gratitude and tossed his head around. Harry's eyes were wide.

Shelley laughed. "Come on, Harry. Let's get you up on Slappy's back. I use a western saddle for the kids so they can hold on to the pommel. I'll keep hold of the reins."

Abbie lifted Harry and settled him in the saddle. Harry clutched the pommel.

"Give him a pat on the neck," Shelley instructed Harry. "Tell him he's a good boy. He's just like the rest of us, happy to be complimented."

"You're a good boy, Slappy." Harry's voice was flute-like and tremulous. Abbie was proud of him for not being paralyzed with fear.

"Okay, here we go." Shelley led the horse into the corral and began to walk him around the ring.

Howell and Abbie leaned against the fence, watching.

"Look at his face," Howell said. "He's *shining*." For a moment he rested his hand on Abbie's back. "Thank you for this, Abbie."

Abbie had brought her digital camera. She snapped a dozen photos. "I'll print these off on my computer and make a couple into posters for his room."

"God, what a good idea. You're wonderful, Abbie." Howell's smile was tender. "In so many ways."

Abbie gazed back at him, and for a moment their look was a kind of embrace.

Shelley always had patience for her horses and anyone who loved horses, and she led Slappy in circles around the ring for a good fifteen minutes. Then she helped the little boy dismount and took him into the barn to introduce him to the other two horses. She gave Harry a curry comb and showed him how to groom Slappy. Harry brushed the horse—he had to reach up to get to the animal's side—his face tight with concentration.

Finally, Shelley said, "Okay, Harry, I've got some boring old paperwork waiting for me in the house."

Abbie thanked her friend and hugged her. As they drove away from Shelley's, Harry chattered away, reliving his moments of glory.

"Slappy liked me! He really did! He was so big! I didn't fall off! Did you see how I went all around the circle, Dad?"

"I did. You were brave, Harry. I'm proud of you."

"Howell," Abbie suggested, "show Harry the pictures I snapped." She reached into her bag and handed the camera over the seat back to Howell.

At Howell's suggestion, Abbie drove them back into town so they could stop at the library and get horse books for Harry. Howell limped along into the adult section and checked out a few for himself. Then he settled on a bench in the Atheneum garden while Abbie took Harry to the Nantucket Pharmacy for strawberry ice cream cones. She returned to the garden, gave Howell a cone, and sat on the bench with him while Harry devoured his ice cream. Then he changed into a horse, galloping in circles over the grass.

Abbie sat next to Howell, watching, content in the shade of the crabapple tree.

"This is a perfect day," Howell told Abbie. "Well, almost perfect. I wish I could hold your hand. I wish I could put my arm around you. It's all I want to do—touch you."

Abbie smiled. "I know. Me, too."

Howell leaned back against the bench and stretched his arm out so that it was behind Abbie, just barely touching her. She almost whimpered with lust.

An older woman carrying a book bag and walking with a cane

toddled past them toward another bench set under a tree. Harry galloped up to Abbie and Howell and whinnied. Abbie held out the
last bit of her cone on the flat of her hand, and Harry the Horse nib-
bled it up, shook his head, and galloped away.

The old lady smiled at Abbie and Howell. "You have an
adorable little boy."

Abbie's face went hot.

Howell said simply, "Thank you."

Abbie's heart leapt. *They could be a family*, Howell, Harry, and
Abbie.

At the end of the afternoon, Abbie drove Harry and his father back
to their house near Brant Point. She helped Harry out of the SUV
while Howell negotiated his exit without banging his ankle, then
she hefted the bundle of Harry's library books and held his hand as
she led him to the house. She would fix something special for dinner, she thought. Harry didn't like vegetables, but she thought she
could get him to eat carrots now, since Slappy had eaten them. She
was pleased with herself for the thought, pleased with herself for giving the little boy such a special day, and she was looking forward
with a kind of dreamy confidence to this evening. Harry would fall
asleep easily tonight. Then she and Howell would make love.

She unlocked the door, shoved it open, and ushered Harry inside, then held it wide for Howell to limp through. As she did, something caught at the edge of her senses, something—

Howell's wife stood at the end of the hallway. She wore white
biker shorts and a crimson halter top, and her black hair swayed as
she walked toward them.

"Surprise," she said coolly.

"Mommy!" Harry ran down the hall and threw himself on his
mother.

She lifted him up in her arms. "Hello, Big Guy."

"I rode a horse and he liked me and I got an ice cream cone
and—"

Howell limped past Abbie, who had come to a frozen standstill
by the front door, to his wife's side. He kissed her cheek. "You're
home early."

"Mmm. I missed my boys." She snuggled her son closer.

Harry chirped, "And we went to the library and I got lots of horse books and I was a horse in the garden and—"

"Would you like to go for a little swim?" Howell asked.

"No, it's too late for that. I'll tell you what I would like." Sydney smiled up at her husband, a teasing expression on her face. "I'd like Abbie to take Harry off for a little evening out." She aimed her gaze at Abbie. "Howell will give you some money. You can take Harry to eat at any restaurant you choose. Show him the big yachts along the wharves. Whatever. Keep him out for a good couple of hours, okay?"

Howell stalled. "Maybe today's not the best day for that, Syd. I mean, Harry's been away from the house all afternoon."

"Well, I've been away from *you* all week," Sydney said. "And now and then an adult's needs come before a child's." She flashed a glance at Abbie. "Isn't that right, Abbie?"

Abbie was too shaken with emotion to speak, but she managed to nod an affirmation.

Sydney bent down and set her son on the floor. "Abbie's going to take you out for a special treat. Go on with Abbie now. Mommy and Daddy will see you later."

Harry's lower lip quivered. "But Mommy, I want to stay with you."

"Harry, I'll be with you all weekend, I promise. Run along now, Mommy and Daddy have some—work—to do."

Harry trudged toward Abbie, his face contorted in a pout.

Abbie forced herself to squat down to the little boy's level. "Come on, Harry, we're going to have fun!" She was proud of the lightness of her voice. Actually, she was proud that she wasn't bursting into tears of jealousy and rage.

Sydney leaned against Howell, wrapping her arm around his waist. "Poor baby," she cooed. "Let's get you off your poor ankle and settled somewhere nice and comfortable."

Howell winced as he limped toward the living room.

"Not there," Sydney said. "I want you upstairs." Her voice was silky, seductive. She glanced at Abbie, who stood paralyzed in the hallway. "All right, good-bye, see you in a couple of hours. Take your time."

Abbie had no other choice than to take Harry's little hand and lead him out of the house.

31

·····

Emma

When Emma woke on Sunday morning, she lay in bed listening to the birds sing in the maple tree just outside her window. The summer had grown hot, so she slept naked. Her old soft sheets were luxuriously smooth against her skin. Cinnamon lay purring at the foot of the bed. She stroked him with her toes. He yawned and rolled over.

The aroma of freshly brewed coffee floated tantalizingly up from the kitchen. She didn't work for Francine today, but she'd agreed to help out her friend Marcia with some landscaping work, and before that, she had her share of the housework to do. Still, she allowed herself a few more minutes to luxuriate in the sultry summer morning.

A peculiar thing was happening to her. She allowed the thought to surface like a diamond from the dark depths of her mind. She turned it from side to side, watching it flare and sparkle. She was actually *glad* to be back on Nantucket. No, more than that—it was as if she were getting to know the island for the first time. With Millicent Bracebridge and Spencer, she was learning and relearning Nantucket lore, and every time she walked around the town, she remembered the island's past—the whaling captains' brick houses, the windmill—and she remembered her own past as well.

She was oddly happy. She was enjoying her life.

And she realized, with a start, that she'd been lying here lost in her reflections for at least ten minutes, and she hadn't thought of Duncan or Alicia or the investment firm once.

It was almost a miracle. Certainly, it was a kind of rejuvenation.

Throwing back the cotton sheet, she rose, dressed in shorts and a tee, and padded barefoot down the stairs and into the kitchen. Abbie was standing in front of the refrigerator.

Emma smiled. "Good morning!"

Abbie slammed the refrigerator door shut. Her face was dark with anger. "There's no milk." She seemed on the verge of tears.

Emma wanted to back away from the zone of Abbie's black mood. "Well, I'll bike over to Cumberland Farms and grab a quart."

"No. I'm going to wake Lily. She can damn well go get the milk. Shopping for groceries is her responsibility."

"Oh, come on, Abbie. It's only seven o'clock. She probably stayed out late last night at one of her functions. I'm up and I don't mind."

Abbie was adamant. "Lily made an agreement with us to do her share of the necessary chores around the house. Honestly, Emma, Lily's not going to grow up if we keep doing her work for her!"

Emma squinted at her older sister. "Something else is going on. Something else is wrong."

Abbie flushed and averted her eyes.

"Look," Emma said quietly. "It's Sunday. We've got the morning off. I'd like to sit out on the deck and enjoy the day." She had a brainstorm. "Hey. I'll bet Marina could loan us some milk."

Abbie sulked. "She's probably not awake."

"She is. I can see her. She's sitting under the tree." Without waiting for Abbie's decision, Emma opened the kitchen door. "I'll be right back with the milk."

Emma strolled down the backyard, enjoying the soft brush of green grass against the soles of her feet. Marina was settled in the red chair, a mug of coffee on the little table next to her, a book in her hands. She wore a slinky silk caftan in a pale blue that made her blond coloring angelic.

"Hi, Emma." Marina put her book on the table and stretched her arms high. "Isn't it a glorious day?"

"It is. Or it will be once we've had our coffee. I've come to ask if we could borrow some milk."

"Of course. Help yourself."

"Thanks. I'll bring you a fresh carton. I've got to go to the grocery store today. Lily forgot to go."

"Are you working today?" Marina asked.

"I am. For a friend who's a landscaper." Emma stared up at the cloudless sky. "I'd better remember my sunblock. What are you doing today?"

"Later on I'm going over to Sheila's to work on my lightship basket."

Emma nodded toward the driveway. "Dad's truck is already gone."

"I know. I haven't seen him since I invited you girls to dinner." Marina laughed. "I think he's terrified that I'm trying to get serious."

Emma laughed, too, surprised and pleased that Marina would speak so openly about her father. "No, Dad's just really busy in the summer. He's OCD about every nail on every board on anything he's building." She slipped into the cottage, found the milk, poured some into a pitcher, and went back outside. "Thanks for this. Maybe I'll see you later."

"We could go for a swim tonight," Marina suggested. "Maybe Abbie and Lily would like to go, too."

"Good idea. I'll ask them."

Back at the house, Emma presented Abbie with the pitcher of milk. They stirred their coffee and went out onto the deck to lounge in the morning sun. Cinnamon was already there, stretched out on a wicker rocker, drugged with the heat.

After a few moments of silence, Emma said, "Okay, Abbie, what's wrong?"

Abbie shrugged. "I'm fine. Just tired, I guess."

Emma studied her sister. "It's that man, isn't it? That married man."

"You know nothing about it."

"It's because it's the weekend. His wife's home."

Abbie sniffed and refused to answer.

"You don't want to be a home wrecker, Abbie. They've got a little boy."

"Yes," Abbie said, and all at once she was spilling with emotion.

"Emma, Harry's mother is a world-class bitch. She's cold and heart-less and domineering. She's an absolute Nazi mom. If you saw how happy Harry is when he's with me, you'd understand. The poor kid is so fragile mentally, he's like a turtle hiding in a shell, but when he's with me, he's secure enough to emerge. I took him over to Shel-ley's on Friday and he got to ride a horse, and he was so brave! He was so proud of himself!" Abbie began to cry.

"Oh, honey." Emma went into the kitchen, grabbed a box of tis-sues, and brought it out to Abbie. After a moment she said, "Abbie. You need to find your own husband. You need to have your own children."

Abbie shook her head rapidly as she blew her nose. "No. You don't understand. I've never felt like this about any other man. Howell and I are soul mates. He's in love with me, Emma. He told me he's in love with me. He's not in love with his wife. But things can't be changed with a snap of the fingers. I know that. I trust him. It's just hard to be away from him and Harry. They are where I *be-long*."

"Yes, well, I thought Duncan was where I belonged," Emma re-minded her sister. "I thought the investment firm was where I be-longed. Sometimes your instincts are just off."

"Fine." Abruptly, Abbie stood up. "I've got to clean the upstairs and you've got to clean the downstairs, and Lily has to get out of bed and go to the grocery store."

"Abbie. It's early," Emma objected.

But Abbie stormed off, letting the screen door slam behind her as she charged into the kitchen.

Emma sipped her coffee and willed herself to relax. She had housework to do before she joined the landscaping crew, but she wanted to take just a few more minutes to enjoy the serenity of the summer morning. Love was such a mystery, she thought. Certainly she'd been as sure of Duncan's love as Abbie was of Howell Parker's, and Duncan hadn't been married to someone else. Duncan had asked Emma to marry him. Duncan had given Emma an engage-ment ring. Thinking of Duncan made something inside her cramp with grief. She was learning to *think* without sorrow, but when would she ever be free of the bitter stings of jealousy and regret?

Damn. Her mood was spoiled. She was worried about Abbie and

that married man, and she was a little pissed off at Lily, too. Emma had never felt responsible for Lily like Abbie always had. Abbie had really been a kind of mother to Lily, but they were all adults now, and Abbie was right, Lily needed to grow up. Obviously, the eighteen months Abbie was away had changed her. Her life was no longer centered—*anchored*—in this house, this family. Lily hadn't seemed to realize that yet. Perhaps she didn't want to, and Emma understood. She missed having a mother figure around, but Abbie had never been that for her. Emma had grown accustomed to living with that loss. It was an ache, and a yearning, that she carried in her body like an injured limb.

Abbie came out of the house, letting the screen door slam. "She's not here. Her bed hasn't been slept in. So she's with some man, and I'll bet you a hundred dollars she'll forget her share of the work."

Emma stood up. "I'll go to the grocery store."

"*You* shouldn't have to! It's Lily's job. And what about your job, cleaning the downstairs? How are you going to do that?"

"Now who sounds like a Nazi?" Emma retorted. "The downstairs is clean enough. No one's going to run a home inspection on us. *I'll* get the groceries, and *you* calm down!"

By the time Emma had gone to the store, bought the groceries, carried them into the house, and put them all away, it was time for her to meet Marcia at the Prestons' house. It was going to be such fun, working at the Prestons'. Their yard was a showplace, an acre of land on the cliffs overlooking the harbor, complete with a rose garden, a maze with topiary, a vegetable garden, and a flower garden circling a reflecting pool and fountain. The job was a plum, enhancing the reputation of any landscaper, and Emma was glad. Marcia had been one of Emma's best friends in high school.

Emma biked out to the Prestons' house and found Marcia unloading tools from her truck. Marcia had the field-hockey swagger of a healthy, bossy woman. Her dark hair was in braids and she was already darkly tanned from outdoor work.

She hugged Emma. "Emma, you're a lifesaver. I can't get enough help in July and August." She nodded toward her male clone, a big, broad-shouldered man with his dark hair cut short. "You remember Brian, right?"

Emma grinned. She'd had a crush on Marcia's older brother all through high school. He'd been captain of the football team, leading the Whalers to victory, and all the girls had crushes on him. "Hey, Brian. What are you up to these days?"

"I've joined my dad's plumbing business, just like everyone thought I would," Brian said. "And on summer weekends, I turn into my sister's slave."

Marcia snorted. "I wish. Help me lift the wheelbarrow out." While her brother easily hefted it up and onto the ground, she said to Emma, "I'm giving you the easy job today. All you have to do is weed the flower garden around the reflecting pool. Take this basket. Pile the weeds in it, and when it's full, dump it in the truck. Brian and I will be trimming the topiary. One more thing, the Prestons often have lunch served on their deck. If they do, stop weeding there and go to the vegetable garden. The Prestons don't like to have workers in sight when they're entertaining."

Emma saluted her friend, grabbed the basket, and set off walking around the enormous house and down the lawn toward the pool. The garden was vibrant with daisies, foxglove, delphiniums, globe thistle, and phlox. The variety of colors was stunning. Emma looked toward the deck, and seeing no people there, began to weed at the end closer to the house. She'd forgotten to bring her iPod with her and she found she didn't mind. There was something very satisfying about kneeling among the flowers, feeling the hot sun on her shoulders and the tug of the weeds between her fingers.

She was halfway down the length of the pool when she heard voices. She saw the glass door sliding open from the house to the deck. A group of people came out and a woman in a maid's uniform followed, carrying a tray of drinks. Emma quickly gathered her tools and basket and slipped away from the pool and through the hedge toward the vegetable garden.

She was on her knees among a row of tomato plants when she heard someone speak her name. Shading her eyes with her hand, she looked up. Spencer Bracebridge stood there, looking like a GQ ad in his white flannels and blue blazer.

"I thought that was you," Spencer said. "You're really a jack of all trades, aren't you?"

Emma felt awkward as she squatted there in the dirt in her shorts and tee shirt and long-billed scalloper's cap. There was something a little too Lord of the Manor and Peasant Girl in the moment to suit her. She stood up, stretching to release the tightness of her back.

"I prefer Jacqueline of all trades," she quipped. "How are you, Spencer?"

"I'm good. And I'm working right now, too, actually. The Prestons have agreed to hold a fund-raiser for the historical association here at the end of the summer and we're going over the details."

"Cool." Something in the way Spencer looked at Emma made her tingle. But what was she thinking? She was sweaty and had dirt smeared on her clothes and probably on her face, too.

"Actually, I was out on the deck and saw you and I just wanted to, um, come out to say hello."

"Well," Emma said. "Hello." She couldn't stop smiling at him. She told herself that he was undoubtedly used to women gawking at him.

Spencer seemed slightly tongue-tied. "Um, it's getting hot."

"It certainly is." His shyness was turning her shy, too.

"Did I ever tell you how grateful I am that you brought my grandmother to my talk?"

"Oh, well, I was glad to do it." Emma thought Spencer was sort of leaning toward her. Was he attracted to her? He did come to lunch every day at Mrs. Bracebridge's. His eyes were so warm on her face.

Spencer touched her arm. "She really likes you, and believe me, she doesn't like everyone. And she and my mother act like a pair of wet cats with each other."

Emma laughed. "They're both strong-willed women."

"I know. You're so great with them. I really . . ." Spencer paused. "I wonder if you'd ever like to . . . Well, you probably just . . ."

Was he trying to ask her out? The heat between them was not all caused by the sun. Emma leaned closer to him.

"Spencer?" From the deck, a woman called. "Lunch is served!"

"Oh. Damn. I've got to go," Spencer said. He became formal again. "It was so nice to see you here, Emma."

"Nice to see you, too."

"Emma—" He hesitated, then plunged ahead. "I wanted to tell

you—if you ever have to choose between doing what my mother says and what my grandmother says, choose my grandmother. Or if that's a problem, call me. I want you to know you can always call me."

So that was it. He had only come out to talk to her as an employer giving her instructions. Emma pulled away from his hand. "Good to know, Spencer. I've got to get back to work." She turned her back on him and knelt back down among the tomato plants.

"Okay, well, see you tomorrow," Spencer said.

Emma focused her energy on the weeds, working fast and hard. Hadn't she learned her lesson with wealthy boys? What was she thinking! Imagining that Spencer Bracebridge was interested in her. Really.

By the time she'd finished the vegetable garden, she was trembling with fatigue.

Marcia loped up next to her. "Wow, Emma, you are one maniac weeder. I want all the hours you can give me. Come sit in the shade and drink a lemonade with me and Brian."

Emma rose and followed Marcia out to the truck. Brian was already there, hauling his tee shirt off, exposing his tanned, muscular chest. The three of them sat on the bed of the truck, drinking cold bottles of lemonade from the cooler.

"Brian's got something to celebrate," Marcia announced.

"Really?" Emma arched an inquisitive eyebrow.

Brian rolled his shoulders and groaned. "Oh, come on, Marsh, give me a break."

"But, Brian, it's a big deal!" Marcia protested.

"No, it's *not* a big deal," Brian insisted.

Emma laughed. "Can you at least tell me what isn't a big deal?"

"Brian got his Mass plumber's license."

"Congratulations, Brian," Emma said.

"It's no big deal," Brian grumbled.

"Yes, it is," Marcia insisted, aiming her words at Emma. "Now Brian can take over from Dad. Dad only likes to do the little jobs for the people he's always known. Brian can take on some big fat new jobs for the new trophy houses."

"That's great, Brian," Emma said.

Brian grinned at her. His teeth were very white against his

tanned skin. "It is, actually. I'm making a ton of money. I've bought a piece of property out in Dionis, and before long I'm going to build myself a trophy house of my own."

"Then you'll need a wife to fill it with kids," Marcia told her brother, and winked at Emma.

32

· · · · ·

Lily

Lily had no idea where she was. The bed, the room, the very smell of the air, were all unfamiliar to her. She shut her eyes tight and took a moment to listen to her body. Nope. She wasn't hungover. She hadn't passed out at a party. She'd only done that once, anyway, back in college, and once was enough; she'd never let herself get that drunk again.

But where was she?

She opened her eyes. She was facing a plain brown wall. No pictures. She smelled a dampness in the air, a kind of basement smell . . . and then, in a rush, it all came back to her.

She was in Jason's apartment. She was in bed with Jason.

Last night rolled past her in a blur of memory. She'd attended two cocktail parties, and a concert. Jason had been waiting for her in his truck after the concert, just as he'd promised.

He'd stepped out of the cab and come around to open the door for her, a gentlemanly touch that pleased Lily.

He'd been smug. "I've got a surprise for you."

He'd driven them over to Wild Rose Drive and parked in front of an old, three-story shingled house. This close to town, all the parking places on the street were filled, but he steered his truck into the driveway of the house, turned off the ignition, and came around to open the truck door. He took her by the hand and led her to the back of the house, in through a door, and down a set of steps, where he unlocked a door.

"My year-round apartment!" he announced.

Lily had stepped inside. "I don't understand."

Jason strode through the room, turning on lights. The apartment was small, basically a living room with a galley kitchen attached, and a boxlike bedroom with the world's smallest shower-stall bathroom. It was furnished scantily—a bed, a futon for a sofa, an ancient and obviously wobbly table.

"I just rented this!" Jason waved his arms triumphantly.

"In the summer? It must cost a fortune."

"Mrs. Fischer's a friend of my mother's. Her husband died a month ago, and she wanted to have someone in the house she can trust. They used to use this place for their grandchildren, but they're all grown. She gave me a great deal on the rent."

"But you don't have to pay rent at your parents' house," Lily pointed out.

Jason came toward her, smiling. "True. But there's no *privacy* in my parents' house. You're not the kind of woman I want to keep— *seeing*—in a pickup truck. You deserve a palace, Lily. Until I can afford that, I can at least offer this." He took her hand and pulled her into the bedroom. "The sheets are brand-new. And I washed them."

Lily sank down on the bed. A wooden chest stood at one end of the room. Curtains with sailboats on them spanned the high, narrow windows.

"I haven't had time to fix it up yet," Jason said. "And I want to paint over this gross brown, too. But for now—my parents gave me the bed from our guest room. It's hardly been used at all." A pair of candles stood on the chest. Jason lit them. He left the room, returning with two flutes and a bottle of champagne. "Let's celebrate."

She didn't even need the champagne to feel intoxicated. It was enough to have Jason next to her. It was ambrosia to know that he cared enough about her to rent his own apartment.

Now, next to her, Jason snored gently. He'd hooked one of his legs over hers and his body warmth almost disguised the chill of the basement walls. Lily shifted onto her back and checked her watch.

It was after eight, but this was the one morning of the week when she didn't have to hurry. Except she did have a lot to write up. Last week had been filled with activities, and it would take some time and concentration to be sure the right names were matched with the people she'd photographed.

Plus, she had some serious atonement to do with her sisters. Emma didn't seem too upset about Lily forgetting to go to the grocery store, but yesterday Abbie had turned into a drama queen, storming past Lily, head high, not speaking. Having Abbie back home wasn't the unmitigated pleasure Lily had anticipated.

What a confusing summer it was turning out to be! Emma was sad, Abbie was huffy, and the Playhouse was inhabited by a woman with designs on their father. And Jason—oh, this thing with Jason was happening so fast! He had rented an apartment just because of her! Last night when they were making love, he had told her he loved her, and she had told him she loved him. And she did. But she didn't want to get serious yet, not so soon. And not—she allowed herself to be brutally honest in her secret thoughts—not with a man who could only afford a basement apartment. She wanted to live in a house on the cliff, a house like Eartha's. Thank heavens for Eartha, she was the only part of the summer that came close to matching Lily's dreams.

Her thoughts made her restless. She slithered out of bed and slipped into the bathroom to dress. When she came out, Jason was still sleeping. She wrote him a note and tiptoed out of his apartment and up the stairs to the street.

The morning air was fresh, the sky bright blue. As she strolled along the narrow lanes and over cobblestone streets to her own home, she fished her cell phone out of her bag and listened to her voice mail.

Invitations to a few more events—good.

A snippy message from Abbie: *No milk in the house. God, you are such a spoiled brat.* Ouch. Lily would have to go to the store today.

Then, Eartha's raspy voice: *Honey, some friends of mine just arrived on their yacht and want me to come to dinner tonight. Wanna go with me? You might like their son.*

Oh my God, Lily thought! Her heart leapt. Dinner on a yacht?

With Eartha and a man Lily might like? As she walked, she clicked in Eartha's number and agreed to meet her employer at Straight Wharf at six.

When she walked into her house, the only sound Lily heard was the vacuum running upstairs. That would be Abbie. Lily rushed through the house, grabbed the grocery list off the refrigerator door and the keys off the hook by the back door, and hurried out to the car. At the Stop&Shop, she filled the cart so full she could scarcely push the damn heavy thing. When she got home, Abbie was gone, and so was everyone else. Hurriedly she put away the groceries. She raced up to the bathroom—she had to admit, it was awfully nice that Abbie had washed the towels and put out fresh ones—showered and washed her hair, then slipped on shorts and a tee shirt and grabbed up her digital camera and her laptop. She grabbed a banana and a Diet Coke for her breakfast and went out to the patio. She linked her camera to her computer and downloaded the photos while she ate, then opened her notebook and began to write.

The phone rang, breaking her concentration.

"Hey, Lily." Jason's voice was rumbly, warm, and masculine. "Why'd you leave? You should have woken me. I wanted to take you out to breakfast."

"Oh, Jason, I'm sorry, but I had to get home and go to the grocery store. If I didn't, Abbie would absolutely detonate."

Jason laughed. "How about lunch, then?"

"I can't. I've got to write up a bunch of stuff for the magazine. I should have done it last night, but you—*distracted* me."

"Can I take you out to dinner?"

"Oh, Jason, I'm sorry. I've got another event." It was only a white lie, Lily told herself. And God knew, dinner on a yacht certainly ranked as an *event* for her.

"Damn. I won't get to see you at all today?"

She closed her eyes, allowing herself a moment to envision his mouth, his lips, his hands, his body . . . "But I'll come over tonight," she promised. "As soon as I can. And I'll spend the night."

33
. . . . .

Marina

Sunday evening, Marina settled out beneath the apple tree with a glass of wine and the Sunday papers. She'd had a good day. She'd gone to church, and chatted with people at coffee hour, had a pleasant lunch at the Boarding House, then spent a few hours in Sheila's studio working on her lightship basket. In the late afternoon, she'd gone for a swim, and now she was showered and pleasantly relaxed.

And she'd only thought about Jim seventy-five or eighty times.

She'd been aware all day that Jim was around. All morning he'd hammered away, repairing the steps at the front of the house. Later, she'd heard Abbie and Jim talking and laughing as they washed the windows.

Now she couldn't help noticing that Jim's red truck was parked in the driveway. Maybe another woman had picked him up in her car. Well, good luck to her, whoever she was. Jim was a gorgeous man, but he seemed emotionally imprisoned by his daughters. She'd considered not sitting outside, because she didn't want to seem to be telegraphing her availability to Jim, if he happened to be watching from the house. But she'd rented the cottage. She wasn't going to hide inside, as if she'd done something wrong. It was cool there, so pleasant.

She took her time reading the papers and sipping her wine. She heard the door slam on Foxes' house, but didn't allow herself to observe who was coming or going.

At least, she decided, if she was obsessed with Jim, that was better than being obsessed with Gerry and Dara and their baby. Which was due any minute, she thought.

The light was fading from the sky as Marina folded the newspapers and carried them into the house and the recycling box. She decided to have a sinfully big bowl of ice cream for dinner—surely she could allow herself to indulge after a day of biking and swimming. She curled up on the sofa with a novel, but by ten her eyes were closing, so she climbed the loft to bed and fell asleep at once.

She woke at eleven. The moment her eyes snapped open, she knew she was doomed for one of her insomniac nights. She went down the ladder to the main room, picked up her novel, and settled in for a long read. She had nowhere she had to be tomorrow, she reminded herself. She could sleep all day if she wanted to. At least she knew enough by now not to lie in the dark with her eyes closed—that would guarantee that her obsession with Gerry and Dara, and now, Jim Fox, would buzz through her thoughts like a plague of mosquitoes.

The novel was a page-turner mystery by a writer she enjoyed. She yawned and stretched out on the sofa, feeling cozy in the circle of light cast by the reading lamp.

Someone knocked on her door.

"Marina? It's Jim."

She was wearing only her nightgown, a little bit of emerald silk which was held up by two thin straps and ended at her thighs. She thought about going up to the loft to find her wrapper, but decided the hell with that. If he was going to come here at this hour, he could take her as he found her.

She opened the door. She'd forgotten how handsome he was.

"I saw your light come on." Jim wore a white tee shirt and baggy khaki shorts and he smelled like soap. "I can't sleep. I thought perhaps you couldn't sleep, either." He was leaning toward her, as if expecting to walk in.

The tug between them was powerful, but she didn't want to seem eager. "I'm reading."

He put his hand on the doorjamb. "Marina, I want to talk to you."

"You don't have to explain anything, Jim."

"For Christ's sake, Marina!" Jim growled. He stepped forward, pulled her into his arms, and kissed her hard, crushing her lips, pressing her head back, forcing his body against her.

She tightened her arms around his neck and lifted herself against him.

Holding her to him, Jim entered the cottage, slamming the door shut with his foot, and he half walked, half carried her to the sofa. He kissed her mouth, he clutched her hair with his hands as he kissed her neck and collarbone.

Then, abruptly, he pulled away. He held her from him with both hands on her shoulders.

"I want to talk to you," he said. "I need to tell you some things."

"You don't have to," she protested. "I'm sorry if I rushed you, I—"

"Listen to me," Jim insisted. *"Listen."*

Marina shifted slightly away from him and turned so that she could sit with crossed legs, facing him. "I'm listening."

He took hold of her hands. "I've been trying to figure out how to say this." He cleared his throat. "I've decided that you are like music to me. You know how you go along, busy with life, and then one day you turn on the radio and a song hits you and your whole body responds, your heart and soul and body, and you think—why have I been living without that? How have I been living without that? I need that every day in my life."

Astonished, Marina said, "That's quite a compliment."

"It's not a compliment. It's not a line to get you into bed. It's the truth. It's a fact. Ever since you came to the cottage to see about renting it, I've wanted to be with you. The moment I saw you, it was as if I knew everything I needed to know about you. But I wasn't thinking about your side, about you knowing everything you need to know about me." Now he dropped her hands and turned away. "I haven't told *anyone* this before."

Marina held her breath. She could sense his struggling.

"I was having an affair when my wife died." He clenched his fists. "She drowned. I don't know, I'll never know, if Danielle found out and that's why she committed suicide. If it *was* suicide. The autopsy showed she'd taken an overdose of her medication. Perhaps she just made a mistake. Sometimes . . . sometimes she thought she could swim forever." He ran his hand over his face, then continued.

"Danielle always had emotional troubles. She tried everything, psy-chiatrists, medications, exercise, super blue-green algae—but it all got worse and worse for her. She was difficult to live with. She was difficult for herself to live with. And she had this spiritual side. Or maybe I should call it mystical. She wasn't happy here. She often talked about being *there*. And all I can hope is that she's *there* now. She loved our daughters with all her heart, but it just wasn't enough."

"Oh, Jim." Marina wanted to touch him consolingly, but held still.

"She started Prozac, and for a while we thought she was getting better. One night I went to Gretchen's house. I told Danielle I had to double-check a house I was caretaking. It was early September, still hurricane season. I was just gone for an hour or so. When I came home, Danielle was gone. I waited up all night. I drove around the island, searching for her." Jim was nearly bent double now, sitting with his head hanging low and his arms crossed over his knees. When he spoke, his voice was scarcely audible. "I didn't even think of notifying the police. Sometimes Danielle went off without telling us. Thursday I got the girls dressed and fed and off to school like al-ways, and then I called some of our friends. No one had seen her." He paused. "That evening the police came to the house. Danielle's body had washed up on the beach out at Surfside."

"I'm so sorry," Marina whispered.

"It was devastating for the girls." His face was grim. "The pain of losing their mother—oh, God, it was so hard. I don't know, I'll never know, if Danielle found out about me and Gretchen. It only happened twice, but it happened the night Danielle died, and I don't think I'll ever stop feeling guilty. Forget being with another woman, *if only I had stayed home*. If only I had stayed home, I would have kept Danielle from going out. We might have fought. We often fought. But she would have stayed alive. The girls would have had their mother." He buried his face in his hands. "The girls don't know about the affair. I don't think anyone on the island knows, or knew. It was just a couple of times, it wasn't *love*—but I know I'm still a shit for doing it."

Marina rose, went into the kitchen, and set about brewing tea. Now she knew why the British made tea in every mystery she'd ever read. It provided a moment, a space, to step back from the anguish and catch your breath. It gave you something sensible to do, as if you could ever do anything that mattered.

She carried the tea tray over to the table.

"Thanks," Jim said, his voice husky. "But I'd rather have a brandy."

"I've only got wine."

"That's fine."

She poured them both a glass, set one before him, and returned to her place on the sofa.

"Gretchen left the island shortly after Danielle's death." Jim took a sip of wine and a deep breath. "I haven't heard from her since. She was the only one, as far as I know, who knew about her and me. Not that there was a 'her and me.' It was just two times. And she wasn't in love with me. She was an actress, she was on her way to California." He drank more wine. "The only other person I've spoken to about all this is a counselor I went to see in Boston a few years ago. For years I focused my whole life, my time, my thoughts, everything, on raising the girls. I know I can never make up for the loss of their mother. For a long time I didn't date or see any women. I felt I shouldn't; it seemed to me that being celibate was what I should do, what I deserved to do, to atone for Danielle's death."

"I can understand that."

He looked at Marina. "So now you know why we're such an odd family."

She objected gently, "I don't think you're odd at all."

"Well." He nodded. "I guess the girls have turned out remarkably well, given what they went through. Sometimes it seems a long time ago. Well, it was years ago, and the loss is part of our lives. We're used to it. The girls have grown up. They're competent, happy—well, perhaps not so happy right now. I mean, Emma's miserable since that creep Duncan dumped her. But we manage to roll along okay together."

"I like your daughters. I think they're charming."

"Thanks. Sometimes they can be . . . rather opinionated."

Marina touched his hand. "Jim, have you never dated another woman since your wife died?"

"Well, I've *seen* other women." His face went crimson for a moment. "But to be honest, not very often and I've always kept that secret. I haven't brought another woman into the house. Into my life. Into *our* lives." He turned to face Marina. "But I never wanted to until now. That's why I'm here. I don't know exactly what I'm saying here. I don't want to rush anything. But I want to have you in my life. I want you to meet my friends. I want to go places with you." He smiled bashfully. "I don't know why, but you just fascinate the hell out of me."

Marina laughed. "And you fascinate the hell out of me."

"And there's something else," Jim said.

She shivered at the intensity of the moment. "Yes?"

"This." He leaned forward and kissed her. "There's this."

"Jim," Marina said. "Wait."

He pulled away. "I don't want to rush you—"

"Rush me all you want," Marina said. "First, just let me turn off the light."

34

· · · · ·

Abbie

Abbie didn't sleep. She tossed in her bed, tortured with thoughts of Howell making love with Sydney. She rose early in the morning, while the others were still sleeping. She would have liked it, she admitted to herself, if Lily had forgotten to go to the grocery store again. It would have felt so good to yell at someone. She kicked herself for that thought. Still, it would have been something positive to do, to buy groceries. But the shelves were stocked. She settled on putting together a stew in the Crock-Pot and making a carrot cake with buttercream frosting. For the first time ever, she wasn't tempted to lick the icing off the beaters.

She biked over to the Levins, and after making more mistakes on the computer keyboard in ten minutes than she usually made all morning, she got herself in control and concentrated on her job, which made the time go faster.

Finally, it was time to bike over to the Parker house. She biked around their block a few times, trying to get her breath in control. She didn't know if Sydney would still be there. Probably she'd gone back to New York.

But when Abbie tapped on the door and then slipped into the front hall, there was Howell's wife. Sydney looked whip-thin and brittle in her black suit and crisp black hair.

"Hi, Abbie. Come into the living room with me. I need to talk to you."

Oh, man, Abbie thought. She swallowed. "Okay." She held her head high as she followed the other woman into the living room.

Sydney shut the door. "I understand you took Harry horseback riding."

Abbie's blood pressure dropped back to normal. "That's true. I have a friend—"

"I don't want you taking him again."

"But he loved it!" Abbie protested. "He *loves* horses!"

"I'm well aware of that. He is my son, after all. But he's only a little boy, and he's a particularly fragile child. Oh, for Christ's sake, don't look so horrified. I don't mean he has a *condition* or anything like that. But he's clumsy. He's not naturally athletic. And he takes everything to heart so terribly. He needs to toughen up, and I mean mentally as well as physically, before he does anything serious like horseback riding."

"We didn't let him go off on his own," Abbie assured her. "My friend Shelley was with him every minute. Harry didn't really ride. He didn't hold the reins. Shelley held the reins and only led him around the ring."

Sydney crossed her arms and tapped her foot. "I appreciate your kindness and your friend's kindness. But I don't want it to happen again. Is that understood?"

Abbie took a deep breath. It was odd, being spoken to this way by someone pretty much her own age. But Sydney was Abbie's employer. "Yes. I understand."

"And you won't take him horseback riding again." She glared at Abbie, waiting for her to parrot back her words.

"No. I won't take Harry horseback riding again."

Sydney sent Abbie off to the beach with Harry. She had already packed a basket for them and dressed her little boy in bathing suit and flip-flops. Abbie had to leave the Parker house without even seeing Howell.

Dutifully, Abbie helped Harry build an intricate sand castle. She walked on the beach, collecting shells with him. She continually slathered him with sunblock. Time seemed to stand still even though Harry was especially animated and brave today. But at last she took the little boy back to his house.

Sydney was gone.

And Howell was there.

Howell reclined on the sofa, his ankle in its cast propped on a pillow. Harry raced in, jumped into his father's arms, and reeled off a list of the adventures he'd had with Abbie that afternoon.

"Abbie." Howell's eyes were warm on her face. "Can you stay for dinner with us tonight? Please? I need to talk to you."

"All right." Abbie turned away to hide the hope that she knew must be glowing from her eyes.

In a kind of trance she prepared dinner and got Harry fed and bathed and ready for bed. Howell read Harry a story and tucked him in, and the little boy fell asleep easily.

Quietly, they left the room and went downstairs. Howell sat on the sofa, but Abbie sat in a chair across from him.

"Abbie," Howell said. "I'm sorry about the way Sydney treated you on Friday."

Abbie couldn't speak. She could only wait. She was like a prisoner waiting for a verdict.

"Abbie, listen to me. I don't want you to imagine that I made love with Sydney this weekend—"

Abbie dug her fingers into her palms, fighting for dignity, but unable to keep quiet. "How could I not? She was so obviously—in the mood—for you."

"It was an act, Abbie. A show. If I'd objected, we would have fought, and I hate having Harry see us fight. Anyway, all we did was argue, but not too much, because she'd made plans to go out for dinner with some New York politicos who were here for the weekend and she needed me as her willing accessory. Believe me, it's in public, not in private, that she wants me to play the role of the adoring husband."

Abbie searched Howell's face, hoping he was telling the truth, needing him to say more.

He leaned toward her. "Abbie, I'm going to ask Sydney for a divorce."

Her heart leapt. "Oh, Howell."

"But I need time," Howell continued. "There's a lot to figure out. I don't know where I want to live. I don't know that I want to keep the job I have or take one of the offers I've received. Most of all, there's Harry. I need to think about how to do this in the best way for him." Howell frowned. "I don't want Harry ever to think I left Sydney for you. I want him to like you. I want him to love you. I want him, most of all, to feel safe with you."

Abbie said, "I see." She struggled to appear sympathetic and concerned when really, she wanted to jump to her feet and cheer. *Howell wanted to be with her! He was going to divorce Sydney!* She would spend her life with this man and she would give real nurturing love to little Harry. She'd provide the warmth and consistency and maternal affections the little boy needed. She wanted to hug herself and laugh with glee like a child on Christmas morning.

"But we have to go slowly," Howell continued. "It would be a disaster if Sydney suspects how I feel about you before the divorce takes place. Can you trust me with this, Abbie? Can you understand—I don't want Harry to connect our divorce with this island. We need to take our time. The more Harry gets to know you, the better." He smiled suddenly. "And the more I get to know you, the better for me."

He looked at her then with such love in his eyes that Abbie could do only one thing. She went into his arms.

35

. . . . .

Emma

As she did every day, five days a week, Emma opened the unlocked front door and stepped into the Bracebridge house. From the living room came the sound of angry voices. She shut the door behind her quietly and stood for a moment, trying to decide what to do. Emma didn't want to be eavesdropping, but she did want Sandra Bracebridge to know she had arrived at work on time.

"It *is* my Elizabeth Rebecca Coffin painting!" Millicent Bracebridge insisted. "*Mine*. My parents gave it to me for my twenty-first birthday. And if I want to give it to the historical association, I can and I will!"

She was speaking of the illustrious oil painting that hung above the fireplace in the living room. It was called *Gathering Seaweed* and featured a horse and cart on the beach with a young man and a pitchfork. It had been painted around 1900, and it glowed as if lit within. Certainly it was the focal point of the room. On the other hand, so many other treasures and antiques were gathered in the room, it was hard to focus on one.

"Millicent." Sandra Bracebridge's voice was honeyed. "Darling, I know what you're doing. You want to give the painting to the NHA so that you'll help Spencer's career along. But he doesn't need you to do that. He's doing perfectly well on his own."

"Of course he is!" Millicent snapped. "I know that. That is *not* why I want to give them the painting now. I want to get it out of this dark old house and exhibited where people can see it. I'm getting old. My vision is going. I can't see it. I shouldn't be selfish."

"Well, then, Millicent," Sandra cooed smoothly, "why not *sell* it to the NHA? Or sell it to someone else. If you don't want to be selfish, then think of your children."

"My son left you a very healthy inheritance," Millicent reminded her daughter-in-law.

"That's true. And I'll always be grateful to him for that. But if you don't want me to have any more money—although may I remind you that in this economy, money isn't worth what it used to be—at least think of your grandson. You should give Spencer the painting to sell. He could use—"

Spencer spoke up. "Mother. If Grandmother gives me the Coffin painting, I would give it to the NHA. That's where it belongs."

"Oh, of course you want to seem high-minded!" Sandra's voice grew shrill.

Hearing Spencer's voice spurred Emma into action. She opened the front door and slammed it shut loudly. "Hello!" she called.

"Oh, for God's sake, that girl's here," Sandra snapped.

Spencer stepped out into the hall. "Hi, Emma. Come on in. We're just having a little family discussion."

"Not anymore, we're not." Sandra grabbed up her lightship basket bag. "I'm leaving. I'll talk to you again when you're in a more reasonable mood." She stormed out of the house without speaking to Emma.

Spencer grinned at Emma. "I don't suppose you ever fight with your mother."

She hesitated. This wasn't the time to tell him her mother had died years ago. She decided to let the question slide. "I have two sisters, and it seems we fight constantly. In the nicest possible way, of course," she added, returning his grin.

"I hope you will be as fortunate as I am," Millicent said. "I have children I love and grandchildren I adore."

"That's because we're so adorable," Spencer joked, kissing the top of his grandmother's head. "Okay, I'm going to get back to work."

"Take the painting with you," Millicent ordered.

"Not now. If I do take it, it has to be done with some ceremony. If you do give it to the historical association, there should be an article about it in the papers. Some fuss should be made."

"I hate fuss!" Millicent complained.

"Maybe you don't want fuss, but this painting deserves it. I'm not talking about anything complicated. Just perhaps having the director of the association over for a glass of champagne and a photograph."

"Oh, really, Spencer. Why can't you just take it?"

"Because it's an absolutely magnificent and historically important gift. I'll give you awhile to think it over," Spencer said. "Bye, Grams. Bye, Emma."

Millicent's hands were trembling as she rearranged herself in her wheelchair. "I don't think my daughter-in-law will ever have enough money," she grumbled. "I suppose some people just always want more."

"How about a nice quiet Agatha Christie murder to calm you down?" Emma said.

"Yes, please." Millicent allowed Emma to tuck the blanket around her legs. "That Agatha, she did know what she was doing, didn't she? In her books, family members were always killing one another for money."

Emma settled on the sofa and opened the book. "We've got only about thirty pages left of this one."

"Spencer really likes you," Millicent said.

Surprised, Emma answered, "I really like Spencer."

"Don't pretend you're naïve, dear, I know you're not." Millicent leaned her head back against the chair, closed her eyes, and was asleep at once.

Emma began to read, slowly, in a low droning voice, the kind Millicent slept best to. After awhile, she allowed her eyes to travel the room, lighting on all the objects and artifacts Millicent had collected over the years. Sailors' valentines hung on the wall. The lightship baskets were lined up from smallest to largest in the bay window. The lustrous Coffin painting hung above the fireplace—

Wait a minute.

Something was wrong here. Something had registered with Emma's brain, something *tugged*.

She scanned the room slowly. Across from her, Millicent rustled in her chair.

Quickly Emma returned to the book. " 'Hercule smoothed his mustaches.' " She continued to read aloud, slowly, while scanning the room again. She'd spent so many hours in this room, it was as if each item had imprinted itself on her subconscious, and some detail was wrong here, something nagged at her like a chipped nail on ten otherwise perfect fingers. She tried not to think so hard, to let it come to her, and it did.

Seven lightship baskets still stood in a formal line on the window seat, ranged according to size, from largest to smallest. The outline was the same.

But the color was off. Five of the lightship baskets were lighter in color than the others. Millicent's baskets were all old and valuable, but now five of them were just slightly, but noticeably, lighter . . .

"Why have you stopped reading?" Millicent was awake, and cranky.

"Sorry," Emma apologized, faking a little cough. "My throat is dry. If you don't mind, I'll get some iced tea for you and me."

"Very well." Millicent closed her eyes.

Emma hurried into the kitchen and prepared the tea, then carried the tall glasses and the plate of cookies into the living room. Millicent seemed to have fallen back asleep. Emma set the tray on the coffee table and quickly walked to the window at the front of the house, pretending to adjust the draperies.

Yes. Now that she was so close, it was obvious that five of the lightship baskets had been replaced. They were much lighter, and one of them had a fake ivory decoration that was similar to the real one, but just a little different.

Millicent spoke up. "I thought you were thirsty."

"I just needed to stretch my back." Emma hurried back to hand the older woman her tea. Now Millicent was awake, and eager to hear Emma read. She would have no more opportunity to check out the baskets. But in the back of her mind, she worked on the puzzle: Why were the lightship baskets different?

36
· · · · ·

Lily

Emma rapped on Lily's bedroom door. "Hey, Lily. I just got a phone call from someone who needs a babysitter tonight."

"Sorry, I'm busy tonight." Lily was on her knees, digging into the back of her closet for a pair of strappy open-toe sandals that were torturously uncomfortable but killer sexy.

It was the middle of August, and the island was caught up in the full force of summer activities. Beaches, stores, restaurants were crowded and so many boats were moored in the boat basin you could practically walk from the harbor to Monomoy without getting wet. Lily had never been so busy, and she loved it, loved all the parties, luncheons, receptions, events. Her boss at the magazine piled the work on and she did it all, and so well he actually praised her.

Her days were full. She would wake early to make love with Jason, rush home to shower and dress, type up her notes and email them to the magazine, then bike over to Eartha's. She'd help Eartha with her wardrobe or her correspondence—she was teaching the older woman how to use a computer and the Internet—then bike home to change her clothes and head off to a gallery opening or party. Late at night she'd go to Jason's, where they lay in bed, recounting their days for each other. And they would make love again.

When she had the chance to think about it, Lily admitted to

herself that she was not doing her share of the household chores. On the other hand, she hardly ate anything at home, and she did all her own laundry, when she found the time.

Emma persisted. "She needs someone for every night this week, actually. I could do a couple. Can you do any?"

"Emma, I really can't. I've got parties to cover for the magazine."

"I thought you wanted to be part of Nantucket Mermaids," Emma snapped.

"I do! But Emma, you know I have to work almost every night!"

"Right, and you can't work in the morning because that's your time with Eartha, and you can't do afternoons because you have to do your nails or something."

"That's not fair!" Lily found the shoes and stood up, holding them in her hand. "Oh, no, I'd forgotten, the heel's broken." She almost wept. "Emma, can I borrow those open-toe high heels of yours? Just for tonight?"

Emma put her hands on her hips. "You are just hopeless."

"Please?"

"No." Emma turned her back on Lily, stalked off to her room, and slammed the door.

Lily's thoughts were all in a tangle. Emma had never been as caring to her as Abbie was but now Emma was just being mean. Her sisters had ganged up and started a "Let's Count Lily's Flaws" campaign. She wished she hadn't begged Abbie to come home.

Now Lily pounded on Emma's door. It was locked. Lily said, "You just don't respect the work I do! You know *you* had to dress well for your precious money job in Boston. Well, *I* have to dress well for my job, too! I'm not just some vain little idiot!"

No response.

Lily leaned her forehead against Emma's door. "Emmie . . ."

No response.

"Well, see if I ever do anything nice for you!" Lily shouted. She heard how childish she sounded, and it embarrassed her. She wanted to cry, but more than that, she wanted someone to hold her and comfort her and at least tell her she was hot no matter how old her shoes were.

She went back to her own room, plopped down on her bed, and mentally scanned her clothing. *Carrie!* she thought with a hit of excitement. Carrie's shoe size was pretty close to Lily's, and Carrie had lots of great shoes. And Carrie had a baby, so she wasn't going out much. She snatched up her cell phone and called her friend.

She spent two hours at Carrie's, two duty hours from Lily's point of view. Carrie gladly loaned her several pairs of drop-dead shoes from her carefree single days, but she also talked endlessly about baby Olivia, who was teething, and not sleeping through the night, but was still pretty cute with her drooly little smile. Lily tried to tell Carrie about her job, but her friend hadn't seemed very interested, and why would she be? Carrie never went anyplace anymore.

With her backpack full of shoes bumping against her back, Lily biked home. She wheeled her bike into the garage and went up the steps and into the kitchen. It was after five, and she had to be at a cocktail party at six.

"Hello!" she called out as she always did, letting the screen door slam behind her.

"Hello," Marina said.

Surprised, Lily stopped dead.

Marina was at the stove, stirring something. Her blond hair was tied up high with a shoestring and her feet were bare. Her slip of a sundress showed off how slim she was, but Lily could see the lines at her eyes and the beginning of lines around her mouth. Marina was *old*.

"What are you doing here?" Lily demanded.

Marina smiled. "Fixing dinner. I hope you can stay. It's my favorite new recipe."

"Why aren't you fixing dinner in the cottage?"

"Because your sisters and your father are joining me, and the cottage is too small for us to eat in comfortably. Plus, this meal is too elaborate to be prepared in the little kitchen." She opened the freezer door and gestured inside. "I made baked Alaska for dessert. So scrumptious and cold, perfect for a summer evening, don't you think?"

Lily turned away, pretending to have difficulty slipping her backpack off, but really to hide her irritation. Who did this woman think she was, cooking in *their* kitchen? Opening the freezer door as if she had every right to use it?

"You look hot," Marina said. "I made sangria. Would you like a glass to take up while you shower?" Opening the refrigerator, she took out a pitcher full of fruit and rose-colored liquid.

"Okay." Lily grudgingly accepted. What had been going on here while she was so busy with Jason and Eartha and her work? Her sisters hadn't told her anything, but for the past two weeks Lily hadn't had a moment to sit down with them and talk.

Anyway, how could she ask it? *Are you sleeping with my father?*

Marina filled a glass with ice, poured the sangria over it, and handed Lily the glass.

"Thank you," Lily said quietly.

"Hello, ladies!" Lily's father came in through the kitchen door. Seeing Lily, he gave her a quick peck on the forehead.

Then he crossed the room and gave Marina a quick peck.

On the mouth.

"God, this smells good." Lily's father was covered with sawdust and his arms and face and neck were sunburned. "I'd better take a shower."

Marina held up the pitcher. "Would you like some sangria?"

Lily's father's expression was skeptical. "Um, what's in it?"

"Red wine, a little brandy, a little club soda, and lots of healthy fruit." Marina leaned against the kitchen counter as she talked, as if she were offering herself as well as the drink.

"I think I'd rather have a beer." Jim reached into the refrigerator and grabbed a Heineken. "Okay, ladies, see you later." He took off for the upstairs and his shower.

"You seem very chummy with my father," Lily said.

"Oh, well—" Marina began to reply but stopped when Emma swept into the kitchen.

"Hi, Lily, how's it going? Oh, wow, Marina, that smells fabulous!"

"Paella," Marina told her. "And—" she held up the pitcher triumphantly. "Sangria."

"You are the best," Emma said. "And man, do I need a drink." She took the glass Marina offered and plopped down in a chair at the kitchen table. After a long sip, she said, "I need your advice on something."

Lily's eyes went back and forth between her sister and this

strange woman who seemed to have enchanted everyone. Why would Emma need advice from Marina? Why didn't she ask Lily? Lily was family!

Marina poured herself a drink and sat down at the table. "Shoot."

Lily sat down, too.

"You're making a lightship basket with Sheila Lester, right?"

"Right."

"Well, you know I'm reading every afternoon to Millicent Bracebridge."

"Yes, you've spoken about her a lot. And also about her grandson, Spencer." Marina waggled her eyebrows teasingly.

What the hell! Lily thought. When did Emma tell Marina all this?

"You know Millicent has a lot of valuable Nantucket heirlooms. Oil paintings. Sailor's valentines. And seven lightship baskets, very old, probably by José Reyes, probably worth thousands of dollars. I mean each one. She has them arranged according to size on the windowsill in her living room."

"I'm with you so far," Marina said.

"Well, today while I was reading, I glanced at the collection and it seems to me, no, I'm *sure* of it—five of the baskets have been exchanged. Five of them are lighter than the others."

"Have you asked Millicent about them?"

"No. No, I haven't for several reasons. For one thing, she has macular degeneration, so she wouldn't have noticed the change. For another, she treasures all her Nantucket antiques, and I'm sure she'd never sell them or give them away. I think someone is stealing them and replacing them with cheap reproductions."

"That's a pretty serious accusation," Marina said. "Do you have any idea who's doing it?"

Emma looked grim. "It's got to be Sandra. I've gone over and over this in my mind. I know Cathy Evans, she's the housekeeper, and she would *never* steal anything. Nor would Patty LaFleur. She's the home health nurse who comes in to help Millicent every evening. Feeds her dinner, gets her into the shower, in and out of her clothes, into bed, spends the night with her and gets her up and going in the morning. Both these women have been on the island forever and have sterling reputations and great families. They just wouldn't steal. I'd stake my life on it. No, it's got to be Millicent's daughter-in-law, Sandra."

"What are you going to do?" Marina asked.

"Well, that's what I wanted to talk to you about," Emma answered.

Lily shot up from her chair. "I've got to get to work." She left her drink on the table and stormed from the room. Why did Emma want to talk to Marina about this problem! Why didn't Emma want to talk to *Lily*? Or at least wait and talk to Abbie! What was going on? Emma was acting as if Marina was a good friend. Confiding in her. Asking her advice.

Emma was almost acting as if Marina were her mother!

For sure, Marina was driving a wedge between Lily and the rest of her family.

At the cocktail party, Lily's thoughts about Marina revolved on an obsessive hamster wheel, hampering her work. She forgot to write down the names of a couple she'd just met and worst of all, she missed the opportunity to snap a photo of a television anchor who briefly dropped in to the party. But Eartha arrived, with much drama, as always, and Lily cheered up. She loved the way Eartha embraced Lily and whispered in her ear. She knew others were watching them, wondering what fabulous bit of gossip Eartha had now.

"I'll get you a martini," Lily told the older woman, once Eartha was ensconced on the sofa.

"Thanks, dawling." Eartha spread out the skirts of her fuchsia silk dress and flashed a welcome smile to the friends who were flocking to see her.

Jason had told her he was bartending at this party, still it gave Lily a little shiver of delight to see him there behind the table, handsome in his white shirt and black tie, flashing his great smile at people. A willowy brunette approached Jason to ask for a drink, leaning forward over the table so he could hear her—and so he could catch a view of the remarkable cleavage exposed by her dress. *Sorry, honey, he's taken,* Lily thought smugly.

"Ah, Lily. How nice to see you here."

Lily turned. Bancroft Stone stood there smiling at her. She'd met Bancroft the night Eartha took her to the dinner party on the yacht. Bancroft had just finished at the London School of Economics and was working with a hedge fund company based in London and New York. Even though his hairline was receding, he was handsome enough. And his British accent—genuine, one of his grandmothers lived in England—thrilled Lily. She returned the greeting and easily fell into a conversation with him. He hadn't paid special attention to her at the dinner party, so she was surprised at how he lingered next to her now, treating her as if she were the center of the universe, leaning toward her—of course, that could be because the noise level was so high all around them. Still, she thought he seemed to be flirting with her. What would it be like to date this man? He was smooth, cultured, cosmopolitan. The kind of man who could take her to the opera in New York, to polo matches in Connecticut, to ski at Vail. He would never marry Lily, she was certain he was from the sort of family who only married among their narrow social set, but she wouldn't want to marry the man. Date him, yes. Sleep with him? Perhaps.

"Want to go out to dinner later?" Bancroft asked.

Dumbfounded, Lily blinked and stammered. "Well, I–I . . ."

Jason loomed up. "Hi, Lily. What can I get for you?"

She turned, flushing like a schoolchild copying from a friend's paper. "A martini for Eartha, all gin, and I'll have a white wine, or red if it's easier." She knew she was babbling. She couldn't tell whether or not Jason noticed Bancroft's attentions, but really, that didn't matter. Lots of men flirted with Lily, just like lots of women of all ages flirted with Jason.

"Coming right up." Jason set to work and quickly handed Lily the glasses.

"Is the martini for Eartha?" Bancroft asked.

Lily nodded. "I'll just take it to her."

"I'll join you in a minute." Bancroft turned to Jason. "Waiter, I'd like a martini just like that one."

Lily's thoughts spun as she squeezed her way through the crowd to Eartha. One of the reasons her boss liked her work was that she knew how to schmooze, to make connections with the wealthy and the slightly famous and infamous. Last year she'd charmed her way into doing a photo essay on a billionaire's waterfront estate. This year—well, imagine who Bancroft Stone knew! Couldn't going out to dinner with Bancroft be considered work? Of course it could! She certainly wasn't going to go to bed with him.

Was she?

37

· · · · ·

Marina

Marina and Jim lay entwined in each other's arms, even though this August night was really too hot for such intimacy. They were in the loft of the Playhouse, with a fan playing over them, slowly sweeping back and forth, humming hypnotically. The drift of cool air across her bare skin was just another sensual pleasure for Marina. The world seemed full of sensual pleasures now.

She lay with her cheek on Jim's chest. Idly, she ran her finger through the hair on his belly. When he spoke, she could hear his words rumbling.

"I've got a question, Marina."

"I've got an answer," she replied. She felt him smile.

"You might want to take awhile to think about this," he said. "What I want to ask you is—why don't you move in with me?"

She was glad he couldn't see her expression. She knew she was smiling, probably ear to ear. She cleared her throat before speaking. "For how long? The rest of the summer?"

"Yes. And the fall. And the winter. And the spring." Gently he lifted her away from him, changing positions so they could face each other. "I know it's too early to ask you to marry me. I know you're still raw from your divorce. Perhaps you think this has all gone too fast for us. Perhaps it has. But I trust it, what we've got between us. I want you to be in my life."

Marina couldn't control the tears that suddenly flowed down her cheeks. "I don't know what to say." She sat up, reached over to the bedside table for a tissue, and blew her nose.

Jim sat up, too. He studied her face. "Well, have I terrified you? Freaked you out?"

"No. Oh, no. No, Jim, you've made me happy. But moving in with you—it's a complicated subject. I mean, what about your daughters? It was only a few weeks ago that you were upset when I invited them to dinner with you."

"I know. And I apologize. I was afraid to hurt them. Sometimes I forget that they're grown women, not little girls."

"We're all probably a little child deep inside," Marina said. "Maybe we should wait until they're settled in their own lives before doing something so drastic."

Jim chuckled ruefully. "Believe me, I've thought about that. I don't know if we'll live long enough for all three of my daughters to be settled in their own lives. I mean, Emma came home because she lost her job and her fiancé, but I don't know if she wants to stay on the island for the rest of her life. I don't have any idea why Abbie came home or how long she wants to stay. As for Lily . . ."

"Lily doesn't like me," Marina said bluntly.

"Lily's always been pretty self-centered," Jim told her. "She acts like a brat around you, but she's a good kid, really. And I'm not about to let her ruin any chance I have of happiness."

"All my things are in Missouri," Marina said. "All my friends are in Missouri."

"Really? Seems to me you've made a few friends here. Sheila Lester, for one. And I think you can count Abbie and Emma as your friends, don't you?" He put his arm around her and nuzzled his mouth against her temple. "Not to mention, I feel pretty friendly toward you."

"What would I do here?" Marina asked, adding, "I'm just thinking aloud, Jim. I mean, I intended for my visit to Nantucket to be a kind of holiday, a time away from real life, when I could think about the future."

"Maybe it could be the beginning of a new life," Jim said. "Maybe it could be the beginning of your future."

"I think I'm overwhelmed," Marina told him honestly. "Let me think about it?"

"Absolutely. Take all the time you need. No deadline. No penalty."

The next evening, Marina fixed dinner again, in the Fox kitchen, preparing enough barbecued chicken for however large a group showed up for dinner. Jim was working hard—August was a prime month for him—and so were his daughters. Marina found she really enjoyed shopping for groceries, making not just a meal, but a delicious meal, a treat for everyone after a long hot day.

Tonight Jim and all three girls came for dinner. As they sat around the table, the conversation was casual and fast, everyone complaining about the humid heat and the traffic, sharing anecdotes from their day. Even Lily seemed friendly, or at least relaxed, resigned to Marina's presence. Perhaps she just needed to get used to the idea.

Abbie had a babysitting job and left right after dinner. Lily excused herself to dress for yet another party.

"Go watch the Red Sox, Dad," Emma said. "I don't have a job tonight. I'll help Marina clean up."

Jim glanced at Marina.

"Go ahead," she said. "I'll join you in awhile."

Emma was the daughter Marina felt most comfortable with, and as they moved around the kitchen, clearing off the table, stacking the dishwasher, putting away leftovers, they fell into an easy, natural rhythm.

"I've had an idea about Millicent Bracebridge's lightship baskets," Emma told Marina once the work was done.

"Share?" Marina held up the wine bottle, which had just enough left for each of them.

"Thanks." Emma held out her glass and leaned against the counter. "I'd like Sheila Lester to check them out. If she says they're fake, then I can tell Spencer about it and he can do something."

"Do you want me to ask Sheila if she'd appraise them?" Emma asked.

"Would you? I know her, but not as well as you do."

"Oh, I wouldn't say I know her well . . . but I know her well enough," Marina decided. "I'll phone her tomorrow."

"Oh, that would be great, Marina. Thanks."

After the kitchen was clean, with the dishwasher gargling along, Marina went in to watch the baseball game with Jim. She'd only sat down when Emma stuck her head into the living room.

"Want to take an evening swim with me, Marina?"

"That's a great idea." Marina turned to Jim. "Want to join us?"

"The Red Sox are tied with the Yankees," Jim said, keeping his eyes on the screen.

Marina laughed. "Okay. See you later."

As they walked through the moonlit streets, Emma said, casually, "You and Dad seem to be getting along nicely."

Marina chose her words carefully. "Your father is a pretty special man."

Emma laughed a full-bodied laugh and linked her arm through Marina's. "I am *not* five years old! I can tell my father's in love with you."

Startled, Marina said, "You can?"

"Gosh, yes. In fact, I think Lily knew it even before he did."

"What? That doesn't even make sense."

"Yes, it does. Lily noticed the way Dad always brought you fish, when you first rented the cottage. She saw the way he looked at you, and how happy he was after he'd seen you. It freaked her out, actually. She emailed me and Abbie, all in a dither."

"Oh, dear."

"Don't worry about Lily, Marina. She's the baby of the family. It just takes her a little longer to adjust to things."

Should she tell Emma that Jim had asked her to move in with them? Marina wondered. No. No, she should let Jim broach the subject with his daughters. But she wanted to tell Emma something of her feelings. "I really like your father," she said carefully.

"I can tell that. It kind of cheers me up. If you can find someone you enjoy being with so soon after getting dumped, maybe there's hope for me, too."

"So you don't mind that I'm—dating—your father?"

"God, no! I'm glad! He hasn't had anyone make a fuss over him for years."

They arrived at the beach and kicked off their sandals to walk barefoot over the sand to the water's edge. The night was hot, the water still. Music floated out from boats moored in the harbor and in the distance the lights of the ferry floated toward them like a slowly moving spaceship.

Marina waded out into the shallows. The water was warm against her skin, and then, as she went deeper, the water became cool. Beside her, Emma dog-paddled, flipping her feet, clowning around.

"I'm so happy!" Emma laughed. "I don't know why, Marina, but right now, I'm happy."

Marina laughed. She felt as if she could swim forever. "I'm happy, too," she told Emma, and rolled over to do a lazy back crawl so she could gaze up at the moon.

38

· · · · ·

Abbie

The relentlessness of the late August heat and humidity was irritating even the happiest of tourists. Main Street was crowded, you couldn't walk along the sidewalk without bumping into people. The grocery stores were so packed, you couldn't get down the aisles. Marine Home Center sold out of window air conditioners. All over the island, car alarms seemed to blare incessantly, and babies wailed as mothers pushed the double-sided strollers along, making everyone else get out of their way.

And Harry had morphed into a little brat. He wouldn't eat any vegetables. He couldn't sit still. He screamed like a two-year-old in the grocery store when Abbie wouldn't buy him a box of cookies. Wednesday evening he wouldn't get out of the bath, so Abbie sat on the bathroom floor for thirty minutes until the child gave up. Then he didn't like his summer pajamas, and he didn't like any of the books Abbie wanted to read to him when she finally got him tucked into bed. By the time she got him to sleep, she was ready to lie down next to him and sleep herself.

Instead, she went downstairs. Howell was at his desk, tapping at his computer.

"Coffee?" she asked. "Or a beer?"

"I've got to get this done," Howell told her. He stretched and yawned. "But I'll take a break." Rising, he walked over to Abbie and enfolded her against him.

"How's your ankle?" she asked.

"Perfect. Not even a twinge. Which is a good thing, since I've got to go to this conference."

Howell was flying out Thursday morning to a conference in Seattle. He had arranged for Abbie to spend Wednesday and Thursday nights with Harry; Sydney would fly in Friday evening. Howell wouldn't be back until Sunday night.

As they settled on the sofa, Abbie asked, "Do you think Harry's so moody because you're leaving?"

"Maybe. Or maybe it's more than that," Howell told Abbie. "I think Harry's aware of the tension between me and Sydney. I don't think he *knows* anything, but he certainly senses something. Be patient with him, Abbie, please."

"Of course I'll be patient with him," Abbie assured Howell. "I love Harry."

"And I love you," Howell whispered and kissed her lips, and her throat, and her collarbone. "Let's go to bed."

It was like a dream life. And it was a glimpse into her future.

Abbie slept with Howell all night through, but made sure to set her things around in the guest bedroom so that Harry would think she'd stayed there, just as she would that night.

In the morning she made breakfast for Harry and his father, and dressed Harry for the day while Howell finished packing for his trip. She tucked Harry into his car seat and drove Howell to the airport, and she stood holding hands with Harry as they waved to Howell when he walked out to the plane. She gave Harry a perfect day—beach, library, ice-cream cone, stories—and when she went to bed at night, she couldn't fall asleep for happiness. This was what it would be like when she married Howell.

Friday was the first day of the traveling fair that visited Nantucket annually. It was small, but that only made it seem quaint and perfect for little children. Knowing how easily Harry got overexcited, Abbie opted to take him to the fair in the morning, to give him plenty of time to calm down by evening. When Abbie parked in the sandy lot, she saw lots of other mothers with little children. Good. That made it seem she'd made a good decision.

The day was hot and bright, and the ground was dry and dusty, but once they'd walked through the balloon-covered arch, they entered a fantasy world of rides and arcades and music. Abbie held tight to Harry's little hand, partly because she didn't want to lose him in the crowd, and also to give him a sense of safety. She could tell he was overwhelmed.

She knelt next to Harry. "What shall we do first? How about a ride on the train?"

Harry held back. "Can you sit with me, Nanny Abbie?"

"No, honey, I can't. Look, the seats are just right for someone your age, and the train doesn't go very fast." As she spoke, the little train clacked around the track. The conductor waved and blew the whistle, which made Harry jump.

What a strange little life the boy had had, Abbie thought. He'd ridden in jet airplanes and limos, but hadn't seen much television and he'd certainly never been to an amusement park.

"Why don't we go try our hand at one of the games?" she suggested.

It took fifteen minutes of patiently watching other children throw balls at plastic ducks, all of them walking away with a stuffed animal, before Harry tugged on Abbie's hand and whispered that he'd like to try it.

They got in line, and waited their turn at the wildly decorated stand. The game operator spoke gently and encouragingly to Harry. Eyes wide, Harry threw the balls three times. The third time, he knocked over a duck and got to choose a stuffed animal. He chose a seahorse with a stiff satin mane and hugged it to his chest, triumphant.

Abbie felt pretty triumphant herself as she continued around the little fair. Harry was now brave enough to climb up inside the bright red fire truck, where he himself could push the button that activated the siren as the operator pushed another button that made the truck rock back and forth. After that, Harry was ready for the train, and he liked that so much he asked if he could go around three more times. Abbie was delighted. She'd bet that the seahorse Harry had clutched to his chest was providing him with courage, or at least a sense of companionship. Sydney was so wrong to deprive Harry of the experience of horses!

The tantalizing aroma of hot dogs drifted through the air. Abbie was pretty sure Harry hadn't had a hot dog at a fair before. She bought one for each of them and laughed to see how quickly Harry devoured his. He was still hungry, so she prudently bought him a cup of milk, and then allowed him a cone of cotton candy for his dessert. Harry's eyes nearly bulged out of his head when he was allowed to choose either pink or blue, and when he tasted the concoction, he broke into a surprised smile.

"This is really good, Nanny Abbie," Harry said. "Would you like a taste?"

She almost cried with pleasure at his offer. "No, thanks, Harry. It's all for you."

It was noon, and the sun beat down fiercely. She took Harry to the little Porta Potti, which was an adventure in itself for the child. She wiped his hands and face with the hygienic wipes she carried in her purse, and spread more sunblock over his nose and cheeks and insisted he wear his baseball cap to shade his face. He obeyed easily, as eager as any other child to get back to the amusement park. She loved it when other mothers saw Abbie and smiled—as if Abbie were Harry's mother!

Which she kind of almost was.

Harry went on the train two more times, and then sat in a helicopter as it jolted back and forth, making a whirring, whapping sound even though the blades didn't really move. The Ferris wheel was very small, but the seats were large enough for adults as well as children, so Abbie and Harry sat together, Harry clutching her hand tightly as they rose high into the sky. Or what seemed high to Harry—Abbie thought it probably didn't go more than twenty feet off the ground.

"How about the carousel?" Abbie asked next. Harry had stared at it in consternation when they first arrived. Loud music overwhelmed him, and the carousel music was loud.

"Okay," Harry announced bravely. "If you come with me, Nanny Abbie."

"Of course!" Abbie waited until the carousel stopped, then led Harry up onto the platform. "What color horse would you like to ride? Black? White?"

"The Appaloosa," Harry announced, proud of knowing the word.

Abbie led him to the painted horse and lifted him onto its back. "Now hold tight, right here on the pommel of the saddle," she instructed.

Harry clasped the pommel in one hand, but kept hold of his seahorse with the other. He gawked openmouthed at all the painted horses with their jeweled saddles and arched tails and streaming manes, and all the other children who were being lifted up onto their own horses.

"Why don't you let me hold your seahorse so you can use both hands on the reins," Abbie suggested.

Harry only shook his head.

Abbie hooked her bag over her shoulder so she could keep one hand on Harry's back and hold on to the pole with the other. "Your horse has spots, Harry. What do you think his name is?"

"Slappy!" Harry crowed, laughing.

Abbie laughed back, loving it that he'd remember the real horse Shelley had let him ride.

With a jolt, the merry-go-round began to revolve. Harry's face lit up as his horse dipped and rose.

"This is fun!" he yelled, laughing. "We're going fast, Nanny Abbie!"

"I know! Hang on tight!"

They circled around, the music tinkling, while mothers and fathers and grandparents stood on the ground waving at them. Harry grinned from ear to ear.

Suddenly, "Oh, no!" he cried. He had dropped his seahorse.

Abbie saw it land on the wooden board between two horses.

"Don't worry, Harry. I'll get it," Abbie said.

She bent to pick up the stuffed bit of satin.

As she stood up, she heard Harry scream.

She caught a flash of his leather sandal as the little boy slipped sideways off his horse, his thin legs whipping into the air. Helplessly she watched his head knock into the horse next to his. She tore around the moving horse but Harry slammed to the platform of the carousel before she could break his fall.

"Harry!" Abbie threw herself next to the child, trying to gather him into her arms. The movement of the carousel unbalanced her and threw her sideways. "Stop!" she yelled.

Harry was caught between the poles of two horses, his arms and legs flailing. He was screaming at the top of his lungs.

"Harry, Harry, you're okay, honey, Harry, let me help you." She leaned forward, and the carousel's motion made her lurch, falling against the child. She steadied herself with one hand. "Harry, you're okay."

But she could see that he was bleeding from his head.

The carousel was slowing now, the spinning easing, the horses pausing. Abbie reached out to pick Harry up.

The little boy fought away from her, a little whirlwind of flailing arms and kicking legs.

"Mommy!" he cried. "Daddy! Mommy!"

"Harry, Harry, calm down, let me help you—" She tried to sound both soothing and authoritative.

"Mommy! I want my mommy!" The child arched his back and twisted away, inadvertently kicking Abbie hard in the stomach.

Harry was out of control, shrieking in a full-force tantrum. Abbie was aware of the other adults and children watching them. Judging them. Sweat trickled down her face, all her skin seemed on fire with embarrassment.

"We'll get your mommy. Calm down, Harry, let me help you get off the carousel and then we'll go call your mommy."

"I want my mommy!" Harry's shrieks were lessening. His little body convulsed as he sobbed. "I want my mommy! I want my mommy!"

Abbie finally was able to get her arms around the child. She held him against her and staggered to her feet. Someone put a guiding hand beneath her elbow, steadying her as she lurched around the horses and stepped down onto the ground.

A crowd had gathered around them. Someone said, "Here's a bench. Sit down."

She half fell onto the bench. Harry was sobbing relentlessly in her arms.

"I'm a nurse." The woman was older, gray-haired, comfortably plump. "Let me look at him."

"Thank you," Abbie said gratefully.

The nurse tried to peel Harry away from Abbie, but he clung to Abbie, digging his fingers into her shoulders. His knees jammed into her rib cage and one foot kicked her arm hard.

"Stay there," the nurse said. She walked around to the back of the bench and squatted down.

Harry's face was pressed against Abbie's shoulder, but the nurse could see his temple.

"He's got a big goose egg," she said. "That's good. The swelling's gone out, not in. He's scraped his cheek. That's where the blood is coming from. He just needs a pack of ice." Standing up, she said to the crowd, "We need ice. Other than that, he's okay. You can all leave now."

As if sensing the power of her authority, the crowd began to disperse. A young man ran up with a silver ice pack in his hand. "We keep some here, for accidents like this," he said. "You think he's okay?"

The nurse bent toward Harry, attempting to put the ice pack next to the child's face, but when he felt it, Harry screamed louder and threw himself away from the nurse, almost propelling himself out of Abbie's arms.

"I guess no ice," the nurse said. She came around and sat down next to Abbie. "I think he's okay. He didn't lose consciousness. His eyes are tracking fine. The scrape on the side of his face has already stopped bleeding. Children's heads and faces bleed a lot, don't let it worry you. You need to keep an eye on him for about twenty minutes. He might throw up. If he does, don't worry, as long as it's only once or twice."

"*I* might throw up," Abbie muttered.

Harry had subsided against her again, his sobs weakening, his little body calming.

"I want my mommy," he cried pitifully. "Please, Nanny Abbie. I want my mommy."

Abbie thought her heart would break.

39

· · · · ·

Emma

Emma sat at the kitchen table with her father and Marina, eating the seared garden vegetables and sausage Marina had prepared. Cinnamon crouched beneath the table, purring as he ate the bit of sausage Emma had slipped him.

"Too spicy?" Marina asked.

"No, it's fine. I'm just wired." She gave Marina a quick, complicitous glance. Marina grinned.

The front door slammed and Lily hurried into the kitchen. "Is there anything to eat? I'm starving!" She threw herself into a chair and bent over to remove a high-heeled stiletto sandal. "And do we have any Band-Aids? I've got a blister from Carrie's shoes and it's killing me."

"Yes, there *is* food," Emma informed Lily, "thanks to Marina. She went to the grocery store, and cooked dinner."

Lily ignored her. She had her foot in both hands and was scrutinizing the blister. "If I can't wear the silver heels tonight, my whole outfit will be ruined."

"Actually, Lily," Marina said apologetically, "I only made enough dinner for the three of us. Abbie told me this morning she wouldn't be home for dinner, and I wasn't sure about you—you've been gone for the past few nights. But there's plenty of cheese and bread and veggies."

"I guess that will be okay," Lily said.

Emma flashed a look at Marina and then at her father, who had gone into deaf robot mode, focusing on his food and not on the conversation. Emma put down her fork.

"Honey," she said gently to Lily, "why don't you fix your dinner yourself? Marina's eating now and probably doesn't want her food to get cold."

"Yeah, and that could happen fast on a *cold* night like this," Lily muttered sarcastically.

Jim dropped his napkin on the table, pushed back his chair, and rose. "Well, ladies, I'm off."

"Where are you going, Dad?" Lily asked.

"Poker night with the fellows." Jim pecked a kiss on top of Emma's head and Lily's and then a longer kiss on Marina's cheek. "Great dinner. Thanks, Marina."

"Have fun," she told him.

"See you later," he told her.

Emma rolled her eyes at her father's gooey tone. She pushed her plate toward Lily. "You can have mine if you want. I'm not hungry tonight."

"Thanks," Lily said, and began to eat.

Marina asked, "So what time do we have to be there?"

"I think about nine. It shouldn't take more than a couple of minutes to get in and out, and we can park the car a couple of houses away. It should only take a few minutes to drive to Sheila's. I told her we'd be there around nine-thirty."

"What are you two talking about?" Lily asked.

Emma flashed a warning glance at Marina. "Oh, nothing." She stood up and opened the cabinet with the first-aid supplies. "Here's a Band-Aid. What are you doing tonight?"

Lily folded her arms over her chest and stubbornly insisted, "Come on, Emma. Tell me what's going on!"

Emma hesitated. Marina was carefully studying her plate. Emma gave her points for keeping out of it. "Look. If I tell you, you have to keep it a secret."

"Fine."

"I mean it, Lily. It's important, really."

"I can keep a secret."

Emma sighed. "All right. It's no big deal. More of a romp. I think someone's taken Millicent Bracebridge's antique lightship baskets and replaced them with new, less valuable ones. Millicent hasn't noticed because her vision is so bad. I told Marina, and Marina got Sheila Lester to agree to evaluate the baskets and give us her opinion. But she won't come into the house uninvited, so I'm going to smuggle them out tonight—and then smuggle them back in after Sheila's seen them."

Lily narrowed her eyes. "And Marina's helping you?"

"Right."

"Why didn't you ask me?"

Emma laughed. "Honey, you're never here. You always have so much going on at night. Like what do you have on your schedule tonight?"

"The library fund-raiser," Lily admitted. "It's a very important occasion. Could you do it another time?"

"No, we've got Sheila on board for tonight." Emma changed the subject. "Are you staying over at Jason's tonight?"

"Probably." Apparently satisfied, Lily began to eat. "Where's Abbie?"

"I think she's spending the night at the Parkers'," Emma said. "Both parents are gone so she's doing a couple of overnights with the little boy." Emma settled her chin in her hands and said to Marina, "I'm so worried about Abbie."

"I know," Marina said. "But maybe things will resolve themselves after Labor Day, when the Parkers have to go back to New York."

"Why are you worried about Abbie?" Lily asked.

Again, Emma and Marina exchanged glances.

"What!" Lily dropped her fork with a clatter on the table. "*You two* are keeping *another* secret from me?"

Marina got up and went to the sink to begin washing the pots and pans.

Emma reminded herself that Lily was her sister, not Marina's. And Lily looked crushed.

"Honey, we're not keeping anything from you."

"Then *tell* me."

"Abbie has a crush on her employer, that's all."

Lily grinned. "Abbie's having an affair with a married man!"

"I didn't say she was having an affair. As far as I know, Abbie is *not* having an affair, so get that out of your head. I said Abbie has a crush on the dad, that's all."

Lily laughed triumphantly. "What an idiot. She ought to know better than to get involved with a married man."

Emma snapped. "Lily! This is just why I never want to tell you anything! You always spin it out to the most extreme." She shoved her chair back and carried her utensils and glass to the kitchen counter. "Let me scrub those, Marina. You did all the cooking and I need to work off some cranky energy."

"I'm not hungry!" Lily dropped her fork on the plate with a clatter and stomped from the room.

Marina tore off the rubber gloves and handed them to Emma. "I'm going out to the cottage to change clothes."

Emma grinned. "Black. Thief colors."

Without explaining exactly why, Emma had asked her father if she could have the pickup tonight—no way could they carry everything on a bike, and Lily had dibs on the Old Clunker.

A little after nine, Emma turned off Main Street onto Hyacinth Lane, killed the lights, and parked the car two houses down from Millicent Bracebridge's home.

"Have you got the key?" Marina asked.

"Right here." Emma held up her wrist to show how she'd attached the key to a rubber bracelet so she wouldn't have to worry about dropping it. "Okay, here we go!"

They walked in watchful silence as they passed the houses next to the Bracebridge home. Lights were on all up and down the street, but Emma had done some research and she knew all the people in this neighborhood were older. Not as old as Millicent Bracebridge, but up there in their sixties. Probably all seated in front of the television set now, or reading.

Millicent Bracebridge would be in bed, asleep. Millicent was an early-to-bed, early-to-rise kind of gal. Her home health nurse, Patty LaFleur, would be tucked away in bed right across the hall from Millicent, with both doors open so she could hear Millicent if she called. Patty had a small TV on a stand near her bed that she watched with the volume turned low so it wouldn't bother the older woman; it would be just loud enough, Emma thought, to cover the sounds she and Marina would make.

She and Marina had discussed and planned every step. Now they walked toward the Bracebridge house at a normal pace, as if they belonged there, not skulking or sneaking up the brick path. Emma had a key.

Emma turned the key in the lock, opened the door, and stepped inside. Marina followed.

Emma shut the door and the two women stood still for a moment, listening. They could hear a slight ripple of TV laughter from the second floor. No other sounds. No lights were on downstairs, although the green light from the microwave clock shone at the end of the hall.

As silently as possible, they crept into the living room. Marina had agreed to follow Emma closely, because Emma knew how to make it through the crowded room without bumping into one of the antiques. The difficulty with smuggling the baskets was that they were large and stiff and bulky. Emma could carry three at one time. Marina could carry the others and they'd be in and out of there in one trip. Plus, Emma was glad for the moral support.

Streetlight and starlight fell through the window onto the far end of the room where the baskets were lined on the sill.

Emma walked toward them, picked up the first one, and slid it over Marina's outstretched arm. She put the next one on Marina's other arm, and gave Marina a basket to hold in each hand. Then she slipped two of the smaller baskets on her left arm and held the smallest basket in her left hand. She kept a hand free for the front door.

She and Marina carefully traded places so that Emma could walk in front of Marina.

The baskets made a clicking noise as they bumped together on Marina's arm. Both women stopped. Emma turned and adjusted the baskets. They walked.

They stopped for a moment in the hall. Without needing to speak, of one accord, they held their breath and listened for any sign of commotion upstairs. Footsteps? No. A voice calling out? No.

Good. They were almost halfway through with their mission. After Sheila evaluated the baskets, they would have to sneak them back into the house.

Emma could see Marina's eyes shining in the darkness. She nodded once. She opened the front door. They stepped outside. With infinite care, Emma pulled the heavy front door closed.

They hurried quickly down the slate path to the street. Everything seemed peaceful—except a car was approaching. They stepped off the street and onto the grass to let it pass.

But instead of passing, the car stopped alongside the two women.

It was a police car.

"Miss?" A police officer got out of the car and stood next to Emma. He shone a light in her face. "What do you have there?"

40

·····

Lily

The August night was muggy, but inside the Debenham house the air was cool, dry, and scented with hundreds of flowers cut from Mai Debenham's garden. They were throwing a fund-raiser for the library, so Lily, who had learned a few things over the past year, snapped several good shots of the museum's board members with the Debenhams before she even allowed herself to get a drink.

She worked her way through the crowd, taking photos, jotting down names, smiling, smiling, smiling. Her emotions were all over the place. Like a deep roll of approaching thunder, guilt for the telephone call she'd made earlier rolled toward her.

God, how she wished she'd hadn't made that call—it had been a spontaneous and completely childish act. With all her heart she wished she could take it back, especially since she'd forgotten about caller ID and the policeman who took the call had been in Emma's high school class.

She had two other parties to cover before she could find out what had happened. And she was staying the night at Jason's. Thank heavens for that. Emma would no doubt go ballistic. Perhaps Lily could call home late tonight, to find out what happened—but no. She wanted to let Emma cool down before facing her. After all, what could Lily say? What was Lily's excuse? Jealousy, plain and simple. Sometimes it seemed to Lily that her emotions dragged on her as powerfully as the moon moved the tides.

"I love your dress!"

It took Lily a few seconds before she realized the glitzy girl was complimenting *her*.

"Oh, thanks. I like yours, too."

"Where did you get it?" the girl asked.

"New York." She wasn't lying. The dress had been sent to Eartha from New York.

She felt her cell phone vibrating inside her little evening clutch. Emma? Already? Couldn't be. She didn't need to answer it. She didn't want to answer it. Still, she stepped into the downstairs powder room and held the phone to her ear.

"Lily?" It was Abbie, but her voice was choked.

"Abbie? Are you okay?"

"Oh, Lily, no," Abbie wailed. "I'm not okay. Everything's terrible. Do you know where Emma is? She won't answer her cell."

"I think she's . . . she's gone off somewhere with Marina."

"Oh, God." Abbie's voice broke off into sobs. "I need Emma."

"Abbie, where are you?"

"I'm at the Parkers'."

"Are you hurt?"

Abbie sobbed harder. "Not me. Harry."

"Harry's hurt?" Abbie was crying so hard Lily couldn't understand her. "I'm coming over right now."

Her hands shook as she steered the Old Clunker through the streets. She couldn't believe the child Abbie was caring for had gotten hurt. Not under Abbie's watch. Abbie was übercapable and really good with children.

Lily realized she'd never heard Abbie cry like this, as if her heart were broken. Not since their mother died.

The second floor of the Parker house was dark, but lights shone from the first floor, and the moment Lily's hand touched the front door, it flew open.

Abbie stood there, and she looked a million years old. Her eyes were red and swollen, her nose crimson at the tip, and her entire body sagged.

"Abbie! What happened?"

Abbie put a finger to her lips. "I don't want to wake him. Come into the kitchen."

Lily followed her sister through the house, pulling the kitchen door shut behind her. "Abbie, *tell* me."

Abbie wrapped her arms around herself as she paced around the kitchen. "Lily, I don't know what to do. She'll be here any moment. I'm terrified to face her."

"Who will be here? And why are you terrified? And what happened to Harry?"

"Oh, Lily!" Abbie's face crumbled. "Harry fell off the horse on the carousel. He hit his head. He has a bump. He wants his mommy."

Lily flew to her sister's side and wrapped an arm around Abbie. "Where is Harry now?"

"He's in b-b-bed."

"In bed? So he's not in the hospital?"

"I took him to the emergency room today, after he fell. He was checked out by the doctors and they said he was okay. But he wanted his mommy. He was hysterical, and he was so frightened, and he wants his mommy."

"Okay, and so is his mommy coming, is that who's coming?"

"I called her, but she was in court. She didn't get the message until this afternoon. She tried to fly, but the airport's been fogged in all evening, so she's on the late boat."

"Well, that's good. Abbie. That's good, right? The doctors said Harry is okay. And his mommy is coming." She thought her sensible words would calm Abbie. Instead, Abbie began to sob so hard her body shook.

Lily stared at her sister, horrified and full of pity, and also a little scared. "Abbie." She put iron into her voice. "Abbie, stop that right now. She'll be here any minute. You've got to pull yourself together. You don't want her to see you like this."

"Nothing matters anymore," Abbie cried.

"Lots of things matter. Come on, calm down." She nudged her sister into a chair. She ran a paper towel under cold water, turned to Abbie, and washed Abbie's face. "Hold this over your eyes," she instructed. "You've got to get the swelling down or you won't be able to see."

Abbie held the cool towel over her eyes. After a moment, she calmed down. She wiped her eyes and blew her nose into the paper towel.

Lily took it from her and handed Abbie a glass of cold water. "Drink this. God, have you been like this all day? You must have scared the little boy out of his wits."

"Of course I wasn't like this!" Abbie snapped. "I would *never* let Harry see me like this!" Indignation replaced hysteria. She drank some water and took the new wet paper towel Lily handed her. After a moment, she said, quietly, "I held it together until he was asleep. I can't keep it in anymore." She cast a wry smile at Lily. "Sydney's a bitch from hell. She's going to rip me apart."

"What about Harry's father? Where is he? Have you told him?"

Abbie's face flushed with emotion. "He's at a conference in Seattle, giving a paper today. Yes, I phoned him. He and Sydney talked and agreed she would come home. He'll stay at the conference since the doctors said Harry's okay."

Outside, a car door slammed.

"Sydney's taxi," Abbie said. She stood up, straightened her shoulders and walked down the hall to the front door.

Lily followed. Her heart skipped a beat when the front door opened.

Sydney Parker stepped inside, a compact force field of energy. She wore a perfectly tailored black suit, high black heels, and she carried a briefcase.

"How is he?" she demanded.

"He's asleep. He's fine. He ate all his dinner, and played in the bath. He didn't throw up, he didn't complain of dizziness or a headache or anything. But he kept asking for you. This is my sister Lily, she only just got here, to drive me home—"

Abbie spoke to the other woman's back, because Sydney was rapidly climbing the stairs. Lily waited at the bottom of the stairs, then couldn't stand it and walked up a few steps, until she could hear them on the second floor.

"Harry?" Sydney's voice was low but authoritative. "Harry. Wake up. Mommy's here."

Lily could see Abbie standing just outside the bedroom door. She was wringing her hands and chewing on her lip, but she held her head high.

"Hey, Big Guy." Sydney's voice became sugary. "Hi, Harry."

"Mommy. You came!"

"Of course I came, Silly Willy."

"Mommy, I fell off a horse! I have a *bump*!"

"Well, let me see this terrible bad bump you got. Oh, my. You know what, Harry? It looks bad, but I think it will probably go away pretty soon and you'll never know it was there. Want Mommy to kiss it for you?"

Lily saw Abbie wrap her arms around her stomach, as if it hurt her.

"There. All better now. And I'm so glad Nanny Abbie was with you. She knew just what to do, didn't she? Now lie back down and have a good night's sleep. I'll be here to have breakfast with you in the morning."

Lily saw Abbie put her hand to her eyes.

"Good boy, Harry. Mommy loves you. Night-night."

Lily hurried back down to the hall. A few moments later, Sydney came down the stairs, with Abbie close behind.

"I need a drink." Sydney stalked into the dining room, picked up a decanter of Scotch, poured herself a drink, and tossed back a big gulp. Noticing Abbie, she said, "You look like hell."

Abbie said, "I was worried about Harry. I watched him carefully all day. No dizziness. No headaches—"

"Children can scare the shit out of you, can't they. Well, go on home. I'll be here all day tomorrow. We won't need you until Monday."

"You want me to come back?" Abbie asked.

"Of course. It's too late in the summer to get a new nanny. Anyway, we don't want Harry thinking I fired you because you're incompetent. He's already a nervous child. It won't help him if he learns he can't trust his caregivers."

"I'm sorry about the fall," Abbie said. "It happened so fast—"

"What, you expect me to forgive you? Tell you everything's okay? Believe me, I don't have that in me." She tossed back another slug of Scotch, then muttered, "This fucking island. There's not one professional on it."

"I'll just run up to the guest room to get my things," Abbie said.

"Fine." Sydney turned away, to pour herself another drink.

Lily followed Abbie up the stairs. She stood watching as Abbie collected her nightgown, hairbrush, and paperback novel. Abbie went into the bathroom and came out again with her toothbrush and dental floss in her hands.

"I'm ready," Abbie said.

They found Sydney in the kitchen, peering into the refrigerator. She'd stepped out of her high heels and stripped off her suit jacket. Suddenly she seemed younger, and tired.

"I made a veggie casserole," Abbie offered. "You could microwave it—"

Sydney waved an impatient hand, and turned, and they saw that she had her cell phone clutched to her ear. "No, you don't need to come home," she was saying. "I've seen Harry. He's just fine. Wait a moment. I've got to say good-bye to the nanny." Glancing at Abbie, she said, "We'll see you Monday." She turned her back. "I know, honey," she said in a low, soothing voice. "Me, too."

Abbie seemed paralyzed there in the kitchen.

"Abbie," Lily whispered, and tugged on her arm.

"Wait," Abbie insisted. "I just need—"

Sydney flapped her arm again, shooing them away.

Lily took her by the arm and pulled her down the hall, out of the house, and into the car. Abbie curled up in the passenger seat and began to cry again, in relentless, heartbreaking sobs.

"Oh, Abbie," Lily sighed.

"Let's just go home," Abbie said.

Lily started the car and drove slowly through the narrow streets of the town. A strange sensation rose within her, a kind of pride that made her lift her chin and feel oddly happy—although she stifled her smile because it would be just too odd to be smiling while her sister cried. She was realizing that tonight *she* had helped *Abbie*. Tonight Abbie had needed her, and she had come. Well, actually, tonight Abbie had needed Emma, but Emma wasn't available. Lily had gone. *Lily* had left her party, left work, and flown to Abbie's side. She'd comforted her older sister, she'd helped her pull herself together, she'd provided emotional support when Harry's mother arrived, and she'd gotten Abbie out of the house when Abbie was absolutely dithering with emotions.

It was as if Lily had stepped over an invisible threshold tonight. If *she* could help *Abbie*, then she could do anything at all. A small childish part of her, the part that had been so overpowering only a few hours ago, wanted to tug on Abbie's sleeve like a child who craves attention and praise, boasting: I *helped* you, Abbie! *I* helped *you.*

But the ripened, capable, and even perhaps slightly wise Lily understood deep within herself that this knowledge, this pride, needed to be sheltered inside her own heart and soul, protected like the fragile trembling radiance of a newly lighted flame.

41
· · · · ·

Marina

It wasn't really funny, Marina knew, but adrenaline was still flooding her system, urging her to giggle nervously as she sat, trying to appear dignified and law-abiding, in the interview room of the police station.

Riley O'Hara, the young officer who had arrested them, and the accompanying officer, Sean Shreve, sat on the opposite side of the table from Marina and Emma, who sat side by side without speaking. The purloined lightship baskets were clustered together at the far end of the long table. In the relentless overhead fluorescent lights, the difference between the color of the cane was obvious.

Sean Shreve kept shifting in his chair as if he were the guilty one. He was trying to get Emma to look at him, but she was slanted back in her chair with her arms crossed over her chest and her jaw clenched.

During their ride to the station in the back of the Crown Vic, Emma had informed Marina in a loud, angry voice that Sean had grown up on the island. Emma had actually dated Sean in high school. Emma could not believe that after her explanation, given in whispers in the dark night on the street in front of the Bracebridge house, Sean had insisted the two women be brought into the police station.

"We have to do it," Sean had pleaded with Emma. "It's the law.

It would cost me my job not to do it. We had a phone call, Emma. It's logged in. We have to respond. We have to bring you in."

"Yes, and *who* phoned the station, Sean? I'll tell you who—*Lily*, right? *Lily* phoned you or how else would you know exactly where to go?"

"That's the point, Emma," Sean had retorted. "Lily didn't phone *me*. She phoned the station."

At the station they made one phone call each. Marina phoned Jim, who said he'd walk down immediately. Marina asked Jim to call Sheila Lester, too, and to ask her to come to the station to confirm that she was planning to evaluate the baskets. Emma phoned Spencer Bracebridge. Then they were shown into the interview room, and now all they could do was wait.

"Would you like some coffee, Emma?" Sean asked.

"If I had it, I'd throw it in your face, Sean Shreve," Emma muttered darkly.

The door opened to the hall and a woman police officer escorted Sheila Lester into the room. As she was being seated, Jim appeared in the hall, talking with a man who, Emma told Marina, was Chief Coffin. The two men remained in the hall, murmuring in low rumbling voices, until the last person arrived. Spencer Bracebridge hurried in, dressed in khakis and a polo jersey, looking concerned.

"All right, folks." Chief Coffin entered the room, which seemed cramped with all the people in it. "Have a seat, everyone. Let's see what we can get sorted out here." He nodded toward the arresting officers. "Riley?"

Riley opened his notebook and cleared his throat. "At eight-thirteen, the station received a phone call from Lily Fox, stating that at nine o'clock, a robbery would be taking place at 135 Hyacinth Lane. Miss Fox said she had overheard two women plotting to steal some lightship baskets. Sean Shreve and I drove to the location. We saw the two women leave the house carrying a number of lightship baskets, which are present at the end of the table. We apprehended the suspects and brought them into custody."

Emma snorted. *"The suspects,"* she echoed under her breath.

Chief Coffin leaned back in his chair. "All right, Emma, why don't you tell us your story."

"My story?" She was white with anger and her freckles stood out on her face. "My *story* is that I've been employed by the Bracebridge family to read to Millicent Bracebridge five days a week. I've become very fond of Mrs. Bracebridge, and I respect the love she has for all the Nantucket antiques and heirlooms in her house. I've been noticing that the lightship baskets—she has seven of them, all very old—looked different. They're lined up on the window seat of the front bay window. Mrs. Bracebridge has macular degeneration and can't see very well. She can probably see well enough to know shapes, objects. She can tell, I think, that seven baskets are there, but not whether or not they are the original ones. It wouldn't occur to her to even wonder about that, anyway. But *I* could tell that five of them were different. I suspected that someone was stealing the baskets and replacing them with cheaper, newer versions. But I didn't want to worry Mrs. Bracebridge or tell Spencer about it unless I was sure. So I asked Marina to ask Sheila if she would evaluate the baskets and she agreed to do it, but she refused to come into the Bracebridge house without permission, so I said I'd bring them to her."

Chief Coffin interrupted Emma. "And Marina is?"

"Marina Warren. She's my friend," Emma said stoutly. "She's renting our cottage, and she's taking lessons from Sheila. She said she'd help me. And that was what we were doing—taking them to be valued, and then we were going to put them back, all without bothering Mrs. Bracebridge."

Chief Coffin leaned down the table. "Sheila?"

"Everything she said is true," Sheila confirmed.

"Could you examine the baskets and tell us if you have any idea whether or not they're old?" Chief Coffin asked.

"Easily." Sheila smiled. "These baskets are not original. I don't have to check the bottom for a signature. I can tell by one glance. I don't think they're even handmade."

Chief Coffin sighed. "Well, then, Spencer, what do you think of all this? Do you want to press charges?"

"Absolutely not," Spencer said. "I'm grateful to Emma for bringing this to my attention, and I appreciate her sense of discretion. I'll sit down with my grandmother and tell her about the baskets. It might spur her into being more realistic about the heirlooms she's got tucked away in her house."

"You need to be aware that someone is stealing from her, Spencer," Chief Coffin said. "Perhaps these women weren't, but someone is."

"Yes, Chief, and I think I know who it is," Spencer replied. "But it's a private matter."

Chief Coffin slowly scanned all the faces at the table. "Does anyone want to say anything else?" He waited. He put both hands flat on the table and studied them for a moment then announced, "Well, then, everyone is free to go." He stood up.

Marina turned toward Emma, but Emma had approached Spencer.

"Spencer, I'm sorry," she said.

"It's all right." Spencer frowned. "Let's talk about it later."

Emma turned to Sheila. "Sheila, thank you so much for coming down here. I'm sorry to spoil your evening."

"Wouldn't have missed it for the world," Sheila said. Leaning over a chair, she hugged Emma. "Honey, in a few years we'll all be dining out on this story."

Marina thanked Sheila, and they hugged as well.

The door was opened and they filed out of the room. After a whispered consultation with Spencer, Emma carried three of the baskets and Spencer carried the others. As they walked past Officer O'Hara and Officer Shreve, Emma muttered, *"Little weenie."* Officer Shreve blushed.

It was after eleven when everyone left the police station. Spencer drove Emma, Marina, and Jim back to Jim's truck, still parked near the Bracebridge house. If she had been alone with Emma, Marina thought she would have burst into relieved and even hysterical laughter. But both Spencer and Jim were somber, and Jim was obviously steaming.

When they arrived at the Bracebridge house, Emma said, "Spencer, I'm really sorry. I didn't handle this well. I was trying—"

"It's okay, Emma," Spencer interrupted. He turned to Marina and Jim. "I would be grateful if you'd help me keep this quiet. Frankly, I'm not sorry this happened. My mother has been helping herself to some of the family heirlooms, and she needs to stop. I'll see that she stops. But I'd hate to see her or my grandmother embarrassed publicly."

"We won't say anything," Jim promised solemnly.

Next to him, Marina nodded, enjoying the rush she got from hearing Jim say "we."

Emma asked, hesitantly, "Would you like help putting them back?"

"That would be great," Spencer said. "Then I'll drive you home, Emma."

They all awkwardly bid one another good night. Emma and Spencer headed toward the Bracebridge house with their arms full of baskets.

Marina climbed into the cab of Jim's pickup and looked over at him. His profile was stern, unsmiling.

She took a deep breath. "You seem upset."

Jim drummed his fingers on the steering wheel. "You're going to have to decide, Marina, whether you're my person or Emma's."

"What? What does that mean?"

"I'm Emma's father. Emma might be a grown woman, but I'm still her father. She's still my daughter."

"Are you upset about the baskets?"

"Of course I am!" Jim's voice darkened. "She was caught stealing. If she hadn't been fortunate enough to have everyone concerned ready at her beck and call to come down and help her out, who knows what would have happened."

"Oh, Jim, please—"

"You and Emma act as if this was some kind of *lark*."

"Well, for heaven's sake, Jim, we hardly committed a *crime*. In fact, we were in the process of discovering a crime. We should have been in and out of there with no one knowing about it. Emma planned to talk privately with Spencer. We wouldn't have been found and arrested if Lily hadn't phoned the police station, which I have to say is a pretty crappy thing for her to do to her sister."

Jim was silent for a long time. They rode together in a steamy détente until he came to their house. He parked in front of it, turned off the ignition, and faced Marina.

"Lily's my daughter, too, Marina."

"I know that."

"I don't like to play favorites. Now all three girls are grown up, and I'm doing my best to stand back and stay out of their arguments.

I'm their parent, Marina. And if you are going to move in with me, you have to decide whether you're going to move in as a friend of the girls or a friend of mine."

"Why can't I be everyone's friend?" Marina countered.

"Marina. I am twelve years older than you. You are ten years older than Abbie, twelve years older than Emma, and eighteen years older than Lily. Maybe you should be with a man closer to your age."

"Oh, Jim!" Marina went speechless.

"I need you to be on my side against these girls," Jim continued. "I can't even consider what it would be like otherwise. Have you thought ahead to what's going to happen when Emma confronts Lily?"

"But Lily was *wrong!*" Marina insisted. "She acted like a little rat, a little weasel! Calling the cops on her own sister!"

"More like calling the cops on her own sister and you," Jim quietly pointed out.

"What does that mean?"

"Think about it. Did Emma confide in Lily? Did she ask Lily to go with her to get the baskets? No. Emma confided in you. She teamed up with you. And now, when we go into the house, you're going to be on Emma's side, against Lily."

"But Lily—"

"If you move in with me, it will be like Emma having an ally and Lily having an enemy."

"Oh, my Lord." Marina leaned her head back against the seat. "This is like some labyrinthine medieval conspiracy."

"Well, that's a pretty accurate description of what it's like, having daughters. Having children in general, I'd imagine." Reaching out, he gently stroked Marina's shoulder, relenting. "I'm not saying it's always like this," he chuckled. "Sometimes it's the three of them against me."

Marina laid the side of her face against his hand.

"I'm not saying you would ever be called upon to discipline one of the girls. I mean, they're women now. They come and go, they're inventing their own lives. When the summer's over, they might all be gone, or they might all stay on. If you move into the house with me—"

"*When,*" Marina corrected, brushing her lips against his hand.

"When you move into the house with me, you can bet there'll be some kind of dramatic crisis, probably with lots of weeping and name calling. I mean, remember how rude Lily was when she saw you had on that bedspread of Danielle's."

"She was a bit extreme."

"I know that. And I love her just as much as I love Abbie and Emma."

Marina considered this. "I'm not sure I can love all three girls the same."

"I'm not asking you to," Jim told her. "I just want you to love me the most. I just want you to be clear about it, that you're on my side."

Marina nodded. "I can do that. I want to do that. I want to be on your side, Jim." She moved toward him. "Actually, right now I'd kind of like to be on your—" leaning over, she whispered the word against his lips.

The house was unusually still. At the end of the hall, light bloomed from the kitchen. They walked through the house and found Abbie and Lily seated at the kitchen table, both obviously exhausted.

"What's going on?" Jim asked.

Abbie stared, without speaking, at the table.

Lily answered. "Abbie took Harry, the little boy she's been babysitting, to the fair. He fell off his carousel horse, hit his head, and scratched his face. It terrified both of them. She took him to the hospital—" Seeing the fear on her father's face, Lily hastily added, "Harry's okay. The doctor said he was okay. And he was normal all day, and now he's asleep and his mother is with him."

"Oh, Abbie." Marina put her hand on Abbie's shoulder. "How frightening for you. But he's okay, that's the important thing."

Abbie said, in a dull voice, "I know."

"Was his mother mean to you? Did she—"

Jim interrupted. "Marina, let's go out to your cottage and get that article we talked about."

Puzzled, Marina said, "What article?" Then she saw his face. "Oh. Right."

They went out the back door and walked in silence to Marina's cottage. Once inside, Marina turned to Jim. "Is there a problem? Did I do something wrong?"

"Marina—" Jim ran his hand through his hair and paced across the small space, stopping at the other side of the room. "I've heard the girls talking. I'm pretty sure Abbie's having an affair with Harry's father. No one's asked my opinion, Abbie hasn't come to ask my advice, she hasn't confided in me, and she's an adult now, and God knows I've made my share of mistakes. But I don't like Abbie being involved with a married man."

"I see." Marina crossed the room and leaned against Jim, wrapping her arms around him. "Goodness. What a dramatic evening your women have given you. Aren't you exhausted?"

He nuzzled his chin on the top of her head. "I'd like to take you to bed right now. But I think we'd better wait until Emma comes home."

Marina paused. Part of her really wanted to join Emma when she got back, to tell Abbie about their adventure with the lightship baskets. Emma would be furious at Lily, but she would calm down. Marina could imagine all of them sitting around the kitchen table, laughing. She felt she had become part of their lives. It seemed only natural for her to be with them.

But really, it was Jim she wanted to be with, to belong to. He had asked her to choose between him and his daughters, and she understood the wisdom of that choice.

"Let's sneak in the front door and into the living room and see if the Red Sox game is still on," she suggested with a grin.

"Brilliant idea," Jim agreed. He put his arm around her shoulders and they walked together, companions, through the night to the front of the house.

42

. . . . .

Abbie

After Marina and their father left the kitchen, Abbie remained at the table, paralyzed by her emotions.

Lily bustled importantly around the kitchen. "Here, Abbie." She set a mug in front of Abbie. "Drink this."

"Not thirsty."

Abbie couldn't stop her mind from relentlessly replaying the events of the day: Harry dropping his seahorse, Abbie taking her hand from his back for just a moment, bending down, the tinkling music, the way the horses rose up and down and up and down, the terrible sound of Harry's head hitting the horse and his body hitting the wooden platform. Harry, limp in her arms.

But Harry was okay. He was fine. He had not been seriously hurt. That was the important thing.

But not the only thing. Harry had wanted his mommy. All day long, he had wanted his mommy.

Perhaps tomorrow Harry would ask to see Abbie. "Where's Nanny Abbie?" he would ask. Abbie's eyes welled with tears. But when he was hurt, when he was scared, he wanted his mommy.

The truly terrible thing was that deep in her deepest heart of hearts, Abbie's own feelings were hurt. She was jealous, jealous of Harry's need for his mommy, jealous of Sydney's irrevocable position in Harry's life, jealous of the way Sydney spoke with Howell tonight on the phone, jealous of the original basic triangle of mother/ daddy/child. Her jealousy provoked a blizzard of questions and fears: What right had Abbie to think she could step into the middle of Harry's family? If she *really* loved Harry—and she did—then how could she even consider causing a divorce between the child's parents? She knew only too well how painful life could be when the normal family pattern was torn apart. The only logical, loving, right thing to do would be to step aside, away from Howell and Harry.

Near her, Lily continued to babble cheerfully, like some kind of bizarre nurse in her high heels and gorgeous silk dress. "Drink the tea, Abbie. You need it. And when did you eat last? Never mind. I'm making you some cinnamon toast."

Lily prepared the toast just the way the sisters loved it, bread slathered with butter and sugar and cinnamon and put under the broiler for a few seconds, until the sweet smell swirled through the kitchen and everything had melted into a luscious thick crunch. The toast was the smell of comfort, the taste of love, the warmth of healing.

When proudly Lily put the plate of toast in front of her, Abbie discovered she was actually hungry. She looked at the clock. Good grief, it was almost midnight. She took a bite of the toast, and flavor flooded her mouth.

"Thanks, Lily," she said. "And thank you for leaving a party to come help me."

Lily smiled. "You're welcome. I was glad to do it. Abbie—"

The front door slammed and Emma stormed into the kitchen. When she saw Lily, her eyes went wide.

Emma glared at Lily. "You little bitch. I can't believe what you did."

Lily's voice was suddenly small and high. "I'm sorry, Emma."

Abbie dropped her toast on her plate and looked from one sister to the other. "What—"

Emma shook her head. "Don't you dare go into your little girl routine, Lily. You're not any of that. You're not a little girl. You are a woman. A woman who makes decisions. And you decided to hurt me as much as you could—and why? What did I ever do to you?"

"I don't know," Lily said miserably.

Abbie asked, "What's going on?"

"Oh, you don't know?" When Emma turned to face Abbie, her freckles stood out on her skin as if they'd been drawn with black markers. "You haven't heard? Didn't Marina tell you that she and I were *arrested* because Lily called the police?"

"You were *arrested*? For what?" Abbie glanced from Emma to Lily, seeking an explanation.

"Marina and I planned to smuggle Mrs. Bracebridge's lightship baskets from her house tonight and take them to Sheila to be valued, because I was pretty sure some of the baskets had been stolen and replaced with new ones." Emma was spitting as she talked. "I wanted to be sure of this before telling Mrs. Bracebridge about it, or rather, Spencer, because I thought it was his mother who was doing it, and I didn't want to upset everyone if I was wrong. And Marina said she'd help me carry them, they're so bulky, and we called Sheila and agreed on a time to bring them over, and Marina and I went over there at nine tonight—and *Lily* called the fucking police to tell them there would be a theft at the Bracebridge house!"

Abbie gawked at Lily. "God, Lily. Why would you do that?"

Lily bit her lip and cringed.

Emma continued, "We were taken to the police station! We had to ride in the back of the police car with those scary doors that don't open from the inside. We had to drag Sheila into this, and Spencer and Dad. What kind of person calls the police on her sister?" Emma demanded. "Tell me, Lily. What the hell were you thinking?"

"I don't know." Lily's chest heaved. "Maybe I was just jealous that you chose Marina instead of me. I never dreamed they'd *arrest* you. I only thought they'd give you a good scare. I didn't think it through." Lily's face was blotchy with emotion. "I am so sorry. I am so so sorry."

"Well, I'll never forgive you for this, Lily. I'll never trust you again in my life."

"Hey, Emma, come on." Abbie rose from the table, crossed the room, and put one arm around Lily, who was crying now. "Back off, Emma. Calm down. Come on. You're not in jail, are you?"

"Oh, *nice,* Abbie, side with *her,* protect your little baby sister. *The little princess.*" Emma took a few steps away from Lily and stood for a moment catching her breath. After a long moment of silence, Emma confessed, "I was so *frightened* in that police car. I had a panic attack. It was awful. It's *awful* being trapped in a car and you can't get out; all I could think was what if there's an accident, I can't get out!"

"Oh, Em, I never meant for that to happen," Lily said. "I didn't think anything like that would happen."

"It was so *mean* of you, Lily," Emma said and now she was weeping. "Why would you do something so mean to me? You must hate me."

"But I don't hate you!" Lily protested.

"Well," Emma's voice was thick with emotion. "*I* hate *you*." She turned and left the room.

43

·····

Emma

Emma had agreed to help Marcia with her landscaping business this weekend, and as she dragged herself out of bed at five-thirty Saturday morning, she was glad. She hadn't slept well, and it was a relief to see the dawn, to leave her hot, tangled sheets. She wanted to get out of the house before either of her sisters woke. She was so mad at Lily it made her jaw clench until her teeth ached, and she wasn't pleased with Abbie, either.

She poured herself a glass of orange juice, slugged it back, and was ready at the curb when Marcia and Brian drove up in the green pickup truck. She squeezed into the cab next to Brian. Marcia was driving. The air was rich with the aroma of coffee and sugar, and to Emma's delight, Brian handed her a traveling mug filled with hot coffee and a bag of Downy Flake doughnuts.

"Thanks, guys," Emma said. "I need this."

"Well, I need *you*," Marcia said. "I can't believe Karen just took off like that. She'd promised she'd work for me through August. Instead, she left the island without giving me one day's notice."

"Not to mention," Brian added in his low rumbling voice, "everyone wants their gardens to look perfect, and we haven't had rain for a week, and no one considers that they might wander out and water their gardens all by themselves!"

Emma sipped her coffee, listening to Marcia's chatter, aware of

Brian's low chuckle and also of how his muscular thigh pressed against hers. They were crowded in the cab; he couldn't help it. She didn't mind it, really, and he smelled good, like Ivory soap and Barbasol. Idly Emma wondered if brothers and sisters had less friction between them than sisters. Would Brian ever try to get his sister in trouble? She doubted it. He seemed like a pretty easygoing guy.

Their first stop was on Wolf Lane. Brian mowed the lawn while Marcia and Emma weeded and watered. The day was hot and humid, and an irritating gusty wind yanked plants from Emma's hands and slapped branches into her face. The humidity turned her hair into a giant ball of frizz, and when she tried to pull it back, her rubber band broke. Sweat washed away her sunblock and she knew her nose and shoulders were turning lobster red.

Really, she knew she was most angry at herself. In her own twisted, warped, pathetic way, she had allowed her attraction to Spencer Bracebridge to create some kind of bizarre and hopelessly doomed scenario. She'd imagined how she would discover that the lightship baskets were fake, and she'd tell Spencer, and he would be impressed by her acute perception and her deep concern for island historical artifacts and for his beloved grandmother . . .

And what? What then? What had she imagined? She hadn't thought how horrified Spencer would be if it really was his own mother who was stealing the baskets. He might hate Emma for exposing his mother and putting them all in such a difficult position. Emma was only an *employee*—who did she think she was, to pry into the lives of such an important, respected island family?

At the next job, Brian trimmed the high privet hedge with electric trimmers while Marcia and Emma pulled out the annuals the owner was tired of and planted flowers in the colors the owner desired. Tearing healthy plants from the ground just seemed wrong, and it sent Emma's mood tumbling. She couldn't believe what Lily had done. She couldn't believe that Abbie had defended her. She couldn't believe that she'd thought Spencer Bracebridge would ever be interested in her, and her only consolation was that she'd never allowed her feelings for him to show, not to him, not to Millicent, not even to her sisters.

Her cell phone, tucked into the pocket of her cargo shorts, vibrated. She glanced at the caller ID. It was Millicent Bracebridge's home. Her heart leapt. Perhaps Spencer was calling—

"Hello?"

"Is this Emma Fox?" It was Sandra Bracebridge's chilly voice.

Emma closed her eyes, as if against an oncoming train. "Yes."

"I'm calling to tell you you are relieved of your duties here. I don't want you to set foot in this house again, do you understand?"

Emma swallowed. "I understand, Mrs. Bracebridge. But I'd like to tell your mother-in-law good-bye."

"Did you not hear what I said? You are not to come into this house again. If you do, I'll phone the police and have you forcibly removed."

Emma snorted with surprise. What was it with everyone phoning the cops on her?

"I'll send your paycheck in the mail," Sandra Bracebridge concluded, and without saying good-bye, disconnected.

Emma squeezed the cell phone so hard she was surprised she didn't crush it. She wanted to throw it hard against a brick, but she stuck it back into her pocket and savagely attacked an azalea bush.

What was she doing on this island?

What was she even doing on this planet?

No one was choosing *her*! Marina had gone off with her father. Abbie had sided with Lily. Duncan had dumped her for Alicia, her Boston firm had fired her and kept other people, and now she'd lost her connection to Millicent Bracebridge and the island, not to mention Spencer, because she'd never had any real connection to him.

She was a total loser.

She could understand for the first time how her mother had done it, why she had done it. Sometimes it all got to be too much, and there was nothing hopeful in sight. Then how did a person go on?

44

.....

Lily

Lily woke on Saturday morning with misery sitting on her stomach like an elephant.

Last night after her sisters went to bed, Lily had phoned Jason to tell him she was sleeping at her house. She and Emma had had a fight, she'd told him. She'd explain it later.

She'd hoped that in the morning Emma would be less angry and more forgiving. She and Emma had fought before. A good night's sleep would calm her down.

But the house was empty. Her sisters had already left for work. Without making coffee.

Crankily, Lily brewed a pot of coffee and drank juice, considering the day before her. The Life Saving Museum fund-raiser, the last big event of the summer, was tonight. After this weekend, families began to pack up in preparation for returning home. The weather was still hot and sunny, but hurricanes were spinning near the southern states, threatening to spiral north, to loom overhead, darkening the sky and kicking up high winds that made the ferry and plane trips uncomfortable and sometimes even terrifying.

The sense of a long, idyllic summer was ending. Everyone's thoughts were turning to fall.

For Lily, it had all gone too fast. She felt she was only now hitting her stride, learning how to move among the truly wealthy as if she belonged there. The approaching storm, the flickering of the light as the winds batted the summer leaves, made her anxious about her future.

Low laughter drifted through the kitchen window. Lily leaned against the sink, curious.

Her father and Marina were walking away from the Playhouse. Her father's arm was around Marina's waist, a possessive and sexual grasp. He was looking down at her, and she looked up at him, and they stopped right there in the middle of the yard where anyone could see them and kissed. *Really* kissed. A full-body press, movie-moment kiss.

Gross, Lily hissed. Yet she couldn't wrench her eyes away. Horrified, mesmerized, she watched as the couple walked on, leaning toward each other, to her father's truck.

Everyone liked Marina more than they liked her. It was a childish thought, but Lily couldn't ignore it. Eartha would be going back to New York any day now. Most of the parties were over. Was Marina going to go back to Missouri? Or would she stay here? And where did Lily belong?

Put on your big girl shoes and stop whining, she told herself. She had a ton of notes to type up for the magazine, so she got out her laptop and notepads and set to work. That helped.

She called Jason again. He was working all day on a deck. She called Carrie and took lunch over to her house and then, on the spur of the moment, she offered to take the baby for a walk for an hour or so, to give Carrie time for a nap. Carrie was thrilled and grateful, and as Lily pushed the stroller along the sidewalk, she felt helpful and generous and quite pleased with herself.

The house was still silent when she returned home. She had time for a good long soak in the bathtub and plenty of time to set and arrange her hair in the smashingly attractive sleek do that made her feel like a movie star.

At the fund-raiser, she snapped photos and jotted down names. Now, at the end of the summer, lots of people knew her. *Important* people. They smiled at her, and air-kissed her, and chatted with her. Her dark mood lifted. She actually felt rather glamorous. She went to Jason's to spend the night, still on an emotional high.

Sunday she and Jason slept late, then spent a lazy afternoon at the beach. Sunday evening, for the first time in weeks, she had nothing scheduled for work. Jason ordered a pizza and suggested she kick back, watch TV, and relax.

But the basement was dank and mildewy with the worst of the summer's humidity, and she got cranky again. Her shorts and baggy tee shirt seemed hideous. She kept checking her cell phone, and no one had called her, not Emma, not Abbie, not Eartha. It made her feel so unwanted.

"Stop checking for calls," Jason told her. He padded barefoot to the refrigerator, got out two cold beers, and levered off the caps. He took a long cool drink, then returned to hand her a beer. "You deserve a little time off."

"I wish I could get time off from my thoughts." Lily yanked her long hair up off her neck with a rubber band.

"Emma will forgive you," Jason assured her. "You know she will. You're sisters. And Marina's lease on the cottage is up in December, right?"

Lily snorted. "That doesn't mean she'll leave in September. I'm afraid she's never going to leave."

"All right, then, is that such a bad thing? Think about it rationally, Lily. It might be nice for your dad to have someone in his life. Someone serious, to live with him."

"*I* live with him," Lily reminded Jason.

Jason laughed. "Honey, you don't want to live with your daddy all your life. That's just sad."

Why did his words hit her like a blow? Lily couldn't understand her own emotions. "I know that. I just—it's like I don't belong anywhere, Jason." She felt tears well in her eyes. "Oh, God, I am so sick of myself."

Jason contemplated her for a moment, then rose and went into the bedroom. She heard the dresser drawer open and close. Jason returned to sit next to her.

"I was going to wait until some romantic occasion," he said. "But we don't have to do that clichéd stuff, do we? You don't have to worry about where you belong, Lily. You belong with me." He held out a small black velvet box. "Let's make it official."

Lily took the box, opened it, and saw, ensconced in black velvet, the smallest diamond ring on the planet. She stared at it as the world closed in on her, and this moment engraved itself in her memory. This was how she would always remember Jason asking her to marry him. Sitting here, in a rented basement apartment, wearing old baggy clothes, her hair straggling around her face, no makeup, a box of pizza and a bottle of beer on the coffee table.

"I know the diamond's small," Jason explained. "But I want to save as much as possible so we can make a down payment on a house here someday. I was even thinking that if Marina does move in with your father, you and I could move into the cottage, and we'd save on rent and have more money piled up sooner."

Jason was so earnest, his eyes so full of love. "We've only known each other three months, Jason," she said softly.

"We've really known each other our whole lives," he said. "We've been in love for three months. We're not kids anymore. We're old enough to know what we want. Who we want. I want you, Lily."

"And I want you, Jason. But—"

Jason's face lit up. "Then marry me."

She thought out loud. "I've always wanted a big wedding."

"Well, we can have a big wedding." He took her hands in his. "Lily, we can have any kind of wedding you want, any time you want. A Christmas wedding? A June wedding? Yeah, how about a summer wedding, on the beach, barefoot in the sand, with the ocean all around us." He studied her face. "Lily, we don't have to decide all that now. We can take the time to plan just what you want. But I want you to feel secure. I want you to know you have a place, and it's with me, wherever I am. And I know I don't have a lot of money right now, but we're young, Lily. We're young and strong, we're hard workers. I love you, Lily. I want to marry you. I want to protect you. I want to take care of you."

"Oh, Jason," Lily said helplessly. "You're so sweet. You're the sweetest man on the planet."

"Then will you marry me, Lily?"

She smiled, and she was crying now, too. "Of course I'll marry you, Jason."

"Then let's seal the deal." He slid the ring on her finger.

She held her hand up. If she wiggled her hand just right, the tiny diamond caught the light and sparkled.

45

·····

Marina

Sunday evening, Marina took the pie from the oven, feeling quite pleased with the way the tips of the meringue were toasted to a caramel gloss, the crust a perfect golden brown. She was coming to cooking late in life, and she found it engaged many of the creative energies and attention she had once paid to her work. She was gaining weight, she noticed, but she didn't mind. Jim didn't, either.

She smiled, thinking of Jim. He had a talent for enjoying the day, and she was learning from him. And with each day she came to understand how right Jim had been when he talked with her about his daughters. It would be almost impossible, Marina thought, not to favor one woman more, and one woman less.

Earlier today, Marina had gone through the empty house, organizing it after the weekend. She carried glasses and plates back to the kitchen, newspapers out to the recycle bin, and swept and mopped the kitchen floor. She started a load of wash, emptied a load of laundry from the dryer and carried it up to Abbie's room. She took a couple of towels out of the hamper in the bathroom, wondered where the others were, and guessed where they were at once. She didn't want to intrude uninvited, but with one quick glance, she found most of the towels in Lily's room, some still damp, tossed on a chair or the end of her bed or on the floor, mixed in with the mounds of discarded clothing. She gathered them up, washed and dried two loads of towels, and folded and put them away. She liked thinking of what a luxury it was to come home from landscaping or taking care of a child on the beach, to have a shower and step out to find a fluffy clean towel waiting. She tried not to think judgmental thoughts about Lily, but it was hard.

It was almost six o'clock, so everyone would be arriving any moment. At least Jim would be. Marina sliced cucumbers, carrots, and zucchini and set them out with a light yogurt dip. She'd start the bluefish baking when they were here—this recipe would take exactly twenty minutes. She'd gotten pretty good at cooking fish.

She popped into the downstairs bathroom to check her reflection in the mirror. She looked great, tanned and relaxed and happy. If she could run a business, she could run a family!

The back screen door slammed, and Jim called hello. She went out to greet him with a kiss and a hug. He grabbed a beer and sat at the table, and then Abbie came in.

"Hi, Abbie. I'm about to open a bottle of wine. Want a glass?" Marina held up a bottle of chilled Vino Verde.

Abbie shrugged and collapsed in a chair. "That would be great. Thanks."

Marina had heard about the frightful fall the child Abbie was caring for had taken on the carousel, but Abbie had not asked her advice about it, and Marina was restraining herself from offering advice. After all, she'd never had a child. But it made her sad to see how the sparkle had gone out of Abbie.

Emma came in just then, and she seemed even sadder than Abbie.

"Do I have time for a quick shower before dinner?" Emma asked as she kicked off her gardening clogs. She'd spent the day working with Marcia on landscaping jobs and her skin was plastered with dirt. She even had leaves in her hair.

"Sure." Marina loved it, how Emma just assumed Marina was there. "Want to take a glass of wine up with you?"

"Thanks, Marina." Emma took the glass and padded barefoot out of the room.

Marina put the fish into the preheated oven and began to set the table. Jim sat relaxed in his chair, telling Abbie about a friend of theirs who'd gotten so thoroughly covered with poison ivy he'd had to be hospitalized. Marina checked the lobster pot—the water was simmering—so she sat down next to Abbie, handed her an ear of corn, and they stripped the husks off a dozen ears of sweet Nantucket corn as they talked.

"How was your day?" Marina asked Abbie.

Abbie shrugged. "I spent the day helping the Fitzhughs pack up and close up their house. What did you do?"

"I finished my lightship basket," Marina announced. "It's quite handsome, if I do say so myself."

"Did you enjoy making it?" Jim asked.

Marina considered. "It requires a lot of patience and repetition, you know. Let's just say I'm glad I made one but I don't think I want to make another one."

"Gee," Abbie said, "I was hoping you'd make one for me."

Marina was surprised at how pleased she felt to hear Abbie joke like that in spite of whatever crisis was going on with her. "Honey, if you want one, I'll make you one," she said.

Emma returned to the room, dressed in a clean tee shirt and shorts, her hair wet and curling.

"Perfect timing," Marina told her. She dropped the corn into the boiling water, took the fish out of the oven, and set it on a hot pad in the middle of the table. She tossed the salad with a vinegar and oil dressing she'd made herself, dumped the rice into a bowl, and set out butter dishes for the corn. By then the corn was ready. She'd organized it perfectly!

"Shall we wait for Lily?" Marina asked.

"Are you kidding?" Emma answered.

"We don't even know if she's coming to dinner," Abbie said, sensibly.

They sat around the table, eating the hot juicy corn and the flaky white fish, hardly talking except to murmur appreciatively. Marina felt as proud of herself as she had when she'd done a great ad campaign presentation for a client. She couldn't make life easier for the girls, but at least she could nourish them, and their pleasure nourished her.

"Hi, guys!" Lily exploded in the back door, so exuberant she seemed to throw off beams of light. Jason came in after her, grinning like a kid.

"Hi, Lily. Sorry we started without you," Marina began.

"Oh, never mind about that!" Lily waved her left hand at them. "Jason asked me to marry him! We're engaged!"

"Oh, Lily!" Abbie jumped up from the table and hugged her sister. "Hold still and let me see the ring! Oh, Lily, it's stunning."

While Abbie hugged Jason, Lily approached Emma. Only two days had passed since the disastrous night at the police station and Abbie had told Marina how angry Emma was at Lily. Marina glanced at Jim to see if he was concerned.

But Emma took Lily's hand and scrutinized the ring, turning Lily's hand this way and that. She stood up and hugged her sister tightly. "This is spectacular news, Lily. Congratulations." She turned to Jason and kissed his cheek. "Welcome to our crazy family!"

This sister thing, Marina thought, is as complicated and incomprehensible as particle physics.

"Thanks, Emma." Lily did a little jiggling dance of happiness. She turned to show her father the ring.

Jim stood up and hugged his daughter. "Congratulations, Lily." Reaching out, he shook Jason's hand. "Congratulations, Jason."

"Oh, Dad, I'm so happy!" She linked her arm through Jason's, smiling up at him. "We've got to go tell his parents! And Carrie. And—"

"Wait, Lily," Emma said. "When is the wedding?"

"Oh, I don't know, we just got engaged." Lily held out her hand and turned it, making the diamond flash.

"Oh my God!" Abbie said. "Do you realize this means Lily will be the first sister to get married?"

Lily laughed a theatrical, triumphant laugh. Everyone talked at once about which church they'd go to, would it be a beach wedding, who would officiate. Marina sat at the table, smiling and watching and thinking how odd it was that no one noticed that Lily had not deigned to show Marina her engagement ring.

46

. . . . .

Abbie

Monday afternoon, Abbie let herself into the Parker house, walked straight through into the kitchen, and found Harry and Howell there, finishing their lunch. They were dressed alike in white tee shirts and khaki shorts. When Howell saw her, the connection between them sparked like a Roman candle.

"Hi, Nanny Abbie!" Harry's piping high voice was full of excitement. "Daddy came home last night and he brought me a *giant octopus!*"

Abbie pretended to shiver. "A live one?"

"No, silly Nanny Abbie!" Harry giggled. "A rubber one." He wriggled in his chair. "I'll show you—"

"Finish your lunch first, Harry." Howell tapped the side of his son's plate.

"How's the noggin, Harry?" Abbie slid into a chair next to the little boy's and checked out his head. The bump had disappeared. Only a bruise-colored mark remained.

"He's right as rain," Howell told her. He moved his leg under the table so that his bare foot touched her ankle.

The touch took her breath away.

"Mommy took me to Victoria's house!" Harry announced. "Victoria has a kitten! We might get a kitten."

"That would be terrific, Harry," Abbie told him. She smiled a friendly kind of smile at Howell and moved her leg away. She was determined to carry through with her decision, her logical, responsible decision, even though her heart and her soul and her senses all flowed toward Howell, craving his touch, the sound of his voice, the flesh of his body. She clenched her fists beneath the table, digging her nails into her palms. "How did your conference go?"

"Very well. I didn't trip over my own feet to or from the podium, a respectably large audience attended my talk, and no one fell asleep or stormed out of the auditorium while I was reading my paper."

Abbie forced a laugh and winked at Harry, who was watching her face. "As if you were really worried."

"Hey," Howell retorted playfully, "have you ever spoken before three hundred of your peers, most of whom are praying for the opportunity to discredit you?"

Harry slid halfway out of his chair. "Daddy, Nanny Abbie, I'm through with lunch!"

"You can get down," Abbie told him. She stood. "Let's get you ready for the beach, kiddo."

Howell rose, too. "I'd love to go with you, but I've got piles of email to deal with."

Abbie flashed him another fake smile. "We'll be fine."

Because the wind was whipping in from the northeast, Abbie tucked Harry into the SUV and drove to Miacomet Pond. The pond side was sheltered, and most people went up over the dune to the ocean side, so Harry had a large plot of sand to himself. He brought his rubber octopus and Abbie stationed it in the shallow water, weighting its middle down with sand, its eight legs floating free.

At three she called him up to their little nest beneath the beach umbrella. He had his snack of fruit juice and crackers, then curled up for a nap with a beach towel over him. Abbie lay next to him, on her side, just looking at him. He was the most captivating child she'd ever seen and she loved him with a love she couldn't comprehend, but after his fall from the carousel horse, she knew she'd been absolutely wrong to think she could ever be more to him than a nanny. He already had a mother. And he was a child who needed his family intact. What child didn't?

Then it was time to gather up all the beach things and head back home. At the Parkers' house, Abbie gave Harry a quick rinse in the outside shower, then brought him inside.

Howell came into the hall and squatted down to hug his son. "Hi, guys, how was the beach?"

"Nanny Abbie made the octopus swim!" Harry told his father.

"Nanny Abbie is very clever." Howell looked up at Abbie. "Can you stay for dinner?"

She shook her head. "Not tonight."

Startled, Howell stood up. "Really? Are you sure?"

She took a step back. "I've got another babysitting job this week. Every night. So . . . I'd better be going." She kissed the top of Harry's head. "See you tomorrow, buddy."

"Abbie, wait." Howell put his hand on her shoulder. "Abbie . . ." Suddenly aware that his son was watching him, he dropped his hand. "Is everything okay?"

"Everything's fine!" she responded brightly. "Bye, Harry." She hurried out the door.

In fact, she actually had a job lined up every night this week. The children she babysat were older than Harry, and less enchanting. The job was easy enough, though. All she had to do was make popcorn and watch DVDs with them until their parents came home at eleven.

At home, she found Emma standing at the kitchen sink spreading peanut butter on crackers.

"Hey," she said to Emma.

"Hey," Emma said back.

Abbie collapsed in a chair. "You look awful."

"I am awful," Emma mumbled with her mouth full. "Sandra Bracebridge fired me."

"Oh, Emma. That's too bad. Is that why you seemed so wretched last night?"

"Yeah. I was going to tell you, but I didn't want to rain on Lily's parade."

"Because of the lightship baskets?" Abbie asked.

"She didn't explain, but I'm sure that's the reason. She fired me by phone. I can't even go say good-bye to Millicent. That makes me feel really terrible. God, why can't anything go right?"

"Oh, Em. You'll find lots of other jobs."

"Actually, I'm already working for Marcia, landscaping. She pays well, and it's nice to be outside."

"Well, that's good then, right?"

Emma shrugged. She screwed the lid back on the peanut butter jar, rinsed her hands, and settled into a chair across from Abbie. "You look pretty terrible yourself."

Abbie said, "I'll be okay." But she began to cry. "Oh, Emma, I'm such a fuckup."

Emma laughed. "*You?* Please."

"What happened to us?" Abbie asked. "Did we all just go *mad* this summer? I mean, I've worked with lots of children before, and I never felt as charmed by them as I did by Harry. And I certainly never fell in love with any of the daddies before."

"Hang on, Abbie, you're getting things all out of proportion. Harry fell off his horse and hurt himself and wanted his mommy. That is just not tragic. It's normal."

"If you could see her, Emma. Sydney is such a coldhearted bitch. But she is *Harry's mommy.*" She shook her head savagely. "What was I even *thinking?*"

"What are you even thinking now?" Emma countered.

"That I was a *fool* ever to dream I could be with Howell and Harry. I'm stepping back, way back. I'm stepping away."

"Have you told Howell this?"

"No. No, I haven't had the opportunity."

"But Abbie, if he loves you, if you love him—"

"I think he does love me. I know I love him. But honestly, Emma, I love Harry more. And Harry's innocent. He's vulnerable. He's helpless. And he's fragile. When he fell, I realized how frightening it would be for him if his parents divorced."

Emma drummed her fingers on the table. After a moment, she said, "I'm not a big fan of divorce, you know that. But as your sister, Abbie, I've got to say I've never seen you in love the way you were this summer with Howell. I hate to see you throw that away. And you told me that Howell doesn't love his wife. Should Harry live with parents who don't love each other? What does that teach him about families, about life? Don't make this decision so hastily. Lots of kids have divorced parents. It might be great for Harry to have his mother and father and you, as well, to love him."

"I don't want to be a home wrecker," Abbie said.

"But Abbie, *you* matter, too. Your happiness matters, too."

Abbie rubbed her eyes. "I think I really need to get some sleep." She stood up, then impulsively leaned over and hugged her sister. "But thanks. Thanks for being here."

Emma

Now at the end of August there was not as much work to be done in the formal gardens of Nantucket. Most required only simple maintenance—watering, mowing, deadheading. Many of the home owners had already left the island for the city, or were busy packing up. Emma wondered if Marcia had hired her out of sympathy, but when she asked Marcia about that, her friend had snorted.

"Are you nuts? You think I could do this all alone? Oh, please get over yourself."

Being around Marcia was good for Emma. Her friend was honest, no-nonsense, blunt, and cheerful. Marcia was engaged to an island man. They were saving toward building a house, and it would be a long frugal time before they could afford that. But Marcia didn't complain about money, or much of anything, really. She and her brother seemed content with their lives. Emma envied them for that.

Now Marcia removed her gardening gloves and stretched to release her back muscles. "Okay. We're done here. Emma, I'm meeting Brian and some friends at Miacomet. Want to come along?"

With the summer rush over, their work hours were shortened. It was only a little after four, but Emma was hot, sweaty, tired, and sad. "I wouldn't be very good company."

"Hey," Marcia said, "all you have to do is sit back and drink a cold beer."

Emma considered this as they carried the tools to the truck. She suspected that Marcia was trying to get a romance going between her brother and Emma, and perhaps at some other time in her life she'd be interested. He was a hunk and a really good guy, but Emma's heart was somewhere else—foolish heart. Still, she didn't want a lopsided attraction to cause misunderstandings between herself and her friend.

"I'm really beat," she told Marcia. "Another time, maybe."

Marcia dropped her off at her father's house, but instead of going inside, Emma left her backpack on the porch and grabbed her bike. She pedaled away from her house, through narrow lanes and along tree-lined streets until she came to Surfside Road. The bike path was good, and it was easy sailing past the high school, the elementary school, and the outlying wooded neighborhoods.

She was going against the tide of traffic. Everyone else was headed back into town after a day at the beach, and when she arrived at the southern shore, she was surprised at how empty it was. A few people sprawled on beach towels, and in the distance a group of four-wheel drive vehicles clustered together, but it was the end of summer and the end of the day. She was glad. She wanted to be alone.

She locked her bike to the bike rack, kicked off her sandals, and padded barefoot down the dune toward the shore. She ambled along at the edge of the water, letting the cool waves break over her feet, and it felt so good that she surrendered to temptation and walked right out into the ocean, gasping as the water slapped her thighs, stomach, chest. She dove under a wave and swam for a while. The waves were rough and churning from a recent storm. The struggle was engrossing, but she knew how wicked the undertow could be here, so she bodysurfed up to the beach and thrashed her way free of the water and back onto the safety of the sand.

After taking a moment to catch her breath, she walked east along the shore. Her shorts and tee shirt clung to her, and the teasing breeze chilled her. Clouds surged over the sun, making the light glare and dim in an erratic dance. Gulls shrieked as they rode the wind, skimming low, searching for food left by picnickers.

On this side of the island, the ocean rolled free and unobstructed all the way from Portugal, gathering a force and density seldom seen on the calmer Sound side. This was the wild side, deep, forbidding, mysterious. Anything could be hidden in its depths. Whales could be looming nearby—a forty-six-foot-long sperm whale had been stranded in Sconset only a decade ago. Even the air was different here, more electric with ions, charged and fickle and exhilarating.

Over the years, Emma had heard many stories about tourists who came to the island and found their lives changed forever. They were healed of sorrows, or they fell in love. They came here to marry, because the island was romantic and magical for those who didn't live here.

But what about those who *lived* here, who had grown up here? Was there any magic for them?

Emma thought that returning to Nantucket had been good for her. The small-town atmosphere charmed her. The pace of life was more comfortable here. It was good to be back with her sisters, even with that tattletale Lily. It was good to be around her father, too, and it was nothing short of a miracle, the way Marina had made her father brighten up. Okay, she told herself, there was an example of an island resident finding magic. Her father had found love with Marina, and love was magic.

Perhaps Marina was magic. Emma treasured their late-night swims, and the enchanted atmosphere Marina spun around herself with music and wind chimes and sky-blue walls. Marina had recovered from a painful divorce; she provided a role model for Emma. Perhaps Marina could help Abbie figure out what to do with her love for Howell Parker.

Perhaps Marina could help Emma survive the disaster with Spencer Bracebridge. Ironic, really. Finally, Emma was over Duncan—because she'd met Spencer. What an idiot she was!

Suddenly tired, Emma turned back. The waves had already washed away her footprints.

But the tide had left something: a small creamy rock shaped like a heart, polished into a dull gleam by sand and water. Emma picked it up and held it in her hand. Her mother would say: *The sea has given you a sign.*

But actually, it was only a rock.

Emma swung her arm, to toss it back into the ocean. Then she hesitated, and tucked it into the pocket of her shorts. As she strode up the beach and back to her bike, she felt the little solid bump against her hip, a kind of message in a language she could interpret any way she wanted.

48

·····

Lily

Wednesday morning, Lily wheeled her bike up to Eartha's house, let herself in the front door, scratched Godzy's rump, and hurried to Eartha's bedroom. To her surprise, Eartha was up and dressed and wading through piles of clothing.

"God, darling," she greeted Lily. "I don't know what to take back and what to leave here." Suddenly she collapsed on the side of her bed. "It's all too much."

Eartha's blond hair, as always on awakening, was skewed to one side and up. From one perspective she looked almost Marie Antoinette-ish, with the pouf of yellow cotton-candy hair, but from the other side, she looked absolutely *old*. Without the glitz of jewelry and makeup, her brave gaudiness was not there to distract the eye. An arrow of sympathy pierced Lily's heart.

Lily bent to pick up some of the garments. "When are you leaving?"

"Within the week, I suppose. If I can get sorted out. It's just too complicated. I agreed to go to Paris almost immediately. I have some friends there who are opening a new restaurant."

"Oh, that sounds like fun!"

"Sure, kid. But still . . . to tell the truth, sometimes I wonder if I have the energy for it all." Her body sagged. "Everything was more fun when my husband was alive. Julius and I used to have more fun than a Judy Holliday movie. And when we got home, he'd whip up a plate of scrambled eggs and we'd sit up and dish till the sun rose, then we'd go to bed. And dance? Julius could have made Fred Astaire jealous. And he was so gorgeous in a tux." She wiped her eyes. "Without him, it's just not the same."

Lily stood quietly, not sure what to say or do.

"Oh, Jeez," Eartha said. "What's worse than a maudlin old broad? Give me a cigarette, Lily. The pack's over there." She blew her nose and immediately went into a fit of coughing.

Lily thought: Why not? The worst she could do was fire her, and summer was almost over. "Eartha. I think you should stop smoking."

Eartha snorted in surprise. "You do, do you? Well, thanks for that health alert, but give me my cigarettes."

Lily hesitated. "Couldn't you just cut down?"

"Give me a smoke and I'll think about it."

Lily accepted defeat. She crossed the room, grabbed up the pack of Sobranies, and handed them to Eartha. "I'll get your calendar and we can sort out just when you're going to Paris, and how long you're staying. That will help you decide what to take."

Eartha sucked in a big drag of tobacco. As she exhaled, she squinted at Lily through the swirling smoke.

"I should take you."

Lily blinked. "What?"

"I should take you. Hell, yes, what an idea! Why didn't I think of this before! Lily! I should take you with me."

"To Paris?" Lily thought her heart had stopped beating.

"Yeah, to Paris. New York, first, to help me get organized there. Then Paris for oh, about six months should do it. Christmas in Paris is a gas."

"Would I be, like, your maid?" Lily asked.

"Oh, for heaven's sake!" Eartha snapped. "When have I ever treated you like a maid? No, you'd be my, oh, shit, let's just say my social secretary. My assistant. Something like that." She cocked her head. "You want to know how much you'd get paid, right?"

"Well, yes, I suppose so. This is all new to me . . ."

"It's all new to me, too, kid. But I can improvise. You know I'll have to buy you some new clothes and a few more pieces of jewelry. And you're young, you won't want to hang around me every minute of the day, and I like my solitude now and then as well. I don't know how to figure it by the hour. But in general, oh, I don't know, room and board and clothes and air fare and stuff plus about five thousand a month salary? Does that sound reasonable?"

Lily's legs buckled. She sat down hard on the floor. All around her mountains of clothing rose in satin heaps. "That sounds reasonable." Her voice wouldn't work.

Eartha scrutinized Lily for a long, breathless moment. "What's that on your finger?"

Lily blinked. "Oh! Oh, this is an engagement ring." As she held out her hand for Eartha to see, she hated herself for feeling embarrassed that the diamond was so small.

"So who's the guy?"

"Jason Clark."

"Tell me about him." Eartha scooted on the bed and lay back on her pillows.

"Well, he grew up on the island. Just got out of the army. He was in Iraq, but he doesn't talk about it. He's a carpenter. Got his contractor's license this summer, and he's building up his business. He's really handsome. And really nice."

"Do you love him?"

"Oh, yes, I do. And he loves me."

"Will he mind if you take off for six months?"

Lily hesitated. "I don't know, actually."

"How old are you?"

"Twenty-two. Jason's twenty-four." She felt her heart expand under the sunlight of Eartha's interest. "We've known each other, kind of, all our lives—"

The phone rang. Eartha grabbed it, checked the caller ID, and clicked it on. "*Darling!*" she roared. "God, wasn't last night *divine!*"

Lily waited for a moment, until she realized that Eartha was going to keep talking. She stood up carefully, like someone in a new atmosphere. Everything was the same. Everything was different. Brighter. Gilded. *Enchanted*.

She saw no cup or plate or tray, so she went into the kitchen and prepared a light breakfast for Eartha. When she brought it back, Eartha was still on the phone, so she set it on the table next to her and began the task of picking up, smoothing out, and folding the clothes strewn across the floor. Some were obviously summer clothes, sleeveless and loose and lightweight. She set those in one pile. Others were dresses Eartha had worn in the evening, and those Lily put into a separate pile. Eartha might not want to wear them twice. But if she was going to be someplace different, with people who hadn't seen her on the island, she might want to wear them, especially this black silk that was so flattering to Eartha.

As she worked, she felt light-headed, even giddy. It was the most *amazing* thing, to have a dream come true. She had fantasized about Eartha giving her clothes and jewelry, and Eartha had. She had day-dreamed about leaving the island for more glamorous places, and suddenly, as if an angel had flown overhead and dropped a present into her lap, here was her opportunity. It was so astounding, so *magical* . . . She couldn't believe it, actually. She was afraid to get too excited. Eartha could be capricious. What if Eartha changed her mind?

And what if Eartha *didn't* change her mind?

She thought she could convince Jason to understand how much she wanted this. Six months away wouldn't kill them, wouldn't change the love between them. Perhaps Jason might worry that Lily would find city life too tempting, or that she might fall in love with someone else, or have an affair. She had to admit it, the thought of having an affair with a Parisian made her heart race. What if he was a count or something? Why not dream big? Her dreams seemed to be coming true! What if he was a count with a little old castle outside Paris?

Slow down, Lily ordered herself. Get real. Think about this: What would it be like to live with Eartha? Every day. Not to be able to go home to relax and kick back in her own familiar place? Would they get on each other's nerves? Of course they would. They were only human. What if Eartha sent Lily packing? So what? Lily would have at least had the experience of living in New York and Paris. And living *posh*. She wouldn't be cramped in a garret like an au pair or foreign exchange student. Eartha would stay in five-star hotels and ride in limos and attend concerts and operas.

She and Eartha did have fun together. True, Lily was a kind of servant to the older woman, but she was also a kind of friend, and perhaps even a bit more than that. What was she? Lily couldn't be a nurse. She didn't even know CPR. If she was going to Paris with Eartha, she'd better learn that. Would the word companion describe her relationship to the older woman? That came close. Over the past weeks, Lily had come to feel a wary, unsettling affection for Eartha, and she thought Eartha felt the same for her. It certainly wasn't mother/child. Eartha wasn't a thing like a mother. It was actually more like Lily was taking care of Eartha. But of course Eartha was paying her for it.

Oh, things were all mixed up!

49

·····

Marina

How did the Fox family celebrate Labor Day, Marina wondered. She was lolling in the deck chair beneath the apple tree, with a cookbook and a pad and pen in her hand to provide her with the illusion that she was accomplishing something. It would be a pleasure for them, Marina thought, if she prepared an elaborate holiday meal, with lots of munchies they could enjoy all day as they lounged around reading and talking, and she wanted to roast something long and slowly, so the aroma would drift through the air. She would make a special dessert, something complicated, something chocolate . . .

"Marina!" Suddenly Emma surged down the yard. She plopped down on a chair next to Marina. "I have to talk to you. You have to help. It's about Abbie."

"Oh, dear. Is she okay?"

"No, she's not! She's so much in love with Howell Parker, and just because of the little boy—who she loves, by the way—she's decided she can't be with him."

"Oh, Emma, I'm not sure your father would like me to get involved."

"Are you kidding? For heaven's sake, Marina, you might become our stepmother. I know you love our father and respect his opinions, but that doesn't mean you have to walk two steps behind him with your mouth shut!"

Marina grinned, but said nothing.

"Abbie is so so sad." Emma perched on the edge of her chair, unable to relax. "I hate to see her like this. And you have to understand Abbie. She's never allowed herself to get involved with a man. I don't know why. Sometimes I think it's because our mother died. Maybe Abbie doesn't want to love someone because she knows how much it hurts to lose someone."

"You're a rather odd advocate for divorce," Marina said gently. "You know how much it hurts to have a man dump you for someone else. And so do I."

"Oh, I know, but come on, Marina, sometimes divorce is a good thing. From what Abbie's said, Sydney Parker is a jet-propelled bitch. She's not even nice to her son. And Howell told Abbie he loves *her*. He doesn't love Sydney. And you are the *perfect* example of how a divorced woman can pick up her life and start all over again. Look at you! You've met a wonderful man."

"That's true." Emma didn't need advice as much as simply someone to listen to her, Marina thought. And she could do that.

"Well, Abbie says Sydney's gorgeous. So Sydney will meet someone else, and Harry will have lots of people to love him. And Abbie and Howell will be with each other, and Abbie already loves Harry and Harry loves Abbie. Everybody wins."

"That's oversimplifying. You know that if Harry's parents get divorced, it's bound to hurt him."

"I don't agree! If they handle it well, he'll be fine!" Emma jumped up and paced back and forth beneath the tree. "Marina, please, listen to me. I think Howell Parker is the love of Abbie's life. We can't sit back and let her throw her chance for happiness away."

"But Emma, what can we do?"

"I don't know! That's why I came to talk to you. Surely there's *something* we can do. Marina, all her life Abbie's taken care of other people. Just for once, she needs someone to help her." Emma hurled herself back down into her chair. "Talk to her, at least, Marina. Just talk to her, okay?"

Marina reached over and took Emma's hand. "Okay. I'll talk to Abbie. But tell me, Emma, are *you* all right?"

Tears sprang into Emma's eyes. "Oh, I don't know." She jerked her hand away from Marina's, and suddenly her voice was trembling. "This summer has just turned out so weird. I guess I'm still smarting over Sandra Bracebridge firing me like that. I didn't get to say good-bye to Millicent, and that just feels *wrong*."

"And did you say good-bye to Spencer?" Marina could tell her words hit home by the sudden flush that reddened Emma's cheeks and neckline.

"Oh, that doesn't matter. He probably thinks I'm an idiot, thanks to Lily's nasty little trick."

"He didn't act like that at the police station. In fact, Emma, I think he's rather taken with you."

"Right," Emma scoffed. She shook her head angrily. "I didn't come here to whine and snivel about myself. I'm here about Abbie."

"I don't know what I could say that would change things."

"Still . . . talk to her, okay? At least talk to her."

"All right," Marina agreed. "I'll do that."

"Marina?"

From behind her, a man spoke.

The sound of his voice made Marina gasp.

She turned. For a moment, she couldn't believe what she was seeing.

"Gerry?" She stared, amazed.

"*Gerry.*" Emma echoed the name. She rose, too.

It was as strange as if a fish had come walking down the driveway. Marina's ex-husband stood there, with his boyish shock of blond hair and his come-fuck-me blue eyes. He wore a lightweight blazer and gray trousers and leather loafers. She had been with him when he'd bought that blazer.

And he was holding a little bundle that looked very much like a baby.

Marina was paralyzed with shock. She was grateful when Emma stepped forward, crossing the few feet of grass between her and her ex-husband.

"Hello. I'm Emma Fox." She didn't offer her hand. Instead she planted herself between Gerry and Marina, hands on her hips, suspicious.

"I'm Gerry Warren. I'm Marina's husband."

"Ex-husband, I believe," Emma said.

Gerry didn't take his eyes off Marina. "I'd like to speak with Marina alone."

"Why?" Emma demanded.

Marina found her voice. "It's all right, Emma."

"Fine." Emma took a few steps toward the house, then turned back. "*Dad* will be home soon."

"I know," Marina assured her. She couldn't take her eyes off the bundle in Gerry's arms.

Gerry came closer. "This is my son." He held out the baby.

Marina could sense something moving toward her like a dark wave, a tsunami of important information, she could feel it loom and cast its huge shadow over her life. She was trembling.

Marina gasped, "What are you doing here? What do you want?"

"May I sit down?"

"No."

"Marina, please. Marina—" Gerry's voice broke. "Dara died."

"What?"

"Dara died. She developed an infection, but she didn't tell anyone in time, and it spread like wildfire, and she died. Marina, Dara's *gone*." Gerry began to weep, without restraint, without shame.

She could see that his knees were about to buckle. "Sit down." She took his arm and pulled him forward to the lawn chair.

Gerry collapsed in the chair. Marina sat, too, and ran her hands over her face. What was he doing here, telling her this, that Dara had died. That couldn't be right!

Holding the baby to his chest, he sobbed, bent double, folded over with grief. "Oh, God, Marina, oh, God, it's so awful, it's so terrible! I can't believe it happened! I loved her so much! I can't believe she's gone."

A high mewing noise filled the air. Gerry sniffed and straightened and held the baby away from him. "Sorry, Garfield, sorry, little boy."

Marina blinked. "You named your baby *Garfield*?"

"You know it was Dara's father's name." Gerry gently pulled the blanket away from his son's face. "Hold him." He offered the baby to Marina.

Marina hesitated, then took the baby. The warm bundle stirred in her arms, nestling against her breast. With one finger, she opened the blanket so she could see the baby better. He was so small! He moved his head, and his eyes locked on hers. He seemed to be regarding Marina with wonder, just as she was regarding him.

Marina had never seen anything more precious than this child. She cooed at the baby and gently stroked her finger over his cheek, which was so soft, it was like the surface of water. "Hello, little Garfield," she whispered.

The baby responded to her voice by pursing his lips and making sucking motions with his mouth.

That small instinctive response broke Marina's heart open. "Oh," she said, and a geyser of emotion shot from deep in her body. Gazing down at the infant, she wept. Her tears fell on his blanket.

"I know," Gerry said. "I know. Oh, Marina, I loved her so much. I can't believe she's gone."

"I didn't know people could die from infections anymore."

"They do all the time, the doctors told me. Not that it makes any difference, it's no comfort. Dara is still dead."

"I'm sorry, Gerry." Marina tried to smother her weeping, but all she could do was to choke back the urge to wail. She didn't want to frighten this innocent, helpless baby. "I'm so sorry." She had already lost Dara this summer, when Gerry left her to be with Dara. And perhaps she'd lost Dara long before that, when Dara began her affair with Gerry. *Dear old friend*, Marina thought. To lose her life so young—to lose the chance to live with her little baby! "It's terrible," Marina said.

She could see how her emotions were affecting the infant. She swallowed her tears and shifted the baby so that he lay lengthwise on her knees. She made small bouncing motions with her legs, swaying the baby, and immediately he registered this change. He looked puzzled, but content. His blond hair was almost invisible, swirling like curls of light over his pink scalp. She opened the blanket more and studied his little arms and legs, his crooked knees, his seashell fingernails.

"At least you have him," Marina said. "And he's quite something."

Gerry pulled a white handkerchief out of his pocket and blew his nose. "I know. I know. And Marina . . . I want you to come home with us. I want you to marry me again. I want you to come home with me. I want you to be his mother."

50

. . . . .

Abbie

As she'd done for so many summer afternoons, Abbie entered the Parker house, went down the hall, and into the kitchen.

Howell sat at the kitchen table with a cup of coffee and a newspaper.

His son was not in the room.

"Where's Harry?" Abbie asked.

"Hey, Abbie." Howell pushed back his chair and stood up. "I've sent Harry off with another babysitter."

"Oh," Abbie said in a very small voice. "So . . . I should leave?"

He stepped toward her, and reached out his arms to hold her, but she moved away.

"Abbie. No, I don't want you to leave. Harry's with another sitter so I can have some time alone with you. I want to talk to you. I've tried phoning, but you won't pick up or return my calls. What's going on?"

Abbie took a few more steps so that she had a chair between her and Howell. His worried expression and the intensity of his gaze tugged on her like a lifeline.

"Howell . . ." Her voice cracked. She started again. "Howell, we can't do this. It isn't right. We need to think of Harry."

Howell ran his hand through his hair, tousling it into an almost comical disarray. After a moment, he said, "Abbie, will you just sit down at the table and talk with me? Please?"

She nodded. Her heart was so full she thought it might break. She took the chair farthest from Howell. He sat, too, and for a moment he just studied her face.

"You've changed," Howell stated bluntly. "Have you stopped loving me?"

"God, no!" The words burst from her before she could think. She closed her eyes and focused on reining herself in. After a moment, she opened her eyes and tried to be calm. Clear. "Howell, I don't think I'll ever stop loving you. But while you were gone, when Harry was hurt, I realized how much he needs his mother, how much he needs *both* his parents." Urgently, she added, "How much he needs both his parents together."

Howell rubbed his hands over his face. "That's one of the reasons I love you so much, Abbie. Because you truly love my son." He thought for a while. "I will always love Harry more than anyone else in the world. I will always put his needs first. I will always try to do what is best for him. And I honestly believe that what would be best for him would be for you and me to be together."

"Oh, Howell—" Abbie started to object, but Howell interrupted her.

"No, listen to me, *hear me*, Abbie. Sydney and I are miserable together. We don't love each other, hell, most of the time we don't even like each other. We go to intricate trouble to avoid each other. That can't be good for any little boy, to live with parents who can scarcely stay in the room together."

"When he fell off the carousel, Harry was so glad to see her, he *needed* to see her."

"And you felt second best? Is that what this is about? You couldn't console and reassure Harry the way his mother could? Abbie, Harry has known you for about two months. He's known Sydney forever. She'll always be the center of his life. I'm his father, and I'm on the periphery, and sometimes it makes me jealous, but I don't think it's all that unusual, really. Kids just need their mothers."

Abbie closed her eyes for a moment. "I know," she said softly. "I know."

"But Harry doesn't need *only* his mother. He needs me, too, and he needs you. Maybe I can't kiss his owie and make it better, but I can teach him how to throw a baseball. And think of the things *you've* taught Harry this summer. Think how being with you has brought him out of his shell. It's made him a stronger little boy. You *know* that, Abbie."

His words made her smile while tears streaked down her face. "Oh, Howell, I'm so confused."

He grinned. "Good. That means you're thinking about all this. You're not just slamming the door on what we could have together."

Abbie said, "Tell me this. If I walk away from you, will you stay with Sydney?"

Again Howell took some time to think about his answer. At last he spoke, slowly and carefully. "Abbie, over Harry's four little years, we have had lots of babysitters. A couple of them have been as good-looking as you, and they've all been competent with Harry. I haven't lusted after them or fallen in love with them or shared anything with them like what I've shared with you. So, before I met you, I never seriously considered leaving Sydney. My life is full. I like my work, and it's important to me, and I have to believe it's important work to be doing. I could fill up every hour of every day and night with my work, and sometimes I want to. In a way, I've been too busy, too preoccupied, to consider whether or not I'm happy. I mean, in a way, happiness, for me, isn't an option. *Wasn't* an option, until I met you and discovered what it's like to be in love. To be loved."

"You're saying you would stay with Sydney."

"I don't know. Maybe I'm saying, why would I leave if I couldn't be with you?" With a rueful smile, he added, "I don't know if that makes things better or worse in your mind."

Abbie dug a tissue out of her shorts pocket and blew her nose. "I don't know, either. I'm pretty confused, to tell the truth."

"Good. That gives me hope." Howell leaned forward eagerly. "Abbie, let me tell you how I envision our life together. We'd have a house outside the city, so that Harry can have a yard with a swing set and a basketball hoop and maybe even a dog. Do you like dogs? We'd live there with Harry. He would go into the city on weekends to be with Sydney. During the week, I'd go into the city to my office, and you would take care of Harry." He was watching her face carefully as he talked. "And I know how much you love traveling, and I have to do a lot of traveling, so when I have to travel, you'd go with me and Harry could stay with Sydney. And we'd travel wherever you wanted to go, too, of course. And Abbie, we'd have our own children. Brothers and sisters for Harry."

Abbie was stunned by his words. After a moment, she said, "Wow. You really know how to seduce a girl."

Howell said, "I sincerely hope so."

Abbie allowed herself to meet Howell's gaze. His eyes were shining with love. She felt his love waiting for her, like the mysterious enormity of the sea. Her fingertips tingled, her heart raced, she trembled—she felt as if she were bodysurfing, waiting for the crest of a wave to sweep her up on a thrilling ride. She felt terrified, and exhilarated, and brave.

Her voice shook. "I don't want to gain my happiness at Harry's expense."

"You'll be giving more happiness to Harry, not taking it away." Howell was trembling, too.

She felt as if she were being broken open, to see this man she loved making himself so vulnerable, showing her how much he wanted her. Her joy felt very much like pain—and it was laced with fear. "I don't want to take Harry away from his mother."

"You won't be. He will still have his mother. And he'll have you."

"I'm afraid," Abbie confessed.

"I'm not." Howell stood up. He came to Abbie and took her hands in his. "Maybe you're not, either. Maybe what you think is fear is hope." Gently, he tugged her hands. "Take a chance, Abbie."

She stood up, smiling now—how could she not meet his expectant smile? "All right."

His voice was hoarse. "Abbie, this means you have to marry me."

"Oh, Howell, yes." She was crying, too, she felt the tears well and shiver down her cheeks, as she stepped forward into his warm embrace.

They sat together, talking about their future until the front door flew open and in came Harry and a young woman wearing a U. Mass tee shirt.

The moment Harry saw Abbie, he raced to her, jumping into her lap. "You're here, Nanny Abbie, you're here!"

She squeezed the little boy tight. "What did you do this afternoon, Harry?"

Harry touched the bracelet on her wrist, turning the beads. "We went to Jennifer's house. She let me watch TV."

Abbie saw a shadow of disapproval cross Howell's face. It was a fresh, sunny day, not the kind of day for a child to be stuck in front of the television. As Howell paid the girl and said a cool thank-you, Abbie couldn't help but feel slightly smug.

"Listen," she said to Harry, "I've got to go home. I've got another job this evening. But I promise I'll be here tomorrow. We'll spend all afternoon together. Maybe I'll even take you to a beach you've never seen."

"I don't want you to leave, Nanny Abbie," Harry protested, snuggling against her.

Howell swooped down and grabbed up his son. "I don't want her to leave, either, Big Guy, but she has to. And she'll be here tomorrow—and I'll go to the beach with you."

Abbie kissed Harry good-bye and smiled a kiss at Howell. She walked home, her head and heart so full she scarcely noticed where she was going. She was almost frightened by her happiness. Could she trust it? Was it real?

As she walked closer to her front door, she could hear sounds coming from inside, and the odd thing was, it sounded like a baby was crying. God, was she so overwrought she was hallucinating?

She opened the door and went inside.

Over the baby's cries, she heard Emma's voice.

"I *won't* go away, Marina. I'm not going to leave you alone with him. He dumped you, he hurt you, he left you. You came here, you are here, and I won't let you leave!"

Abbie walked into her living room. It took a moment for her mind to make sense of what her eyes saw. Marina was holding a baby! A strange man was digging around in a diaper bag. And Emma was pacing back and forth behind the sofa, waving her hands and raving.

"What's going on?" Abbie asked.

"Abbie!" Emma almost shrieked. "Thank God you're here." She snatched the diaper bag from the man and grabbed up the crying baby from Marina. She thrust them both at Abbie. "You know how to diaper babies and warm up a bottle. I've got to stay here and protect Marina from this—this *man*."

Abbie took the baby and automatically brought it to her shoulder, snuggling its tummy against her and leaning her cheek against the tiny hot head. "Emma, calm down. Tell me what's going on."

"That man is Marina's ex-husband," her sister said. "*Ex*-husband. His new wife died and he wants Marina to come back and take care of him and the baby." Emma hung the diaper bag over Abbie's shoulder. "And I'm not going to let that happen."

51

· · · · ·

Emma

And call Dad," Emma told Abbie. "Tell him to come home."

"Emma—" Abbie began, but the baby began to wail in earnest, drowning out Emma's words.

Emma turned back. Gerry sat down on the sofa next to Marina and reached for her hand.

One small rational part of Emma's brain warned her that she was spinning out of control, but a stronger emotion, a survival instinct, overpowered her.

Emma stepped right over the coffee table and stood between Marina and Gerry.

"Don't you sit so close to her," she ordered Gerry. "You have no right to sit close to her. You shouldn't be here at all."

The man was amused, he was almost laughing. "This has nothing to do with you!"

"It has everything to do with—" Emma began.

"For God's sake." Gerry stood up so fast he almost knocked Emma over. With his nose practically in her face, he said, with quiet arrogance, "Will you please just go away and leave us alone? This is between Marina and me."

Emma was trembling with rage. "You're wrong. *Nothing* is between Marina and you anymore. You forfeited your right to Marina. You left her. She's going to marry my father. She's ours now!"

He didn't back up an inch. He was extremely handsome, and his blue eyes were smug.

He sneered. "Why don't you let Marina decide for herself?"

"Because it's not just about her," Emma retorted hotly. "She's part of our family now. She loves my father. And when he gets home, you'll see what a superior person he is, and how *he* deserves her love more than some vain, smarmy hot dog like you!"

Gerry shook his head, as if completely perplexed. He stepped away from Emma. To Marina he said, "Can we go somewhere private to talk?"

"No!" Emma clenched her fists. "You have no right!"

"Emma." Marina stood up and put her arm around Emma, holding her tightly. "Emma, it's okay. Emma—"

The front door slammed. Lily floated into the room, blithe and summery, in a little pink-checked sundress, with her luscious red hair drifting around her head.

"Guess what! Eartha's asked me to go to Paris with her!" Seeing a strange and handsome man in her living room, she flounced forward, holding out her hand graciously. "Hello. I'm Lily Fox."

Gerry muttered, "Good God, how many of you are there?"

Abbie came back into the room. The baby was tucked carefully against her breast, and with her free hand she held the bottle to the infant's mouth. He was sucking eagerly. "Oh, good, Lily, you're home. I was going to make iced tea for all of us but we're out of tea and lemons—"

Lily's jaw dropped. "Where did you get that baby?"

Marina released Emma and strained forward to see the baby in Abbie's arms. Marina's face radiated a pleasure Emma had never seen before.

Emma's heart sank.

"Oh my God," Emma whispered. "Of course. *Of course* you're going to choose a baby. Who would ever choose us?"

She stepped back over the coffee table. Blinded by tears, she pushed past silly Lily and Abbie and the perfect baby.

"Emma, wait," Marina called.

But Emma didn't stop. She wanted to get out of that room. She wanted to turn her back on Marina before Marina turned her back on them.

She fled up the stairs and into her room. She shut the door and fell on her bed, where she curled up in fetal position, hugging her knees to her chest. She hurt so much it was almost intolerable. A high burning pain flamed between her breasts.

She hated Marina. *Hated* her. She wanted Marina to die, it would be better for Marina to just die than to leave Emma's father for another man, but of course Marina wasn't leaving Emma's father, she was leaving Emma's father and his three obnoxious unlovable daughters.

After years of loneliness, their father had fallen in love, had found happiness, and now Marina was going to just walk away from him. And Abbie would give up her chance at love, and Lily would do whatever the hell she wanted, and Emma and her father would live out their lives, spinster and widower, two rejected and unloved human beings.

She had thought, when she arrived home at the beginning of the summer, that she had reached the most extreme point of misery. But she'd been wrong. That had all been a minor rain shower compared to the tempest of grief and self-loathing that descended on her now.

"Emma?" Abbie came into the room. She sat on the edge of Emma's bed. "Are you okay?"

Emma snorted. "Sure. I'm peachy keen."

"Marina has taken Gerry—and the baby—out to her cottage to talk."

"To *talk*. Right."

"You think they're going to jump into bed together? Give Marina some credit, Emma. She's not an idiot."

"You saw how she drooled over that baby."

"Well, babies are adorable. Nature made them that way. But it's not about Marina choosing the baby over us, Emma. It's about whether she really loves Dad or still loves Gerry."

"He's so handsome."

"So's Dad."

Emma wanted to wail. She rolled over and threw herself onto Abbie's lap. "I don't want Dad to be hurt!"

Abbie cuddled Emma against her. She smoothed Emma's hair. "I don't want him to be hurt, either, Emma. But you and I can't do anything about it. It's up to Marina."

"I hate her."

"No, you don't hate her. You love her. So do I."

"I want to stab her. I want to stab her in the foot."

Abbie laughed. "I understand your thinking. You're not crazy enough to kill her, but you'd like to hurt her."

"I would. I would like to hurt her as much as she's hurting us."

"But, Emma, she hasn't decided anything yet."

"Emma?"

The door opened, and for a moment Emma's heart leapt with hope, but it wasn't Marina. It was Lily who walked into the room.

Emma said, "Go away."

Lily said, "Emma. Millicent Bracebridge is on the phone. She wants to talk to you."

52

. . . . .

Lily

Emma stared at Lily for one long moment. Then she sat up and held out her hand for the cordless phone. She smothered the receiver with a pillow as she cleared her throat. When she said, "Hello?" her voice was surprisingly normal.

Abbie grabbed Lily by the arm, escorted her out of the room, and shut the door behind them.

"Let's go to your room," Abbie said.

They opened Lily's bedroom door. She'd forgotten how messy it had become over the last few days of the summer. Well, of course, she'd had to sort through things fast when she packed to go over to Jason's. Still, it was a shambles.

"Oh, Lily." Abbie turned around. "Let's go into my room."

Abbie's room was the anti-Lily's. All her clothes were tucked away out of sight and her bed was made with nunlike perfection.

"You live in a convent," Lily said.

"You live in a pigpen," Abbie shot back without any particular venom. She waved at the chair by the window and threw herself down on her bed. "What did you say about Paris?"

"Abbie, Eartha asked me to go with her to New York, and then to Paris. She wants me to stay with her for six months, maybe more. She'll pay me five thousand dollars a month, plus I'll get room and board free, *plus* I'm sure she'll give me more clothes."

Abbie smiled. "Sounds like a dream come true for you, Lily."

Lily fingered her engagement ring. "But what will I do about Jason?"

Abbie was taking off her clothes as she talked, and her mind was clearly not on Lily or even on Marina and the baby. "Have you mentioned Eartha's suggestion to Jason?"

"Not yet, I—"

"Better do that first." Abbie reached for the robe hanging on the hook on her closet door. "It may not be any kind of problem at all. He might be glad for you to have the opportunity to travel awhile before settling down."

An odd kind of panic seized Lily. "But what if he doesn't?"

"Then you'll have to make a decision, won't you?" Abbie smiled. "I think you'll be surprised, Lily, at how good it feels to just . . . *jump*."

Lily stared at her sister. "Abbie . . . are you okay?"

Abbie smiled mysteriously. "I'm fine, honey. I've got to be over on Farmer Street in twenty minutes, and I need to take a shower and change. Let's talk later." She pulled on her bathrobe and headed off to the bathroom.

Lily wandered back down to the living room. She was disappointed to see that it was empty. Hurrying to look out the kitchen window, she saw Marina and Gerry walking toward the Playhouse with the baby. It gave her an unpleasant twist in her heart to see them like that. What if Marina went back with Gerry? What would that do to their father? He had been so happy lately, so much more *there*. Lily was seized with a sudden desire to rush outside, grab Marina by the shoulders, and apologize for the way she'd acted about their mother's bedspread. About the way she'd acted all summer. Not showing Marina her engagement ring. It would be terrible if Marina chose Gerry instead of their father because Lily had made her feel unwanted!

Marina, Gerry, and the baby disappeared inside the Playhouse.

Lily took a deep breath. Now she had to deal with her own choice. Now she had to tell Jason.

She had planned to meet him at his apartment around six. They weren't going out to eat tonight; they were saving money toward their wedding. For the first time in a long time, Lily didn't have an evening function to attend. The summer was winding down. People were returning to work and to organize their children for school and college. Around Labor Day there would be another rush of events, but tonight, this summer night, she was free.

She walked over to Jason's place, let herself in, and checked the cupboards and refrigerator. She'd make spaghetti, she decided. She found a bottle of inexpensive red wine, opened it, and poured herself a glass to drink while she cooked. Jason came in as she was putting together a salad.

"Hi, babe," he called. "Smells good." As always, he headed right for the shower.

In a few minutes, he came out, smelling like Ivory soap and shampoo, wearing clean jeans and a white tee shirt. His hair was still damp, his face brown from working in the sun. Lily kissed him, and he kissed her back, thoroughly.

She'd spent enough evenings with him by now to know that whatever she wanted to discuss could wait until after he'd eaten, so she handed him a beer and tossed the salad and set the table. As they ate, he talked about his day and Lily told him some of what had gone on for her. Not until they were through eating did Lily say, "Jason, there's something else I need to talk to you about."

He was getting another beer from the refrigerator. "So hit me."

"Eartha's asked me to go to Paris with her this fall."

"Cool, honey." Jason threw himself down on the couch and put his feet up on his old beaten-up coffee table. "For how long?"

Lily swallowed. "About six months."

"Six months!" He swung his legs to the floor and turned around to face Lily. "Six months?"

Lily hurried to sit next to him on the couch. "Jason, she's going to pay me five thousand dollars a month! Plus room and board, plus I know she'll buy me some *sublime* new outfits."

"Hell, Lily, what do you need expensive clothes for? You're fine just as you are."

"But, Jason, I *like* expensive clothes—but that's not the point."

"No, the point is, you'd rather be with that rich old broad than with me."

"The thing is, Jason," Lily said quietly, "I haven't been anywhere."

"Well, I have, and let me tell you, Nantucket is as good as it gets." He swallowed hard. "And if you really loved me, you wouldn't want to leave. For *six months*."

"I do really love you," Lily protested.

But Jason stood up and began to pace the room. "I was afraid this would happen. I could see it coming."

"What are you talking about?"

"That Yardley woman's going to give you a taste for the kind of luxury I'll never be able to give you."

"That's not true!" Lily insisted. "I don't see why you're so upset! I just want to have a little adventure before settling down."

Jason skewered her with his stare. "Six months, Lily? Six *months?*"

He was so handsome, so sexy, and she never wanted to hurt him. Lily crossed the room, wrapped her arms around his waist, and pressed herself against him. "Jason. I love you. I want to marry you. Think of how much money I'll make." She moved her hips against his.

"Don't start with that," Jason said. He put his hands on her shoulders and pushed her away. "You want too much, Lily. You want two different things at the same time. And you can't have that, Lily. You're going to have to make a choice."

Jason turned his back on her and went out the door, slamming it hard behind him.

"Don't go," Lily begged, but he was already gone.

She ran her hands through her hair. She sat down on the couch and sipped some wine, then immediately stood up, restless with her emotions. *He'll come back,* she told herself, *of course he will. He just needs time to walk it off, to think.*

She cleaned the kitchen, did the dishes, and made herself a cup of tea. She tried watching television, but her attention was all over the place, she kept thinking of things she wished she'd said to Jason, things she wanted to tell him right now. An hour passed, and then two hours, and she began to freak out a bit. Where was he? It really wasn't fair of him to just walk out on her like that, just to leave without talking things over!

And what had he said? That she wanted too much? That she wanted two different things at the same time? That she had to make a choice?

She couldn't stay in the little apartment any longer. She

grabbed up her purse and went to the door, stopping for a moment to consider whether she should leave her engagement ring on the table. That would scare him! she thought. Maybe he'd be more flexible about their plans if he thought he would lose her.

Or maybe he would believe their engagement was off.

She kept the ring on, and hurried through the dark night back to her house.

53

· · · · ·

Marina

Marina opened the door to the cottage and stood back for Gerry and his son to go in. Instead, Gerry handed the baby to her. The warm weight of the child made her heart turn over.

"I'd better bring my luggage in. The cabdriver left it at the end of the driveway."

Indignation shot through Marina. "You brought *luggage?*"

"Of course I brought luggage. Believe me, you can't travel across the room without piles of stuff for the baby. Not to mention, it's a hell of a long trip out here to the middle of nowhere." Gerry walked off.

Marina sank onto the sofa and gazed down at the sleeping infant. *Oh, Dara,* she thought mournfully. Dara's parents and brother must be devastated. She hoped it brought them some solace that this child of Dara's was here on earth.

Gerry returned, dragging behind him a large suitcase and lugging a duffel bag. He dropped them by the table and came to sit next to Marina. Together they looked down at the sleeping baby.

"He's so beautiful," Marina whispered.

Emotions flooded through her—envy, self-pity, confusion, wonder, and doubt. Was what she'd always wanted being offered to her now, at last, by Fate? Certainly, here was a fresh, new beginning. So much she was familiar with, so much that she loved, waited for her where this baby belonged. Her old friends, her old surroundings, her

old life. The rolling green and wooded hills of Missouri, the streams
and forested beauty, as well as the more civilized enticements of the
city with its elegant plaza, art museum, concert halls, and parks.

But what of the life she had begun here, spun with such diligent
industry from her own determination and hope like the shimmering
threads of a spider's complex and optimistic web? What about this
present beauty, the sparkling blue ocean, the golden beaches, the
small-town charm? Most of all, what about Jim? Did she love him?
Could that love be compared to what she had once felt for Gerry?
Certainly Jim was the more honest, trustworthy man. She did love
him. And she felt safe with him.

But this baby . . . he was so small and vulnerable. How would he
fare without the soft, maternal embrace of a constant female presence? Gerry was certainly not going to stay home with the baby. He
would continue to run the agency. He was all about the agency. And
even with all the love in his heart, he could be only one parent, not
two. Marina gazed down at the baby, swaddled in a light blanket,
and envisioned the future: rocking the infant, feeding him a bottle,
carrying him against her heart in a Snugli, reading him books, pushing him in a stroller, clapping her hands when he learned to crawl or
eat creamed food or walk . . . He would know no other mother. She
would always be his mother. They would belong to each other. She
could keep him healthy, happy, and safe.

But something within her bridled at this dream. Her feelings
were confused, swirling in a kind of maelstrom that pulled on her
heart.

Carefully, she lifted the infant and laid him in his father's lap.

"I'm glad you have him," Marina told Gerry.

"Marina—"

"He's irresistible," Marina continued. "You won't have any trouble at all finding someone to love him, and you."

"Wait, Marina," Gerry protested softly. "You haven't given this
any thought at all."

"I don't need to *think*, Gerry. I know how I feel. I feel profoundly
sorry for Dara, and for this little boy, and for you. But my life is here
now."

Gerry made a scoffing noise. "You've been here, what . . . three
months?"

"About that."

"How can you leave everything you've known all your life to live out here in the middle of nowhere?"

"How could you leave me for Dara?" Marina countered mildly.

"Oh, come on, Marina, it's not like you to be vengeful. There are more important things involved than your wounded pride."

"It's not about my wounded pride," Marina told him. "Perhaps last spring it was. But I've moved on, Gerry. I've changed. And I've fallen in love with someone else."

"Please. You've known him for such a short time, how can you possibly choose him over me, over me and my little baby?" Before she could respond, Gerry bent to lay the baby in the corner of the sofa. He arranged a pillow next to the child as a safeguard.

He went down on his knees in front of Marina. He took her hands in his.

"Marina, please listen to me. I love you. I still love you. I've always loved you. I don't know what got into me, and I'll regret every day of my life that I hurt you. But I can't regret loving Dara—because she brought Garfield to us. Don't you see, Marina, it's one of those crooked miracles. Dara has given us our baby."

Marina studied her ex-husband's earnest face. He was so very handsome. He was so very smooth.

Gently, she pulled her hands away. "What a spin doctor you are. What an ad man."

"I'm serious, Marina. I love you. I want you. I need you, and our baby needs you. Please." Tears welled in his eyes. "I flew all this way, Marina. I can't go on without you. I know I've made a lot of mistakes, and I'm so infinitely sorry, but there is so much at stake here. We could be happy, Marina."

Marina stood up. She moved away from Gerry. "The answer's no, Gerry."

He stood up, too. "You're making a mistake. At least think about it, okay? Give me the night."

"There's no way I'm having sex with you."

"I didn't mean it that way. I mean, sleep on it. Make your decision in the morning. It's too important to be rushed."

Marina hugged herself with her arms and briefly closed her eyes. "All right. I'll sleep on it." Before Gerry could say anything else, she continued, "I'll sleep on it up in the main house. You and your son can stay here." She gestured to the little kitchen. "There's plenty of

food. You can make your own dinner." She went to the door. "I'll
come back here in the morning with my decision."

Thoughts whirling, Marina hurried across the lawn up to the house
and entered by the back door. The kitchen was empty. On the
chalkboard above the telephone, Abbie had scribbled a note:
Babysitting till eleven. Emma had scribbled: At Millicent Bracebridge's, home sometime tonight. Lily hadn't written anything, but
Emma knew by the empty atmosphere of the house that she was out
somewhere, too.

She poured herself a drink and sank down into a chair at the
kitchen table. She felt cranky for allowing Gerry to make her put off
her decision. And somewhere in the midst of all her turbulent emotions, she was still shocked about Dara's death. She needed to think
about that, to mourn Dara.

"You look pensive." Jim came in through the kitchen door. He
smelled of sunshine and sawdust and his nose was burned red from
working all day in the sun.

"We have visitors," Marina told him. "Nothing to do with the
girls. It's my ex-husband, I'm afraid. Gerry and his baby."

"*What?*"

"Sit down. I'll explain."

Jim took a beer from the refrigerator and sat at the table in the
chair farthest from Marina. He frowned but listened quietly as she
told him about Gerry's surprise appearance, about Dara's death,
about the baby.

"I told him about you." Marina leaned across the table and
touched Jim's hand. "I told him about *us*. I told him my life is with
you now."

"But he's still here?"

"He's leaving—they're leaving—tomorrow morning. I gave him
my decision, but he asked me to sleep on it, and actually, Jim, I don't
think that's unreasonable. I think I'm just a little bit in shock about
Dara's death. And I have to admit, no one's ever offered me a nice
new baby before." She smiled, trying to lighten the moment. When
Jim didn't smile in return, she continued, "I'm sleeping here
tonight. I'm sleeping with you tonight. Gerry and the baby will be
in the Playhouse."

"Which seems strange to me," Jim told her.

"Oh, Jim, I didn't know what to do. It's August. It's after six o'clock. He has a little baby. I doubt whether he could find a room in an inn on the island, or a seat on a flight to Boston . . ."

"He managed to get himself here," Jim reminded her. "I think you should admit it, Marina. You're not one hundred percent certain that you want to be with me." Abruptly, Jim pushed himself away from the table and headed for the door. "I'm leaving."

Marina was so shocked, she laughed. "You're leaving? What do you mean? Jim, this is *your house*."

"I'll sleep somewhere else tonight. I'll sleep on the boat."

"Wait, Jim, listen to me." Marina stood up. "Don't be so damned John Wayne, don't turn up your collar and head off into the horizon like that."

He paused with his hand on the doorknob. "What are you talking about?"

"You can't go all quiet and manly and proud right now. I know you're mad that I let Gerry stay, and perhaps it was the wrong decision, but everything happened so fast, and it's all huge, Jim, it's enormous. And you can't just go off and leave me alone now. I'm sorry that it hurts you that even one percent of me would consider going home to be the mother of that baby, and that's what it's about, Jim, it's not about Gerry, I don't care a fig about Gerry. The important thing is that I told him I'm in love with you, that I'm going to move here to be with you, that I won't go back with him, baby or not. Isn't that the important thing?"

She caught her breath, watching him.

After a moment, Jim let his hand fall. "All right. I'll stay."

Marina crossed the room and leaned against him, wrapping her arms around him. He didn't hug her back, but he didn't push her away.

"Actually," she joked, trying to lighten the moment, "I was kind of hoping you'd challenge him to a duel for me."

Jim didn't respond.

"Let's go out to eat," she suggested. "Let's go buy cheeseburgers and French fries and watch the sun set. Then we'll come home and go to bed, and tomorrow morning Gerry will be gone."

Jim nodded. "Good idea."

Marina said, "I'll just write a note for the girls."

54

.....

Emma

Emma changed from her shorts and tee shirt into a pretty sundress before she walked over to the Bracebridge house. It was a funny thing to do, she supposed, since Millicent Bracebridge could scarcely see, but Emma wanted to look her best for this conversation. The older woman wanted to have a talk with her, that was all she'd said, but Emma was pretty sure Millicent wanted to hear for herself about the lightship baskets. Perhaps Millicent would ask Emma to continue working for her. She hoped so.

When she reached the Bracebridge mansion, she paused, admiring the high white building with its symmetry and elegance. It was one of the most historically important houses on the island, Emma knew, and she was fortunate to have been able to work there, even for the summer.

She went up the brick sidewalk, raised the silver door knocker, then opened the door and stepped inside, calling, as she had so many times, "Mrs. Bracebridge? It's Emma."

She found Millicent Bracebridge in her usual place, seated in her wheelchair by the fireplace. The older woman wore a long-sleeved dress in pale blue linen and pearls around her neck.

"Thank you for coming," Millicent said formally. She gestured toward the table near her right hand. "Would you pour us some sherry, please?"

Emma poured the sherry into the platinum-rimmed etched glasses and handed one to Millicent, taking care that the older woman had a good grip on it before removing her own hand and settling onto the sofa across from Millicent.

"It seems we have had a little drama," Millicent began, "that concluded with you quitting your job. I can understand your decision, but I'm disappointed that you didn't bother to discuss it with me first."

"But Mrs. Bracebridge!" Emma objected. "I didn't quit! Your daughter-in-law *fired* me. She phoned me, she told me never to come to the house again." She realized she was almost yelling and moderated her voice. "I told her I wanted to say good-bye to you, but she said if I tried, she'd call the police and have me forcibly removed."

Millicent's face fell. She took a moment to gather her thoughts, then spoke with fierce dignity. "This house has been in my family for twelve generations. A Bracebridge has lived here continually for over two hundred years. I had hoped one of my children would live here to take over the stewardship of this house, but unfortunately, my son died and none of the others wishes to make this island her home. It is isolated, I understand that. My daughter-in-law finds it boring. I understand that. History is not for everyone." She paused to sip her sherry, then continued. "It is a difficult thing for someone as entrenched in traditions as I to realize that someone outside the family values my possessions, and me, more than my own daughter-in-law."

"Oh," Emma murmured. "I don't think—"

Millicent gave a demure little snort. "You don't need to think that. I know that. I may be blind, but I'm not blind." She laughed briefly at herself. "I'm aware of many things, Emma, some of which you obviously aren't aware even with your excellent sight."

"I'm sure you are—"

"For example, I'm aware that my grandson is in love with you." Emma was speechless.

"Do you imagine he used to rush over to have lunch with me almost every day before you were around?" Millicent smiled. "I wish I could see your expression now." Then she continued briskly, as if she hadn't just given Emma the surprise of her life, "It took a bit of courage, not to mention a rather unusual imagination, for you to sneak those baskets out of the house like that. I understand that you didn't want to tell me, but I am surprised that you didn't confide in Spencer. Of course, you were probably trying to protect his pride. He would have known immediately that his mother was taking them. She's taken things from this house before. In a way, she sees them as her possessions to do with what she wants."

"I apologize for the way I handled it," Emma said softly. "I should have told Spencer. But I wanted to be certain before I mentioned it . . ."

"The question for me is, were your actions an indication of respect and affection for me, or for the objects themselves?" Millicent took another sip of sherry. "I'd like to think the answer is both." The older woman suddenly leaned forward, her black gaze aimed at Emma, and it gave Emma the eerie sense that she was seeing directly into her soul. "You do not give yourself enough credit, my dear. I might be blind, but you're the one who doesn't see. It would make an enormous difference to me if I knew that someone who cared about the history of this house and this family were carrying on the traditions."

Emma frowned. Was Millicent getting senile? Suddenly nothing she said made sense. "Mrs. Bracebridge—"

"Hello, Grams!" The front door slammed and Spencer came into the room. Seeing Emma, his face brightened. "Hello, Emma. I didn't know you were going to be here."

Emma stared at Spencer and for the first time she *got it*—how happy he was to see her.

"I've been off-island," he told Emma. He sat on the couch next to her. "I brought back a figurehead from one of the whaling boats that a Falmouth family had in their barn."

"Your mother fired Emma," Millicent said.

Spencer looked dismayed. "Oh God, Emma, I'm sorry." He glanced at his grandmother, then back at Emma. "I know she's embarrassed by the whole lightship basket thing. She's taken things before when she's wanted a little money, and we've let it slide . . ."

"But taking the baskets was too much," Millicent said sternly. "And firing Emma without talking to you or to me—no. This can't go on." She shifted uncomfortably in her chair. "The two of you really need to settle things so that I can enjoy the rest of my days in tranquillity." She rang the small brass hand bell next to the sherry bottle.

Almost immediately Patty LaFleur appeared in the doorway. "Are you ready for me, Mrs. Bracebridge?"

"I am," Millicent said. As the nurse wheeled her out of the living room, she said, "Shut the door behind me, if you please."

For a moment, there was only silence in the living room. Emma felt herself growing warm, her senses tingling, her throat dry. Could it be true, what Millicent said, that Spencer was in love with her? She felt slightly drunk, and it couldn't be the sherry.

"Your grandmother—" she began.

"Emma, I want to talk—" Spencer said at the same moment.

They both laughed, and Emma gave a little shiver as Spencer reached for her hand. He was so handsome with his pale skin and black hair and eyes. He was dashing, really, *vivid*, and her heart double-timed in her chest.

"Actually, I don't want to talk," Spencer said quietly. "I want to kiss you."

She was turned toward him as they sat on the couch. He moved closer to her, and touched her cheek and the side of her neck, and sensation sparkled all through her body. He leaned forward and pressed his mouth against hers. Lightly first, and then insistently. She kissed him back and accidentally made a little whimpering sound as her body woke up and strained toward him. He pulled her close to him, he ran his hands over her shoulders, down her back, and pressed her hard against him. She reclined against the arm of the couch, and he was half-lying on top of her, kissing her neck, her chin, her ears, then, again, her mouth. She put her hands in his glossy raven black hair and moaned at the silk of it against her palms.

He kissed her breasts through the cotton of her dress.

"Wait," she said, pushing him away. "We can't do this on your grandmother's couch! Not with her so nearby!"

Spencer gasped. "I'd bet Grams knows exactly what we're doing and heartily approves." He stood up, tucking his rumpled shirt into his pants. "But you're right, we can't do it here. Let's go to my house." He held out his hand.

Emma took it.

55

. . . . .

Abbie

A nervous wind swept over the island all through the night, and when morning came, the blue sky was hidden by flying clouds that let in brief, bright flashes of sun. It was hurricane season now, and storms in the south spun the wind and waves up north into a blustery turbulence. Often the summer season ended like this, with an abrupt temperature drop and a cool snap of fall in the air. It was the season of change.

Abbie heard the wind during the night—she hardly slept. She was so amazed at what Howell had promised her, at what she had promised Howell. She lay on her bed in a kind of happy stupor, revisiting each word he said, each gesture he made. Could she trust this happiness? What if he changed his mind? So many people fell madly in love on the island in the summer, only to find when they returned to their real lives that the love had been only a summer fantasy. She didn't think this was what would happen with Howell. He'd had the opportunity to let her go; she had offered. But he wanted her to stay. He wanted her to marry him. He wanted to have babies with her. And Harry would be her stepson. She hugged her pillow, silently squealing with joy.

At six, she gave up the pretense that she would ever fall asleep. She tiptoed down to the kitchen and made coffee, moving quietly because she knew others were sleeping. She hadn't gotten home from babysitting until midnight, when everyone else was in bed.

She wondered how the Marina-Gerry situation had resolved itself. She hoped, for her father's sake, that Marina had decided to stay on Nantucket, but as she slipped outside to drink her coffee on the patio, a light came on in the Playhouse. She saw a man's profile. Gerry, perhaps warming a bottle for his darling baby? So he had spent the night in the cottage. Where had Marina slept?

And where would Abbie sleep tonight? She had no other jobs today, and if someone called, needing a babysitter, Emma could take it, or even Lily.

She wanted to be with Howell.

Setting her coffee cup on the kitchen counter, she went quietly up the stairs and dressed for the day. She wrote a note on the kitchen chalkboard telling her sisters where she would be, and let herself out into the windy morning.

Honeysuckle fell in great white fragrant heaps over fences and walls as she walked through the streets and rose of Sharon bushes tossed their white and magenta flowers in the wind. The air was bracing, full of salt and movement. For a moment, Abbie worried that yesterday had been a dream.

When she arrived at the Parker house, she saw that a light was on in the kitchen. So Howell was awake. She knew he was an early riser. She knocked on the door, her heart fluttering in her chest.

Howell opened the door. "Abbie." He pulled her inside as if she were life itself. "Abbie." He held her to him, and she could feel the racing of his pulse. "Abbie," he said again. "I asked Sydney for a divorce."

Her knees buckled. *So it was real.* "My God, Howell. How did she react?"

He led her into the living room. "I did it over the phone, which seems cowardly, I know, but I wanted to get it *done*. Of course she was furious. She called me a lot of names, and threatened a lot of things—"

"Oh," Abbie said, suddenly afraid.

"It's all right. It's understandable. She needed to vent and attack; she was like a trapped animal. It was more about her wounded pride than any love she has for me." He smiled ruefully. "Believe me, she made her low opinion of me crystal clear."

It was happening so fast, Abbie thought. Her head was spinning.

"We didn't talk about the future much—and that makes sense.

She needs time to calm down and think." Howell paced away from Abbie, across the room, then back to her, as he organized his own thoughts. "Chances are she'll throw me out of our New York apartment, and believe me, I'll be glad to go, except for Harry. Harry starts school next week. I'll have to spend some time in the city, for work, of course, but I'm thinking I can come back here, and Harry can come here on weekends. It will be a familiar place for him, rather than a nondescript apartment. And you'll be here for him, too."

"How long do you think the divorce will take?"

Howell frowned. "Honestly, Abbie, I don't know. New York State doesn't have no-fault divorces. They're usually protracted and expensive. Sydney might be mad enough to make it a hellish process."

"Oh, Howell," Abbie said. "I wish it didn't have to be that way."

Howell took her hand. "I can deal with it."

"Daddy?" Harry called from the stairs, and suddenly he entered the room, small and endearing in his rumpled dinosaur-print pajamas, rubbing his eyes.

Then he saw Abbie. "Nanny Abbie!" He ran to sit in her lap.

Abbie hugged him tightly. "Good morning, Harry. What about some pancakes for breakfast?" She felt so euphoric, she thought she could conjure breakfast out of the air.

"Yay!"

They went into the kitchen. Abbie set out the butter and the mixing bowl. Harry crawled under the table, playing with his horses.

"We have to leave this weekend, you know," Howell told Abbie.

Abbie's heart thudded. "Will you close up the house?"

"Absolutely not."

"Harry, your breakfast is ready," Abbie told him. "Let's put Thunder on the table. He can watch you eat. See, I made a smiley face with blueberries." She set his food in front of him.

Howell's cell phone rang. He checked the number, flashed a glance at Abbie, and answered.

"Right. Okay. See you."

He clicked off the phone, and said in a careful voice, "Harry, that was Mommy. She finished her work early." With a wry smile at Abbie, Howell added, "The woman she represented in the divorce case has reconciled with her husband, leaving Sydney's schedule suddenly free. She's in a cab, she'll be here any minute."

56

·····

Marina

Marina lay in her bed with her arm over her eyes to block the growing light. She wasn't sure she'd slept at all during the night, but lay awake with her thoughts tumbling through her mind. She knew she was testing the limits of Jim's patience by allowing Gerry to spend the night in the cottage, but she still thought it was the right thing to do. It wasn't every day Fate offered her an adorable little baby. She remembered all the times she had wept, begging Fate or God or Nature to give her a child. Never had she imagined something like this.

She heard movements in the hall. Someone was quietly padding down the stairs. Lily or Abbie, Marina thought—she didn't think Emma had come home last night.

At last, Marina slipped from the bed. Jim slept on, turned to the wall, away from Marina. She pulled on a tee shirt and shorts and tiptoed down the stairs. She could hear the birds waking, chirping away, as she flicked on the kitchen light, and she jumped at the sight of someone already there in the kitchen.

"Lily! You're up early."

Lily sat with her knees tucked under her chin and her arms around her legs. "Couldn't sleep." Lily wore a pink polka-dot sundress that made her look younger than her years.

"I couldn't, either. I'm going to make some coffee. Want some?"

Lily shrugged. "I guess."

Marina cocked her head. "Is something wrong?"

"Eartha wants me to go with her to Paris for six months."

"Why, that's fabulous, Lily."

"Yeah, well, I told Jason, and he's furious."

Marina poured water into the coffeemaker, flicked the On button, and sat down at the table across from Lily. "Why?"

"He doesn't want me to go. And it's just not fair! I do love Jason, I really do, and I want to marry him, but I'll never have another opportunity like this, to live in Paris!" Lily dug a tissue from her pocket and blew her nose.

"Why doesn't Jason want you to go?"

"He says I'll get a taste for luxury that he can never provide me."

Marina studied the young woman. "Is he right?"

Lily wiggled her shoulders. "No! Maybe. I don't know." She sighed, admitting, "I do love wearing cool clothes and real jewelry."

Marina smiled. In the early morning light, Lily looked inexperienced and fresh, and Marina considered her words carefully. "You seem to love your magazine work. You seem to thrive on parties and an extensive social life."

"What, are you saying I'm superficial, a social climber?"

"I'm not putting a value judgment on anything, Lily. I like parties, too. I like nice clothes and jewelry, too—"

"Then you shouldn't be with Dad."

"Wait, let me finish. I'm older than you, Lily, and I've sort of had my fill of parties and froufrou and baubles. I don't want all that so much anymore, I don't *need* it, but if I'd never had it, then I'd be wishing for it now."

"Are you saying I'm too young to know what I want?" Lily demanded.

Marina thought a moment. "Yes, yes, I guess I am."

Lily pouted. "Jason said I want too much. He said I have to choose."

"What are your choices?"

Lily snorted. "Well, *obviously*, Eartha or Jason."

"Really? That sounds sort of extreme. Isn't there any middle ground?"

"What do you mean?"

"Well . . . maybe you go for a shorter period of time. Maybe Jason could join you for a couple of weeks. Maybe he could meet you and the two of you could go off together without Eartha. To London, or to Rome."

Amazed, Lily let her feet fall to the floor and sat up straight. "Marina, those are really good ideas."

Encouraged, Marina continued. "And maybe you could have Jason and Eartha meet. Invite them here for dinner some night."

Lily squirmed. "Oh, I don't know about that. I don't know if I want Eartha to see this house."

"It's a nice house, Lily. It's where you grew up. Where your father lives. It's part of you."

The coffee was ready. Marina poured a cup for each of them, set out a pitcher of milk, and handed Lily a spoon.

"Unless," Marina continued thoughtfully, "unless you want to leave all this behind. There's nothing wrong with that, you know. I'm going to leave Kansas City behind. Oh, I might visit occasionally, but I'm ready to start a new life here."

"But I love Jason!" Lily protested. "We're engaged to get married!"

"Does that mean you're willing to give up posh clothes and jewelry?" Marina asked. Seeing the conflict on Lily's face, she added, softly, "You may not know the answer to that question yet, Lily. There's nothing wrong with that. You may need to experience another way of life before settling down. That's a smart thing to do. You don't want to marry Jason unless you're sure, and if he loves you, he should be able to let you go, at least for a while."

Lily frowned down into her cup. Marina leaned back in her chair and sipped her coffee. Outside, light flooded down, opening up the day. Upstairs, footsteps thudded on the floor and water ran. Jim was awake. Marina had decisions of her own to make.

Lily stood up. "I'm going to go talk to Jason." She crossed the kitchen and started to leave, then stopped and turned back. "Thanks, Marina. For the coffee and the advice."

"You're welcome." Marina smiled.

Lily left. Marina sat for a few moments, feeling pleased with herself. She'd done a pretty good job of counseling, she thought.

Jim came into the kitchen, his hair still wet from his shower. He mumbled good morning, poured himself a cup of coffee, and stared out the window at the Playhouse.

"He's still there." Marina went to stand behind Jim, wrapping her arms around his waist. He was so satisfyingly solid and strong. She laid her cheek against his back, soaking in his warm, clean smell. "And I'm still here."

Jim didn't reply.

She continued, "I've just been talking with Lily. It was a good conversation. It made me realize something, Jim. I do want to marry you, but I also want to be involved in your daughters' lives. They need a woman's opinion, and I give good advice. And I like being part of their lives. Okay?"

Jim turned around and met Marina's eyes. "I think I'd agree to almost anything. I don't want to live without you in my life, Marina."

She stood on tiptoes to kiss his mouth lightly. "And I don't want to live without you." She stepped back. "So I'll tell Gerry that I've slept on it, and my decision remains. I'm staying here."

"Good," Jim said. "Let's go tell him now."

"Don't you need to go to work?"

"Are you kidding? I'm driving that man to the airport and personally escorting him onto the plane!"

Marina laughed and took his hand, tugging him toward the door. They walked down the lawn together. Marina knocked on the cottage door.

"Come in," Gerry called.

Overnight the cottage had been transformed into a nursery. Used and clean paper diapers littered the furniture, baby bottles stood on the kitchen counter, and Gerry's suitcase was open, spilling his clothes and his son's clothing onto the sofa. Gerry was dressed, sort of, his shirt half-tucked in, his hair tousled, and he'd missed several spots when shaving. He looked overwhelmed and disoriented, and when Marina walked in the door, his face lit up. Then he saw Jim and his face fell.

The two men studied each other in silence.

"Jim, this is Gerry, my ex-husband," Marina said quietly. "Gerry, this is Jim. We've come to take you to the airport."

"Marina, wait." Gerry began to argue.

Marina interrupted. "I did what you asked, Gerry, I slept on my decision and I'm still one hundred percent certain that I'm staying here with Jim. I didn't invite you here, and I'm sorry about Dara, but I know you'll be fine, and actually, Gerry, I just want you to leave. Can I help you pack?"

At that moment, the baby wailed. The three adults turned toward the infant tucked into one corner of the sofa.

"You can change the baby while I finish packing," Gerry said.

Marina almost laughed. Gerry was a master manipulator who loved a challenge. And she had to admit, privately, this was a challenge. Still, she organized the baby wipes, the paper diaper, the tiny blue and white romper, setting them on the table next to the sofa. She sat down and leaned over the baby, cooing and smiling at him.

"Hello, Garfield, I'm Marina. I'm going to change your diaper."

Garfield gazed up at her with his serious questioning face, studying her, and then he smiled and kicked his feet and the sudden compelling connection between them made love blossom in her heart like a flower. What a happy, trusting, little boy. She could love him so very much. She removed the soiled diaper, cleaned him and put on a new diaper, and bent down to kiss his fat little belly. The baby shrieked with glee. Here was this new life, pure and eager, and she snapped on his clothes, then lifted him to her shoulder and felt his sweet baby weight against her. She was aware of the two men in the room, both of them carrying their burden of history, their charms and flaws, their heaviness and guilt, for no adult was ever really without guilt of some sort. The baby snuggled against her. She knew instinctively how to support his bum and his neck. She gave herself a moment to breathe in his clean baby fragrance, to feel the warmth of his hot little head. She closed her eyes and silently prayed: *Bless you, little boy. May your life be good.*

She had to force herself to act relaxed and calm as she turned back to Gerry and Jim. Gerry's suitcase was packed and at his side. Jim held the cottage door open.

"All ready," Marina said brightly.

They walked out to Jim's truck. During the ride to the airport, Marina sat in the passenger seat, holding the baby.

Gerry leaned over from the backseat. "I meant to tell you, Marina," he said amiably, "Colin Finster has been dating Eloise."

Marina didn't reply. A year ago, she would have laughed at this news, for a year ago Colin and Eloise were employees of hers. But all that was a world away, and irrelevant to her now. She would not share anything with Gerry in front of Jim.

The rest of the ride was in silence. When they arrived at the airport, Jim parked the truck in the ten-minute loading zone in front of the terminal. Gerry got out, and Marina gave the baby to Gerry while she got out, and then Gerry handed the baby back to her while he put on his backpack.

She looked down at the infant in her arms. "Good-bye, little boy," she whispered.

The baby cooed softly to her. He grabbed her finger in his fist and clutched it tight. This was what babies did, she told herself, it didn't mean anything. Still, when she handed the baby to Gerry, her heart lurched and spilled a stream of distress into her blood.

She didn't want to let the baby go. They stood on the pavement outside the terminal. All around them people came and went, pulling luggage, chattering brightly about the summer.

"Marina," Jim said quietly, "come on."

"Perhaps we should wait . . ." Marina felt as if her heart were being torn open. "Help . . . until the plane leaves."

"He managed to get here from Kansas City all by himself," Jim reminded her. "I think he can handle it from here."

She nodded. Jim was right, of course he was right. She ripped her gaze away from the baby boy. She looked at Gerry, and that helped, that lessened her regret just a little, loosened the bond of her longing enough for her to reach out and grasp Jim's hand.

"Okay," Marina said. "Let's go. Bye, Gerry. Take care of him."

She knew that Gerry waited on the pavement, watching, holding the baby, as they got back into the truck, and that he was still standing there, waiting, as they drove away. She didn't allow herself to look back.

"Marina," Jim said quietly. "You can cry."

"Thanks," she said, "but you know what? I wish you would hold me a minute."

Jim steered the truck to the side of the street and parked. He held out his arms. Marina unclipped her seat belt and slid next to him, but the console between them made their embrace awkward.

Still, she was grateful to be held so close, to be held so dear as she cried. She was grateful for the steady beating of his heart.

57

·····

Lily

Lily let herself into the apartment with the key Jason had given her.

"Hello!" she called.

But he was already gone. No surprise, really. His crew started work at six.

Frustrated, Lily paced the small living area, trying to think what to do next. She didn't like having things up in the air like this, it made her feel absolutely *itchy*. What house was he working on now? She admitted to herself that she didn't always pay close attention to Jason when he told her about his work. Sometimes, if he was renovating a fabulous house, he invited her out to give her a little tour, a peek into how the superrich lived, but she thought he was building an addition to a fairly modest house out in Madaket—yes, that was it!

Should she go there? It was a long way, about five miles. She could bike there, but she'd arrive all sweaty and exhausted. Who had the Old Clunker today? Could she take it without making her sisters angry? Should she even do it at all; would he hate it if she showed up at the site, interrupting his work? But she was so *uncomfortable* with the way things were between them now, she was miserable, really, and she knew he was miserable, too, and she hated that, and she supposed this meant she was truly in love with him. She felt as if she were on fire with alarm. She didn't want to lose him. She had to do anything, everything, to keep him here with her.

She needed to tell him and tell him *now*.

She pretty much speed-walked back home. Her father's truck was gone, but the Old Clunker sat in the driveway. She went in through the kitchen and stood for a moment, listening to the house. Silence. So everyone had gone, although she wasn't sure about Emma, perhaps she was still sleeping. Lily clattered up the stairs, not trying to be quiet; if Emma was still asleep, well, it was time for her to wake up! She waited outside Emma's closed door for a moment, then opened it.

The room was empty. Perhaps Emma had gotten up early and gone off to work already. If so, she'd been picked up by Marcia, which meant she didn't need the car.

Lily took a few moments to touch up her makeup, not that she wore much in the morning. She brushed her hair and changed her shirt for one that showed a little more cleavage. Then she hurried down the stairs, grabbed the keys, and raced to the car.

Much of the island traffic had left, and the streets were clear and easy. Goldenrod and asters bobbed along the verges of the narrow road winding out to the west end of the island. The light slanted slightly, bronzing the landscape, and today the air was cooler than usual. Just a taste of fall in the air. Tonight she'd be able to use the turquoise pashmina she'd found at the thrift shop.

Her friend Carrie bought things at the thrift shop all the time. She dressed her baby in thrift shop clothing; she'd gotten her maternity wardrobe there. So many wealthy people donated clothes, some of them brand-new, it really was a satisfying experience to shop there, but did Lily want to live the rest of her life in thrift shop clothing?

What had Jason said? That she was fine as she was. Lily smiled, remembering that, and then immediately she frowned, for he had also asked her what she needed expensive clothes for, as if that were some sort of strange desire.

You want too much, Lily, Jason had said. *You're going to have to make a choice.*

But really, she didn't see why. She drove past the turnoff on Cliff Road, leading past the Tupancy land with its spectacular views of the Sound and remembered the fund-raiser she'd been to there. She'd met Jimmy Buffett! And he had really *looked* at her, and even if he was an old guy, he was cool, and she'd loved being young and desirable in her sassy little cropped top and her long dangling earrings.

Next she passed the road to Dionis and the gorgeous mansions resting on the edge of the cliff, with their splendid views of the Sound. She'd never been in one of those houses. She'd always wanted to, and perhaps, if she worked for the magazine next year, she would, or perhaps Eartha would invite her to accompany her to a party there . . .

Why should she have to give up all that in order to be with Jason? If he loved her, why couldn't *he* change? If he really loved her, then didn't he love the part of her that desired gorgeous clothes?

She was thinking so hard she almost ran off the road.

Jason would never be able to afford one of those trophy houses. Even though contractors made a lot of money, they didn't make millions and millions. She didn't care about that, she didn't need millions and millions. But she did want just a taste of it, just a few pretty clothes, and she did want to go to Paris before she settled down.

Suddenly she was in Madaket, the small colony of houses and marinas clustered at the end of the island. Instead of turning onto the street where Jason was working, she went on down to a dirt road leading to the harbor and turned again, onto another dirt road that dead-ended in a forest. She turned off the engine and sat there in the silence, trying to calm herself.

What was she going to say to Jason? *I'll give it all up to marry you?*

That just didn't seem right. But she didn't want to lose him, and she tried to think clearly about why she loved him so.

First of all, she just *did*. She'd fallen totally, completely, helplessly, sexually, romantically, in love with the man, and she trusted that, she trusted whatever surging insistent power it was that had brought her this man, that had brought her this kind of love. It was real, enormous, and unlike anything she had ever known before. It was *momentous*.

And it was right. She could step away from her passion and enumerate the other reasons she loved Jason. He was a good man. He was reliable, honest, kind, funny, he was trustworthy, and he wouldn't fool around. He was in many ways, all of them good, like her father. She liked being with him. She felt at home with him.

And if she thought of someday having a child with him—it made her shiver with helpless joy to even think of that.

But she wasn't ready for a baby yet. She wasn't ready to settle down, buy appliances, and spend her days working in a shop in order to pay for a new sofa or a mini vacation. She was who she was, young, probably naïve, certainly not completely formed. But she was not just a helpless bit of driftwood being tumbled into shape by the power of the ocean; she did have some say in her future, in what she would become.

She didn't want to lose Jason. She didn't want to lose herself, either.

She started up the car again, did a three-point turn, and headed for the farthest road in this little town. She came to a modest white Cape with its splendid view of Madaket Harbor. Jason's truck was in the drive, another truck behind it.

She parked and stepped out into the sunshine. The clean smell of sawdust floated past on the breeze and she heard hammers pounding. She walked around the side of the house to the addition Jason was building, past the pile of plywood and the sawhorses with two-by-fours lying in wait to be cut to size. The new room had been framed in. Now they were pounding up the walls.

Jason was up on a ladder. It was one of his crew, Patrick, who spotted Lily first.

"Hi, Lily," Patrick called.

Jason's head whipped around. When he saw her, he smiled. "Lily! What are you doing here?"

"I just wanted to talk to you for a minute," Lily told him.

He climbed down the ladder, tossed his hammer onto a pile of plywood, and came over to her. "It's nice to see you."

"Can we just walk down here a little way?" Lily asked.

"Sure." He put his arm around her shoulders as they walked away from the house, closer to the beach and the harbor, its water sparkling in the sunlight.

She stepped back a little, away from the shelter of his arm. She faced him head-on. "I just want to tell you I love you, Jason. I don't want to lose you. I don't want to lose us."

He smiled down at her. "Okay. Me, too."

Lily took a deep breath. Her heart thudded in her chest, in her throat. "But I do want to go to Paris. Maybe not for six months—" she hurriedly added. "Maybe just for three months, or two, I have to figure it out, and maybe you could come to Paris and stay with us and you and I could have a romantic time in Paris together, and maybe you could meet Eartha, because whatever I am, part of me does really like her, she's kind of fabulous, Jason . . . I guess what I'm saying is, I don't want to have to make one choice, black or white; I want you and me to work this out together somehow. Can we do that?"

He was listening to her carefully. She felt his resistance harden when she mentioned Eartha and Paris, but when she stopped talking, she saw how his shoulders relaxed, just a bit, and the muscle stopped jumping in his jaw.

He said, "I love you, too, Lily. And I want you to be able to see Paris. I've been thinking. I was wrong to want to deny you that. I guess I'm afraid you won't want me if you go to Paris—"

"Oh, Jason! I'll always want you!" Lily cried and tried to hug him.

He put his arms on her shoulders and held her away from him. "We don't need Patrick to witness everything," he told her gently. "I'm glad you came out here, Lily. I'm sorry I stormed out of the house; it was a childish thing to do. I want to work things out with you, okay? We can both compromise a bit, right?"

Lily smiled. "Right."

"I'd better get back to work. See you at home tonight?"

She nodded. Jason dropped a light kiss on top of her head, picked up his hammer, and went back up the ladder. She watched him for a moment, loving the lines of his body, the strength of his arms, the muscles in his back. She saw how he was building something new with his hard physical labor. He was good at that, at building something new. And she could learn to be good at that, too.

She drove back home, and her thoughts still raced, but her heart was calm.

58

. . . . .

Emma

The sound of running water woke Emma. As she surfaced from her warm ocean of sleep, she was aware of a sense of extraordinary happiness growing within her. She didn't want to wake from this blissful dream. Then she opened her eyes . . . and the dream was still there. Even more happiness rushed through her.

She was in Spencer's bed. The sound of running water was Spencer in the shower. They'd slept the night together here, in his house.

Sighing with pleasure, Emma sat up in bed, stuffing all the pillows behind her for support. When they came in last night, she hadn't really paid attention to Spencer's house—it could have been the Taj Mahal or a refrigerator box and she wouldn't have cared.

Now she let her gaze wander around the room. It was a quaint little chamber, tucked up on the second floor of this old house. The entire house was a low-ceilinged, beam-and-plaster jewel box, built in the late eighteenth century and remodeled and modernized as the decades passed. The front door opened directly off a narrow hidden lane into a long room that served as living and dining room, with a galley kitchen downstairs and the bathroom upstairs built on the back of the house in what the islanders referred to as "warts." It was Spencer's house. He'd bought it with money left to him by his grandparents, and loving history as he did, he cherished the house.

The room was sparsely furnished with a double bed, an old bureau, a chair, and on the wall several paintings of Nantucket by island painters. No curtains hung at the small, many-paned window. It was open, and the dewy air of early morning drifted into the room.

Last night had been amazing. Emma closed her eyes and hugged herself, remembering. When they first got to the cottage, they'd gone directly to bed, but later, after they made love, as they were ravaging through Spencer's refrigerator and making grilled cheese sandwiches, they'd talked and talked, getting to know each other better, sharing secrets and plans and dreams.

Later, around two, they'd gone back to bed again. They'd made love again. It was very late when, exhausted, satiated, and content, they finally fell asleep.

Now Emma's gaze fell on the clock on the bedside table. It was after seven-thirty. Oh, heavens, Marcia must have gone to Emma's house to pick her up for work. Emma jumped out of bed, grabbed her purse from the floor, and dug out her cell phone. She hit Marcia's number and got her voice mail.

She held the phone to her ear and leaned against the little window, peeking out at the bright day.

"Marcia? It's Emma. I'm sorry, I can't come to work today. I'll explain later. Sorry."

"Good God!"

The woman's voice, so close to Emma, made her nearly jump out of her skin, and it was only her skin that she wore. For a horrified moment, Emma stood there, stark, raving naked, gaping at Sandra Bracebridge, who loomed in the doorway bristling like a giant hedgehog. Spencer's mother wore a Lily Pulitzer dress in a geometric pattern and from her arms, neck, and ears several pounds of gold glittered. She carried a lightship basket purse, one of the new styles with a strap handle.

"What are you doing here?" Sandra demanded.

Emma was seized by an almost irresistible desire to laugh as various answers flashed through her head. She started to say, "Sorry," but realized that actually, she had nothing to apologize for. She crossed back to the bed, yanked the top sheet off the mattress, and wrapped it around herself.

"Mother?" Spencer stepped out of the bathroom, a towel around his waist, steam drifting behind him into the bedroom. "What are you doing here?"

Sandra Bracebridge drew herself up to her full belligerent grandeur. "I've been talking to your grandmother and I need to talk with you. Obviously things have progressed further than appropriate."

"Oh, for God's sake." Spencer's face darkened. "In the first place, Mother, it's not *appropriate* for you to just appear in my bedroom unannounced. We've gone over this before, it's my house, not yours, and you should call me before you barge in."

Sandra was undaunted. "If you were in danger, wouldn't you want me to 'barge in'? If your house was on fire, wouldn't you expect me to—"

Spencer turned his back on his mother. "I've got to get dressed."

His mother glared at him for one long moment. "I'll be waiting downstairs."

Spencer tugged open a bureau drawer, pulled out a pair of boxer shorts and stepped into them. "Emma, I apologize. Mother has never just burst in on me like this. Give me a few minutes to talk to her and I'll get rid of her." He yanked on a pair of trousers and pulled on a white button-down shirt, then strode across the room barefoot to kiss Emma quickly on the mouth.

Stunned, Emma sank down on the side of the bed. She wanted to take a shower, but she also wanted to hear what Spencer had to say to his mother, and curiosity won out. She remained very still, hardly breathing, and listened.

"I'd like you to give me my key back now." Spencer's voice was calm but firm.

"Nonsense. What if you need me to fetch something when you're off-island—"

"In that case I'll give you a key before I leave. I want my key back now. Or I'll change the locks."

"Why are you acting like this! You have no right to speak to me this way!"

"I have every right, Mother. I'm an adult. This is my house. I bought it with my money. I—"

"Very well, I apologize. But really, Spencer, consider it from my perspective. I hardly slept last night, not after I phoned Mother and she told me you'd gone off with that girl."

"Her name is Emma, and I'm going to marry her."

Emma nearly fell off the bed.

"Oh, Spencer, you can't be serious! She's just an island girl, she's not one of our kind."

"Thank God for that," Spencer said. Sandra's voice had risen a few octaves, but he sounded mild and reasonable. "Mother, I've got things to do. You need to leave."

"Spencer, I'm your mother. I'm only concerned about your welfare. I—"

"Believe me, I've never been happier. Now please go."

"You can't shut me out like this."

"Please go."

"Promise me you'll come to my house for a drink this evening. By *yourself*."

"I can't promise that. I have plans."

"It's your grandmother who's instigated this, isn't it! Millicent is always trying to turn you against me."

Now his voice was cold. "Please. Go."

Emma heard the hard click of Sandra's heels against the floorboards, and then the firm slam of the door.

Spencer came up the stairs, two at a time. "Damn, that woman makes me crazy! My brother and sister have both moved to the other side of the country, and now you know why. She's so controlling, she's so infuriating, she's like some kind of giant household pest!"

Emma just smiled. She couldn't stop smiling.

Spencer gawked at her, then suddenly smiled back. "So I guess you overheard our conversation." He sat next to her on the bed and took her hand in his. "I suppose that was not the most romantic marriage proposal in the world."

"But perhaps the most unusual," Emma assured him.

Spencer laughed. Then, more soberly, he said, "I'm not trying to rush you, Emma. I don't want you to answer yet. I wouldn't blame you if you didn't want to marry me. I know I've got the strangest, most dysfunctional family in the world. You've seen my mother in action. And I want to live on this island, and that means I'll always be within Mother's striking range. Does that frighten you?"

Emma started to reply, but the question was a serious one, and she took a moment to consider it. She had never discussed the thorny subject of money with Duncan. She had always glibly pretended to be comfortable around people with lots of money, and for the few years she'd lived in Boston, she'd felt certain she was going to make a nice fat bunch of money for herself and her family and belong to that golden group.

"I do think," she said slowly, thinking aloud, "that your mother will never accept me. I don't come from money. Our family doesn't have the kind of money you do."

"Let me just remind you that my mother doesn't even have the kind of money she acts like she has. That's why she tried to steal those lightship baskets. She's always trying to sell off something so she can have more ready cash."

Emma nodded. "Still. Still . . . Spencer, I think I'm a little afraid of people like you."

"Because we have an old family name? I am proud of being a Bracebridge. It's one of the reasons I know so much history. But other than that—my father is dead. My mother is a terrible snob. My brother and sister have moved away and hardly keep in touch. Plus, they don't give a fig about Nantucket. My mother fights with my grandmother all the time. Since my brother and sister have abandoned me, my mother focuses way too much of her energy on trying to run my life. And I'm afraid I love my grandmother more than I love my mother." He paused, and with a wry smile said, "Actually, now that I've enumerated all our charms, I can see why you'd be afraid of us."

Now Emma smiled. "Oh, Spencer, I've got a pretty odd family, too. Perhaps everyone thinks their family's odd." She laughed. "Perhaps every family *is* odd."

"You can't build a straight house out of crooked wood, but you can build a very cozy crooked house," Spencer said. "Grams used to say that all the time. The house Grams lives in will have to be sold when she dies, and the money will be divided up among my siblings and me. I'll never be rich, Emma, but I think I'll be comfortable."

"Comfortable," Emma echoed. She ran her thumb over Spencer's hand. "I like this, Spencer, I like talking about all the real stuff." Suddenly, sitting there naked with a sheet wrapped around her, she remembered—"Actually, my own family is in its own crisis right now. My father has met someone, at last, a really nice woman who makes him happy. Spencer, I need to take a quick shower and get back home."

"I'd like to meet your family. Outside of the police station, I mean." He grinned.

"Oh Lord," Emma moaned.

Spencer stood up. "You shower, I'll make coffee."

59

. . . . .

Abbie

Abbie took Harry upstairs to help him brush his teeth and dress for the day. She really wanted to tuck him under her arm and run. Or maybe just hide in the closet. She heard the front door open and slam shut.

"Mommy's home," she told Harry.

"*Mommy!*" Harry raced down the stairs.

Abbie followed, her heart triple-timing in her chest.

"Hello, Big Guy. " In the front hall, Sydney performed an admirably graceful squat, given the tightness of her suit and the height of her heels. Harry ran into her arms. She hugged him and kissed the top of his head.

Then she noticed Abbie standing on the stairs. "What are you doing here so early?" she demanded.

"Sydney." Howell came into the hall, a kitchen towel in his hand. "We need to talk."

Sydney narrowed her eyes. She glared at Howell, then at Abbie, then back at Howell. She rose up, tall in her high heels, thin as a whip. "So that's what's going on." She snorted. "Unbelievable! You and the nanny are having a little fling."

"It's not a fling," Howell objected, adding, "and let's not do this in front of our son."

"I think *fling* is actually a rather perfect way of putting it," Sydney snapped, "and why not do it in front of Harry? I imagine you two have been doing lots of things in front of Harry."

"Harry!" Howell reached for his son's hand. "We're going to have some adult time, so you get to watch television."

Harry pulled away, reluctant.

Howell persisted. "In fact, I'm going to give you the remote control. You can change channels all you want."

At this, Harry's face lit up.

"I'll be in the kitchen." Sydney stalked away from the rest of them.

Howell led Harry into the living room and settled him on the sofa. Abbie took a deep breath and followed Sydney into the kitchen. Howell's wife was leaning against the counter, her arms crossed, her face bitter.

Sydney raked her gaze over Abbie's face. "Well, aren't you the little multitasker. I have to say I'm surprised you've caught Howell's eye. You're hardly a femme fatale."

Abbie didn't reply. She understood Sydney's anger.

"It's a cliché, you know," Sydney sneered. "The boss screwing the help."

Howell entered the room. "Sydney, let's not talk that way."

"Oh, listen to you, so civilized and refined. You can screw the nanny but you don't want to talk about it."

"I want to marry Abbie," Howell announced. "I love her, and I think she's good for Harry."

Sydney shook her head like a boxer who's been stunned by an unexpected blow. "You want to *marry* her? Good God, Howell, you really are full of surprises." Then she smiled triumphantly. "And *she* is why you want a divorce?" Sydney really had a remarkable voice, as clear as a bell, and full of confidence. "Howell, you are such a loser. *I'm* the one who wants a divorce! You want to shack up with a babysitter. But I'm going to marry the next senator for New York State."

Howell seemed genuinely amazed. "Everett Candelli? You've been seeing Everett Candelli?"

"What?" Now Sydney's voice was gleeful. "You think someone that important wouldn't notice a little ol' lawyer?"

Oh, man! Abbie felt like a kite swept up in a gale of fresh, intoxicating air. *Oh, man, Sydney wants a divorce, too!*

"I'm impressed," Howell said. "Everett is a remarkable man and a great public servant. I'm glad for you, Sydney."

"The hell you are. You're just relieved that you won't have a nasty divorce and custody case to deal with."

"Well," Howell admitted, "that's true, too."

"Daddy," Harry called. "The remote doesn't work."

Howell looked frustrated. "Okay, kid, I'm coming." He left the room.

Abbie found Sydney's angry eyes latched on to her face. She sucked up her courage and found her voice. She said the one true thing that would matter to the other woman. "I love Harry. I want you to know that."

"Like you have any idea what maternal love is," Sydney snapped. "Sweet little you, all innocent and eager! You're just a hopeless girl, you can't imagine what it takes to be a mother."

"Actually, I can," Abbie began.

"Being a nanny is *nothing* like being a mother!" Sydney exploded. "You worry all the fucking time! Vigilance, intelligence, all your best intentions, none of that matters! It doesn't stop when you go to sleep, it never stops! You are going to be so *swamped* if you take on Harry. You won't sleep at night, you won't know what to do when he gets sick, hell, *you* can't even take him on a fucking carousel! It's hard work, sometimes it's hopeless and heartbreaking! You feel like you never get anything right! But look at you, you think you know how to be a mother!"

Abbie could understand the woman's rage, and it was with consideration of the mother Sydney was that Abbie said quietly, "My own mother died when I was fifteen. I pretty much raised my two sisters."

"That's hardly the same!" Sydney retorted. Suddenly she collapsed in a chair and rubbed her hands over her face. "But that's too bad. It must have been hard for you." She studied Abbie for a long moment, her eyes penetrating and critical. Finally, she said, "Oh, fuck it, what do I know? You've been good with Harry. I can tell he feels loved by you. Damn it all, you'll probably be a decent stepmother."

"I will," Abbie promised in a hushed voice.

"All right, do me a favor," Sydney said. "Take Harry somewhere so Howell and I can talk. We've got a lot of details to iron out."

Abbie hesitated. "Okay."

Howell and Harry were still in the living room, struggling with the stalled remote control. They looked up at her, the lines of their faces, the fall of their hair, and their hopeful expressions so much alike it made Abbie smile.

"You know what?" Abbie said. "Forget the TV, Harry. I'm going to take you to my house to meet my family."

Howell looked relieved. "Good idea." He added, "Come back by lunchtime, okay?"

Abbie nodded and took Harry's hand. "Okay."

They stepped out into the gusty day. Abbie's spirits swirled like the wind and she was almost running, tugging Harry along. "You'll love my house, Harry. I've got lots of cool things for you to see. We've got seashells and dolls and a cat named Cinnamon and a Playhouse!"

"You're silly today," Harry giggled.

"Harry, I'm absolutely slaphappy!" she agreed.

60
· · · · ·

Abbie, Emma, Lily, and Marina
and Harry, Spencer, and Jim

Marina said, "I'm okay, now, Jim." She pulled away from him, slightly embarrassed that they were sitting on the side of the busy airport road, wrapped up in each other like a pair of high school lovers while half of Nantucket drove past, gawking.

Still, Jim's embrace was very nice.

"Ready to go home?" he asked.

She liked the sound of that, going *home*. "Absolutely."

He pulled the truck back out onto the road and headed back to town. He steered with one hand and kept the other on Marina's thigh. "I think I'll skip work this morning."

"Really?" Marina turned toward him and touched the side of his face. She felt so close to him, so happy with her choice, as if finally she'd stepped away from her past and crossed the threshold into her future.

"Well . . ." For a few moments, Jim seemed at a loss for words. "Marina. I know what kind of a decision you made just now. How hard it must have been for you. And God, I'm glad you chose me. Us. Here. I think you were brave. I don't think this is any kind of a normal day, and I don't want to go rushing off to work."

Marina touched his face gently with her fingertips. "Jim."

He pulled into the driveway and turned off the engine. "Besides, I've just had a contract signed and a payment made for a major ren-

ovation on a huge old house, so I can take a little time for myself."
He turned to Marina with a grin. "And you know what? I'm starving. I feel like I haven't eaten for days."

Marina laughed. "I'm hungry, too. I bought eggs yesterday. I'll
make us scrambled eggs . . . protein for energy!" She was so *pleased*
with how hungry she felt, hungry and euphoric and healthy and
right.

"What's so funny?" Jim asked.

"Nothing," she told him. "Everything. I think I'm a little
berserk. The past few hours have been pretty intense. And now I
just feel really good!"

They held hands as they walked to the house. The warm aroma
of coffee still lingered in the air, but the house was quiet.

"The girls have gone," Jim said.

"I don't think Emma was here last night," Marina told him. She
got out a mixing bowl and the eggs, and it was so satisfying, how perfectly an egg fit into her hand, how smooth it was, how real and
comforting and nourishing, this simple thing.

"Hello!" The front door slammed and a moment later Abbie was
there, holding hands with a little boy.

"Hi, guys!" Abbie lifted the child up into her arms. "This is
Harry! Harry, this is my dad, Jim. And Dad's friend, Marina." As
everyone said hello, Abbie studied her father and Marina. "So
they've gone?"

"We just put them on the plane," Jim said.

Abbie whooped with glee and did a little salsa, bouncing Harry
in her arms. He giggled. Abbie said, "Marina, I'm so glad."

Marina blushed. "Thanks. Want some scrambled eggs?"

"No, thanks, we just had pancakes," Abbie told her. She set
Harry on the floor. "Maybe some fruit, though. I'll make a fruit
bowl." She opened the refrigerator.

Marina smiled and began cracking the eggs into the mixing
bowl.

The back door opened. Emma and Spencer stepped inside.

Emma's eyes widened. "Marina! You're here!"

Marina winked. "Yup. Jim and I took Gerry and the baby to the
airport first thing this morning."

"Hallelujah!" Everyone was staring at them. Emma collected

her wits and said, "Everyone, this is Spencer. Spencer, this is my dad, Marina, my sister Abbie, and—" She squatted down next to the little boy. "You must be Harry."

He looked amazed at her clairvoyance. "I *am* Harry!" He laughed.

Emma said, "And I've never met a Harrier Harry than you." She stood up. "Oh, wow, Marina, are you fixing breakfast? We're starving."

"Coming right up." Marina took out a block of cheddar and grated a pile to add to the eggs. She put four pieces of bread into the toaster, and set the butter out to soften. She took a package of bacon from the freezer and organized it for the microwave. She said, "Emma, could you pour the juice? Jim, could you make more coffee?" She found the blueberry jam and set it with a spoon in the middle of the table. *I've found my element*, she thought.

The microwave pinged. Marina took out the bacon. "All right, everyone, breakfast is ready. Grab a seat." She put the bacon on a platter and loaded plates with a pile of steaming-hot buttery, yellow eggs. She grabbed the second round of toast, spread it with butter, and set it on the table.

"I might be a little hungry, too," Harry announced hopefully.

Jim said, "Here's a trick." He picked up a pile of cookbooks and set them on a chair, then lifted the little boy up. "Just the right height," he said, pushing the chair close to the table.

Emma looked around the table. With so many people here, they were crowded arm to arm, and she liked it. She saw Spencer talking to Marina, and thought: *Maybe we're not the weirdest family in the world.*

The back door opened and Lily stepped into the kitchen. Her face fell. "No one told me about a party."

Emma laughed. "Lily, it's just breakfast!"

Marina motioned to the chair next to her. "Sit down, Lily. There's plenty here."

Pleased but confused, Lily sat.

"Where's Jason?" Marina asked as she dished up eggs for Lily.

"He's working," Lily said. She leaned close to Marina. "I talked to Jason. I told him we could compromise, he could come to Paris, too—"

"Who's going to Paris?" her father asked.

"Oh, well, I am, Dad." The eggs smelled so good she took a bite before continuing. "Eartha's going to take me. This fall. For six months. And Jason's not thrilled."

Her father looked perplexed. "I thought you were going to marry Jason."

"Well, I am. But *first* I'm going to France."

"This is marvelous, Lily," Marina said.

"I know!" Lily wiggled with delight. "Maybe you can come visit. You and Dad." She looked around the table. "Maybe you can *all* come visit!"

Emma squeezed Spencer's hand under the table. "Perhaps we will," she told her sister. "It's a possibility."

Harry slipped out of his chair and went to the shelf holding the beach treasures. "Nanny Abbie, what's this?"

Abbie knelt next to him. "It's cool stuff we found on the beach. That's a rock we liked. And that's an oyster shell. You can pick it up. When I was your age, Harry, I used to pretend it was a cradle for my little troll."

Harry's eyes went wide. "You had a little troll?"

"Yes. I made them out of rocks. Let me show you." Abbie took the small, smooth rock from the trophy spot and drew a face on it with a blue felt-tip pen. Harry watched, entranced.

"You have a lot of people in your family, Nanny Abbie!" Harry said, looking over at the table where the others were eating and talking and laughing.

"That's true," Abbie agreed.

After a moment, Harry said solemnly, "Nanny Abbie, I like your family."

Abbie paused to consider her answer. She wanted to tell the child he was going to be part of her family, but this morning was too soon for that announcement. It would only confuse him. So she kissed him on his cheek and said, "You know, Harry, I like my family, too."

Abbie, Emma, Lily, and Danielle, Kind of

It was Abbie's idea.

In the cool of the evening, they climbed into the Old Clunker and headed out to Surfside beach. Abbie drove. Emma sat in the passenger seat, holding the picnic basket. Lily sat behind Emma. She didn't have her seat belt on because she was perched on the edge of the seat, leaning forward, trying to subdue Emma's long curly hair.

It was just after seven, and when they arrived at the parking lot at the top of the bluff, they spotted few other cars. The concession stand was closed. The air was tinged with early autumn coolness.

They didn't speak as they went down the sandy hill, although Abbie said aloud, to herself, really, "Why did I bother to wear sandals?" and stopped to take them off.

When they came to the wide beach, they all just stood for a moment, gazing out at the infinite expanse of ocean. The breeze came from the southeast, so the waves rolled dramatically, crashing onto the shore in a scatter of white froth.

"Mom would like this," Emma observed.

Abbie nodded. "You're right. She always loved big waves, stormy seas."

"So that's one more thing I don't know," Lily said sadly.

"What do you remember?" Abbie asked. She handed Emma a corner of their ancient beach blanket and together the sisters spread it on the sand. Abbie weighted one corner with the picnic basket.

Lily said, "Mostly I remember her singing me lullabies."

"Well, there you go, Lily." Abbie nodded encouragingly as she took the glasses out of the basket. "*That's* a memory *we* don't have. Mom stopped singing me lullabies when I was about eight."

"Me, too." Emma was working the cork off the champagne.

"She sang me lullabies all the time." Lily chewed her lip, remembering.

Abbie smiled. "And you were seven. You were her last little baby. She adored you."

The cork exploded out with a loud gunshot sound.

"Hooray!" Emma held up the bottle. "Glasses, everyone." She poured champagne into three glasses.

"I officially declare the opening of the First Danielle Fox Memorial," Abbie pronounced solemnly.

The sisters clinked their glasses and drank.

Emma looked at her sisters. "All right. Who starts?"

"You," Lily decided. "Because Abbie and I already had a memory."

Emma agreed. "Okay. I've been thinking about this, and I've got a good one. I remember how Mom used to make clothes for my dolls—"

"That's right, she did!" Abbie said.

"Except she made *weird* clothes. None of my friends ever had clothes like my dolls had. She turned one of my Barbies into a Gypsy. With shawls and lots of sequins."

"That's kind of cool, Emma," Lily said.

"Actually, it was embarrassing," Emma told her. "I loved my baby dolls. I just wanted lots of baby clothes for my dolls. I didn't even like my Barbies, and I at least wanted clothes just like my friends had. Malibu Barbie. Cinderella Barbie."

"Oh, gosh!" Abbie shrieked. "I'd forgotten that! Remember, she made one of my Barbies into Wicked Stepmother Barbie! With an old black shawl and a little basket with apples in it. The apples were cinnamon red hots."

"She didn't make clothes for my dolls," Lily recalled.

"No, *you* were her doll. She made dress-up costumes for you, remember?" Abbie prompted.

Lily thought. "I had a princess outfit."

Emma said, "Right. With a tiara."

The three sisters were silent for a moment, caught up in memories. Then Lily said, carefully, "Mom was really kind of bizarre."

"She was *artistic*," Emma corrected.

"She was *different*," Abbie insisted. "We agreed we'd be truthful out here. And we never have talked about the bad stuff."

"It wasn't so bad," Lily hurried to protest. "It's not like she ever hit us."

Abbie looked at her youngest sister. "No. You're right. She never hit us or said mean things to us."

"But she acted like she hated us, sometimes," Emma said softly.

"No, she didn't!" Lily exclaimed.

"Okay," Emma continued, "maybe not you, Lily. You were so young. But she would say things . . . I remember coming home from school my first day in seventh grade. I was excited because I was taking French. I said something like *bonjour* to Mom, and she got that sad look in her eyes and said, 'I always wanted to live in France. If I weren't stuck in this house on this island, I could go to France. Now I'll never get to go.' Gosh, I felt so terrible, like I'd ruined her life."

Abbie nodded. "That was getting near the time she died. She had a really bad couple of years then with depression. She was fighting it but it was winning."

Lily burst out, "She should have loved us most! She should have wanted to be with us! We loved her! Dad loved her! Why wasn't that enough for her?"

Abbie countered, "Okay, Lily, listen to yourself. *You're* the one who's postponed your wedding so you can go to France with Eartha."

Lily chewed her lip.

Emma said, "Hey. We agreed not to talk about the present and not to criticize one another."

"I wasn't criticizing. I was only saying."

"It sounded like criticism." Lily pouted.

Emma changed the subject. "Doesn't it scare you? I mean, do you ever think that depression might be inherited? That we'll suddenly get slammed by it?"

Abbie said, "I think about that a lot. But it helps to remember how levelheaded Dad is. He's calm, content with life. I guess I think maybe his genes and Mom's mixed. Anyway, when I get depressed, I can get out of it pretty fast."

"She used to shout at Dad," Emma said, almost whispering.

"I remember that," Lily said. "It was scary."

Emma continued, "She used to have rages. She'd throw things. Remember when she broke the vase we gave her for her birthday? It wasn't expensive, but we were young, we didn't have much money. We were so proud when she put it in the living room on the front table where everyone could see it. And then she broke it—"

"She didn't know what she was doing," Lily insisted.

"She felt terrible the next day," Abbie said. "She cried and cried. She apologized to us over and over again. She glued it back together."

"She *tried* to glue it back together," Emma clarified. "It was in so many little pieces, and she cut her finger on a shard—"

"I remember that," Lily whispered. "I remember all the blood."

The sisters fell silent, each staring out at the roiling seas. Evening was drifting toward them like a dark cloud, staining the water with indigo.

"Okay." Abbie took a deep breath. "This is why we're here. We've never done this before, and it's hard, it hurts, but I think we need to do it. So let's each say the *worst* memory we have of Mom."

After a moment, Lily said, "I think the vase thing was the worst for me. The entire incident. The way she screamed at Dad. The sounds of things breaking. You came and got me," she said to Abbie, "and took me out to the Playhouse. Me and Emma. We were *in bed*. In our *pajamas*. It was scary to go to the Playhouse at night like that."

"I didn't want you to have to hear," Abbie said.

"Dad yelled, too," Emma recalled. "That was always the most frightening thing for me. Dad was so good with her, he listened to her for so long, he kept asking her if she'd taken her medicine, he tried to get her to just calm down. But he ran out of patience and yelled at her."

"*What do you want me to do?*" Abbie said in a low voice. "*What in the* hell *do you expect me to do? Jesus, Danielle, I'm trying!*"

"We fell asleep in the Playhouse, remember?" Emma shifted in the sand, unsettled by her memories. "You slept on the sofa, with your arms around Lily. I slept on the floor."

"The next morning, Mom served us pancakes with all the maple syrup we wanted." Lily smiled ruefully. "She promised it would never, ever, happen again."

"Well," Abbie said bitterly, "she kept her promise."

They were quiet again.

"I hate her," Lily declared. "I was a little girl. She left me."

"She left us all, and Dad, too," Abbie said.

"But you were grown up! I was so young!"

"I think she was in agony," Abbie said slowly. Very quietly, she told them, "Once I caught her trying to cut her wrists in the bathtub."

"Oh, Abbs, I never knew that," Emma gasped. "How terrible for you."

"Dad was out fishing. It was late. I had to pee, so I just walked into the bathroom . . . She was naked in the bathtub with a knife. She dropped it when she saw me. I said, 'Mom.' She said, 'It's all right, Abbie.' But I couldn't move. I was paralyzed. I needed Dad to help. I was terrified."

"What did you do?" Lily asked.

"I just stood there like a big dummy, frozen. Deer in headlights. Finally, Mom stood up, dripping water, and wrapped a towel around her and got out of the tub. She hugged me really tight for a long time. She said, 'It's okay, Abbie. You go on back to bed. You have school tomorrow. I'll be fine. I'm going to go to sleep, too.' But I still couldn't move. I'd forgotten this—I was turned to stone. I couldn't even speak. I was fifteen. I knew I should do something. And I was embarrassed that Mom was naked, her towel kept falling off her. And she kept making these big fake smiles and telling me everything was fine."

"So what happened? Did Dad come home?"

"Not then. Later. Mom finally dried off, and pulled on a night-gown and took my hand and said, 'Come on, honeybun, let's get in bed together and cuddle up like we did when you were little. I'll scratch your back like I used to.' So somehow I could move and we lay in bed together for a long time. I didn't fall asleep. Mom didn't, either, I could tell by her breathing. But she was calm. Then Dad came home, and I went to my bedroom and fell asleep."

Lily said, "That's awful, Abbie." She drank some champagne as she sorted her thoughts. "I've been so jealous of you—and Emma— because you got to have more of Mom than I did. Years and years more. But you got the hard stuff, too. I never thought of it that way."

Emma's voice was low and husky. "Remember, a few weeks before she died, how we woke up one morning with her jewelry on our pillows next to us?"

"Oh, I remember that!" Lily cried. "I was so excited. I'd always wanted her amethyst bracelet. I put it on right away." She sobered quickly. "It never occurred to me that she was giving us her jewelry because she was planning to . . . not use it anymore."

"You were seven," Emma reminded her. "But I was thirteen, and I thought it was just creepy."

"Dad should have gotten her into a hospital that day," Lily said.

"It's not Dad's fault," Emma protested.

"I'm not saying it was," Lily began.

"Dad tried so hard to get her to check herself in for long-term treatment, but she wouldn't even hear of it."

"Okay," Abbie straightened up and her take-charge voice returned. "I think the three of us need to make a pact. We need to keep in touch with one another, wherever we are, and if one of us starts showing signs of serious depression, we'll fight and kick and scream until we get help."

"That's a good idea," Lily said, "but how do we judge a serious depression? When Emma came home this summer, she was flat out in bed for days."

"And you emailed me, and I came home," Abbie reminded her. "But really, that was a situational thing."

"I think we'll need to talk to our husbands or roommates or whoever is living with us at the time," Emma suggested.

Abbie said, "Right. Like when you marry Spencer, he should know to call me and Lily and we can figure it out together."

"But if I tell Jason I might have crazy genes, maybe he won't marry me!" Lily wailed, distraught.

"Oh, come on," Emma chided. "Jason is wild about you."

"Still, you should mention it to him," Abbie said. "Anyway, it won't be a huge surprise to him. Everyone in town knew that Mom was eccentric."

The sky and ocean were dimming into a luminous field of gray. The wind was rising, playing with the corners of the blanket.

Lily shivered. "I'm getting chilled."

"Okay," Abbie said. "One more memory each, and then we'll go."

"I remember how much she loved summer," Emma said. "Practically the moment the snow stopped, she'd be outside stringing up the shell lights around the deck and setting up the deck chairs. She'd go swimming every day. She just lived in her bathing suits with a shirt of Dad's buttoned over them."

"She loved Christmas, too," Abbie said. "She'd blast Christmas music all over the house and make fifteen different kinds of Christmas cookies and a *bûche de Noël* and she always bought the biggest tree she could find."

"And she put three angels on top of the tree." Lily choked up as she spoke. "She always said we were her three angels, so she had to have three angels on the tree."

"I'd forgotten that." Abbie was growing teary too. "It was a cool idea, but it always looked kind of odd."

Emma raised her glass. "Here's to the memory of Danielle Fox."

The sisters touched glasses and downed the last swallow of champagne.

For a few moments they were silent, lost in their own private thoughts.

"Okay." Abbie wrapped her glass in a paper towel and laid it in the basket. "Let's go."

As they shook the sand off the blanket and folded it into a neat rectangle, Lily asked, "Do you ever think that maybe Mom's really out there? Somewhere? That she can see us?"

Emma chuckled. "It's a nice thought, Lily, but there are times when I wouldn't want Mom to be watching me."

Abbie swirled her toes in the sand. "Remember the things Mom said when she brought us beachcombing? She told us to always believe in something *more*. She told us to look at what was right in front of us, and we'd see that even a grain of sand was a miracle. That even a bit of glass was a message, that the universe was full of tricks and clues and signs."

They gazed out at the water in silence for a moment. The sun was low, lighting the tips of the waves with points of light.

"Come on," Emma said.

They slogged up the steep sand dune, carrying the basket and blanket.

Lily said, "But do you, Abbie? Believe in something else?"

"Oh, I don't know, Lily. I guess in my head I think it's not possible, but in my heart I want it to be true. So I guess I believe, in a vague kind of way." Abbie turned to look out at the sea one more time.

Something flashed in the water. Something like a gleam of skin. She gasped.

"What, Abbie?" Lily stopped and turned, too.

"Oh, nothing," Abbie decided. "It was just a trick of the light."

62
. . . . .

The Family

It had been a gamble, and as the wedding day approached, the suspense was nerve-racking for everyone. Jim checked the weather on his iPhone every hour and still went outside and stared up at the sky. They had rented the house on the beach so the bride and her bridesmaids could have a place to dress, and they were prepared, if necessary, to hold the ceremony inside. Marina and the girls had decorated the expansive downstairs living room with shell lights and had buckets of flowers waiting, just in case.

But the April day dawned clear, bright, and unseasonably warm. It was a gift of a day, and the wedding party were elated, as if the day was a message from nature, and who, Abbie insisted, could say that it wasn't?

Earlier, Jim and Howell and Spencer and Jason drove their four-wheel drives onto the sand and set up rows of handsome white folding chairs borrowed from the yacht club in a semicircle, facing the ocean. Abbie and Lily created a low altar out of driftwood and set buckets of pink tulips and yellow daffodils on either side. The boardwalk from the house came right down to the beach through the beach grass, and they set vases of flowers here and there along the way.

Now cars and trucks were arriving, parking along the side roads, and the wedding guests in all their bright colors made their way, in sandals or barefoot, over the sand to the chairs. Inside, on the second floor, the bride slipped into her gown. The guitarist was still playing softly, and the notes of "The Water Is Wide" drifted up to the house.

On the first floor, Abbie gathered her skirt with both hands and knelt down next to Harry.

"You can do it, Harry," she assured him. "Just like last night at the rehearsal."

Harry twisted one foot around the other leg and looked miserable. It wasn't his navy blazer and tie making him unhappy. He actually thought it was cool to wear such grown-up clothing, especially since he was also barefoot. He was just having an extreme fit of shyness.

Abbie took a deep breath and looked questioningly up at Howell.

"We'll all be right there with you at the front, buddy," Howell assured him.

Harry squirmed. "Too many people."

It was understandable. Last night the beach had not been crowded with what seemed like half of Nantucket Island. Now all the folding chairs were filled, and waves of conversation and laughter drifted toward them.

"I have an idea," Abbie said. "What if Bill walked with you?"

Harry's eyes lit up. "Yeah! That would be cool."

Howell shook his head. "I'm not so sure that's a good idea. He's only a puppy."

"But Bill is so calm," Abbie reminded him.

"Should I ask Marina or Jim?" Howell wondered. "They might think it's too, oh, I don't know, daffy."

"Sure." Abbie took Harry's hand. "You double-check with them. Harry and I will go get Bill."

She and Howell had gotten the puppy for Harry for Christmas. They thought it might help the little boy feel older, more responsible, if he had an animal to care for, and the mixed-breed orphan from the MSPCA had turned out to be a perfect fit for their newly evolving family. Harry had named the dog Bill. He was a placid, good-natured, unexcitable little animal with black-and-white markings and one floppy ear. He always looked content, even amused, by

his small doggy life. When Harry came to Nantucket for his time
with Howell, he was allowed to have Bill sleep in bed with him. Boy
and dog had become best friends.

Howell's new Jeep was parked in the drive. Bill was curled up on
the front seat, sleeping, and when Abbie opened the door, the little
dog cocked his head.

"Come on, Billy Boy," Abbie said. "You're going to walk down
the aisle."

She fastened the leash on the dog's collar and handed the leash
to Harry. Then, with a laugh, she said, "Wait, Harry." Kneeling
down, she took one of the white magnolia blossoms from her hair
and fastened it carefully to the top of Bill's collar.

"Perfect!" she said.

She held Harry's hand as they walked back up the path to the
house. Now she could see the wedding party gathering on the deck
overlooking the beach.

Emma leaned on Spencer as he ushered her out to the deck. He
looked splendid in a tux, while Emma looked, well, *impressive*, in
the sky-blue chiffon gown they'd had to alter to fit her enormous
girth.

"I'm waddling," she said.

He gave her waist a squeeze. "You've never looked more beautiful."

She laughed. "You know, I sort of think that's true. And you've
never looked more handsome."

Emma knew Spencer's mother was gale-force wind with fury because Emma was pregnant and they weren't yet married, but Millicent didn't seem bothered. After all, when, in November, they had
planned their wedding for the summer, they hadn't known that
Emma was pregnant, due in May.

Emma and Spencer had tried to convince Sandra to come to
this wedding. Soon they would all be part of one big family, they reminded her, but Sandra was enjoying her ire too much and refused
to attend. But Millicent was here. Spencer had brought her to the
beach himself, and settled her in one of the front rows, next to
Sheila Lester and her husband. Millicent had attired herself quite

regally for the wedding, in a silver wool suit and a silver wide-brimmed hat trimmed with feathers and rhinestones and pearls.

Emma and Spencer were living in the big house with Millicent for the next few months. The baby would be born in the hospital, but it was reassuring, having a home health nurse around at night, and during the day when Spencer was working. Emma was working part-time for the historical association, helping Millicent unearth, sort through, and catalog her enormous collection of Nantucket arts and crafts which, when organized (for tax purposes, to assuage Sandra), Millicent would give to the historical association. Emma still read to Millicent during most afternoons. Sometimes she read from contemporary books about pregnancy, which made Millicent bark with laughter.

"Gosh," Spencer said now. "Look. I think Bill's going to take part in the wedding."

Emma laughed. "I love our crazy family," she said.

Lily checked her reflection one last time in the mirror. Marina had wanted her bridesmaids to wear sea colors. Abbie's gown was almost indigo blue, Emma's was sky blue, and Lily's was turquoise. Lily thought her color was hands down the most stunning. She wore the dangling turquoise earrings Eartha had given her, and she'd had Jason take lots of photos with his digital camera so she could email pictures to Eartha to show her just how fabulous she looked. Eartha was invited to the wedding, of course, but she was still down in Sarasota, visiting friends. She didn't want to come up to the island until July, when the social season really got under way.

With a final smile of approval at herself in the mirror, Lily turned, lifted her gown in her hands, and stepped out onto the deck. She felt like Cinderella as she went down the steps, there *was* something about holding her skirt up that made her feel royal, princessy.

Jason was waiting for her on the deck, looking like a movie star in his tux. She was quite aware of the looks other women gave him, the way even some of her *friends* invented problems with their houses and begged him to come over to help them. Some of the women were even married—but most of them weren't. Lily knew she was going to have to stop stalling and make a decision. Jason wouldn't wait forever. He'd enjoyed their two weeks in Paris, but he was an island guy, the island was in his blood and bones and heart and soul. Jason would never leave the island, not even for Lily.

Lily didn't know if that was enough of a love for her. Paris had been a revelation, and the few weeks she spent with Eartha in New York had been confusing, challenging, and exciting. She knew she needed to spend some time living and working in New York before deciding to settle down with Jason. And perhaps Jason would decide that Lily didn't love him enough. It was a chance she had to take. She was learning—slowly, with lots of anxiety and trepidation—that she could do pretty well on her own.

But today wasn't about Lily. It was about Marina and Lily's father.

Marina had been drinking champagne for the past hour, trying to calm down. She was so happy, and the day was so absolutely dazzling, she was afraid she'd cry, just right out *blubber*, with joy.

They had decided—they had *all* decided, for the girls were probably at least as interested in the ceremony as their father—to have the wedding on the beach. The girls had helped her choose this drop-dead-gorgeous, form-fitting, ivory silk sarong. On her feet were the thinnest of white leather sandals. Her hair was adorned with a glittering tiara the three girls had made for her out of seashells and beads.

And the girls looked stunning, all of them together in their coordinating sea colors. It was hard to look at them and not burst into tears.

In just a month, Emma was going to have a baby. Emma had asked Marina to babysit four afternoons a week, while she worked with Millicent. In her secret heart of hearts, Marina sometimes thought she was more excited about Emma's baby than about her own wedding, but of course she'd never say such a thing to Jim.

And now that Abbie was living with Howell, there had been several occasions when they'd asked Marina to stay with Harry so they could go out to dinner or a movie, and of course all of them, Howell, Abbie, and Harry, came to dinner often. Marina was learning how to create healthy food that was fun to eat, as well as the cookies and cupcakes she decorated for each season. Harry was gaining some much-needed weight, and Marina thought that just a few ounces could be attributed to her culinary creations. In a funny way, Marina was becoming a grandmother without ever having been a mother.

Lily was the one daughter with whom Marina still felt uncomfortable. They didn't quite "get" each other yet. But Marina had come a long way to achieving Lily's approval by having the clothes she'd put in storage shipped to the island. She'd invited Lily to join her as she unpacked all her horribly expensive, black designer suits. Lily had almost drooled on them, and she had screamed with joy when Marina told Lily they were all for her. They hardly had to be altered at all, and Lily looked fabulous in them.

Now they were all waiting for her. Jim, Spencer, Jason, and Howell went down the boardwalk to the beach, where the minister stood waiting in his white robe, the breeze playing with the hem. Marina's bridesmaids, Lily, Emma, and Abbie, were on the deck, all huddled together down at little Harry's level, giving him moral support for his trip down the aisle as the ring bearer. Their skirts billowed around them in a lovely flurry of blues.

Marina stepped outside.

"Marina!" Harry called. "Look! Bill is going to help me walk down the aisle!"

"Why, what a clever idea," Marina told him. "Harry, I'm so proud of you."

"I can hold his leash in my left hand and the rings in my right hand!" Harry assured her.

"Perfect." Marina nodded to the three sisters, who lined up for the procession. Here we are, Marina thought, four women, one little boy, and a dog. Perhaps an unusual wedding procession, but after all, there were so many kinds of weddings on this earth, and so many kinds of families.

The guitarist began to play Beethoven's "Ode to Joy." The congregation rose. They turned, looking so expectantly—so happily!— toward Marina, who lifted her head, smiled radiantly, and followed her family down the aisle toward the beach. As she walked, she could see, just behind the altar, the wide blue ocean sparkling in the sun.

Beachcombers

A   N O V E L

NANCY THAYER

A Reader's Guide

A Conversation with Nancy Thayer

Random House Reader's Circle: What made you write this story?

Nancy Thayer: The ideas for my books all come from deep within my heart and my life. In many ways, *Beachcombers* is about dealing with loss—of a parent, or like Marina, of a husband and best friend, or of an important job, income, and fiancé. We all face loss. Sometimes loss makes you dig deep into yourself to find what you never realized was there.

My mother was ninety-one and failing when I started writing *Beachcombers*. My sister, Martha, a nurse, visited my mother in her nursing home every day. When she was younger, my mother had worked for the development department of a hospital; she was capable and logical. She loved music and reading above all things. One time when I was a teenager, she was driving a car and I was sitting next to her, in the front seat. She had the radio on, playing classical music, when suddenly, Mother said, with joy, "Nancy, look at those birds!" She pointed to the sky. "It looks like they're flying in time to the music!" Then she drove the car into a tree. (We weren't hurt.) In some ways, my character Danielle is like how my mother was, loving, but often forgetting us because she's hearing other music.

My sister often called from the Kansas City nursing facility to talk with me here in Nantucket. Mother, Martha, and I discussed so many memories. Later, while driving away from the nursing home, my sister would call and we'd talk about other memories of our mother. I knew we would be losing her soon. I began to wonder what it must be like to lose your mother when you are still very young, and that was the germ of *Beachcombers*.

RHRC: In *Beachcombers*, you delve into four very different female perspectives. Did you find any one woman harder to write than the others?

NT: Lily was the hardest character for me to write, not because she wasn't like me, but because she was so very much like I was when I was in my twenties. True, I was the oldest of three children, so I did a lot of nurturing and caretaking like Abbie. I'd once lived in Kansas City, been divorced, and started my life over on Nantucket like Marina. I was practical, hardworking, and history-loving like Emma.

But when I was young, I was *so* Lily. I desperately wanted to leave Wichita, Kansas, where I grew up. I wanted to live in Paris or New York City. My best friend and I were going to run away, wear black turtlenecks, recite our poetry in coffee houses, and have mad affairs with dangerous men. If I had met Eartha when I was Lily's age, I would have been her servant in a flash. When I look back at myself in my late teens and early twenties, I see someone who didn't care a fig for keeping house or being on time and responsible. I wanted glamour, bright lights, sexy clothes, martinis! (Kansas was a dry state; I'd never had a martini.)

Knowing my past, when I wrote *Beachcombers*, it was hard for me to give Lily a break, because she was so much like I had been: kind of an idiot. Or are we all idiots at twenty?

RHRC: Do you begin writing with an idea of your characters in mind or do you allow them to evolve as the story progresses?

NT: I always start with characters in mind, and also a kind of theme, like loss, or as in *Summer House*, generations of family, or how friendships change over time. The characters definitely evolve as I write. They become more fully formed, more definitely *themselves*. In fact, they take over. Sometimes I have to stop typing and say aloud to my empty study, "I really can't allow you to say that in print!" I am incapable of sitting and plotting in advance. I either type, or I go for a walk, and things shift in my brain. I want to say, "Well, why didn't you tell me this in the first place!" Or I phone my daughter, Samantha Wilde, also a published novelist, and ask something like, "Should Joe marry Helen?" Sam will say, "Duh, no, Mom, he's going to marry Sarah." And I'll say, "Oh! I had no idea," but I know instantly she's right, and I hang up the phone and go back to work.

Writing is a mystery, and when it works well, a delight. When it doesn't work well, it goes into the shredder.

RHRC: Reading your novels always makes me want to visit Nantucket. Does the beauty and nature of Nantucket inspire your creativity while writing?

NT: I usually take a walk every day when I'm writing, often an adventure in the winter, but I love the ocean in the winter. It's so dramatic! The white surf pounds. The air sparkles. On Great Point, I walk near harbor seals wallowing in the sand, oinking like pigs from eating so many fish. Once my husband and I saw a group of enormous grey seals with their gorilla bodies and black horse heads hanging out next to the shore like a bunch of adolescent gangsters. They were *fascinated* by us. We studied them. They studied us. They kind of flirted with us. I'm pretty sure they thought we were funny looking. Or maybe delicious looking. It was thrilling. And terrifying. We didn't go any closer. Even the sweet little harbor seals bite. So much of such incomprehensible difference so near to us every day—that shakes the doldrums out of me and stirs me up.

Also, the town of Nantucket is exquisitely beautiful, the houses mostly old and shingled, with small gardens hidden behind hedges or picket fences. Many of the houses are named, with signs called quarter boards above the door. On Fair Street sits FAIRY TALE, FAIR ISLE, and FAIR THEE WELL. Door knockers are mermaids, or whale tails, or scallop shells. Many houses have "widows' walks" where women whose husbands were off at sea watched for approaching ships. Window boxes spill with flowers in most seasons. Walking around Main Street and over to India Street where our magnificent Greek Revival library stands and over to the Episcopal church with its Tiffany stained-glass window is always inspiring. And if I stop in at Even Keel for a mocha latte and one of their chocolate cakes, then I'm *exhilarated*.

I believe that sometimes you just have to *go somewhere else*. Perhaps you've had a tremendous loss and you're sad. Or you've worked very hard and you're exhausted. Or everything is great, but still, something's missing and you can't figure it out. Nantucket is thirty miles out at sea. You have to fly or take a boat to get here. Here, you're surrounded by water. Here, no chains stores, no Dunkin Donuts or ToysЯUs, and if you rent a car, you can't go faster than 25 mph on the narrow roads. History is everywhere; you walk on the cobblestones brought over from England hundreds of years ago. Nature is everywhere. And it isn't only sweet. If you don't watch out, a gull will swoop down and steal your sandwich right off your picnic blanket.

I've seen people come here for a week and leave changed. I've met groups of women who reunite here from all over the country in the autumn to rent a cottage, walk in the sand or on the moors, eat lobster dripping with butter or fresh sweet scallops, and talk all day and much of the night. They go home recharged for the year. I know the nature and beauty of the island changes people. I've heard them talk about it.

RHRC: Why do you think the relationships between sisters are so complex and complicated?

NT: I think relationships between any two human beings are complex and complicated. But with sisters, you've got emotional memories of the intense past to color everything that happens in the present. Children get labeled, even unintentionally, not just by their parents, but by the children themselves. "The Smart One," "The Baby," "The Favorite," "The Shy One." When we grow up, those roles lurk in our unconscious, shadowing our present behavior.

For example, my sister, Martha, is now my best friend. She is nine years younger than I, so she is the baby of the family. I have brown hair and hazel eyes, while Martha is a blond with gorgeous blue eyes. She was always *adored* by everyone, no matter what she did. Once, for example, she ruined my lipsticks. I yelled at her. She cried. My mother always just went gooey over Martha. "Oh, when you cry, your eyes turn turquoise! Nancy how can you be mean to her?" Martha looked like my father, so of course she was the favorite. She didn't have to do chores. She had a canopy bed. Of course, I'm not saying she was spoiled. . . . Wait! Am I getting off track?

RHRC: I love the scene where Marina and Sheila go to Madaket Mall to find treasures. Have you ever found any surprising treasures in an unlikely place like Madaket Mall?

NT: Oh, yes. At the end of the summer, and this is *true*, many of the exceptionally wealthy women who vacation here for a month or two weeks have their maids bring their clothes to the dump because they wouldn't dream of wearing them next summer, which will be a different season. Many of the clothes still have price tags on them.

I haven't gotten clothing there, but I have friends who have. What I do get, although I hesitate to share this information, is British mysteries and British novels. There's a book section in the Madaket Mall, and someone comes here in the summer and leaves brand-new British fiction behind. Bless them.

The thing to remember is that this is an island. The ferries and planes bring supplies over, but on this small island, it makes sense to recycle, and people did it here at the Madaket Mall before it became politically correct. Need a new door? New window frame? New dress? A mirror? Some pretty mismatched china for your rented summer cottage? It's there. It may not fit perfectly, but it's free.

RHRC: Why did you choose that specific line from e. e. cummings's "Maggie and Milly and Molly and May"?

NT: This book begins with loss of all kinds. Sometimes we do lose ourselves right in the midst of a busy life. I think nature is a miraculous restorative. We can walk by the ocean, or hike up a mountain, or swim in a lake. We can weed our backyard garden. When we're out in nature, our minds drift away from the little gerbil-wheel revolving endlessly in our mind. We take deep breaths—of new air, fresh air, different air. We watch the sun sparkle on water. Nature gives us back to ourselves, refreshed. It is ourselves we find in the sea.

RHRC: Do you agree with Danielle's beliefs that the universe is always speaking to us?

NT: Yes. But it's not like a two-way conversation on a cell phone. The universe is not going to solve our problems. I think the universe sends us hints to pay attention, be alive, look around.

Here's an example: Yesterday my daughter, Sam, phoned in tears. She has three little children, she's breastfeeding her baby, and she had two blocked milk ducts. She was in terrible pain and developing a fever. Her husband works and couldn't come home to help. After her call, I was so worried, I went for a walk up and down the wharves, looking at the water, trying to decide what to do. Should I pack, take a ferry, drive three hours, and help her? Should I stay home and work? I was frantic. I kept thinking: *two* ducts! Two *ducts*! I turned the corner and there in the water were two ducks. It made me laugh out loud. I realized the problem was not *terrible*. When I got home, she phoned to say her husband had brought home antibiotics and she felt better. I think the universe sends us hints, clues, puns, and always amazing beauty to remind us where we are. Interpretation is up to us.

RHRC: Where did you get the idea for the Beachcombers Club?

NT: Perhaps deep in all our hearts lies a primitive soul who loves the idea of finding "treasure." Certainly in twenty-seven years, everyone I've ever walked with on the beach has suddenly bent down and picked up a rock or a shell, studied it, and tucked it into his/her pocket. If you go into Nantucket houses, you'll see shells on shelves, under glass, on windowsills, on the sides of the bathtubs. Out of zillions of pebbles and shells on the beach, everyone seems to discover something. "Now here is an interesting rock," they say. Everyone becomes a beachcomber on Nantucket. The idea of a club came from walking with my children on the beach when they were smaller and I needed to find a way to discard some of our finds. (Although I wasn't as peculiar a mother as Danielle was.)

RHRC: What are you working on at the moment?

NT: *Heat Wave*, which comes out in hardcover in summer, is about a young woman, Carley Winsted, who has two daughters and a wonderful life when suddenly she is widowed. In addition, the lives of her two best friends become inextricably tangled, and Carley must choose between them. She discovers she doesn't, and perhaps can't, always do the "right" thing. It's the sort of lesson that's hard for some of us to learn, especially good-hearted Carley. I hope readers will enjoy Carley's company as much as I have.

Discussion Questions

1. Do brothers and sisters fight less and have more easygoing relationships than sisters? Why are the relationships between sisters so complicated?

2. Which of the four women did you most identify with?

3. Given Lily's desire to visit glamorous places and have fancy things, why is she the only sister who comes back home to Nantucket after college?

4. Was Marina running away from her problems by going to Nantucket, or did she need time by herself to heal?

5. Danielle battles her depression in front of her girls, while Sydney is very strict with Harry and is often away from her family. Are either of them intrinsically bad mothers, or are they trying the best they can with the situations they have?

6. If Emma and Marina did not get caught red-handed, would Emma's decision to remain discrete regarding her suspicions about the stolen light baskets seem more admirable, or should Emma have just gone straight to Spencer with her concerns?

7. Were Abbie, Emma, and Jim wrong to shelter and spoil Lily after Danielle's death?

8. If you were in Emma's shoes, would you encourage Abbie to continue her relationship with Howell, given what you know of Howell and Sydney's relationship?

9. Should a couple who is not in love with each other stay together for the sake of their child?

10. Jim says that mothers are the centers of their kid's lives; do you think this is true? Where does that leave fathers, especially single fathers like Jim?

11. As a twenty-two-year-old who has yet to experience the world, is Lily wrong to want as much as she can get?

12. Do you think that being a grandmother figure to Emma's child will be enough to satisfy Marina's longing for a baby?

Read on for an excerpt from

HEAT WAVE

by Nancy Thayer

Published by Ballantine Books

Some days recently, Carley Winsted had experienced moments of actual happiness, when her heart gave her a break. She'd forget Gus's death and focus on the sight of her daughters or the sparkle of sunlight on the ocean—and lightning-fast, guilt zapped her. How could she be happy even for a moment?

She *had* to be happy, because she needed to be a role model for her daughters. She wanted to show them how to get through the dark times, to relish the good in each and every day.

Today she just needed not to be a coward.

It was the end of December, the end of the year. The end of the worst year in Carley's life. High on a cliff overlooking the deep blue waters of Nantucket Sound, Carley stood in her bedroom, her heart racing with anxiety.

Thank heavens her girls were with friends this morning. She couldn't let them see her like this. They had enough to deal with. Their beloved father, Carley's dear Gus, had died a month ago. His death had been unexpected, unpredictable, *wrong*, caused by an undiagnosed heart defect that had been lying stealthily in wait for years. Gus had been only thirty-seven. Carley was only thirty-two.

Cisco was twelve.

Margaret was five.

It was unbearable. Yet it had to be borne.

She'd been doing pretty well, she thought, but this morning her grief was overridden by a gripping panic, which was ridiculous, really.

After all, it wasn't as if she were a peasant being thrown into the lion's den. She was only going to her father-in-law's office to discuss finances with him. Okay, fine, finances had never been her strong suit. She'd gotten married at twenty, she'd never had a real job, Gus had handled the money, she had taken care of the house, the children, food and clothing, their lives. But she was not a financial *idiot*, and Gus knew that. Gus had left this house entirely to her. It had no mortgage. It was completely, legally, hers.

So why had Russell asked her to come to the law office to meet with him? Such a cold, businesslike place—why hadn't he come to her house to talk with her in the living room as he always had? True, Carley had not always been on the same page as Annabel and Russell. They were different in so many ways, and the truth was, her in-laws were difficult to please. But they shared a mutual love for their son, her husband Gus, and for his and Carley's daughters, Cisco and Margaret.

Carley gave herself a careful, critical once-over in the mirror. Her tailored gray suit was loose on her, but that was to be expected. She'd lost weight since Gus's death. So had Russell and Annabel, even Gus's best friend, Wyatt. Carley was tall and lanky, and now whip thin. In this suit, she looked elegant, even haughty, although anyone who knew Carley knew elegant and haughty were so not her. Russell had to know that after being around her for thirteen years.

But since Gus's death, both Russell and Annabel had been . . . different. More openly judgmental. Carley's only defense was to be prepared. She slipped her feet into her highest heels.

Her appointment with Russell was set for eleven o'clock. Her *appointment*! Gus wouldn't have put up with this formal crap. "Come on, Dad, just tell us what you have to say, and we'll work it out." That's what Gus would have said.

Carley met Gus on Nantucket one summer night when she was nineteen. The air was hot and muggy and she was whipped from waiting tables.

She'd just finished her second year at Syracuse with less than sterling grades. She wasn't upset about the grades. No one was upset about the grades—her parents were engrossed with their work and all her life Carley had been advised not to compare herself with her older sister, Sarah, who was brilliant at science and a jock as well, so no one was pressuring Carley to perform.

It was just that now, approaching her junior year, Carley felt a little lost. Sarah had always yearned to be a nurse when she grew up, an emergency room nurse. Her father was a much-respected and eternally busy dentist. Her mother and her best friend ran a day care center.

Carley had no idea what she wanted to be.

She thought she should want to be *something*. Rosie, her best childhood friend, wanted to go into the Peace Corps and become an immigration lawyer. Another friend wanted to teach in elementary school. Carley had believed she'd be inspired by some teacher or subject once she got to college, but that hadn't yet happened. She was listlessly declaring education her major.

One thing was crystal clear to her: she loved being on Nantucket. It was her third summer working here, and it seemed she was always happy here, no matter what her job was. Of course, it was always *summer*, when the days were drenched with sunshine and the air smelled of salt and roses and she was surrounded by friends. She kind of even liked her wait job. Some of the customers were jerks, but most of them were on vacation, tanned, relaxed, happy, and ready to give a big fat tip.

Still, she couldn't make a career out of waiting tables. First of all, her restaurant closed for the winter, but more important, island life was staggeringly expensive. She shared an attic room and tiny shower-stall bath with four other women and rent still took up a large chunk of her paycheck.

She wasn't worried about it, though. Not worried about a thing. Tonight some girlfriends had heard rumors of a party out on Cisco Beach and Carley decided to ride out with them. She smelled like the curried fish stew she'd been serving all evening, so she stripped down to almost nothing—shorts and a halter top, bare feet, her hair skinned back into a ponytail to keep it off her neck. The minute she arrived at the party, she nabbed a bottle of beer and chugged it down.

She was in a restless, devil-may-care kind of mood that summer. She was an accident waiting to happen, and subconsciously, that was probably what she wanted to be.

That night at the beach, she was light and supple, riding the tide of life wherever it would take her, and loving the motion. Bonfires were illegal on the beach, but someone had set up some grills and hibachis that gave off flickering golden lights and filled the air with the rich aroma of roasting hamburgers and hot dogs. Tables sunk into the sand held plastic cups and gallons of wine. Trash barrels stuffed with ice and beer leaned crookedly in the sand. Friends screamed with glee when they saw each other, as if they were reunited after years apart, and as darkness fell, people seemed mysterious, exotic. Music from a CD player had people dancing at the water's edge, with partners or alone.

Carley talked with friends, drank a couple of beers, and then she and Rhonda, one of her roomies, started dancing with their shadows. Oh, that night—the heat of the air, the cold shock of waves lapping over her feet, the sounds of laughter, and the beat of music—she was a primitive thing for a while that night, dancing in and out of the waves that surged up the shore. It wasn't just the alcohol, it was the essence of the night, the sheer joy of being young, and she felt sassy, free, *eternal*, somehow part of the world and still very particularly herself.

Late at night, a man came over, took her hand, and led her up to a log someone had left on the beach as a seat.

"You need a hamburger," he said.

Carley threw her head back and laughed. "I need a hamburger?"

"I've been watching you. You've been dancing for a long time. You're about to fall down. I think you need a hamburger and some water and if you sit here, I'll bring them to you."

As she dropped down on the log, her head spun and her legs suddenly gave way. She landed hard on her bum. "Oops." She grinned up at the man. "I think you may be right."

Carley never had been able to drink much. She went straight from sober to pass out on three glasses of wine, seldom enjoying any kind of high. That night she'd only had two beers, or maybe three. She wasn't exactly drunk. Perhaps she was just a bit tired. And she couldn't remember when she'd last eaten.

The man returned, bearing a paper plate in one hand and a bottle of Perrier in the other.

"Thanks." She chugged the sparkling water. "That tastes sublime! I had no idea I was so thirsty." She held the hamburger with both hands. "Yum."

"I'm Gus," he said.

"I'm Carley," she told him.

They didn't go to bed with each other that night, although around three a.m., when most of the others were dragging themselves away for a few hours of necessary sleep before their workday began, they did begin to kiss. The log was not a comfortable site for romance. Twice they clumsily tumbled into the sand, laughing through their kisses. Rhonda straggled up to Carley, saying she was driving back to town now, if Carley wanted a ride. Gus asked Carley if he could see her the next night, and Carley had chuckled, feeling warm and dreamy and tired and sexy.

"Yeah, and somewhere with lights might be good," she told him. "So we can see what we look like."

The next night, sober, she had liked the way Gus looked. Anyone would. He was striking, with unusual black eyes and thick black hair. He was older than Carley, already a lawyer, working at the family firm on the island. He loved the island, he had grown up here. He knew who he was and what he was, and that impressed the hell out of Carley.

That night, they had slept together. He took her out to dinner at a posh restaurant, then brought her to his apartment. The sex hadn't been amazing, at least not for Carley, but it had been friendly, and that was very nice. Afterward, Carley joked, "Ah. Seduced by a hamburger."

Then Gus took her home to meet his parents, and she did fall in love.

Gus was a Winsted, whose family had helped settle Nantucket in the 1600s. His mother Annabel was a Greenwood, and her family had deep island roots as well. Gus's father, Russell, had grown up on the island in the Winsted family's enormous brick house on Main Street, gone off to Harvard, and returned as a lawyer. Annabel was the only child in her family, and when her parents died, she inherited the Greenwood house, another historic Nantucket mansion, this one set at the end of a road on a cliff overlooking the Sound. Gus was an only child, too. "It had just worked out that way," was as much as elegant Annabel ever offered in explanation.

Russell and Annabel were both striking to look at. Tall and slender, Russell clad his storklike body in elegant pin-striped suits and handmade monogrammed cotton shirts that had belonged to his father and his grandfather. At home, he poured his daily scotch from an antique crystal decanter embossed with silver leaves. And he had that glossy ebony hair, those piercing dark eyes that gave Gus such intensity.

Annabel, Gus's mother, was a lean beauty with honey-colored hair worn in a careless twist and soft brown eyes. She was Carley's mother's age—49—but she went around in jeans and turtlenecks and Docksiders.

Carley knew her own mother would consider Annabel a lightweight, a frivolous and even selfish woman. But it was hard to measure up to Carley's mother's standards.

Marilyn Smith and her friend Bernice ran a day care center in East Laurence, New York. Marilyn was a passionate reformer, trying to bring comfort and affection to as many small children as she could—as long as they were other people's children. She had been a dutiful mother to Sarah and Carley until they turned ten, then Marilyn considered them old enough to take care of themselves. More than that, she considered them lucky, *too* lucky, and had no interest in any of their problems, which were, after all, only the problems of spoiled middle-class children. Carley's father, a dentist, worked hard as well, and came home late and tired. The family seldom ate dinner together but made sandwiches or heated up frozen dinners in the microwave.

But Russ and Annabel relished daily life—that was the mesmerizing, seductive quality the Winsteds had. Everything was centered around the home. Life was about family and friends.

Annabel and Russ both loved cooking. They grew some vegetables and herbs and experimented with sauces. They both had brown rubber waders that they wore when they pushed their way over the sand and through the water to pick mussels off the jetties; one of their favorite meals was mussels steamed with garlic, a warm loaf of homemade bread, a fresh salad, and wine. In the summer, Annabel roamed the moors to pick wild blueberries for pies and jellies; in the fall, she picked beach plums and made jam. Because Annabel and Russ were great sailors, Russ was always taking off from his law firm—it was his family's firm, he could take off whenever he wanted—to go sailing for the day with Annabel on their catboat, often returning with fish for dinner. They were both gregarious and loved entertaining, filling the house with people who gathered in the kitchen drinking wine and talking while Annabel and Russ put together some of their spontaneous catch-as-catch-can pizzas.

Not that they were obsessive about cooking. Sometimes Carley would drop by to find Annabel curled up on a sofa, reading. "I can't put this book down!" she'd say. "We'll have to order takeout tonight." Annabel and Russ were voracious readers. They attended all the lectures the library and museums gave. They loved art, too, and covered the walls of their house with works by island artists. They were involved in politics, and attended town meetings faithfully. The high school plays brought them out for at least one performance and often more. They were right *there* in their lives. They were not trying to get anywhere else; they weren't competitive or envious; they were that rarest of human creatures: genuinely happy people.

Of course, they had started off with more than many people ever had. They had each inherited an old Nantucket mansion. Their lives grew out of the island history like a flower from a new dawn rose, climbing, blossoming, part of a thick twisting stem deeply planted in the island's sandy soil, and proud to be in that sandy soil.

The Greenwood house that Annabel had grown up in—the house where Carley had made her home for the past thirteen years—was a rambling old wooden structure with a definite summer feeling about it. The redbrick mansion Annabel and Russ lived in was the more formal Winsted home. Behind the house, the large yard was walled with redbrick fifteen feet high, making the garden a private enclosure, a little Eden few people ever saw. Here Annabel grew her vegetables and flowers, and played with shaping privet bushes into whimsical shapes, one of her favorite pastimes. Inside, the rooms were large and high-ceilinged, with fireplaces, most of which worked, silk drapes pooling on the floor, and comfortable sofas and chairs mixed in with antique pieces. Like the ones at Carley's home, the kitchen and bathrooms were ancient, floored with ceramic tiles, fitted with claw-foot bathtubs that would have been delightful if the porcelain weren't almost worn through. Both houses required endless vigilance and maintenance, and endless amounts of money.

The first time Carley entered the Winsted house, she didn't notice the paint peeling from the walls or the faded ancient Oriental rugs. She thought the metal kitchen cabinets with the inset sink, considered "modern" in the 1940s, were charmingly old-fashioned. She didn't see the cracks in the plaster around the fireplaces or the way the bookshelves, overburdened with books, leaned dangerously sideways. The house had such a quality of excellence and experience and age. It felt like a wise house, a comforting house, a house that had witnessed holiday festivities and political gatherings and the solemnity of birth and death, and had stood at attention, with pride, through it all.

Carley loved the *idea* of the way the Winsteds lived. She wanted to be casually elegant, too. She yearned for Annabel and Russell to like her. She could imagine spending time with Annabel, learning so very much from her.

The older Winsteds seemed pleased by Carley that first night Gus brought her home. Certainly they charmed her, asked her questions, laughed at her slightest attempt at whimsy, treated her with gentle warmth.

As they drove away from his parents' house, Carley glanced shyly at Gus. "I think they liked me."

"Of course they liked you," Gus replied. "Who wouldn't?"

She smiled contentedly.

Then Gus said, "Although they wouldn't like it if I got too involved with you."

"Really? Why not?"

"Because you're not an islander. Not 'one of us.' "

"Does that really matter?"

"You'd be surprised how much it matters."

Carley chewed on her lip. She was already worried about something that could be a real problem between them. This made her feel even worse. She decided to wait a few days to tell Gus. She wanted to be sure.

NANCY THAYER is the *New York Times* bestselling author of *Beachcombers, Summer House, Moon Shell Beach, The Hot Flash Club, The Hot Flash Club Strikes Again, Hot Flash Holidays,* and *The Hot Flash Club Chills Out.* She lives on Nantucket.

About the Type

· · · · ·

This book was set in Goudy, a typeface designed by Frederic William Goudy (1865–1947). Goudy began his career as a bookkeeper, but devoted the rest of his life to the pursuit of "recognized quality" in a printing type.

Goudy was produced in 1914 and was an instant bestseller for the foundry. It has generous curves and smooth, even color. It is regarded as one of Goudy's finest achievements.

Chat.
Comment.
Connect.

Visit our online book club community at
www.randomhousereaderscircle.com

Chat
Meet fellow book lovers and discuss what you're reading.

Comment
Post reviews of books, ask—and answer—thought-provoking
questions, or give and receive book club ideas.

Connect
Find an author on tour, visit our author blog, or invite one of
our 150 available authors to chat with your group on the phone.

Explore
Also visit our site for discussion questions, excerpts, author
interviews, videos, free books, news on the latest releases,
and more.

Books are better with buddies.
www.RandomHouseReadersCircle.com